JACK DALTON MONSTER HUNTER THE COMPLETE COLLECTION

T S PAUL

**Great
God Pan
Publishing Inc.**

Reading, Writing, Publishing, plicefy and such

Legal Stuff

Editing by Laurie Holding

Formatting by Nina Morse

Dedications

Special thanks to my wife Heather who keeps me grounded and to Merlin the Cat, we are his minions.

JACK DALTON, MONSTER HUNTER

BOOK 1

IN 1914 DARK Witches turned Vampires loose on unsuspecting troops on the Western Front and the world changed. Beings known as paranormals were discovered to be living side by side with the humans of the world. Who knew that Witches, Vampires, Werewolves, and Fairies were real?

Jump ahead now forty-five years to the United States and the establishment of the Magical Security Act of 1959. Against the wishes of FBI Director J Edgar Hoover, the American Congress established an arm of the FBI to hunt down and bring to justice any and all paranormal criminals. This is their story. Or I should say mine.

"Congratulations on the promotion, Jack!" That was what the paper sign hanging in the common room said. Drunk and half-drunk FBI Academy graduates were staggering around the room. The jukebox in the corner was blasting out the latest and greatest tunes by the Platters, Elvis, and Buddy Holly.

I was the man of the hour, but I was sitting in the corner of the room beer in hand staring out at the snow. The promotion sounded good on paper, but it wasn't real. Of course, none of my classmates saw that trap. To them, it was a promotion to a brand new division in a Bureau that was rarely innovative. I remembered my interview with the big man himself, Director J Edgar Hoover and laughed, what a day that was.

"So, you're Jack Dalton. Director Hoover will be with you soon." The secretary was an older woman with bluish-white hair. She looked over her horn rim glasses at me like I was a bug she needed to kill.

The office was nice. Much more elaborate and glamorous than those at the Academy. The walls were lined with pictures of the Hoover busting criminals and posing with famous or infamous celebrities and dignitaries. One of the larger ones caught and held my attention the most. It was Director Hoover standing with President Long overlooking the hole. The public called it the doorway to Hell, but I'd read the unredacted part of the report. Conception, California was the proud owner of a Hellmouth. Much of the public was ignoring the fact that Demons had tried to end our country.

I checked my watch, I'd officially been here for over an hour already. That the reading material in the office was lacking was an understatement. Old copies of Newsmonth and Secret Agent X comic books were scattered on the table in front of me. I remember reading the comic books growing up. I sighed loudly, attracting the attention of horn rim, my new nickname for the secretary.

"Harumph."

That was the only response I had gotten from her in an hour. I thought about taking a nap but knew that would not go over well here. Reaching into my pocket, I pulled out my uncle's journal. Reading it has always helped me pass the time before.

My uncle Tim, had been a tanker during the Demon War. He had seen heavy action in France and Italy. When what was left of the Horde charged the lines following the death of the Demon Prince, he and his unit were killed. But they went down fighting. My aunt still proudly displays both the Medal of Honor and the Presidential Unit Citation. Uncle Tim had been an active proponent of Weres in the military. He always said that using them was the best decision Uncle Sam ever made.

His experiences and those of his units might explain my being introduced to some of his unit's Were families. I spent five years of my childhood in or around one of the reservations. Fighting in the war was the only way to get off the reservations for many of the Were folk. Humans just weren't ready for shapeshifters to be living among them unchecked and unmonitored.

The door to the office opened, making me look up from the journal. The woman entering caused my heart to stop! She was a Goddess among men. Our eyes met, and she actually stared me down! The wry look on her face was one of mirth. She smiled at me, nodded to Horned Rim, and walked right into the Director's office! I looked at the secretary in surprise. She glared at me over her glasses yet again and shook her head.

At least I got a shake. Looking at the door longingly I shook my own head and went back to the journal. Every so often I checked the closed door, hoping to get a look at that woman again.

The next hour or so crawled by. The hands on the clock were moving so slowly I could almost swear time had stopped still. I knew THAT was an impossibility. Magic just doesn't work that way in the real world.

Brrrrriiiing.

The phone of Horned Rim's desk rang suddenly. She picked it up and answered, "Hello?"

She nodded her head as she listened to the voice on the other end. "Yes, Director. I'll tell him."

I looked expectantly at the woman, and she glared at me as she hung up the phone. "Director Hoover will see you now."

Taking a deep breath, I stood up and approached the doors. The woman I was calling Horn Rim got up from her desk and headed me off at the pass. She was going to open the door for me. I still didn't understand why I was even standing here. Behind these doors was the most important man in my new career. It was like just learning guitar and meeting Elvis Presley for the first time.

Mrs. Gandy, I learned her name eventually, opened the door and escorted me inside.

I could feel my eyes widen at the sight of his office. For just a split second I thought I might be in the wrong office. Fluted Etruscan style lamps hung from the ceiling. It was the ceiling that blew me away. My room at the Academy was maybe, six-by-six. The Director's immense office had a ceiling that reached twenty-four feet into the sky! Huge swaths of gold drapes hung all the way down to the floor. Just one section of one of the three windows could have clothed half his Academy class. Or it seemed that way.

I hastily swallowed my own spit. Across the vast room was a

gigantic oak desk. The man himself sat there head down studying something on his desk. The Goddess of a woman I'd seen earlier was here as well. She noticed me before the director did. At her nod, Mrs. Gandy gave me a small push from behind and left the room.

Director Hoover looked up and saw me at the end of the room. "Ah, Cadet Dalton? Good. Step forward please."

The woman retrieved a stack of files and took a single step backward from the desk. She, like Mrs. Gandy, looked at me like a bug needing pinning.

Hoover motioned to the single straight-backed chair sitting in front of his desk. The walls of the room were lined with leather covered padded chairs, but I assumed I was too good for those. Nodding, I walked forward and sat. The unsanded chair felt rough, and I could feel every knot and groove through my pants.

Hoover peered at me across his desk. "What do you know about the Magical Security Act, Cadet Dalton?"

I looked at the head of the FBI in surprise. Laws and reports from Congress concerning our duties was something we had to read up on an almost daily, more so for Cadets and I'd not heard about this one. "Nothing sir. Did I miss a memo?"

Please God, let me have missed a memo! I thought to myself.

"At least that's stayed secret," the Director commented to the woman at his side.

"For now, sir," she replied.

Hoover nodded in response. "It's new. Congress passed it secretly a month ago. The President has signed it into law, and now I'm, we, are stuck with implementing it."

I shifted uncomfortably in my chair. Why was the J Edgar Hoover telling ME this?

The Director leaned back into what looked like a very comfortable leather chair and gazed at me. "One of the many tasks this act encompasses is the foundation of a new division inside the FBI. While we have partial integration of elements of paranormal society in the FBI, Congress in their eternal wisdom believes we need more."

"They have created a Magical Division," he paused and stared at me again. "At the moment there are no guidelines for this new unit. So, we are creating them starting with you, Cadet."

My eyes widened just a bit, "Me, sir?"

"Yes. You. Your file here states that before your recruitment you spent several years living among one of our country's Were packs. Is this true?" Hoover asked as he waved a file at me.

"Yes, sir. In Texas, sir. They were... I mean they served with my father in Europe. Mom thought I'd like knowing them." I flashed on my years living there. The war was over, but many loose Demons threatened the country. She moved us there for protection. I'd grown up as one of the few humans ever to be admitted to a pack.

Hoover frowned and glanced at the woman his side. She nodded and pointed to something in the file. "That is not what this says. Are you still considered a pack member?"

I should have expected them to know. The OSS was pretty thorough sometimes. I tried to answer without answering. Some things were supposed to stay secret. "Yes, sir. I've been a little out of touch with them, but as far as I know, I still have that status."

The woman's eyes flashed, and for just the briefest moment I thought I saw a smile. Hoover nodded and looked at the file in his hand. "Good to know. This new unit is to be composed of agents with connections to paranormal entities. Its job will be to police them."

"Police them, sir?" The current doctrine was pretty brutal. In most states, it was shoot-to-kill for almost ANY infraction. There was a reason the Weres were on the reservations, to begin with.

Hoover grunted and frowned again. "This new Act does several things. It establishes a prison system for offenders and funds a new training center for paranormals. The rules concerning them are about to change. These... These people are citizens, and we cannot just kill them anymore. So because you have prior contact with these elements, we are promoting you."

I just stared at the man. Promoting me to what?

"Don't be too excited Cadet," Hoover looked at me.

"Sorry, sir. What am I being promoted to?" I quickly amended that, "Sir?"

"The new division. You are now its head and solo agent until we can dig up staff for you. For now, you will report to Agent Romanoff here. She will take care of any requisitions and pass along your reports to me. Any questions you have can be answered by her as well," Hoover informed me.

The Goddess of a woman, Agent Romanoff, took the files from the Director. She whispered something in his ear that made the man smile, but his frown returned when he saw me still sitting there. He pointed to the door I came in, "Go on."

Standing, I hurried out of the room as fast as I could without running. Agent Romanoff actually beat me to the door. "This way Cadet. We'll finish this conversation in my office."

Mrs. Gandy sniffed at the two of us but barely looked up from her work. I learned later she somehow knew everything that happened in this building.

My new boss led me down the hall to the elevators. I watched as we cleared security and then traveled to the first floor.

"Come along, Cadet. Just a little further." Agent Romanoff led me past the staff offices and down a little-used hallway. The doors here were for janitorial staff and supplies. At the end of the hall was a freight elevator.

The Agent pressed a button and called for the elevator. I stood motionless for what seemed like hours waiting for the car to arrive.

When the doors opened, I tentatively stepped on board. Agent Romanoff inserted a key into the control panel and pressed not the basement button, but an unmarked button.

I tried not to stare at this agent. There were very few women agents in the Bureau. Even though the charter didn't exclude women, the Director didn't go out of his way to recruit them. He liked single, unattached young men as agents. He wanted everyone to be professional and courteous. Hoover had a specific image he wanted to project.

The elevator car shuddered to a halt, and the door opened. Peering out I could see a darkened hallway with a door at the end. The female agent motioned for me to proceed.

Agent Romanoff opened the door and led me inside. Unlike the Director's office, this one was standard. I could see several doors to either side leading who knew where.

"Sit down before you fall down. He can be a bit daunting the first time," Agent Romanoff sat at the desk.

Sinking into the padded chair, I sighed in relief. No pain.

"You didn't hear it from me, but he saves that chair for anyone that irritates him," at my shocked look she smiled. "You didn't do anything wrong so don't worry. It's the assignment. Not you."

"Then why..." I trailed off. This was way, way, way off any conversation I intended to have at FBI headquarters.

"Congress, the President, state governors, the American people, pick one. Pick more than one. The Director doesn't like being told to do something. Which brings us to you." Agent Romanoff stared me in the eyes until I looked away.

"Good. Work on that skill. Some paranormals like to play games. You aren't the only agent with the background for this. But you are the most expendable. He doesn't think it will succeed, so you are the Judas Goat here," the agent remarked.

My mother ensured I was educated properly, so I understood the reference.

"I, on the other hand, want you to succeed. Whether he wants it or not, we need this division. The Weres are going to be released, eventually. You know it, and I know it. And when that happens, everything that the Alphas keep in check will be loosed upon us." The agent smiled and started to laugh.

"Don't be so surprised, Jack. You may call me Anastasia if you like. You know how Weres are. So, do the governors of the states they're locked up in. They want the workforce and the income they will bring. Before you say it, I am aware of the work release program. But if you look at it from the state government point-of-view any money given to the workers goes right back onto the reservation. They want Weres to spend it in the towns. Which you can't. Get it?" Anastasia asked.

I squinted at this woman, Anastasia, and worked through what she was saying. Slowly I nodded. "OK. I sort of understand what you say."

She pointed upward. "He knows this too. Never, ever, assume that man is stupid. But he wants the entire FBI to deal with what's coming, not a select group. So, by appointing you, he can tell those that ask that there is a division and that you are working. But training takes time, and the regular FBI will pick up the slack."

I understood now. He was never going to give me help. It really was just me doing this.

"Don't take it too hard, Jack. Look at it as an opportunity, not a chore. There are a few perks to the job." Anastasia smiled and held up a folder.

"Free coffee?" I asked.

Anastasia smiled, "No. But I did manage to find you a truck you can use as a command center. One portion of the Act the Director didn't mention was amnesty. If you are to be able to do this job to its fullest, you require amnesty from prosecution."

"Why would agents need that? The FBI has standards and an internal affairs group already." I stated to her.

"It does. What happens to you if you have to kill a suspect? Or even a prominent citizen?" she asked me.

I looked at her with wide eyes. Why was I killing people?

"Think about it, Jack. You now run the Magical Division. It will be your job to apprehend Witches, Weres, Vampires, and any other creepy crawly you find. Dead or alive, remember the laws? They are changing, but for now, when a call comes in, it's you that takes care of it!" Anastasia smiled at me again.

I choked and started to hyperventilate.

Anastasia allowed me to calm down before she continued. "If it's in the commission of your job, you are immune to prosecution. If you take over a case, it's yours. You are the lead agent regardless of rank and file. All law enforcement agencies including local sheriffs and chiefs of police are required to assist you. Be aware that the memos just went out on the national and state level. It will be some time before it trickles down to the local level. I suggest you acquire one of the National FBI directories and start memorizing."

"How? How can I do this alone? It's impossible!" I almost yelled at her.

"You're a resourceful man, Jack. I happen to know at least one instance where you took it upon yourself to do the impossible. This should be easy for you. I know you like challenges," Anastasia remarked.

I froze. How she found out secret what I thought she was alluding to was surprising. No one outside of the pack knew about that. No one.

"There is a file." That was all she said to me.

Shaking my head, I denied it. "Can't be."

"If you share your story, I'll share mine. Trust me. There was a record of it. The packs talk to each other, and we and our counter-parts in the OSS listen. It was unusual enough that a Texas boy was accepted by an Illinois pack. A human boy. While it has happened in the past, it's rare. If you see your mother and stepfather tell them they did a good job with you. Now spill." Anastasia ordered.

I took a deep breath. This was not a story I had told anywhere. Not even a whisper. While it wasn't exactly illegal, the local and tribal police might have looked for a reason to lock me up if they knew. I still had a friend on the reservation.

"I was fifteen. Mom married Chuck Rogers when I was twelve. As you know, he is in the Air Force. Mom likes the structure of the military, and when the Colonel was reassigned, we packed up and went with him." I flashed back to those days in Texas.

"Honey, we have to go. It was the reason Chuck and I got married after all," She told me.

"It's not fair is all. Me and the guys were going to go camping this summer up at Eagle Point." It was going to be pretty cool too. The Were reservation butted up against one of the local Native reservations. Some things were shared.

"You can camp in Illinois, buddy. From what I hear the area around Pacific is filled with trees and stuff." Chuck stepped into the room with a stack of boxes.

"Fine," I stepped around them and went back to my room. The house was very small but suited me fine as I spent any time not in school running wild outside. My parents continued to talk, and I swear I tried to not listen.

"Chuck, are you sure this is the right move?" my mom asked.

"You know it is, Elizabeth. It's too late, anyway. Orders are orders. From what command says, this post is temporary anyway. Roger over in logistics swore to me the defense stations were going to be phased out anyway," Chuck replied to my mother.

"If you say so. At least there's a local pack he can connect with," Mom replied.

"You know my opinion of that, but they might be able to help him socialize. I'll get some more boxes and help you pack the kitchen. The truck is coming in the morning," Chuck stated as I heard his voice fade.

While Chuck was good for mom, he had a different opinion of paranormals than we did. The Army and Marines were the service of choice for most Weres. They like to keep their feet firmly on the ground. Only a very few enlisted in the Air Force. Government service was the only way off the reservation. By joining, you were declared neutral in all things pack and couldn't be challenged for ranking. It was one advantage to joining. My Alpha had promised to put me in touch with a local group that would allow me to stay 'inside' their world.

The truck Chuck mentioned showed up in the morning, and I got to watch several of the largest men I'd ever seen outside of a Wolf-pack move our entire house in a matter of hours and load the truck. They would meet us at our new house which amazed me at the time.

Three days of hard driving with very few stops was the plan. It didn't work out that way, but who was I to complain.

"Honey, can you explain this base you're going to again? I don't understand why there are so few other families." Mom asked as we waited for the gas station attendant to fill the car tires, check the engine fluids, and add gasoline.

"It's called the Belleville Air Station. The base hasn't been there all that long. For the Air Force, it's practically new. We are defending the St. Louis area from any sort of aerial threat." Chuck replied.

"Like dragons?" I asked.

Chuck laughed. "Only if we see one. No one has yet just so you know. Command told me they worry about Thunderbirds and Bat Demons. During the war, that type of Demon could knock a fighter plane right out of the sky. The only way to be sure you killed it was heavy, concentrated fire."

I nodded. I knew more about the Demon War than most of my human classmates because of the pack. The classroom history books barely mentioned the war anymore.

"My base is only one of four that will protect the city in case of attack. St. Louis is a vital port and rail station." Chuck told me.

"What about the other Demons?" I asked.

"That's what the Army is for. I'm supposed to have a bunch of those ground pounders under my command. Inter-service cooperation the General called it. We'll see how that works out." Chuck pulled out his wallet and paid the man presenting him with a bill. "Anyone have to pee?"

"I barely remember that road trip. All I could think about was losing friends and changing schools," I looked at Anastasia.

"I bet. I've moved a few times in my life. Skip ahead some please and get to the good parts." Anastasia ordered me.

I smiled and continued. So much for dragging it out.

"We moved in, and I went to the new school. Unlike Texas, my classes were unsegregated. For me it was refreshing. In my young opinion, people were people. It didn't matter race, color, or species.

"The local pack wasn't a Wolfpack. They were leopards, which is a heck of a shock when you're used to dealing with Wolves. My nickname with them was Dog Boy."

"Hey Dog Boy, wanna go camping?"

I nodded. My integration with this group wasn't as firm as it was back in Texas. The kids were similar to me in what they thought, and that was enough. Plus, I loved camping.

Out of all the friends I'd made, I had two that I hung out with the most, Kevin and Charles. My stepdad liked to call Charles by the nickname of "Chuck" just like he was called, but my dark-haired friend resisted. My stepdad's job was a bit more intensive than he'd led us to believe. What the base was for wasn't a secret even though it was supposed to be. The code name was SL-47DC. What that meant was, they had a large number of ninety-millimeter, anti-aircraft guns and a brand new battery of Nike missiles. Rumor had it among us kids that they were tipped with atomic bombs. Even I thought that was crazy since they would kill us along with the Demons.

So, we went camping. A lot. Pacific, Missouri was next to the Meramec River, and the even bigger Missouri River was near. All sorts of people came through the area. Highway Sixty-six was just spitting distance from where we lived.

The reservation was between the two rivers, but they liked to camp on the bluffs near the Missouri side. We would stay up all night telling each other tales and spooky stories. Charles and Kevin tried to scare me the first time we went out.

According to Kevin, there was a monster that frequented this part of the country. The native Indians had told tales of it for a couple of hundred years. Legend had it that French trappers had even seen it. Over in Illinois, there was supposed to be a big painting of it, but my parents refused to drive all the way over there to see it. It was called the Piasa Bird. Kevin swore it was like a flying bear with teeth and claws that would swoop down and snatch up deer and eat them. The first night we went there they shook me out of bed in the middle of the night to scare me.

Needless to say, I didn't really believe in monsters then. Espe-cially flying bears. Not until I saw one. For real.

It was just supposed to be another one of our camping trips. We were going up river just a bit this time. The area was supposed to be devoid of humans, and Charles wanted to try doing a vision quest along with some hunting. None of us were natives. Kevin claimed to have gotten instructions from a guy he knew, but it was all just made up stuff we got from books. But we were young and dumb.

This time was unusual because we took Charles's dogs with us. Hunting was legal if you were on private land or had a license. We had neither, but where we were going didn't have roads. Kevin said the dogs would alert us and could help chase down the deer if needed.

"Did you get your dad's gun?" I asked Kevin when he came knocking.

"Shhh. Are you crazy?" Kevin looked around for my parents.

I smiled at him. "Mom's at a PTA meeting and Chuck's on duty. Did you get it or not?"

"No, Dad said no way. I did bring my new crossbow. Take a look." Kevin handed me a bundle wrapped in a sheet.

"Your mom know you took her sheet?" I asked as I unwrapped the weapon.

"It's not hers. Found it on the line out there." He pointed across the street.

I shook my head. "Oh, boy. Let's get moving. Those folks over there are mean to kids."

Kevin shrugged and wrapped up his prize. Grabbing my kit and locking the door I followed him through the neighborhood. Charles was waiting for us by the river with the dogs.

"Just where is this place?" I asked.

"That way. We have to paddle. It's not all that far." Charles pointed to a flat-bottomed aluminum boat sitting in the river.

Eyeing the boat I asked, "will we all fit?"

"Sure, come on let's go." Kevin climbed in and told me to toss him the packs and supplies.

With the dogs and us, we just fit.

There was just a bit more rowing and paddling involved than I was told about. After about an hour, Charles announced we were there.

"Where?" I looked up at the river bank. Nothing but trees and rocks as far as I could see.

"Over there, Dog Boy." Kevin pointed to a small island in the middle of the river.

I peered at the tree-lined shore. "Isn't that just a channel island?"

The island was just a chunk of a sandbar that was cut in the channel by the dredging machines. Lots of barges used the river around here.

"It's safe. Unless the river is flooding, it's dry. Trust us, Dog Boy," Kevin really liked calling me that.

I was surprised to find a campsite on the island. They actually told me the truth this time.

Kevin's idea of doing a vision quest was getting rip-roaring drunk and passing out next to the fire. Charles went right along with him like always. I thought that the beer they gave me tasted what I imagined horse piss tasted like. It gave me the shivers thinking about it.

I ended up on the river bank looking up at the moon at three in the morning or so when I first saw it. It was not a flying bear. To my young eyes, it looked like a cross between a deer, a bear, and a dragon. Horns were coming out of its head and sharp claws on its feet. It screeched, and I just about peed myself. Jumping up I ran to wake up Kevin.

Both my friends were dead to the world. I shook both of them and even splashed the remainder of a beer on them. Nothing. The screeching got louder. Looking up I didn't see anything, but the dogs were going crazy! They were barking and whining. We'd brought three of them with us, but only one was a real hunting dog. Charles called him Spot, but he was some sort of mutt without spots.

Spot ran past me growling while the other two dogs tried to hide under me while I was still standing.

"Spot! Spot come back here!" I yelled at the black and gray dog.

From the direction the dog ran, there was a screech and what sounded like metal tearing. I hear a dog yip and then nothing. The moon was behind clouds, and I was too afraid to look. I sat out the rest of the night shivering in the cold clutching the biggest stick I could find.

"Where's my dog?" Charles pushed me over off the log I was sitting on.

I lay on the ground and didn't speak. The other two dogs lay at my feet still shaking with fear.

"What the hell's the matter with you Dog Boy?" Kevin asked me.

"The monster took your dog," I replied.

"What've you been smoking? There aren't any monsters. Where's the dog?" Charles tried to get his other dogs to heel.

"You guys were passed out last night. I saw it, and it attacked us. Go look at the boat if you don't believe me." I pointed toward the river.

Kevin looked at me like I was crazy and Charles just shook his head.

"That was just a story we told to scare you. No such thing as monsters." Charles repeated.

When I didn't move or deny it, Kevin cursed at me and stomped off toward the boat.

"Did he run off? Is that it? He's been known to chase deer or rabbits sometimes? Spot!" Charles called for his dog.

"What the freaking hell did you do to my dad's boat, Dog Boy?" Kevin yelled.

Charles stood up and ran toward the river. His voice joined Kevin's in yelling.

I rolled over and carefully stood up. Picking up my stick I kept it in my hand watching the sky as I walked. Both my friends were exclaiming over the boat and the splashes of blood on the ground.

"I told you. The monster attacked," I told them.

The boat was a wreck. We wouldn't be rowing up-river or even down the river. Somehow the monster had ripped giant holes in the bottom of it. Claw marks scored the sides, and there was also a big, bite-sized chunk gone from the side.

"Why'd you wreck the boat, Dog Boy?" Kevin yelled.

I looked at him in shock. "Me? If it was me, how did I do it? Do you see giant ass claws on me?"

Charles just stared at all the blood. "I raised him from a pup. Old man Webster gave me that dog. He deserved more than this."

Kevin shook his hands and screamed up at the sky.

"What if it comes back?" I asked my friends.

"Monsters don't exist. Those are just stories the tribes tell each other. My dad says so," Kevin yelled at me.

"Even myths have some form of truth to them," Charles muttered as he stood on the river bank.

I looked at my friend. A tear was working its way down his cheek, but he was looking less lost.

"Can we defend against it? Will a crossbow kill it?" I asked.

"Monsters don't exist! Someone came and did this to us. Boles Valley is just over that away. We can swim for it and come back for the dogs later." Kevin pointed toward the opposite shore.

I looked down at the swiftly moving muddy river. People drowned every month in that river. We'd been warned more than once at school about swimming in it. No way I was swimming for it. "Did you guys tell anyone where we were going?"

Charles nodded. "My pop knows."

"Then they'll come looking for us?" I asked.

"Maybe. Pop doesn't listen all that well sometimes." Charles started to pet his other dogs.

"I'm not staying here with you two. I swim really good." Kevin yelled at us.

"What if that's what the monster wants you to do?" I asked.

Kevin looked at me incredulously and started digging in what was left of the boat. He pulled out a Type II life jacket and slipped it over his head. "Just stay here and don't touch my stuff."

The river didn't look all that safe, but Kevin was a shifter. I didn't think that cats swam all that well, but he looked like he was OK. turning to Charles, I asked, "Now what?"

"Build a big fire and hope the monster doesn't come back?" Charles replied.

"You believe me?" I asked.

"No. Kevin is right. Monsters are make-believe." Charles replied to me.

"Explain the boat, then." I pointed to the chunks missing.

"I can't." Charles walked back to our camp and sat clutching his remaining dogs.

"I'm not just sitting here." I grabbed Kevin's pack and bag and pulled out the crossbow he'd brought.

Charles just shook his head. "He loves that thing. If you break it, he'll kill you!"

"He can get in line if that thing comes back." I pulled out two bundles of quarrels and started trying to figure the bow out.

Charles knew a little about it from listening to Kevin talk. He explained how the stock was once part of a .30-.30 rifle Kevin's father once owned. For some reason, the barrel blew up. Charles said it may have been a faulty reload. Kevin's uncle was a gunsmith, and he took the stock and had it made into a bow.

"I can see why he treasures it." I would too if my family made it for me.

"Don't break it," Charles told me as he showed me how to cock it and fire.

Carefully I fired a couple of the short arrows at one of the trees.

"You suck at that," Charles commented as he watched.

"There aren't any monsters in Texas to practice on." I lined up another tree in the sights and fired.

A loud screech sounded just as my arrow hit the tree with a thunk!

Charles looked up, "The hell?"

"Monster. I told you." I scanned the trees above us.

"Has to be a plane or something." Charles stepped out by the river bank.

"Don't go out there!" I yelled at him.

There was another screech, and we both looked up at the same spot. The same monster I'd seen was swooping down at the center of the river. Its sharp claws extended the frighteningly ugly creature skimmed the water for a moment. Suddenly its claws grabbed something.

The biggest fish I've ever seen was in those talons as the monster my friends swore didn't exist flapped into the sky.

"River sturgeon. A big one. There really is a monster, you were right." Charles was totally calm as he watched the Piasa Bird swoop down.

"Should we hide?" I asked him.

"Yup." That was the only answer I got as Charles grabbed both his dogs and ran for the trees.

There was another loud screech, and the dogs started howling. The tree branches above us began to crack and creak. I would almost swear that the monster was right above us.

Another screech split the sky. To us on the ground, it sounded as if there was more than one. Grabbing up Kevin's crossbow I aimed at a dark shape in the foliage above us and fired.

"Did you hit it?" Charles asked me.

"No idea," I fumbled with the quarrels. My hands were shaking so badly I almost misfired the thing.

Sighting at the shape again I fired a second shot. This time there was an immense screech followed by another further away.

"You got it, Dog Boy! You killed it!" Charles jumped up slapping me on the back.

"I don't think I did. It might be back." I quickly reloaded the bow.

It was the act of reloading that saved my life. Neither of us heard the silent wings behind us. Like a giant owl, the creature came gliding in, talons outstretched, aiming right at our heads. I bowed my head just as it struck!

Charles went down like someone poleaxed him! The tip of one of the talons grazed my shoulder and ear leaving a deep scratch. Blood began to well up and drip downward.

Crying out in pain, I hit the ground. My hand came away from my shoulder bloody. The pain didn't match the amount of blood, but I screamed anyway. Crawling over to my friend I gave him a shake. Charles mumbled something but stayed unconscious. His Were healing saved him from sudden, irretrievable death but did not keep him awake.

Craning my neck, I looked up at the sky. I ignored the blood on my shoulder and rolled over. I grabbed the crossbow and reloaded it. There was another screech, and I could see the monster making another pass. Without thought or even a plan, I just fired blindly aiming for the spot in the middle.

The creature screamed again and crashed into the trees surrounding the campsite.

I tried to slow my breathing, but I felt as though my heart would beat its way out of my chest by itself. I climbed to my feet. A pile of feathers and claws lay not more than ten feet from me.

Snatching up the bow I started to load it again. There was another of those things up there.

"Why am I laying in pee?" Charles commented as he tried to stand.

"The dogs were scared and so were you it seems," I told him.

Charles looked past me at the pile of feathers. "Is it dead?"

He poked at it with a stick. The monster didn't jump up and kill him, so he jabbed it again.

"I think so." Charles jabbed the monster a third time.

Stepping closer to the monster I could see that it looked like a giant chicken mated with both an owl and a human. What was that thing? "Is it the Piasa Bird?"

"If it's not, it might be a Demon," Charles replied looking as scared as I was. "Is that blood on your shoulder?"

I looked down at all the dried blood on my shirt and suddenly noticed the pain on my shoulder. "Ouch."

Peeling the shirt away I could see a deep scratch across the middle of my right shoulder. The bleeding had stopped, and it was scabbing up. "I'm not gonna turn into one of those, am I?"

Charles started laughing. "Even if I scratched you, you wouldn't. All those years with the pack and you forget that part?"

My cheeks warmed up a bit. "Sorry. Gut reaction. You guys are born to be what you are. Unless I meet a Vampire, I'm stuck like this."

"Chances are you won't ever see one. They're pretty rare out here." Charles smiled at me.

"Good, I need all my blood where it is," I told him.

The dogs tried to sniff the corpse of the monster, but we both grabbed one and sat down by our fire. If Kevin made it ashore, he would send help.

Just before dark help materialized along with Kevin.

"Charles! Jack! Are you here?"

We had just laid the extra wood on the fire when we heard Kevin yell. Looking toward where the boat was we saw him and a couple of strangers walking into the campsite.

"I brought Mr. Szandor and the sheriff with me." Kevin motioned to the men with him.

"You boys need to be more careful out here. Freak boating accidents happen all the time. I don't like fishing kids out of the river. You two OK?" The largest man was wearing a brown sheriffs uniform complete with a hat.

"Yes, sir. We killed a monster." Charles answered for me.

The sheriff raised an eyebrow and looked back at the other man. "What monster?"

"The one over there. Jack shot it with Kevin's bow." Charles pointed to the lump of feathers behind us.

"You two are crazy! I told you there's no such thing as monsters..." Kevin looked past us and saw the thing. "What the hell?"

"Sorry, I touched your stuff, Kevin. It was trying to eat us," I informed him.

Kevin didn't say anything as he walked around us and stared at the big monster. I didn't pay any attention to him. I was watching the adults.

The sheriff was looking away from us. He and the other man were saying something, but I couldn't hear it. I looked at Charles as he shook his head. Somehow they were whispering things a Were couldn't hear!

"Come away from that thing, Kevin. It might be a Demon. Get your stuff. I'm taking you three back upriver right now. Anton here will take care of whatever that is and guard the site. I have to call the state police now, and I sure can't do that from here. Get moving." The unnamed sheriff started giving orders.

"Who's this guy?" I whispered to Kevin as we started packing up our stuff.

"He was at the farmer's house when I ran up. He's the Franklin County Sheriff. That's what was on his car. The other guy owns the farm over there. First time I've met either of them." Kevin whispered back. "Did you really use my bow to kill that thing?"

I nodded to him. "Yes, I did."

"I'm renaming you Monster Killer. Dog Boy is too tame," Kevin remarked.

I shot him a smile.

"Come on boys. Hurry it up there! I want to get outta here and have you home by dark." The sheriff yelled at us.

Giving the monster a last look, I joined my friends in the motorboat parked next to the remains of ours. "Sheriff? What is that thing?"

The big man gave me a look for just a moment that could melt steel, but only for a moment. His face changed. "No idea, son. You boys were lucky regardless. No coming back here, you hear? If I see any of you out here without a parent or whoever, I'll arrest you for trespassing on Anton's property. He owns that little island over there."

All three of us looked back at where we camped. I didn't remember seeing any signs. He took us down the river just a bit to a raggedy dock sticking out into the river. A police car sat up on the riverbank.

"Let's get you home."

My new boss only smiled at me when I finished.

"Well?" I asked Anastasia.

"What happened when he took you home?" She asked me.

"Not much. My stepdad, Chuck, had a raging fit, but Sheriff Watson calmed him down and said something to him. After that, the matter was done. Any time I brought it up, he shut me right down claiming it was top secret, and I wasn't to speak of it. My mom told me later that the sheriff said it was a military project," I replied.

Anastasia shook her head. "No. It wasn't. Both the sheriff and that farmer were later arrested on charges of Demonic influence. What you killed is called a Harpy. Call it a Greek Demon if you like. Those two and a few others raised it up and set it loose. They figured the Indian legends would keep it safe. Like most things, the Piasa Bird is a lie."

"What happened to them?" I asked.

"Don't concern yourself with them. We have very special prisons for those sorts. Now, you told me yours, I'll tell you mine." Anastasia smiled. It was an open toothed smile, and I could see three-inch-long incisors suddenly come out of the upper jaw!

I tried to scoot backward in my chair but found her holding it tight. I never even saw her move!

"Vampires are not as rare as you think them to be. Calm down. I work for the FBI the same as you." Anastasia walked back to her desk and sat down.

"I've been on his staff since 1945. It's why I'm in a unique position to assist you. It's also why I think you should succeed and not fail. There are way more things that go bump in the night than humanity imagines," Anastasia explained.

I realized I didn't have much choice here. If I refused the posting, my career was over before it began and if I took it, I might be trapped forever.

"How do I get cases?" I asked.

Anastasia handed me a thick file of paper. "You'll call in once a day whenever possible. Information will be given to you and only you. This is a backlog of potential cases as well as a few solved or concluded cases. Those are on top. Just a taste of things. Your authority ends with the Director. You are under his express orders. If anyone questions you, show them your badge first, this authorization second."

She handed me a leather folder with a plastic covered letter inside it.

"Try very hard not to overstep your bounds. Director Hoover isn't the most forgiving man. But keep in mind that he expects you to fail. So a few mistakes are allowed. I'm your direct supervisor for now. At least until you get your feet wet. I do have other duties so you may have to give your report to Mrs. Gandy sometimes."

I frowned at that.

"She's not that bad, just very devoted to the director. Don't cross her or your paycheck could be late. Very late. Any questions?" Anastasia asked me.

"Badge, itinerary, that truck you mentioned, I have tons of them," I told her.

Anastasia pulled open a drawer and tossed me a set of credentials. They'd used my cadet picture. A set of keys flew at my head. "The truck is in the central motor pool, show your badge and the key to the guard. As for an itinerary, you have graduation first. Then you are on your own. My suggestion is flip through the file and pick an easy one. Try to solve at least a couple of cases a month."

And that was it. I looked back at my drunken classmates. They thought my promotion was the greatest thing since sliced bread. It was unprecedented for a cadet to be offered something like this. I wanted it. Keeping America safe from the supernatural was something I was born to do and now I could.

Monsters beware. Jack Dalton is on the case!

JACK DALTON, MONSTER HUNTER

BOOK 2

"Is THIS THE FBI MOTOR POOL?" Jack asked the dust-covered guard sitting in a chair outside a very tall chain link fence.

The older man set down his newspaper and looked up at Jack. Pointing his finger at a sign over his head he spoke. "That's what the sign says. What business do you have here?"

"I'm the new head of the Magical Division, Jack Dalton." Jack held out his hand.

The guard cocked his head to one side and stared up at Jack expectantly.

Jack blushed and bowed his head. Digging into his coat pocket, he pulled out a folded sheet of paper and thrust it forward. "Sorry, I was told to pick up my vehicle here?"

Taking the paper, the guard nodded. He looked down and carefully unfolded the document. Pursing his lips, he nodded again. "If you had to have authorization those are the names to have. Go on in, kid. The man you want is named Charles. He's the one with the key to the garage."

Jack took his paperwork back and stepped through the gate into the yard it protected. Dust and dirt were everywhere. Due to wartime budget cuts and other factors, the maintenance yard and motor pool was unpaved and mostly neglected. It was here official cars were repaired and stored.

As he walked past cars up on blocks and piles of junk that resembled cars, Jack considered the reason he was here.

<<< >>>

"Take this to the motor pool and pick up your official car. It was picked out for you by me." The Vampire known as Anastasia handed him a sheet of paper. "You'll still need weapons and other accouterments. The arsenal is next door to the motor pool. Think big and lean on your experiences when choosing what you need. Remember your training and try to think outside-the-box for this. Weapons like crossbows aren't available in rural America. You can do this Jack. I have high hopes for you. Prove the big man wrong and succeed."

Jack took a second sheet of paper from her. Already the job was a bit surreal. There were rumors at the Academy, of paranormals working inside the FBI but everyone thought they were just rumors.

"Do you understand your parameters and rules? I've taken the liberty of having a packet made up of contacts and general information. It's waiting for you with the car. There is a shortwave radio built into the back as well as parts and equipment needed to send and receive telegraphs. We have a dedicated switchboard set up for you. Call this number weekly for assignment information as well as instructions from me. Build your contacts. Much of what you do will come from the officers out there in the trenches fighting these things. Call me if needed. Understand?" Anastasia caught Jack's eyes and stared at him.

Unable to look away Jack nodded. "Yes, Ma'am."

The Vampire smiled. "You make me feel old. Now I've got one more thing to say and then move you on your way. Come closer."

Jack felt himself move around her desk toward her.

"Closer. Come over here by me. I need to whisper this one. It's top secret information." Anastasia motioned with her finger.

Jack stepped up next to his boss and bent down. He could feel the heat of her breath on his neck as she spoke softly to him. Her cold hands gripped his arm and pulled him even closer to her.

"You and I are going to have a wonderful relationship together Agent Dalton. Agents such as yourself rarely come this close to me. Now let me taste ... I mean, tell you a secret." Jack strained to listen as Ana's face came even closer to his neck.

That was the last thing he remembered. Ana told him one of a Vampire's powers was to implant suggestions in humans. The Director had instructed her to make him loyal to only the FBI and no one else. Or at least that is what she told him.

Jack didn't have any reason to not trust what Director Hoover was saying. Not even a little.

<<< >>>

There weren't any workers in the front part of the yard only wrecks and stripped cars. Mechanical noises could be heard in the distance, so Jack worked his way around to the rear area.

"This must be it," Jack said to himself. There was a very large warehouse surrounded by cars in the back. Men dressed in overalls and jumpsuits were crawling in and under cars everywhere.

Addressing a pair of legs sticking out from under a shiny limo, Jack asked a question. "Excuse me? Is Charles around?"

"It depends on who's asking?" A muffled voice answered. The legs twitched as the body they were attached to rolled out.

"Agent Jack Dalton. I was told to pick up my new vehicle here." Jack held out a hand to the grease-covered man.

Gripping the offered hand, the mechanic stood up and stared at Jack. "Who sent you?"

"I'm the new head of the Magical Division. Director Hoover appointed me yesterday to the position," Jack replied.

The mechanic frowned, repeating the question. "Who sent you to us?"

"Anastasia sent me."

"Good answer. I recommend in the future you listen first before answering, kid. Some things are more literal than others." The man pointed his finger at Jack. "Ana is good people. Hurt her ... and we will hurt you."

Jack blinked a couple of times before answering. How he could hurt a Vampire boggled his mind. Hoover's assistant even more so. "I won't. I promise."

The grease-covered man nodded toward the warehouse at the rear of the facility. "Come on, kid. What you want is back here."

Jack followed along as the man, Charles Taylor, led him to the large building. As they passed other workers dropped what they were doing and joined the procession.

"The big man ordered us to provide you with any old thing, but

Anastasia stepped in and thought you needed more support. We confiscated this vehicle during an illegal weapons sting a few years ago. It's been collecting dust in the back. We made a few modifications, but it already had secrets of its own." Charles grabbed a large metal door and pulled.

Several of the tagalong men ran forward, sliding the bay door open. Sitting in the middle of the room was a yellow and black beauty.

"What year is it?" Jack asked.

"1952. Before the smugglers got it, it was used to deliver auto parts for one of the big national chains. If you look close, you can see the lettering under the paint. The arresting agents wanted it for undercover work, but it was lost in the system. How it ended up here is a mystery, but for you, it should be perfect. It's sturdy, easy to repair, and unlike anything the bureau is driving. We've added the basic logo to the doors and some words to the rear." Charles handed Jack a set of keys.

Jack opened up one of the doors and peeked in. The driver's seat was wider than most, but he could see fine leather stitching holding it together. In place of the passenger seat was a modified file cabinet and desk. "That's different."

"Ana said you were going it alone, so we modified things a little." Charles walked to the rear. Carefully he opened the rear window and dropped the tailgate.

"As you can see we have a shortwave system set up in the back. It's tight, but you should be able to fit a cot in here as well as whatever weapons you find. We weren't sure of your plans, but we put in storage units on the sides and if you look close, a small dresser and portable sink. Your orders are in the glove compartment, Agent Dalton. Blow the horn when you want out. Please tell Miss Ana we kept our promise to her." Charles smiled and left the bay. The other men laughing at Jack's expression closed the bay doors behind them.

Jack stood in the dim light and stared at his new assignment. It was starting to feel real. The words 'FBI Magical Division' was emblazoned on both sides of the van.

————

THE FBI'S WASHINGTON ARSENAL building was next door to the garage. A huge fence backed up by a ten-foot wall surrounded the building. Following the Demon War, it was judged that local agents needed access to weapons heavier than automatics and shotguns. Too many Senators and other politicos remembered the street fighting and deaths caused by the incursion in California. Much of the southern part of the state was still, even now, ten years later, totally devastated.

Because the building housed weapons, there were double and triple the guards usually found on government buildings. Jack's identification, badge, and orders were checked and rechecked. His new command vehicle was checked as well.

"Drive straight and turn right at the yellow pole. No unnecessary stopping. You will be met at the doors. Do you understand?" The agent in charge of security was one of the largest men in government service Jack had ever seen. He was way outside of what Director Hoover thought was standard for most agents.

Jack swallowed before answering, "Yes, sir. I'm supposed to pick up a special package here. Do they have it?"

The big man almost growled at Jack. "Drive straight and turn at the yellow pole. Understand?"

Jack nodded. Best to not see what getting ripped in half feels like.

The armory looked even bigger close-up. The walls were buttressed and looked fortress-like. Turning at the yellow pole as instructed, Jack found himself in front of two enormous steel-banded doors. A lone worker dressed in coveralls, stood in front of them waving at him to pull forward.

"Stop right there." The man pointed to lines painted on the concrete. "Present your document. Stay in the car."

Carefully, Jack passed his orders as instructed out the window.

The name on the suit was Pell. He took the offered page and carefully studied every line and signature. "You're late."

Jack gasped. "What? I just got my orders today!"

Pell looked at Jack over his glasses and smiled. "When you picked up the car from Charles did you come straight here?"

Jack blushed. He felt the heat rising up from his neck all the way to his forehead. This man knew. "Uh, no, sir. I didn't."

"Here's a tip for you, Agent Dalton. Someone is always watching. Keep that in mind, and you may survive in your mission. When the door opens, pull inside." Pell turned and entered the building through a small door on the side.

They knew he had taken the van for a spin before coming here. Jack didn't remember seeing anyone, but he took the lesson to heart for the future. There was a loud creaking noise, and the metal doors in front of him swung outward. Clicking on the headlights, Jack drove into the dark portal of the building.

Boxes, boxes, and more boxes were all he could see. His new van fit nicely in the empty space inside the building, but Jack could see it was meant for a bob-truck or one of the newer army M35 trucks. What the guys on the reservation called a half-ton truck. That style of truck is what he thought he might have gotten for this assignment. When the army was issued the newer M35s, they surplused out the older M135s to federal agencies. Getting a newer delivery van was sweet compared to one of those monsters.

"Agent Dalton, welcome to Candyland for gun nuts. We have it everything in here." Pell held the door open as Jack climbed out.

"Can I pick and choose or are you assigning me weapons?" Jack asked.

Pell gave him a shrewd look. "A little of both I believe. Your boss told us to fit you outright. Come on, I'll show you."

Jack picked his way through the stacks of boxes following Pell. He tried to read the letters and numbers stamped on them as he walked. The smaller man mumbled as they walked.

"We get it all in here. Rifles, shotguns, pistols of multiple sizes. We've got a few pretty nice automatics as well as weapons seized by the OSS and the ATU. To the big boys in the Capitol Building, it made no sense to have more than one arsenal in town. Less efficient is the words they used. As a result, we have this mess. And more every week." Pell patted a few boxes as they walked.

"What happens to the surplus?" Jack asked.

"Scrap metal or surplus. We can't sell frontline weapons to civilians, but police along Highway Six-Sixty-Six have picked up a few. Nobody's seen a Demon since fifty-six, but you just never know now do you?" Pell answered him.

"Can they be killed by regular bullets? I thought we needed special silver and herbs to do the job?" Jack asked.

Pell stopped and looked back at Jack. "You've been reading. Good. You're gonna need that information. Demons can be killed with massive amounts of firepower, but it takes a great deal. Silver and salt are the most common ammo, but silver, salt, and herbs are another option. One of my predecessors came up with the best round. Too bad we don't use it anymore."

"Why not?" Jack asked.

"Not many Demons around. Plus, if you shoot a human with one of them he might die." Pell replied as he stopped in front of a wooden door. "This is it."

"If someone shoots you with a gun, you're going to die. What kind of crazy is that?" Jack stated.

Pell snorted, "You are aware of the concept of spalling?"

Jack nodded, "Sure. It's what happens when a hollow-point bullet enters the body. It flattens as it hits and scatters shards through the body causing damage. We're one of the few countries to use them."

"Exactly. But the type of loads we used to issue for paranormals contained salt, silver, herbs, and shards of wood. The combination of that along with the slug itself can damage too much of the body." Pell replied as he unlocked the door and opened it.

"What kind of wood?" Jack asked.

"Oak, ash, and thorn. Folklore has those three as the most Magical. Trust me when I say if you hit a Vampire with one of those ... he's down for the count. Very effective at close range. Let me show you what we put together for you." Pell stepped inside and hit the lights.

"Oh, my," Jack uttered as the lights came up. A large table stood in the center of the room. A very wide variety of weapons were arrayed upon it.

"We tried to think outside of the norm for you, Agent. We have both the new and the old version of the crossbow. Shotguns will do the job, and certain capture and control gear. You will be on your own for the most part. If you can't bring them in successfully, you will have to put them down. Trust me when I say that many of those THINGS out there don't go easily." Pell had a flash of hatred cross his face for a moment.

"Did you serve?" Jack asked.

"Forty-three to fifty-six. I was in the thick of it from California to what used to be Western Germany. My unit was wiped out fighting the last of the Horde in Death Valley. I hung up my hat and went to work for the Bureau. Less stress working here. Always keep a weapon close at hand." Pell grimaced in memory and casually stroked one of the long rifles on the table.

"Death Valley was the site of one of the last battles with the Horde. Indians native to the area captured several Imps during the earlier battles and were using them as servants. Very much like a parable of keeping a wild animal in your house, they rose up and ate the natives. Troops were sent in to end the decade-long incursion," Pell continued to caress the rifle.

"What's that one?" Jack motioned to the rifle Pell was fondling.

"Mosin-Nagant. This one is configured as a sniper rifle. It comes to us from the Russians. One of the most heavily made guns pre-Demon War in that country. It's not the only Russian weapon we have here. There is an AK-47 as well as a reconfigured Thompson prepared for you. All of the firearms take silver rounds." Pell remarked.

"What about area denial weapons? Can I get a few of those?" Jack asked Mr. Pell.

"Explosives are harder for us to provide to you. There is the potential for unintended casualties with them. We have a few grenades and something new the British Special Service came up with. They call it an incapacitant, a stun weapon. It works on humans but is untested, by us, on paranormals," Pell replied.

Jack thought for a moment. "Can I have any of those? It might come as a surprise to my enemies since it's so new."

"We'll have to install a small explosive locker in the floor so these cannot be reached by civilians. Is that satisfactory?" Pell instructed.

"Will it add too much extra weight to the back?"

"It shouldn't, regardless, we can use the extra space. This way we can give you more of explosive bolts for the crossbow." Pell picked up a clipboard and made a few notes. Finishing he held out his hand. "Keys?"

Jack handed them over to Pell who barely glanced at them as he made more notes on the clipboard.

Pell looked up at Jack, "Come with me. You have a room full of paperwork to fill out. My boys will take care of getting you loaded up. Is there anything else you think you need?"

"Handcuffs, camping gear, flashlights, maybe a stove with a coffee pot, do I need to buy that stuff myself?" Jack asked.

"No. We've got you covered. It's part of the package we have. You're getting Were-proof cuffs, one of the reasons you have paper-work. They make them out of a steel-silver alloy now. Your supervisor made the arrangements. Paperwork calls." Pell pointed toward a distant door.

And what paperwork it was. Jack spent more than three hours signing form after form. At times it felt as if he was signing away his first born and grandchildren at the same time. When he made that comment out loud, the attendant smiled. "You missed one packet there. All of this is necessary, Agent. If for any reason you shoot and kill an innocent, there needs to be accountability. Trust me when I say most FBI agents aren't armed with bazookas and Russian class-three weapons. This is for your protection as well."

"If you say so." Jack signed the last couple of pages and slid them over to the man.

"It's not me, but those that pay me. I believe those same people pay you as well." He looked at the final packet with a smile. "Excellent, Mr. Pell should have your vehicle stocked and loaded by now. Good luck in your new position, Agent. Please do come again."

Jack almost told the man to stuff it but realized quickly where else was he to get silver ammo and exploding rockets. "I will. Thank you."

The black and yellow van was sitting in the same place but was now nosed forward toward the door. Mr. Pell stood next to it wiping the engine cowling.

"Is it all done?" Jack asked.

"Of course. Take a look," Pell tossed Jack his keys back.

Peeking in the driver's side door, Jack could see both a shotgun and one of the pistols mounted with easy reach in the front. A wire mesh wall now separated the front from the rear compartment. Jack frowned as he pulled on it.

"The wireless needed an antenna system. We're full service here. It does double duty to protect what we loaded you with as well." Pell answered before Jack could ask.

Jack could only nod as he opened the rear and looked inside. A collapsible cot sat folded to one side along with a small wooden chair. Lockers and weapons mounts had been added to both sides of the interior walls. Two small safes and a weapons locker took up the passenger side. He could see camping supplies and cookware carefully stored away. The driver's side had the radio as well as places for clothing and food. It resembled a modern chuck wagon he told Mr. Pell.

"That's it exactly. You will be on your own out there, and if you don't carry it with you, you might not be able to find it. The standard ammo you can either buy or requisition from any of the field offices. If you need special supplies, call us and request it be sent. You and only you will be allowed to pick up the items from the office we send them to. This gives you the authorization. Keep it safe." Pell handed Jack a new wallet and several keys. "Codes for the safes are in that wallet. Please memorize them."

"Is that it then?" Jack asked.

"From us. You received a message from the main office." Pell reached into his coverall and handed over a folded sheet of paper.

———

THE NOTE READ "BLADENBORO, North Carolina, and good luck." It was unsigned, but only one person knew where Jack was supposed to be that day. Pulling out a map, he studied the new interstate system. Interstate Ninety-Five was new. Really new. The roads it was built upon were former toll roads that interconnected their way down the entire eastern seaboard to Florida.

From a military standpoint, it made a great deal of sense to be able to send troops anywhere, at any time easily. The only issue was many of the toll roads were still there, and it was going to be really expensive to get to Fayetteville before heading to Bladenboro.

Jack pulled out the petty cash envelope and was halfway through the process of counting when it came to him. He palmed his head and muttered a stupid line from television about tomato juice. How dumb could he be? He was a federal agent. No tolls would be needed.

According to the map, Bladenboro was only six-hundred miles or so from the Capitol, but the road zigged as much as it zagged. It was going to take at least a day to get there.

"This thing is a gas guzzler," Jack muttered to himself as he filled up for the second time. The FBI may have modified the van, but they didn't replace the in-cab fuel tank. It only held sixteen gallons and burned it up in a hurry.

Eyeing the location of the tank, he could only nod. A few other truck models had a tank directly in the rear, just off the bumper. It wasn't unusual for one of those to explode on contact during an accident.

He was more than halfway there, but it was slow going. The map claimed he was only a few miles outside of Smithfield but he hadn't seen many cars along this stretch of road, and it was getting dark.

As he paid for gas, he asked the old timer behind the register, "This is Interstate Ninety-Five isn't it?"

"That's what they tell me. The state came through here a few years ago changing the road signs and informing folks of the new plans. Of course, this stretch here has to wait a few years for upgrades. Where are you headed?" The older man asked Jack.

"Bladenboro, North Carolina. This is the first time I've ever gone this way," Jack answered.

The old man tilted his head and looked out the window at Jack's car. "You hunting the monster?"

Jack started, "What monster?"

"Don't try to josh a josher, young fella. I was there in forty-six when the demons charged the line. You're after the monster aren't you?" The old man stood up from his stool and looked Jack right in the eye.

His entire life Jack had been told to respect his elders and this situation was no different. "Yes, sir. What do you know about it?"

"Just that it's supposed to be dead. Something was out there in the woods and streams killing animals for no reason back in Fifty-four. Almost every hunter in the state went to Bladenboro trying to bag whatever the hell it was. It was killing farm animals left and right. Folks were locking their kids up at night. Two good old boys from one the farms there claimed to have caught a record bobcat in one of their traps. The pictures taken showed a record-sized critter, but folks around here are more of the "see it now" sort. Nobody really trusted those boys." The old man spoke as he gazed out the window.

"Did the killings stop?" Jack asked. He wondered why, if they caught this thing years ago, he was being sent there now.

"For a while they did. But I hear tell it either wasn't dead, or momma is here looking for revenge," the old man commented.

"Five years later? I don't know, monsters aren't people. They don't bide their time." Jack pulled out a notebook and wrote what the man was saying. Better to get what facts he could for now.

"Son, I was in Death Valley and saw things set against the night sky that would curl your hair. Demons are unforgiving. If they catch you, they will either kill you or eat you. Sometimes both. You should turn that fancy rig around and go back where you came from. Safer that way." The old man looked away from the windows.

"If I do that, it becomes someone else's problem. It's my job to fix it the first time." Jack remarked to the former soldier.

The old man snorted. "Self-righteousness can get you killed, boy. Do you even have holy protection?"

Jack looked at him questioningly, "huh?"

"Stupid child. Here, take mine. I want it back mind you. This was given to me by a priest at the mission of San Juan Capistrano just before the Horde took it." The old man removed a shiny bird-shaped amulet from his neck and handed it to Jack.

Looking closer, Jack could see it was intricately designed with a Latin prayer intertwined with feathers and bird features. "You should keep it. This is a work of art."

"You're about to do battle with forces of evil, boy. Use it and when it's over, come see me. We can swap stories and tell some lies. No one should do battle without something to protect them."

Jack knew better to argue with an old soldier. Carefully he slipped it around his neck. "I'll bring it back."

"Of course you will. Now get moving. Take State Eighty-Seven to Tarheel, then Four-Ten straight into Bladenboro. You can't miss it. Be careful. Demons are tricky."

Jack stopped at the first roadside campground he came to. If the forces of darkness wanted a battle, he needed to get rest first. The cot supplied by the armory crew was hard and way too low to the floor, but to someone not used to long-distance driving, it was heaven.

───────

BLADENBORO WASN'T A VERY memorable place. Lots of pine trees and cotton fields dotted either side of the highway. A faint smell of turpentine in the air told the story of what industry was here.

A loud horn shook Jack out of his thoughts making him concentrate on the road. On his side of the highway, there wasn't a car to be seen. Cars seemed to be leaving town in droves. The left side was bumper to bumper the whole way. More than one person blared the horn to tell him to turn around.

Halfway to town, he was stopped by a state highway patrolman and a local county sheriff.

"You need to turn around and go the other way. This road is closed to all traffic."

Jack held out his badge. "Then I'm in the right place. My assignment is Bladenboro."

"Are you really from the FBI?" The local sheriff deputy scrutinized Jack's badge, even calling over the state patrolman.

"I'm here because of your monster problem. Can you tell me more about it?" He asked taking his credentials back from the officer.

"We sent for the army, but they never showed up. The Governor said he was sending the Guard, but now we see you. What makes you so special?" The state patrolman asked.

"I represent the Magical Division. Any cases related to the paranormal is supposed to go through my department. What can you tell me regarding your monster?" Jack asked again.

"It isn't my place to tell you stuff, Agent. Let me call the sheriff over." The deputy climbed back into his car to use the radio.

At more than six feet tall Sheriff Richard Singletary towered over nearly everyone present. As he climbed out of the patrol car, he appeared to get taller. "What's this all about then?"

Quickly, Jack explained the situation and his reason for coming. "What can you tell me concerning the monster?"

Leaning back against his car the sheriff explained. "The beast is supposed to be fake. Mayor Donahoe thought the story might bring in tourists to town. There are always stories of big cats and wild animals that can sneak into your home and steal the souls of children, but nobody listened to those. Five years or so ago, a cat-like creature was spotted killing farm animals and stalking an elderly lady. We put a call out, and hunters came from everywhere. A large bobcat was caught and killed, but it gave the mayor his great idea. Old legends were dusted off and retold. We've got the annual Beast of Bladenboro parade and everything now. Tourists love it. It's not supposed to be real! Not like that thing."

"What does this one look like?" Jack asked. While what the locals had done wasn't illegal, it was unsavory to him.

"Big. Really big. I put five rounds into it when it chased me from town. One of my deputies hit it with his truck," Sheriff Singletary exclaimed.

"I'm guessing it didn't work. Were there deaths?" Jack braced himself for the answer.

"To be honest, we're not completely sure. Most of the town evacuated, but since we aren't in communication with them, we don't know who got out. We know it ate Chuck Williams' prized heifer and the Velasquez family lost their entire flock of chickens. That's how we found it in the first place. Feathers everywhere and one of my deputies got the scare of his life investigating it. We thought it was a cougar or escaped tiger. Half the town was looking for it with shotguns. That was until it showed up at city hall and tried to eat a visiting class from Cape Fear High School. Then we called for help," Singletary explained.

"So, this thing is big. What color is it?" Jack asked.

"Black." All three officers replied at once.

"So big, black, cat-shaped, anything else you can think of?" Jack asked.

"You're gonna think I'm crazy here, but I could've sworn it had sparkling claws and spikes like a porcupine on its back. That was one of the reasons I called the military. We thought it might be one of those Demons on the loose." Sheriff Singletary explained to Jack.

"Let me take a look." Jack turned toward his van, but at the last minute opened up the back. Carefully he removed the Wingmaster eight-seventy from the case and grabbed a pouch of special shells. Better to be safe than sorry.

Once he was safely inside the van, Jack loaded the shotgun. The armory crew had included an extended magazine, and he loaded it as well. Seven shots of the special ammo would kill a Demon. Surely, this cat was no different.

Big was the understatement of the year. Most likely the century. Jack got his first look right on the edge of town. A farm truck complete with trailer lay on its side blocking most of the road. Jack slowed and stopped to investigate.

Shotgun at the ready, he approached the front of the truck. Bending he couldn't see anyone in the cab, but there was what appeared to be blood splattered all over the inside. The driver's side door had been torn off, the hinges ripped and twisted. Gigantic claw marks scarred the vehicle. Cautiously looking around Jack jogged back to get his camera. Documentation was needed for everything.

Measuring carefully, each of the claw marks looked to be three inches apart. Jack tried to imagine what a house cat would look like fifty or sixty times larger. The mental picture wasn't pretty. Where did something like the monster even come from?

Looking at the shotgun in his hands he shook his head. More firepower was going to be needed.

———

THE STREETS LEADING into town were mostly undamaged. A few

cars were overturned, and several blue post office boxes were lying in the street. The devastation didn't start to become obvious until Jack reached the center of town and the courthouse.

"Wow," Jack muttered to himself. The courthouse still stood, but half of the large white columns in front were torn off and destroyed. The grass and park areas were torn and dug up. Piles of what can only be described as cat feces were everywhere.

Parking the van on a side street, Jack loaded himself up. Figuring he might need it, he carefully loaded a backpack with extra silver ammo and two explosive shells for the modified bazooka he found among the van's armament.

The military had used the M20 and its predecessors effectively during the Demon war. Nothing says "hello nice to meet you," like a nine pound anti-tank round. Two of the explosive shells added twenty extra pounds to his load. The launcher itself weighed another fifteen.

Humping the extra weight and guns, Jack hurried to find cover near the courthouse. Somewhere in town was a monster that needed to be killed.

———

CATS BY NATURE ARE HUNTERS. They stalk their prey before pouncing. Bladenboro's beast was no different. The prey it stalked was holed up inside the courthouse. It wanted and needed to kill the human. Pain lanced across its head if it strayed. So far Alderman Sprunt had eluded the large cat, forcing it to stray from the courthouse and the den it had selected to hunt fleeing townspeople.

James was kicking himself for not leaving when he had the chance. At first, the monster was only a rumor. The town had a parade for the blasted thing. Who knew it existed? If only he had listened to his parents, none of this might have happened.

"Son, you're making a mistake. That parcel of land has always been held in trust by our family."

James looked at his elderly father with scorn, "It's potentially prime farmland. If we do it right and drain the swamp rerouting the creek and lining it up, we won't have to irrigate the fields as much. We can double and triple our cotton production. Cotton is king right now. Why can't you see that?"

"Money is all you see. There is much more to life than just wealth. When my grandparents, your great-grandparents, came over from Scotland to settle here a bargain was struck. We were to keep the land inviolate until told otherwise. Our family has lived up to our side of the bargain and have never gone hungry. Now you are bringing upon us the wrath of that which you will never understand, and I pity you." Peter Sprunt could only shake his head at his son's actions. He wife beside him was speechless. While she knew her son didn't value the past, she was shocked he would destroy his heritage so thoughtlessly.

"My entire life you've told me of the trust and beings that never appear. If there were a document I could read or partners I could negotiate with, I would spare it, but you have none of that. Your word is worthless to me, old man. The very moment you signed a power of attorney and allowed yourselves to be placed here was the moment I achieved the first part of my dream, financial independence. Neither you nor some imaginary force is going to take it away from me." James told off his father and never looked back. When both of his parents grew ill several years later, he didn't even bother to visit.

Construction crews were brought in, and they drained the swamp. A body of water that once was half the size of the town was now a tiny shadow of itself. James only allowed a small pond to exist to keep members of the town happy. Frog gigging and fishing were still very popular even among judges and politicians.

The original Beast of Bladenboro was spotted around the time he broke ground, but hunters promptly caught and killed a displaced bobcat. There were no supernaturals or paranormals around here.

When the scratching and digging noises started up again, James hit the floor. It was back! The giant cat or whatever the thing was only wanted one person in town, and that was James. His house, barns, and cotton production facilities were the first to be destroyed. Only his chance stop at the courthouse saved his life.

———

Big, big, BIG cat! That was the mantra Jack muttered to himself when he first caught sight of the beast. It had to be twenty feet at the shoulder easily. Sheriff Singletary was correct in remembering its back was covered in spikes, and the claws looked very sharp as they dug into the concrete.

Something inside the courthouse was drawing it. The cat dug at the main doors trying to get inside for several minutes before running around to the rear, where it attempted the same thing.

"There's someone still inside." It was the only answer. Jack's goal was not to trap and kill the beast. Something of that size was impossible for a lone agent to capture. Stashing the bazooka and shells, he ran back to the van. This called for an experimental solution.

During the drive and one overnight stay, Jack managed to read most of the weapons information provided by Mr. Pell and the others at the armory. The stun grenades were marketed as non-lethal, but they could kill in certain situations. The British government used them for extremist groups and the occasional Demon cult that popped up in their major cities from time to time. One grenade set off in a small room would pop the eardrums of everyone inside and have adverse effects on humans from smoke inhalation. But they might shock the beast and hold it in one place long enough to get a bead on it with the bazooka. He wouldn't know until he tried it. The town was supposed to be evacuated. If he missed, one of the anti-tank shells could do tremendous of damage.

Arriving back at the shattered storefront he used to hide his weapons, Jack realized the glaring hole in his plans. There was little cover between where he hid and the courthouse. To use the stun grenades he needed to get close to the beast. "Well, crap."

Two trees and a park bench were the best covers he could find near where the cat was trying to dig its way into the building. If he set up wrong and it came back the other way he was screwed.

———

JAMES HAD NEARLY GIVEN up hope when he spotted a man dressed completely in green moving around the drug store across the street. At first, he thought the guy was looting the place until he saw the shotgun in his hands. "That's not enough firepower."

It was hard to tell from this far away, but the stranger might be military. That gave James hope he would be rescued. But he could still see only the one man.

Before his brain could come up with a way to warn the man out there, the building shook. "It's back."

Stumbling to the floor, James Sprunt crawled as fast as he could toward the other side of the building. When the cat first attacked, he was on the ground floor inside one of the smaller offices. He'd been searching in the files for a document when a gigantic paw, with razor-sharp claws extended, smashed through the window and attempted to pull him outside. Just as a rat trapped in a maze, the alderman ducked and dodged as he ran for the door, only to find sharp teeth and fetid breath waiting for him.

Half the rear door gave way during the last assault, leaving the second floor James's only option for safety. Like a kid reaching into a cookie jar, the cat had one paw inside reaching for him. He prayed the monster outside wasn't smart enough to know the roof gave better access to the inside.

Bang.

If the window hadn't been open James wouldn't have heard the shot fired because the cat took that time to yowl and screech as if it were a banshee. Gazing out the window, he saw the man in green run across what was left of the courthouse yard and park. A small area of the park was the only section still undamaged.

Yowl! The building shook and trembled as the cat redoubled its efforts to get inside. A loud cracking noise heralded the loss of the other half of the rear doors. The cat could not get its entire head inside the rear of the building quite yet. With the head would come the body and James could soon become kibble.

———

"THIS COULDN'T HAVE BEEN any better if I planned it this way," Jack muttered to himself as he took cover behind the bench and small trees. The monster cat broke through part of the courthouse and left its ass-end hanging out. Whoever it was in the building that the monster wanted, must have done something exceptionally bad to deserve this.

Jack had been a poor football player, but an excellent left fielder in high school. You needed to be able to throw a ball when you played with Weres. They run really fast. Taking aim, he pulled the pins and threw two stun grenades in succession into the building through the broken lower floor windows and hoped for the best.

Blam. Blam.

Any glass that remained on the lower floor shattered outward as both stun grenades exploded. Besides the overpressure effect, there was a two-thousand-degree flash that temporarily blinded the gigantic cat and shattered its eardrums.

The cat shrieked, and its yowl could be heard for miles as it writhed in pain. Jack took a knee and picked up the bazooka. A two-man military team could generally get off six shots a minute using one of the weapons, but Jack was alone. Carefully he loaded the tube connecting the electric firing switch. A magneto in the trigger handle would ignite the rocket. Each shell was supposed to be filled with high explosive, silver flechettes, rock salt, and wood chips from oak, ash, and thorn trees. Each of the elements could kill a specific type of paranormal, but the rounds were primarily set up for Demons.

Squinting, Jack tried to see through the tiny primitive scope. Framing the cat in the circle, he fired.

Whoosh! The bazooka fired tossing Jack backward onto the ground. A huge explosion sounded with parts of courthouse doors flying about.

There was another shriek as the cat bellowed in pain. Blood and other wiggling bits of creature lay scattered around the front of the building.

Peering through the smoke, Jack could see it was still moving. He pulled out another shell and began loading the bazooka. If this didn't kill it, he was in serious trouble.

Squinting through the optical sight a second time, Jack tried to line up with the main body of the animal.

Whoosh! The bazooka fired and once more Jack found himself on the ground from the blast. "There has to be a better way to do this."

The second explosion performed better than the first one. If the cat weren't dead, it would be very soon. Climbing to his feet, Jack approached the front of the building.

Blood and gore dripped everywhere. It was so thick on the stairs Jack didn't even try to climb them. He circled the building with his shotgun at the ready. The front doors were buckled inward but were still locked shut. Peering through the windows, he could see what was left of the 'monster.' It wasn't coming back from that. He had to be sure though. Carefully, Jack climbed through one of the windows and entered the building.

Laying his shotgun beside the cat's head, he delivered a coup de grace, but it wasn't needed. That last blast had finished the monster off and destroyed the stairs to the second level at the same time. Whoever was up there wasn't coming down the traditional way for a while.

Jack pulled out his camera and began documentation. He snapped pictures of the body as well as damage to the courthouse. It was more of a reference point than anything else. The 1959 Magical

Security Act provided amnesty for Magical Division officers in the performance of their duties. Neither he nor the FBI would be on the hook for the damage.

"Anybody up there?" Jack called out.

The upper level was in complete silence. James Sprunt couldn't hear Jack's voice or question. He was huddled under the Mayor's desk in a fetal position with both hands over his ears. A brave man he was not.

"Not my problem anyway," Jack muttered to himself. The beast of Bladenboro didn't resemble any Demon in the official Government books or any known paranormal for that matter. There was nothing but speculation as to where it had come from.

As far as Jack was concerned, he was now the official monster hunter of the United States, and this proved it. Placing the weapons back into his van, he wrote a note as a reminder. More rocket shells were definitely needed.

The roadblock was in the exact place when Jack motored out of town.

"What were all those explosions?" Sheriff Singletary asked.

"Your monster is no longer with us. It was not Demonic, so you should be able to return to the town. There is a bit of damage downtown, but the rest looks OK." Jack leaned out the window of his van and spoke to the police officers.

"Really? What'd you hit it with?" The sheriff asked.

"M20 anti-tank bazooka. Mine is different from the military ones. They're loaded with salt and silver for paranormals," Jack replied.

"The carcass looks to be a regular animal, but I recommend burning it as soon as possible. Other than that, I wish you good luck. Call it in if another one shows up." Jack smiled to himself. He sounded flippant, but he'd just taken out his first monster and was riding an adrenaline high.

"You're not staying to help us?" Sheriff Singletary asked looking shocked.

"No, sir. I need to call this in, make my report, and move on to the next case. Our country is really big, and there is just little ol' me to police it. Have a good day, Sheriff." Jack leaned back inside and put the car in gear. If he was lucky, he could get back to Fayetteville for more coffee and lies.

———

From the shadows of the forest, several figures watched the distinctive black, and yellow van drive off.

"Do you want us to hunt him, my Lord?" The warrior was fierce and wore two swords across his back.

"No. His time will come. The humans like to say that all good things will come to you, eventually. This Jack Dalton will pay for killing the Cath Palug. These humans grow bold with their ingenuity and explosive weaponry. No true knight would use such a weapon. That is the way of dishonor and guilt. Stay your blade for now." The brilliantly garbed Elf Lord stepped out of the shadows to stand in the light of the sun.

"And the other human, the developer? What about him?" The warrior asked again.

"That is a blood debt owed. He is an oathbreaker and deserves the worst punishment possible. I curse him and all his get until the debt is paid. Only full restitution will please those that command me," the Elf lord smiled as he entertained thoughts of blood and torture.

"Allow the curse to play out. Have our scouts spread the word to other enclaves and sithes. There's a new player in the game. Agent Jack Dalton is to be given a wide berth for now." The Fae warriors turned from the human highway and faded back into the trees.

———

"Mission accomplished boss," Jack reported directly to Anastasia using a pay phone outside the gas station.

"So, I hear. The mayor, the sheriff, and about half the town either want to kill you or congratulate you. The Director doesn't know which to do, either. Did you really have to blow up the courthouse?" She asked.

"It was still standing when I left. Only the rear doors are gone as well as the stairwell. I have detailed pictures. It may have been damaged getting the carcass out, but I didn't knock the place down," Jack explained quickly.

"Stop at the first local office you can find and submit your report. Include any film and your thoughts about training for something like this. We need to keep a running record of your missions. Training new agents may become a priority one day. I'm glad you survived, Jack, but now it's time to move on to the next one. Head north toward Maine. There's a Coven of Witches we need you to investigate for us." Anastasia instructed Jack.

"Witches! I thought they didn't want to have anything to do with our government?" He asked.

"They don't officially, but this group is the oldest in the country, and they wield political clout locally in Maine. We want you to intro-duce yourself and poke around the town. It's called Briarwood. Check in again when you get there. Good luck Jack." Anastasia hung up the phone before he could respond to her.

"No rest for the wicked is there, Jack?" The old man told him.

Jack turned and smiled at the old guy. Except for the eye patch, he'd be the spitting image of his grandfather. "No, there isn't. I can't stay long. They gave me another assignment."

"That's a government job for you. Keep the necklace I gave you. Not much call for Demon fighting hereabouts. Watch your six, and you will get through whatever concerns you. Take it easy out there, Jack." Without another word the old man stood and went back inside the gas station.

Jack stood still for a moment after he left. Something about the man reminded him of something, and it wasn't his grandfather. He shrugged his shoulders. More grist of the mill on the long drive north.

Witches. Should be interesting.

JACK DALTON, MONSTER HUNTER

BOOK 3

THERE ARE MONSTERS AMONG US. Shapeshifters, Vampires, Witches, and Demons roam the land unchecked by human law and order. My name is Jack Dalton, and I am America's monster hunter.

The state of Maine was a long way away from Washington, DC. Especially in winter. My truck was holding up fairly well for being both used and rebuilt. Non-military government vehicles generally broke down after long or hard use. Lowest bidder and all that. My newest assignment was taking me toward the frozen north. I was on my way to see a town full of Witches!

Witches. Just saying the word gives me the shivers. At the FBI Academy, we were taught just the bare minimum about them. They were humanoid and could pass for one of us at will. Groups of them liked to congregate and call themselves Covens. And finally, they were scary powerful. General orders were to stay away from them. Really freaking far away from them. Now here I was, going to meet a group on their own ground.

Anastasia, my immediate supervisor, filled in the blanks for me just a little before I left Washington. When the world changed in 1914, dozens of paranormal species were dragged into the light. Witches were just one, but they had an advantage. They looked human and often married humans.

I had realized that Witches were around, but I had been totally ignorant of the existence of groups of non-magical humans that either worshiped magical beings or tried to use Magick themselves. They called themselves Wiccans or Neo-Pagans.

According to my briefing paperwork, there was a worldwide upswing in Earth-based religions at the moment. Analysts at the FBI said it was due to paranormal exposure. I think it's just that people are scared and lonely. Many of the traditional religions aren't cutting it for them. It made me wonder how anyone could tell the difference between real Witches and fake ones. Or if there was a difference at all. I was starting to realize this assignment was going to be a pain in the butt.

One of the best things about my new truck was the cot in the back. While I've got nothing against sleeping under the stars, setting up a tent and then having to take it down is too much trouble. Roadside stops and most campgrounds are right on the main roads, anyway. I never worry about thieves or bandits. There's an arsenal in the back, and the letters FBI on the outside to dissuade most thieves. But there are always a few idiots.

"...when he pulled in. I got a good look, and the back was full. Gotta be a salesman or something. Those guys always have cash."

"I don't know Jake, it says FBI on the side."

"Don't be a dummy. It also says auto parts if you look closely. It must be some sort of delivery van or something. He's got plenty of green. I was there when he checked in. Come on Peter, see if you can jimmy the lock."

I'm normally a light sleeper, and after the last assignment, I've started to carry weapons everywhere. Better safe than sorry. Hearing that one of my new friends was the guy that checked me in made me regret accidentally flashing my cash. There's always a next time to be more careful.

There was a faint sound of metal on metal towards the front of my truck. Those locks don't work the way that others do. The FBI garage did something special to them.

Thunk!

"Shhh. Peter! What the hell are you doing?" Jake whispered to his companion.

"This lock is goofy. No place to access the tumblers. I'm trying to pry it," Peter answered.

"He's in there you idiot! You might wake him up," Jake replied.

"I wrapped a handkerchief around the end. It'll work. Trust me," Peter said as he pried at the door.

Ker-thunk! "Ouch!" Peter almost yelled.

There were a slight sound and a grunt.

"What did you do that for?" Peter whispered trying not to moan as he shook the pain off his fingers and tried to rub his head at the same time.

Jake drew back his hand after whacking Peter across the back of his head. "You're an idiot. You're making more noise trying to be quiet than doing this regular. Come on, we'll try the back doors."

One of them picked up the crowbar, and both men stepped around to the rear. The moonlight allowed me to see them through the back window. I assumed the taller man was Jake. He wasn't rubbing his head like the other man still was.

"Now pry right here next to the window lock," Peter pointed.

While they were discussing things, I carefully unlatched the rear. One push was all it would take to open it.

There was a slight metal on metal noise as the crowbar was inserted then a gasp of surprise. "It's open!"

"Shhh. Quiet you idiot! What do you mean it's open?" Jake whispered.

The back window opened up. "See, it's open already."

Both men leaned in to look at the window and found me staring at them, gun in hand. "Freeze!"

Peter dropped the crowbar and yelped as it hit his foot.

Shaking his head, Jake held up his hands. "Next time, when your sister says to give you a job, I'm saying no!"

Trust me when I say the looks I got from the local police force were priceless. My truck isn't set up for prisoners, so I had the both of them trotting behind the van on wires. It seems the two men had been robbing travelers for several months. The police hadn't a clue it was an inside job.

The police chief looked at my credentials and told his cousin, Jake, he was an idiot. That was my cue to leave town and continue my journey.

It was nice to be back on the road and on the new interstate system. The only part of this that was annoying was all the toll roads. I understand that the highway is needed, and it has to be paid for somehow. It also isn't really my money I'm using.However, it was still irritating.

"Twenty-five cents please," the toll booth attendant held out her hand.

The smile on my face as I looked at the pretty blond girl dropped. "A full quarter? Wow, that's expensive!"

Glancing at my truck and then back at me she continued to smile. "The state of New Jersey wants to continue to have excellent roads for its residents to use."

"Really?" I asked her. That statement was a little too pat.

The attendant's smile dropped off. "Not really. To be truthful, it's to stop all the shunpiking people. But don't say I told you that."

Being from Texas, I smiled at how she pronounced 'you.' It came out as 'youze.' I thanked her and continued on my way.

Highway 95 in New Jersey wasn't any better than the one in Maryland so I couldn't see the ten cent difference. But each state had its own way of paying for things. Reaching out with my right hand I patted the file cabinet in the passenger area. Having funds to pay the toll helped.

Seeing the sign for Maine was heartening. It wouldn't be too much longer now. I still wasn't sure I was up to meeting a town full of Witches. What if they turned me into a frog or something? Eating flies for the rest of my life didn't sound fun.

———

"MARCELLA ARE you sure about this meeting?" Minerva asked as she dug into the backyard planter.

"It needs to be done. The humans grow in strength and power. Our Coven is the most public and vocal of all. It's not just my position on the Council that drives the need for this connection." Marcella pulled back and brushed off her hands.

"The Garden is a full-time job. We all know that around here. But do they? You've seen how the local Maine representatives act when we mention Magick. If we weren't spelling them the moment they set foot in the county, we'd be taxed out of our own houses.

They know we're here. It hurts nothing to speak to them. Besides, we can always spell this man as well."

"True but did it have to be the FBI? They are responsible for so many lies and misunderstandings of late," Minerva replied.

"That's not completely their fault, and you know it, Minerva. Demons are the most manipulative creatures among the worlds, and we were invaded by thousands of them. It's still a great accomplishment for the humans to have been able to beat them down all on their own. Trust me when I say that the Council debated for a long time on whether to help them openly. If they hadn't enslaved the Packs, we might have done much more to help," Marcella pointed out.

Minerva looked at her long-term boss and friend, "Are they really enslaved?"

"What else do you call the situation they are in then? They aren't allowed to vote, each group has to live on one of the reservations, and the only way off is military or government service. To me, that is slavery. This young man that is coming here is supposed to be different though. He was raised among the Packs and is considered a Pack member. He is one of the very few non-shifters to achieve that honor."

After a deep breath, Marcella continued, "Only our power prevents that sort of restriction from happening to us." Marcella added as she looked into her friend's eyes, "You were still overseas when we were revealed in 1914. But I was here and so was Grandmother Verity."

"What did she do?" Minerva asked.

Marcella shifted position, leaning her back against the planter they were weeding. "The town has always known what we were. We Blackmores founded it after all. Telling others outside of the limits is harder. Nobody outside of Salem wants to have Witches in their town. Not real ones like us. So, after the reveal, the state of Maine officials came calling. They'd heard the rumors and were ready to believe much more than usual. Magick is not a secret around here.

The first thing that they tried was to arrest Agnes Huckleberry for casting spells in the park."

Minerva smirked. "Is that why she hates the highway department so much?"

"Pretty much. The idiots just about had Agnes dragged into their car when Chief Middleton arrived. Were you here when he was sheriff?" Minerva shook her head no.

"Big strapping man with long blond hair and a beard. He must have had Viking stock in his background somewhere. Anyway, he came to a screaming halt, his police car siren blasting. It was a huge mess. They had the State Police with them, and they ignored our chief, claiming he was tainted. When they started brandishing weapons, Verity got involved," Marcella explained.

Minerva winced, "She was a force to be reckoned with. What happened?"

"She charged out of the restaurant, which in those days was across from city hall, and hit everyone with a freeze spell. And I do mean everyone. Since she was mad, half the town was stuck for almost an hour," Marcella explained.

"That's it?" Minerva asked.

"No. When all of the humans came out of the spell, they found themselves standing on the edge of town next to their cars. Both the Governor and the Superintendent of Police found a pissed-off Witch in their offices that day. Grandmother paid each of them a personal visit. She never told me what was said, but from then on we've been left alone here. No interference."

Marcella looked past her friend to the very large cat standing on the porch. "I can tell you that we got chocolate and flowers every holiday while those two were still in office."

"And the Feds?" Minerva stressed.

"Nothing. Although, J Edgar Hoover didn't have control of the FBI until 1935. It was the Bureau of Investigation before then. He did control that in the 1920s but they had their hands full with prohibition and smuggling. They pretty much left us alone. We get Feds in here from time to time poking around, but Agnes usually turns them around before they get past the first hill. So far they either haven't noticed the weather around here or are ignoring it. I'm hoping this one is better. That's what the Were say at least," Minerva replied.

———

THE NEW ENGLAND area of the US is delightful to drive through. It's much better than the parts of Texas and Illinois that I grew up in. I spent most of the formative years of my life living in the middle of a Were reservation in a very rural part of Texas. Weres are just like everyone else in America. They go to work, they take care of their families, and they bitch about taxes. The only difference is they turn furry several times a month. The whole full moon thing is just Hollywood fiction. Most Weres can change at will, but only the Alphas can change more than once a day. Alphas can also change infinitely faster than others. You never, ever, want to be on the wrong side of an Alpha with an attitude.

When mom remarried, and we prepared to move to Illinois, the local Pack performed a ceremony inducting me. It totally surprised me that they thought I was that worthy enough to induct. The memory was one that would never leave me.

———

"JACKSON DALTON, present yourself to the Pack." Alpha Dingo announced to the Pack.

I winced when I heard my full name being announced. Only my grandparents called me Jackson. It didn't sound right to my ears, so I didn't use it. The entire pack was here for this ceremony. I could see friends both young and old in the crowd surrounding me. Standing up in the center of everyone, I gave a little wave.

Ron glared at me from the top of the rock formation in the center of the natural amphitheater we were in. Ron Dingo was one of the

Weres in my late father's tank unit. My entire life I'd heard about the unit's bravery in the face of evil. Fighting Demons took a particular amount of courage.

Members of the Pack touched me as I stepped forward. "Sir?"

"Now is not the time for mirth. You are called to the Pack Moot. Do you wish to join the Ghost Pack now and forever?" Alpha Ron asked.

I bowed my head. Even though I was leaving the state, to be a member of a Pack would open doors for me. I also didn't want to disappoint my friends. "Yes, sir. I would be honored to join the Pack."

"Kneel." Ron pointed to a level spot at the base of the large rock.

My friends had mentioned parts of this ritual, but not anything about kneeling. Once I was down, I could see carvings in the rock that looked to be very old. I was confused. The Pack had only been here for less than thirty years.

Spreading his arms wide the Alpha raised his head to the sky. "We present this man-child to the Gods of Earth, Air, Water, and Fire. He is of age and has proven his worth to the Packs of the Western Forest. We ask that he be accepted into our midst and granted everything owed."

I was supposed to keep my head bowed, but I opened one eye and looked skyward in time to see a lightning storm in a clear sky! For less than a minute, lightning flashed, the wind blew, and the earth trembled. My veins began to burn. Clutching my arms to my body, I gritted my teeth and tried to not scream. And then it was gone.

"Do you still breathe Jack?" Alpha Ron looked down at me, concerned.

Swallowing I looked up at him. "Yes, sir. What was that?"

I rubbed my arms searching for what caused the pain but couldn't find anything.

"Our Gods are mysterious and powerful. You have been given something that only a handful have ever been given. Everything in this world has a price. For you, it was a small amount of pain. You bore it well. Welcome to the Pack, Jack." Holding out his hand, Ron lifted me up. Standing on the rock, I could see that it wasn't just the Ghost Pack. It was all the Packs of the reservation.

———

I DIDN'T KNOW it at the time, but I was literally given something rare and unusual. The Gods, if they actually exist, had offered me a portion of the powers that help the Were. I could see, smell, and run better and faster than I could before. It came with a price though. My natural endurance was stronger than before, and I had to train extra hard to learn how best to use my new abilities.

More than once at the Academy, they checked me to see if I was a paranormal in hiding. I might be the only human in America that's been forcibly exposed to sunlight, silver, holy water, and garlic. I've eaten more garlic than most Italians. But being able to run faster and shoot with more skill was a benefit, not a chore.

Throughout this entire trip, I made notes for my files. Where to stop, eat, and where the best gas stations were, topped the list of things I wrote about. Each case I conducted needed pictures and extensive information recorded. I realized halfway through this trip that I was laying the foundation for the division to carry on after I was long gone. Gone were my usual cryptic notes, as longhand became my main style.

Highway 95 took me right into Maine. Getting off the newly built highway and onto an old-fashioned two-lane blacktop was almost a relief. Small towns and backwoods were in my future. Briarwood was where I was headed. It was supposed to be along a river on the Canadian border. That was actually something else I looked forward to. Seeing another country was a treat. Even if it was just across a river.

———

THE ROAD CLIMBED QUITE high in the hills and then dropped down into a valley. The road sign said, "Briarwood Ahead." It was early winter, but the fields looked as green as summer. I stopped and took several pictures. If this was Witchcraft, it was impressive. There was a roadside vegetable stand as well, but I didn't stop.

Briarwood was very much like every small town I had passed in New England. The buildings were old and well maintained, carrying a certain charm that set them apart though. It made me wonder how old this town was. One of the older houses had a sign that announced that it was a bed and breakfast, and it looked very appealing after my trip. Perhaps, it was time to stop sleeping in the truck for a while.

"Welcome to the Briarwood Inn. Do you need a room tonight?" The woman at the counter was bright and cheery.

Smiling back, I replied, "Yes, thank you. I'm not sure how long I'm going to be here but for one person, please."

The woman slid me the registration book and introduced herself. "I'm the owner here, Abigail Mueller."

I carefully filled out the page and reached for my wallet.

Abigail glanced at the register and lightly touched my arm. "No need for that Agent Dalton. Marcella Blackmore will handle your bill. She told us you might be staying with us."

"My expense account can cover it since I'm on assignment," I protested.

"Keep your money. It's covered. I have a nice ground floor room set aside for you with a parking lot exit. Breakfast is at seven. Would you like to get settled in?" Abigail held out a key to me.

It was late in the day, and I was hungry. "I think so. Anyplace around here open for dinner?"

"Of course. The Badger Hole Diner is open every day, rain or shine." Abigail pointed toward the door. "If you leave my place and head toward City Hall, you'll see it. It's directly across from the big statue in the park. Can't miss it."

"The statue or the diner?" I asked.

Abigail chuckled, "The diner. The statue is of Herman Shlock, the supposed founder of the town. Of course, we all know better. The diner just started serving so you might want to hurry. The place fills up pretty quick."

Turning to look, I followed the line of her finger and spotted both the statue and a sign that read Badger Hole. "Why Badger Hole for a name?"

"You would need to ask Marcella that question. It's her family's place. You'd best get a move on. Leave your truck here, it's perfectly safe. No one will touch it," Abigail reassured me.

Wondering how she knew I had a truck since her view didn't include the parking lot, I nodded and started out across the square.

Marcella. I wondered if it was the same Marcella Blackmore I was supposed to meet. There can't be all that many women named Marcella around here, right?

Whoa! For such a small place, the diner was jumping. It looked more like a full-blown restaurant inside the brick exterior. A steak-house feel would be how my mom might describe it. We ate out rarely growing up, and that would have been a big compliment from her.

Entering the diner, I gave my name to the hostess. "Agent Dalton? We have a table prepared for you in the corner," a smiling woman spoke to me.

Did everyone in this town know who I was? I could see people looking at me as I passed and whispering to their tablemates.

The table was what I would call a federal agent special. It was positioned, so someone sitting at it had a full view of the entire room from the safety of the back corner. I could see everyone and not worry about what was behind me.

I had just opened the menu when an older-looking woman slid into the chair across from me. "Hello, Agent Dalton. I'm Marcella Blackmore."

The woman sitting across from me was in no way old. Maybe there were two Marcellas?

"Hello. Director J Edgar Hoover sent me to see you, I think. Is there an older lady I should be talking to?" I asked it even as the back of my brain started screaming at me. Manners. I could hear my mother. Never ask a woman her age.

As soon as the words left my mouth, I instantly regretted them, but Marcella? She started to giggle, then laugh. She laughed loud enough to catch just about everyone's attention for about thirty seconds after which everyone in the restaurant ignored her. That told me right there that I had the proper Marcella Blackmore.

She waved a finger at me as she gasped for breath. "I was warned about you, Agent Dalton. Big Ron said you were both funny and awkward at the same time. I didn't believe him at the time because FBI agents are notoriously dour, but I do now."

I was about to say something, but the mention of Big Ron or Alpha Ron as I know him shocked me to the core. Weres, as a people, are even more closed-mouthed than some of the native tribes. I'd never, ever, heard them discuss any of the other paranormal races. Not even in passing. How did this woman on the other side of the country from Texas know an obscure Pack leader?

Marcella smiled, "Witch got your tongue? I'm surprised. Did you think we wouldn't check you out? I'm sure the FBI has a thick file on me and this town already."

I just nodded, keeping in mind that one of the things that Anastasia told me was this sort of mission was like playing poker. Don't show your hand to anyone. To be truthful, the file wasn't very large. Apparently, none of the early federal officials believed the local Maine legends. Witches were consigned to Salem only in most people's minds.

"Well, then we did the same thing. Just because we're different doesn't mean we can't communicate with each other. Ron and I are old friends. You can imagine his surprise when I asked about you. He sent warm regards on your promotion and asked me to tell you to stop on by the next time you're in Texas. He's very fond of you, you know," Marcella informed me.

"I know. He and my father served together and were friends." I explained.

Marcella smiled at me, "I hope we can be friends as well."

She motioned to the menu, "Eat what you like. The Coven will pay all costs. We really do wish a congenial relationship with the FBI. I know you are hungry and tired of driving. Settle in and get some rest tonight. Tomorrow, ask Abigail for directions to the house. I'll expect you for lunch. Say twelve or so. Try not to be late. We have ever so much to discuss. Enjoy."

I was barely able to get a word in as she hopped up and majestically sauntered out of the diner. Along the way, other patrons nodded respectfully or bowed. What sort of town was this?

———

"WELL?" Minerva asked.

Marcella looked at her best friend and confidant and smiled. "Success, I think. He's interested at least. Name dropping his Alpha's name was what did it."

"And Kassandra wasn't clear at all about this boy? We've managed to stay off their radar for this long. I worry what a closer relationship will bring. Your grandmother would have just zapped him. You're not going to break the covenant are you?" Minerva asked.

Marcella gave her friend a sharp-eyed look. "I may be the head of the World Species Council, but I won't break our covenant. Even though there is some public opinion to the contrary, we were correct to agree to it. Humanity is dangerous enough without our help. At least our trained help. Even I cannot do anything about Russia and some of the far Eastern holdings."

The Covenant was an agreement that Magick folk put in place following the mistakes made during the human's so-called First World War in 1914. The Vampire Purge and what followed was a tragic accident, but it drove home the point that helping humanity destroy themselves wasn't a good idea.

It was the ultimate law for those that signed. No paranormal Magick user, whether they be Witch, Wizard, Mage, or Mystic, would actively help the humans. For some, it cut them off from very lucrative work, but the risk to everyone was just too great for disaster.

Minerva frowned, "Is anything being done about them?"

"Not really. What can we do? All the officials with any sort of power over the general users are dead. I understand their reasoning for breaking the Covenant but the toll upon them..." Marcella trailed off.

The Demon War was devastating to many groups. The Volkhvy of Russia took the hardest hit. With the Demon Horde turning toward them, they helped the humans of their country and performed the second Great Spell of the century. It took everything they had, but they managed to kill and banish the Demon Prince raised by the dictator of the country once known as Germany.

In the aftermath, it was discovered that Germany, Austria, Prussian, and parts of France were wiped clean. After years of demonic occupation, the population had been stripped to feed the never-satisfied demand for food. Humans, animals, paranormals. The Demons were insatiable, and they had destroyed the very structure of the cities in their efforts to harvest the last, surviving living beings. Buildings had been left in ruins, creating a scene of desolation and despair.

Those paranormals that could escape had done so earlier in the war. Fleeing by foot along hidden pathways, slipping through the occasional portal, they abandoned a suicidal stand to attempt to live to fight again. The land was left unprotected and suffered terribly until the Volkhvy's Great Spell.

The Demons enacted their revenge as they were magickally dragged back to the Hell they came from. The Volkhvy were wiped out, eliminating in one blow the entire senior and most skilled practitioners. Magick users still existed in Russia, but they were few and scattered.

Those with Magick tried to teach and pass on what they knew, but without guidance or advanced training, they failed. As a result, they were pushed into tactics of survival that left no room for Covenants or anything that did not allow them to feed their families.

The Russian witches became mercenaries, renting out the only skill that they had in a desperate struggle for survival.

"We could have helped, if they'd asked," Minerva stated.

Marcella nodded. "True. The debate in council chambers was hot and heavy over possible actions. It wasn't the first time Demons visited, and it won't be the last time. Most of the paranormals and Magick users made it out of the exclusion zone before the spell activated. The fact that we allow the mercenaries to exist at all is a form of reparation on the Council's part. Other than human government, there is no one to talk to there."

"I thought the Vampires ruled Russia? Surely they have some influence on the people," Minerva stated.

"Not like what you would imagine. Russia is difficult. The current Tsarina is a Vampire herself. The council of advisors is dominated by them as well. My Vampire advisors suggest we leave them be for now. The mercenary force revenues are the main way that the Russian government earns hard currency," Marcella replied.

"That's already too much in the way of politics for me to track. Russia's just one country. How do you handle all the rest?" Minerva asked.

"Carefully. The Council doesn't have much pull in Asia, but for the rest, I have excellent advisors and assistants. So tomorrow, do you have the luncheon planned out?" Marcella asked, obviously changing the subject.

THAT NIGHT I had a lot to think about. The files I was given were woefully incomplete. I could see that now. They were missing some things, but I wasn't sure what. Making a snap decision in the middle of the night, I jumped in the truck and left town. The roads outside of Briarwood were treacherous at night. It may have been like summer in their little valley, but everywhere else, it was winter. There'd been a snowstorm and ice was everywhere.

Checking my maps, I found what I wanted only a single county over.

"This is very much out of order, son. Let me see those credentials again." One of the many things the Director had put in place was a way for Federal Agents to reach Washington in case of emergency. It was supposed to be used to report suspected espionage or catastrophic events, but my clearance level allowed me to use it. Every State Patrol office was supposed to have a top-secret phone line.

The officer on duty at three in the morning had to wake up his Captain, who didn't find it all that amusing to go out into the cold to help me, but he did it.

"I sure hope this is important for as many folks as you just woke up, son. Everything matches what's here on the paper. Corporal Howard will show you the phone. Now I get to wake up even more people to tell them you used the phone. I hope Governor Reed isn't sleeping too hard. Can you tell me what's this all about?" Captain Chamberlain asked.

I rubbed my chin. "It's not a total secret, but I'm in negotiations with the leaders of the Coven in Briarwood."

The state patrol captain blanched, "Them! Make your calls. I pity you, son, I really do."

It was almost chuckle-worthy, but I didn't laugh. Whatever Marcella's people did to the State Police, it seemed to have worked.

———

THE PHONE WAS inside a tiny closet. There was room inside for a chair and a child-sized desk, but that was all I really needed. I asked for a pad of paper and a pen. There was a special dispatcher who was as surprised as the Captain had been when her phone rang. Getting her to direct my call to the Special Assistant to the Director was the easy part.

"The world better be on fire!"

I couldn't help myself, "I thought Vampires were awake at night?"

"They are, but I'm incredibly busy right now. Jack? How did you get this number?" Anastasia asked.

I took a deep breath. "I used the state patrol emergency line. I wanted to be both secure and get through to you."

The Vampire started laughing. "It's secure, but you kicked over an ant's nest by using it. You do realize that the paperwork associated with this line is like a mile high? We're both going to be signing our names for hours. What was so damn important?"

"I met with Marcella Blackmore tonight and realized the briefing paperwork is missing something," I pointed out.

"Good. It proves to me that you aren't an idiot. What do you think is missing?" she asked me.

"Background history. The founding of the town, demographics of humans versus paranormals, and the relationships that they all have. The state officials are hiding something as well. My file doesn't have any of that covered at all," I informed her.

"Believe it or not, I told Director Hoover that we needed to give you more, but he's still in a snit about you actually being able to do that job. I have no way of giving you anything quickly. I assume you're meeting tomorrow or you would have used a normal phone like everyone else?" Anastasia asked.

"Yes, I have been requested to come in the late morning and have lunch with Marcella."

The Vampire took a deep breath and explained, "The basics are this. Witches live longer than regular humans. Marcella was born sometime in the 1800s. She's run that town since the thirties. Forget Jamestown or St Augustine, Briarwood is the oldest town in America. There was at least one Witch on the failed Roanoke expedition in 1585. When settlers arrived in Maine, the beginnings of the town were already there. More than ninety percent of the people in that town are Witchfolk. They are either Magick users or followers of one form of Wicca or other Neopagan religions. There is a lot of politics involved, but there has been more than one occasion when a Witch from Briarwood has appeared in a Governor's office and scared the bejesus out of them. We like to say that this country hasn't been invaded since 1812, but Briarwood has never been occupied. No British, French or even Native invaders have occupied it. Even we don't know the entire story."

"Marcella is a Power in this world. I won't get into details, but her Coven is THE most powerful one in the entire United States. Step lightly around her. She may look like someone's grandmother, but she's a shark. Just so you know, they were the ones that requested the meeting. And they insisted that you lead the team," Anastasia explained to me.

"Team?" I asked.

"Call it a reward for doing a good job. Be careful Jack. If anyone can turn someone into a frog in this day and age, it's Marcella Black-more. Regardless of the paperwork. If you need me use this phone again."

The phone cut off leaving me staring at it. Looking down I perused the brief notes I took. It was starting to look like I was standing in a minefield all alone.

————

"GOOD MORNING AGENT DALTON! Did you sleep well?" Abigail was awfully bright and shiny at eight AM when I literally crawled from the bed.

I clutched the coffee in front of me like it was the last cup on earth. It was going to be a very long day. "Just fine. I'm not used to soft beds. I usually sleep on a cot in the back of my truck."

"That's terrible! You should tell that Mr. Hoover to pay you agents more then. We still have eggs and toast left, would you like some?" Abigail asked.

I answered her in the affirmative and went back to studying my notes. Marcella and the others obviously wanted something, or they wouldn't have asked me here. Figuring out what they wanted was my primary mission. After that, any of my observations would be an excellent way to flesh out the file. From the reaction of Captain Chamberlain and his man, the State Police did not come here very often. Understanding why might explain a lot.

A plate of eggs and toast was placed in front of me. "Here you are, Agent. Milly, our cook, said she put a little cheese, onions, and peppers in there for you. Texas-style she said. Please enjoy it."

I wasn't so sure about 'Texas Style,' but the food smelled wonderful. Taking a bite, I knew instantly what she had added. They weren't green peppers but Hatch chilies, giving me a taste of home. Texas-style indeed! It wasn't until the last bite that I looked around. Where did someone find those sort of peppers in Maine, let alone the winter? More questions searching for answers.

"Abigal?" I called out.

The smiling woman appeared at the door to the kitchen. "Yes, Agent?"

"How do I get to the Blackmore house from here?" I asked her.

"If you look out that window, you should be able to see it. The family built right on the top of the bluff overlooking both the valley and the town." She pointed out the window behind me. "Take the north road and make a left at the first turn you come to. It's right next to the vegetable stand. Go past the entrance to The Garden and drive up the hill. Only house up there. I believe you're expected at noon. You won't want to miss Minerva's cooking regardless. She's the best cook in the entire valley."

"There's a garden here?" I asked.

"You'll see. The view is best from Marcella's house. She'll explain it to you. Is there anything else?" Abigale asked.

I shook my head and peered out the window. The house looked very impressive from here, sort of like it was watching everyone and everything.

———

"Is everything all set for lunch?" Marcella asked.

Stopping to wipe her hands on the apron around her waist, Minerva answered, "Of course. Would I let you down? I've got all your favorites and a few new things as well. Milly called and said he liked the eggs, so for starters, I've put together a bit of Texas fare, tacos and such."

"Excellent. I want you there as well, we can get some of the girls to serve in your place." Marcella instructed Minerva.

"How's the harvest coming along?" Minerva asked.

"So far so good. There has only been a couple of incursions this week. I've got half the Coven patching holes. We can fix all of this if we can only find Emesh. He's got the ability to mend the fabric of space and time. That is completely beyond the scope of my powers, and you know it," Marcella replied.

"What are you going to tell the FBI about the incursions? If some of those critters get out of the valley, all hell could break loose," Minerva pointed out.

"It's under control. We don't have any..." A yell from outside brought Marcella up short. Both women looked out the window to see a large creature emerge from the garden gate and race across the yard. "Oh, damn!"

Marcella muttered to herself and cupped her hands as she ran from the kitchen toward the very large wraparound porch. Thrusting her hand toward the fleeing creature she shouted. Balls of light left her hands and illuminated the animal. When the light dimmed, it stood frozen in place in front of the lawn maintenance shed.

"What is it? If it's one of those veloc.. velockator...V creatures. Save it for me. They taste like chicken." Minerva yelled at her friend.

Marcella examined the frozen creature. "The word you're looking for is Velociraptor. Somehow the portal in the Garden is either locked onto a world in early development, or it's time traveling for some reason."

"Can't you Magick it closed?" Minerva asked.

"No. It is the unstable one of the pair. The other one goes to a pocket universe that is mostly stable. Time is a bit different in there as well. In a good way though. I really don't want to go for outside help on this, but if the portal is shifting, we need to do something. There are much larger things than this looking for a way in." Marcella pointed to the dinosaur.

———

I HAD several hours to kill, so I drove around. Briarwood was a nice little town. Lots of shops and parks. The people seemed content, and that in itself was a bit unsettling. Out in the rest of the world, some countries were only just now settling down after the Demon War. Trade was coming back, and luxury goods were finally accessible again. Here it was like time had stopped. I didn't see any major industry or activity until I reached the far edge of town. A large industrial building stuck up in the middle of a pine forest. Dozens of the newer refrigeration trucks were lined up to receive fruits and vegetables for distribution. Garden Deliveries was the name on the building. At least now I knew where most of the townsfolk worked.

Following Abigail's instructions, I was able to find the Garden entrance and the road to the Blackmore estate fairly easily. The entrance to the Garden interested me though. Dozens of people were filing in and out of the main gates.

"Is this the Garden?" I asked.

"Of course. How can we help you, Agent Dalton?" A grizzled looking man asked as I approached.

Giving him a funny look I asked, "Does everyone know who I am?"

The man chuckled, "Pretty much. We were told you were coming and since you're the only stranger here..."

"OK. I understand. I was freaking out there a little. What sort of vegetables do you grow here?" I asked.

"We grow all of them. Would you like something specific?" He asked me.

"All of what?" I asked.

"Vegetables. The Garden provides for all and is able to produce all. Is there something you wish of her?" The man smiled and patted the gates he was standing next to.

"No, thank you. Does this road lead to the house?" I pointed to the road and then the house in the distance.

"Yes, it does. They are expecting you. Have fun and tell Marcella I'll be looking into her little problem for her as well. I need to get loaded up first." At my strange look, he laughed. "No worries my friend, just say you met Emesh and she'll understand."

I arched an eyebrow at him but replied anyway, "OK."

Walking back to my truck, it was all I could do to hop in and drive away. This was getting to be a very strange place.

The house on the hill was magnificent. A true Victorian master-piece of architecture. I couldn't imagine what it would be like to grow up here surrounded by these crazy people.

Marcella Blackmore stood on the steps of the house, waiting for me when I pulled up and stopped my car.

"Do you folks have like tribal drums or something around here? I swear everyone knows about me before I meet them," I remarked.

"It can seem that way at times. At the moment, we're a rather close-knit community. The produce plant is expanding soon, and we are expecting some new residents. Being insular is not the way to be. So this is my home." Marcella waved, "It predates the town by a few years actually."

Remembering my notes, I commented, "Not in this form though, right? Construction in the late 1500s would have been log cabins or something."

"Touche, Agent Dalton. You're correct. The first sawmill didn't go up until the late 1600s around here, and they were still using the trench method which was very slow," Marcella informed me.

"Trench method? I'm not familiar with that," I commented. The intricacies of early American industry was beyond me.

Marcella smiled. "You dig a trench deep enough for men to stand in. Using a very large crosscut saw they stand in the pit and cut the log from above. Not efficient and very labor intensive. Parts of the kitchen are from the original house. There's one spot where you can touch the rough cut of the boards. A lot of history in this house."

There was movement just out of my sight which caused me to turn. Instinctively I reached for my guns! "What is that?"

A large lizard of some kind was running straight at us on its hind legs.

"Not another one! How on Earth do they keep getting in," Marcella pulled back her hand and tossed a fireball in the creature's direction.

Pulling both my 1911 automatics, I began firing. Like shooting fish in a barrel, the creature was hard to miss. The fireball hit it, outlining it in flames. The fire and pain distracted it, but my efforts were what brought it down.

The flaming lizard crashed to the ground less than ten paces from where we stood. Rapidly following in the first creature's wake were three other, similar lizards. Quickly I dropped the magazines and reloaded my guns, but I wasn't fast enough. Marcella raised her hand and screamed a word to the sky. Lightning flashed, and all three running animals vanished as if they hadn't ever existed.

"If only we can find Emesh, he's the one that can fix the problem. I can't keep killing these things all the time. Someone is going to be hurt eventually," Marcella muttered.

"Emesh? I met a man earlier who said his name was Emesh." I explained about the man at the gate, including the fact that he had told me to pass his message on to her.

Marcella looked heavenward and muttered something I couldn't hear. "Thank you, Agent Dalton. By just being here you've helped. Emesh is... Let's just say he's a gardening expert who has experience with alternate realities. He will fix the problem of the Velociraptors for us."

"Is that what that thing is?" I pointed to the smoking lizard.

"Yes. It's a dinosaur. I'm getting ahead of myself. Lunch will wait, let me explain the Garden to you. That will help you make more sense of all of this. Come with me." Taking my elbow, she led me across the yard to the edge of the bluff.

"What do you see, Agent Dalton?" she asked me.

Looking down, I saw a different sight than I had expected. Instead of the town, there was an enormous garden laid out before me. Acres of farm fields and masses of vegetation were everywhere. "Where's the town?"

"This is the Garden. When my ancestors settled this land, they planted the beginnings of it. Natural formations of Magickal energy called Ley Lines cross this county at all angles. One strong one called the Kachina Ley crosses over this very spot.

"My ancestors took that Magickal force and infused it into the very earth surrounding this area to allow the garden to propagate. Little did they know at the time that they were creating life." Marcella paused briefly to see if I had any questions. Caught up in her narrative, I was speechless.

After a moment, she continued, "The Garden itself took on... call it a persona. We communicate with it through growth and need. It answers as it sees fit, which is not always the response that we either want or have predicted."

My look of disbelief must have been very apparent because the Witch laughed softly before talking again.

"The Garden has many capabilities and aspects. One of those is its control of access to other places, both on this world and others. There are entryways into other realities called portals that can be used to travel to and from those other worlds that exist naturally in many places here on Earth. The portal opened in Germany was similar to the one in the Garden. It was forced to access the Demonic plane through a little-used channel of Magick. That is where the Demons came from," Marcella explained.

"Demons? You have a portal to Hell here?" I reflexively tightened my grip on the guns still in my hands before I realized that I had just pointed them at the Witch beside me. Shrugging in apology, I put them away.

"Not quite. The portals here could be forced to go to the reality called Hell, but they could go to other more dangerous places as well. My family and the Coven here would never allow that to happen. It is our mandate in fact. We guard the portals. Emesh is just one of many that we work with to prevent dangerous creatures like that from entering our world." Marcella pointed to the still smoldering dinosaur.

"I don't understand. Why tell me about this? When the Director hears about it, he could call up the army, and they'll do here what they did in Conception, California. Then your town, this house, the garden, and all of it would be gone," I explained.

"It's because of that core reason that I wanted you here. We are a resource, not a threat and the government needs to understand that. I know this is hard to take in, but hear me out. The main Portal here is a stable one. We use it to go from here to a sort of way station between worlds called the Badger Hole Bar. The portal that let loose the velociraptors was a temporary one that is being repaired. We watch for those and usually slam them shut immediately. It takes a full Coven to seal something like that unless you're a God, like Emesh," Marcella commented.

"Wait, this Emesh guy's a God? Like, God?" I pointed my finger skyward.

"Magickal beings walk among us every day. Some are spiritual beings, others are just forces of powerful Magick. Why do you find that surprising, Agent? They are living archetypes of our own imagination and belief. I called you here to explain everything to your Director Hoover. I could just pop into his office like my ancestors used to do, but he might take that as a threat," Marcella replied.

Without more than a split-second pause, the Witch continued to explain. "This country has so much potential, and we want to make it so much more than it is. To do that, we need to be able to communicate with those in power. Tell them to leave us be and to trust us. We use our power for the light and to destroy the dark. Can you convey our message for us?"

It was information overload for me, and my head felt like it was simultaneously spinning and ready to explode. How would I tell the Director of the FBI these things and not have him lock me up? In my head, I decided to lay it all out for Anastasia and let her decide. She knew him best.

Realizing Marcella was waiting for an answer, I nodded. Living gardens, dinosaurs, Covens, and Witches, this was a mission to end all missions.

Over lunch, she explained more of the history and purpose of her group which confused me even more. As we finished our meal, the powerful Witch gave me some last instructions and messages to pass on.

"Take the information I've given you back to the Vampire that controls you. Let her inform your government. Tell her that a time will come when she cannot hide from her fate," Marcella instructed.

"I'm sorry, but I don't really understand all of this," I explained.

"We know dear. Take what I've given you to heart and trust us. In the future, you will need our knowledge. Just take what life gives you and roll with it for now. What do you think of the fish? It's local," she asked.

The total non-sequitur threw me off even more. But maybe that was her goal, to begin with. Leave me floundering just a little, but clear on the messages that needed to be delivered.

Instinctively, I trusted the Witch. She was intelligent and articulate, not bullying or applying pressure. Despite all of Anastasia's warnings, this woman was very nice.

My trip back home was going to be a very thoughtful journey, and the writing of my report might take me weeks.

———

"Did you tell him what Kassandra said about him?" Minerva asked.

Marcella looked out at the Garden. She could see Coven members in the fields, and the serenity of that view eased her mind. Emesh was there with his load of vegetables for transport. He waved and pointed to where the random portal had been, and she saw that it was no longer there. Even from this distance, she could see Emesh's satisfaction with its absence.

Bringing her attention back to Minerva's question, Marcella said, "No. Tampering with the timestream is never a good idea. Look what happened to Tesla. All that interference causes is trouble. What will come to pass will come to pass. Or not."

Marcella paused, considering her next words. "Kassandra said he would help the savior of our Coven to achieve her best. If I told him the prophecy, Jack might then have asked what we needed saving from, and there is no answer to that. Not yet at least. Kassandra said other things associated with this Agent Jack that tells me we need to prepare for the future. And I, it seems, must find a man suitable for fatherhood. Who would you pick for that adventure?" Marcella asked.

Minerva smiled and caused her eyebrows to bounce. "What about that British movie star Sean..."

JACK DALTON, MONSTER HUNTER

HUNTER

BOOK 4

My name is Jack Dalton, and I'm a monster hunter.

What is it about Witches that fascinates so? My last mission was to visit an entire town of Witches, and it wasn't even Salem. I passed the information they gave me along to my supervisors, primarily Anastasia and Director Hoover. Why we want an alliance with a paranormal group boggles my mind. Other than the Werewolves none of them will work with us, at least not in any official capacity.

I find humor wherever I can when I'm on the road. The FBI office in Boston was one such case. My orders are such that I'm supposed to use Bureau resources whenever possible to report in, write reports, and requisition materials. But even though Congress and President Long may have wanted a Magical Division, the FBI didn't. I'm a political token. If I want to keep my job I have to earn it and prove I can do it. They had no idea how to deal with me or what I represented.

"You're who?" The agent at the main desk squinted at my credentials.

"Magical Division head, Jack Dalton. I need to call Washington and requisition from you. There are supposed to be instructions associated with my visits," I replied.

The agent stared down at his desk, "Uh..."

"You have a supervisor?" I asked.

The man behind the desk grabbed his phone and pressing a button. "A moment."

I glanced around the entryway as I waited. There were two burly looking guards next to the elevator giving me the evil eye. Smiling, I gave them a wave. Neither of them responded. A large placard on one wall listed the offices and who was where. Behind me was the obligatory Director Hoover portrait alongside that of President Long. It made me remember his campaign.

They called him the 'Kingfish.' He'd been governor of Louisiana since the 1920s and had tried for the presidency at least once previously, but not during the Demon War. His actions using the

Louisiana National Guard brought him national attention, securing his place in history and as a candidate.

The Demon hole in Conception, California opened suddenly exposing America to the Demon threat being battled in Europe. Large swaths of southern California had already been consumed before the first troops arrived on scene. Governor Long had marshaled his forces and recruited large groups of Weres from the three reservations in his state. Using the railroad system, he was able to get both his and the Texas Army National Guard groups to California in time to save some of San Diego from the Horde. Americans value audaciousness. Some of his more extravagant policies were shut down by Congress, but since he gave me my job, I was grateful.

"Agent Dalton?" The new voice brought my attention back to the present. A new man stood behind the desk.

"Yes..." I trailed off as I felt the presence of the two guards on either side of me.

"I'm not sure where you found these credentials, but they are obvious fakes. There is no Magical Division of the FBI. Boys?" He motioned to the two guards who each grabbed my arms. "They're going to escort you to holding until the local police arrive."

A large hand gripped the back of my neck. "You aren't going to cause us any trouble now."

Without explaining any of the charges, searching me, or even allowing me to see a supervisor they dragged me off toward the elevators. Looking over my shoulder, I could see the agent behind the counter smirking at me. "Anyway, we can discuss this, boys?"

"No." The one to my left replied.

I first looked at him then the other one on the right carefully assessing them. Both were big and dumb looking. Director Hoover was trying to change how people looked at the FBI, but these two were either holdover from the old way or bully boys explicitly hired for this sort of thing. I decided to call them Thug One and Thug Two. Either way, I needed to get away from them.

There were three elevators, and we entered the middle one.

Unlike the newer office buildings, this one still had the manual controls in it. The shiny brass box consisted of several switches and a lever. The building looked to have four floors counting the basement.

Pressing the lower button, Thug One gripped the lever to lower the elevator. The doors began to close slowly, and he let go of my arm.

"Before we start, does anyone want to get off?" I asked.

Thug Two looked over at me and replied, "Huh?"

Rapidly, I kicked him in the knee, followed up with a sharp jab to his kidneys. The larger man went down with a gasp as his knee gave way. My punch just added to the amount of pain he was feeling. The hand on my arm slipped off. Spinning quickly, I kicked Thug One in the privates. It wasn't a fair move, but this wasn't a fair fight.

They hadn't bothered to search me, so my guns and other things were still intact. Pulling one of my revolvers, I pistol whipped Thug One as he tried to stand. Thug Two was still gasping on the floor of the elevator.

"Nobody ever listens," I muttered as I pulled out a pair of hand-cuffs. I locked one to the elevator railing, the other to Thug One. "These are designed for Weres. I would advise you not to try to break them."

"Bastard!" Thug Two tried to stand while reaching out toward me with a meaty hand.

I kicked him in the ribs and pistol-whipped him as well. The FBI teaches judo and karate to its agents. The Were Pack I grew up with teaches survival. Fight dirty if you have to and win. Sometimes there is no other way. Especially when it comes to survival.

Supervisory Agent John Rogan had an office on the third floor. That much I remembered from the list on the wall. While I could escape and call Anastasia from an outside line, it wouldn't help my credibility at all. Besides, I was interested to know if the actions being done in Rogan's name were with his knowledge or not. I was just nosy that way.

Watching the man on the floor carefully, I pressed a new button and threw the lever. I'm not a particularly religious man, but I said a prayer to Odin. He was the God worshiped by both my stepfather and the Pack I was a part of. Every little bit helps and I really didn't want to deal with more guards on the upper floor.

There was a slight ding followed by the elevator doors opening. I could see nothing but a wall in front of me, so I leaned out the doorway. On my left was a wall and to my right, I saw an assistant's or secretary's desk. The double doors behind it should lead to Rogan. I smiled to myself about the similarity to Director Hoover's office layout. Some people just wanted to look important.

"May I help you, sir?" The secretary was young, very young. She made Hoover's assistant look ancient in comparison. There was a puzzled expression on her face. At one point she looked past me toward the elevators.

"Is Agent Rogan available?" I asked.

"He's in a meeting, but I can let him know you're here Agent..." She trailed off and looked at me expectantly.

My credentials were still downstairs with the man at the desk. So, I winged it. "Dalton. Jack Dalton. Tell him I'm the Director of the Magical Division."

Still puzzled, the young woman reached for the phone.

"Can you ask him in person? Without calling?" I asked.

"That's just silly. It's easier to call." She picked up the receiver and started to press a button.

Sighing, I drew my guns and pointed them at her. "Just ask him to come out here. No mention of these or me please."

The woman actually squealed as her eyes widened. "Don't kill me. I only slept with him to keep my job."

Smiling I shook my head. "Nothing to do with you. Just ask him to come out here, please? I won't hurt you."

She brought the receiver up to her ear and pressed the button. If she tried to trick me and send more guards, I would deal with them. "John, sorry to bother you when you're sleeping but there is an Agent Dalton that says he needs to speak to you urgently."

I watched as the young woman nodded and replied. "Yes. Yes. Yes, but..."

She shook her head and became more forceful. "John, he says it's a matter of life and death." There was a pause. "Fine. I'll tell him."

Hanging up the phone, she looked at me. "That man only cares about himself, but he's on his way out."

Setting myself up in the corner behind the doors and across from the secretary I drew my other gun and waited. My wait wasn't very long.

"Lavina, what in the hell is so important that you would pull me away from my call with the mayor!" The man I assumed was Rogan, slammed open the door and stood before her.

Lavina smiled at him and nodded toward me. Supervisor Rogan goggled at her.

"Speak up! Who's out here?" He demanded.

I sighed. "She means me, dummy."

"Who said that?" Rogan turned and froze at the sight of me and my guns.

"That would be me, actually. My name is Special Agent in Charge Jack Dalton. Does my name ring a bell?" I asked him.

"You will rot in jail for this! How dare you break into the FBI of all places and hold me up at gunpoint! Criminals will shudder in fear when they hear of your fate in the future. When my men get finished with you, they will ..." Rogan trailed off as I stepped forward.

"Do you recognize my name?" I asked again.

Rogan made a face at me. "Why? Did I lock up your mother or something?"

"No. Your bully boys tried to rough me up and drag me downstairs. Funny how your office here is so cooperative with other parts of the FBI," I explained.

"Who are you again?" Rogan asked.

"Jack Dalton, Director of the Magical Division," I smiled at him.

Rogan smirked, "That group doesn't exist! It's a fairy tale."

"I beg to differ. Lavina, can you dial a number for me?" I looked past Rogan to the young secretary watching us.

"Certainly, Agent Dalton." Lavina picked up the phone.

Supervisor Rogan turned around and glared at her. "You will not! Dial that phone, and you're fired!"

Her hand poised above the phone, Lavina remarked, "He's got the guns."

I smiled and recited a number to her. "Thank you, Lavina. Dial that number and ask for Anastasia."

Addressing Rogan, I explained, "Regardless what you may believe or what your bully boys downstairs think, I am with the FBI. I report to Director Hoover."

Lavina said a few words into the phone and Ana's name. I watched as her eyes widened just a bit. She sat up a bit straighter and explained who she was and better still where she was.

"She wants you, Agent Dalton." Lavina addressed me.

"Can you put it on speaker phone?" I asked.

"Of course." She pressed a button and turned the small gray device toward us.

"Ana? I'm in a bit of a pickle here," I started to explain to her.

"If you mean the report you were supposed to send me half a day ago then yes. Or do you mean something else?" The Vampire asked.

"I'm in Boston at our offices here. There was a slight problem when I tried to speak to the supervisor and to use the phone," I replied.

"They arrested me claiming that there was no Magical Division and that I was a fraud."

There was a moment of silence on the speaker. Supervisor Rogan opened his mouth, but I waved him away by pointing both my 1911s at him.

"Did you explain and show your credentials?" She asked.

"I did. Two big bully boys grabbed me and were going to correct my attitude while the local police were called," I paused for a moment. "Currently I have Director Rogan here under my guns. Want me to shoot him?"

There was the sound of what sounded like laughter. "Did you kill anyone?"

"Not yet. The boys are still in the elevator, but it won't be too long before someone finds them. This place appears to be a snake pit. I'm starting to think I need to kill the head snake," I explained.

"Can he speak?" Ana asked.

I waved my guns at the man in front of me. "Sure. Go ahead, Rogan."

"I don't know who you are, but this man is a maniac! He's assaulted me in my own office. I demand that you have him arrested," Rogan began to shout.

Anastasia listened to his ranting for several minutes and then shut him down. "Supervisor Rogan, shut up!"

Rogan stopped speaking for just a moment and stared at the speakerphone. "Who are you to speak to me like that?"

"J Edgar Hoover's personal assistant," Anastasia replied.

"The Vampire?" Rogan asked.

"Yes. Jack is who he says he is. I know for a fact that memos went out explaining his position and needs. Why is your office not complying?" Anastasia asked.

Supervisor Rogan snorted. "Magical Division, ridiculous. My boss told me to ignore that drivel. We should have deported the lot of you in 1914 and been done with you."

"Your boss? Director Hoover is over all branches of the FBI. If you're working for someone else, then I know we have to replace you," Ana replied.

"Not the GID you don't. We intend to stop this idiocy this very moment." Supervisor Rogan stepped towards the desk and reached for the emergency button.

Lavina Taylor had been listening to the entire conversation with fascination. She knew that the man she worked for wasn't acting true to the values of the FBI because she'd studied the training materials herself to better understand the men around her. Just because Lavina was young and blond didn't make her stupid. When she saw the hand coming right for her and the button she reacted.

"I don't think so!" Lavina batted Rogan's hand away and slammed his arm with the only thing within reach to her, a stapler.

"You bitch!" Rogan howled in pain. The heavy Swingline stapler was like a set of brass knuckles and increased Lavina's swing threefold.

I could hear the crack of bone as the mere slip of a girl broke her boss's arm.

Rogan staggered to one side clutching his arm cursing both his secretary and me.

"Jack! What just happened?" Anastasia asked.

"Rogan was about to hit the emergency button, and his secretary popped him one. I think she broke his arm," I explained.

"Sounds like my kind of woman. I'm sending orders to the US Marshal Service as we speak to take Supervisor Rogan into custody. I need you to control the situation a bit longer, Jack. Something is fishy about this entire incident," Anastasia commented.

"What's the GID?" I asked her.

"It stands for General Intelligence Division, and it's supposed to be defunct. The Director himself dissolved it in 1920, just a bit before my time with the Bureau. The GID was at the forefront of government actions during the Were scare of 1919. They were the ones that established the reservations and placed the Weres in them. The Thompson raids were their claim to fame as well. The Director is going to be upset by this. Whatever you do, try to keep it out of the press."

"We are everywhere, and he has no idea that we even exist. The hammer will rise, and all will be swept away..." Rogan started to shout at the top of his lungs. Then I hit him.

Whack!

"Jack?" Anastasia asked.

"Sorry, he had it coming." I bent down checking his pulse. "It's easier this way."

Anastasia groaned. "Did you ever think that maybe he was telling us stuff we can use against him?"

I looked down at the unconscious man and shook my head. "No."

"Men. Give me all the details. Describe your entire time in that office." Anastasia demanded of me.

Leaning against the edge of the desk I filled her in on all the boring stuff including kicking the ass of the goons in the elevator. "You know I should probably check up on those two."

Taking a few steps forward I looked at the elevator I came up in. The door was closed.

"The cat might be out of the bag, boss," I then explained why to her.

"Just guard the floor. The Marshals shouldn't take too much time," Ana remarked.

An idea came to me as I watched the doors, "Boss? Is there any way we can hire Lavinia here away from this location? She's innocent of the whole thing."

"Is she still here?" Anastasia asked.

Lavina spoke up, "Yes, Ma'am. I'm still here."

The two women started to talk as I moved to a position I could watch both Rogan and the elevators.

True to her word, I didn't have to wait all that long for relief as the Marshals took charge less than an hour later. My credentials were found at the front desk in the trash can.

Anastasia got me out of there pretty quick too. Something about not tarnishing my name as well. Whoever these GID guys were, they faded into the woodwork pretty fast. All information about them dried up leaving the Marshals puzzled.

"Go south toward New Jersey. There's been several sea monster sightings as well as a few disappearances. Chasing a threat should keep you busy and out of the Director's hair for a while," Anastasia explained as she gave me my assignment.

Which is why I was now on the way towards the Jersey shore and all its surrounding chaos.

The FBI had received reports of monster sightings by the Navy and others, but no specific details were given. Any sightings of creatures were crazy because this is December and while it's not snowing presently it's unbelievably cold. At this time of the year, everything usually is quiet which made me wonder, why now? Why not during the height of summer tourist season when food is more plentiful?

———

SANDY HOOK WAS my first stop. The first recorded sighting of a sea monster in America took place there in 1887. I figured if I was hunting the things I should stop there at least.

"You one of those newfangled fish revenuers?" The lone fisherman standing on the pier stared up at me.

The puzzled look on my face should have screamed 'No,' but I answered him, anyway. "I'm with the FBI looking for sea monsters."

When the old guy stopped laughing, he slapped the rail in front of him a couple of time. "Son, that's the funniest thing I've heard in a long time. None of those around here, not lately that is. Town's got a museum of sorts for the sighting fifty years or so ago."

I pursed my lips and stared at him. He was dressed in an old-fashioned slicker with large rubber boots. Sitting on a chair, he kept a bucket huddled between his legs partially covered by a blanket. "Why do you have revenuers here?"

The man gave me a shrewd look then shook his head, "If you were one I guess you'd have fined me by now. It's a new law. This whole area's been crawling with them lately. They're building some sort of new science laboratory out on the point that's attracting them to here. You can't toss your line out without them swooping down asking for a license or some stuff. That's why I'm out here in this cold today. Best time to avoid them."

"Ah. OK. Not really my branch of government. I just chase down monsters. Any idea where I might find one?" I asked.

The old man chuckled, "You are a riot. Willy Gill swears he saw mermaids one night while fishing, but he's also been known to add a touch of whiskey to his oatmeal in the morning. Other than that, we've got nothing for you, Mr. Monster Hunter, sir. Head south, and you might get lucky."

Nodding and wishing him good fishing I moved on. Mermaids weren't what I was looking for, but I would make a note. One day it might be relevant to someone. Nature of the business. Hopping onto the new New Jersey Turnpike, I took the man's advice. South led to many more beaches.

Sometimes when you've thought you'd seen it all, something else pops up. Point Pleasant had a half-sized train set up right on the beach. If the roadside signs were to be believed, it was the Beach Train. A bit further down in Seaside Heights they had a pier. Everything was ice covered, but I passed a carousel and a Ferris wheel.

At each town I came to, I drove or walked the pier, watching the surf. I wasn't sure what I would do if I saw a monster, but I least I was looking for one.

"The only thing we see out here is ships and seagulls. Someone sold you a wagon of sawdust or something. Sea monsters don't exist, don't you know?" The speaker was the keeper of the lighthouse at Barnegat, New Jersey.

I followed his gaze out to sea. Lots of big waves crashing onto the beach but not much else. Winter storms were nasty in the Atlantic.

"There is a monster down in Wildwood, but I think he's concrete." The keeper started laughing at his own joke and waved at me as he returned to the lighthouse.

Shaking my head, I walked back to the truck. I'd seen the signs for the 'monster' of Wildwood. Some entrepreneur had created a twenty-foot replica of a gigantic ape. It was supposed to straddle the Fun Pier in Wildwood. I guess I could have my picture taken with it for Anastasia. Not much else to see so far.

Somewhere round about Beach Haven, I got my first clue.

A fire engine, three police cars, and an ambulance sat outside a crushed house on the beach. My yellow and black FBI van definitely caught their attention as I pulled up.

"What's all this now? Who are you?" The local police officer asked as I got out of the van.

Flashing my credentials, I replied. "Special Agent Jack Dalton, FBI. Do you know what caused this?"

Looking toward the house, I could see more explicit details. It was once a stilted house that seemed to have been right at the edge of the water. A storm surge didn't do this. Neither did wind. The house was almost split in half like something smashed it in two and rummaged through the remains.

The lead cop looked at my ID and shook his head. "Beats the hell out of us. Something sure wanted inside though."

Firefighters in bunker gear were crawling through both sides of the house, but I couldn't see any body bags or injuries. The pilings that once held the building up were broken in half and shattered into wood chips.

"Something indeed," I muttered. The cop, who turned out to be the Police Chief of Beach Haven, shot me a sharp look but didn't say anything. "Any witnesses?"

Chief James shook his head. "Not one that makes any sense. My boys found a couple of transients sleeping on the beach that claim it was Satan himself that did it."

"Why Satan?" I asked.

The chief frowned. "They said it had a flat-faced head with horns and a bristly mustache. One of them told my officer that Satan roared and smote the house with his pointed tail."

"Did they say how long the tail was and the direction that it went after destroying the house?" I asked.

Chief James stopped walking and grabbed my arm. "Who exactly are you, Mister Dalton?"

I looked down at his hand, and he removed it. Gazing into his eyes, I replied, "In 1879, a couple of fishermen had a run in with a large shape just off Sandy Hook in November. They said the shape roared at them and had a large head with horns and a mustache. They also said that it reared out of the water on a long neck. The creature attacked the boat with a very large, sharp-pointed tail. The men estimated the creature to be at least fifty feet long. At the time very few believed the men and accused them of drinking or telling tall tales. But we both know that fishing in winter on an open sea is not the time for drinking. Jump ahead fifty years. We've seen Demons, Weres, Vampires, and Trolls in our country, why not sea monsters?"

"You're crazy. This was a tornado or something. These kinds of houses just fall down sometimes." Chief James shook his head in disbelief.

"Hunting monsters is what I do, Chief. This is my first clue. Have you had other mysterious disappearances or simply people who are just gone of late?" I asked.

The man started to say something but then pulled back. Giving me the eye, he slowly nodded his head. "One. Hattie Peterson."

At my questioning look, he expanded.

"She's a local beachcomber. Been doing it for longer than I've been alive. Earns a pretty good living at it as well. She has a shack out on the very edge of the township limits. Every day she can be seen walking up and down the beaches. Hattie's almost a fixture around here," James explained.

"When did you notice her gone?" I asked.

"Couple three days ago or so. Hattie called me. Said she had something I just needed to see. I didn't have time, so I checked up on her the next day. Her shack was broken into, and there was no sign of her anywhere. Suspicion isn't proof of anything. Hattie disappears every now and then on her selling trips. This might just be one of those."

I stared out at the destroyed house again. "Did Hattie sell stuff to them?"

The chief nodded, "Yes. The Todds owned a curio shop in town. Hattie dragged all sorts of junk to them. She was the best at finding unusual items."

"We need to figure out what Hattie was selling then and if there is more of it. It looks to me as if whatever that item might be, it is dangerous to own. Really dangerous," I motioned towards the destruction.

"I'll start asking around. Hattie gave Todd first crack at things but kept a small list of interested buyers as well. Are you staying in town?" James asked me.

Pursing my lips, I replied, "That I am. Any good campgrounds around here." I looked at the ocean again. "No seaside ones please."

"Yeah, I get that."

The place the Chief recommended was actually pretty nice. It may not have been seaside, but it was called the Seaside Stop. There were shaded slabs with fire rings already installed. Not a lot of business in winter around here so I had almost the whole place to myself.

Morning brought the sun and a host of questions. Sleep is hard with the wind whistling through the van. I stayed up half the night thinking and questioning.

Who else might Hattie have contact with and what hold may they have over her?

What is the item that she found?

If it's a sea monster, why is it attacking dry land?

If it's not a monster, what is it? A Demon? Or some sort of creepy-crawly nobody's seen before?

My final question was this. Where could I get both hot coffee and a meal? The inside of me was about to freeze to the outside of me, and it wasn't going to be pretty.

Melanie's Diner was the solution to my problem. Well, that and three cups of coffee. I sat at the counter watching the locals. Beach Haven wasn't a small town. I would call it a medium to a large one and according to the campground manager, a small city during tourist season. But this was the height of winter, and nobody was moving about.

"Where're all the people?" I asked.

"Gone. Those that can go south for the winter do. The rest just hunker down and tough out the snow and ice. This week is actually much nicer than usual." The waitress smiled at me and continued to wipe the counter down.

The questions I asked myself earlier were still bouncing around in my head. What had Hattie found? Is it just a big coincidence or was I on a wild monster hunt?

A gust of icy cold air woke me up and forced me to turn around. Chief of Police James stood in the doorway, a grim expression on his face. "Agent Dalton, we found something."

Hattie Peterson's place was a lonely house on the very edge of the town being sucked down into the sand dunes. What was left of it that is. Like the Todd house, Hattie's was ripped to pieces.

"I sent a patrol out here early this morning after the conversation we had yesterday. As soon as they saw this the officers called me," James explained.

The roof was gone. A gigantic hole took the place of where I assumed the door used to be. "Any evidence of... anything?"

The Chief shook his head. "I'm not even sure what we should be looking for here. She had so much junk in there that even if we found something, we couldn't know for sure what it was. The only thing my officers can't explain is that over there."

I turned my head to look where the chief of police was pointing. All of the beachfront forward of the house was torn up. It was like several bulldozers, or other earthmovers were loose on it. "Interesting."

"We canvassed the neighbors, what little there are out here. The closest one heard what they thought sounded like the roar of a wild animal. The dunes and grasses around here shield the noise pretty well. One of the advantages of living out here. In the off chance, it was a crazy man on a piece of construction equipment we're checking the surrounding roads and work sites. I don't know what to think, but this might support your sea monster theory. Why did you come here anyway?" Chief James asked me.

Some things are better left unsaid, and I did sign the Secrets Act, but a brief explanation was called for here. "I work for the FBI, but I run the Magical Division. We were created to hunt down rogue paranormal elements and supernatural threats to our country. This is one such threat. My boss in Washington sent me here after there were sightings up and down the coast."

"Sightings by whom?" Chief James asked.

I smiled and replied. "I asked my boss the same thing. She told me the Coast Guard and the Navy were the ones doing the reporting. And before you say it, I'm not sure why they aren't hunting this thing instead of me and my crossbow."

The Chief held up his hands, "Wasn't going to say it."

"Uh, huh. So, we have to ask ourselves this. Why does a sea monster come ashore in the first place and why here? There has to be plenty of food out in the ocean even if it's stormy. What makes a creature do something like this? All the historical sightings were out there," I pointed out toward the ocean. "Not here."

We stood together puzzling it over for a short while as his men wrapped up their investigation.

"Let's get out of this wind and think about it for a bit. I know just the place." The Chief slapped me on my back and pointed toward our cars and town.

It turned out that Melanie's Diner was the unofficial police substation for the town. Everyone that was anyone came to the diner and just hung out. Including the movers and shakers in town.

"Assuming this thing is an animal and NOT a Demon, what drives it?" Chief James asked.

Johnny Watson, the duly elected Mayor and the man who owned half the tourist attractions in town, grunted as he leaned forward. "Animals only care about food."

I shook my head no, "Not quite, sir. They look for food, shelter, and mates. Like humans, sex ... I mean conjugal relations is a priority."

"You think this thing is looking for another one, a mate?" The mayor looked at me in surprise.

"No. I think it's looking for babies or eggs. If you were Hattie Peterson and you found an egg or a strange creature what would you do with it?" I asked the small group at the table.

Chief James nodded, "Hattie survived by the sea. You all know she'd talk about eating seabird or making seaweed soup. She followed the older ways. If she found a critter she didn't recognize, she might try to sell it. Or eat it."

"If she'd eaten whatever it was, only her house would have been destroyed. I think she sold or gave it to Todd. It's why both houses were targeted. Somehow this creature tracked Hattie down," I theorized. "Maybe it can sense its young. Like how some animals can tell their babies from others in a large group. I'm just spitballing here though."

"You might be on the right track, Agent. My cows out at my dairy farm are able to do that. So Hattie found a baby or an egg then?" George McCoy stated.

Chief James shook his head. "More than one George. Why destroy the Todd's house then? Maybe Hattie found a nest or something? Do these creatures nest on land?"

I reached up and rubbed the stubble on my chin. Time to break out the razor. "If they nested on land we, meaning the FBI, would've investigated or discovered them before now. If we had strange creatures other than tourists nesting in New Jersey, it would have made the papers."

All the men at the table chuckled at my small joke. For as much as out-of-towners contributed to the local community coffers, they caused a headache for locals. Too much traffic or sheer simple-mindedness.

Mayor Watson half raised his hand. "Are we sure this thing is a sea monster? It could just be an oversized oarfish or a whale."

Several of the local businessmen turned toward him and frowned. "Johnny, whales don't come on shore on purpose."

The mayor held up his hands in defense. "I'm just speculating like the rest of you. This could hurt the town."

"It could help the town too. I can see the headlines now. Monster found in town. We'd be a tourist attraction like Lake Hopatcong with its diving tower or Wildwood's gorilla. What we do with it is up to us," Travis Hickey mused. He owned the largest hotel in town.

We had dead people, and they were trying to profit off it. It boggled my mind. "Before you start counting your money we need to find this creature first. Remember it's killed at least three people so far."

"Could it be an oarfish?" Police Chief James asked.

Henry Sloan shook his head negatively. "We get a lot of fishermen in the store, and I've only heard of one being caught. Around here they're pretty rare. The biggest one I've heard of was out in California, and that's a long way from here. This thing might have been stirred up by that fishing operation north of us."

A few miles offshore was a commercial fishing operation. I'd considered that angle already. They so far hadn't reported any issues. But, they weren't locals so it would be easier for these people to suspect them.

"We're getting off-track here gentlemen. Other than the Todds, who might Hattie have shown something like this too?" I asked.

"Did you look in her car?" George McCoy asked.

Chief James's eyes widened. "That old thing actually runs?"

George chuckled, "And here you are the police chief. Like clockwork, Hattie comes by my place once a month for ten gallons of milk and as much manure as she can shovel."

"Milk? Why would she want milk?" Mayor Watson asked.

"You know I asked her that once. She didn't have electricity out at her place, and I wondered what she was doing," McCoy stated.

Chief James waved his hands, "And?"

"Cheese. She made cheese wheels and sold them to tourists. Or at least that's the story she told me. Did she own any other properties around here? She had to store it somewhere." The dairy farmer answered.

"Mayor?" I asked.

Johnny Watson looked at me. "What? How should I know where? Hattie was like a hundred years old."

"More like sixty. Can't you find out?" Chief James asked him.

The mayor cocked his head to one side. "Stella's on vacation right now, but her assistant is still around." Watson stood up from the table. Looking around, he caught the eye of the man standing at the lunch counter. "Can I borrow the phone for a local call, Mel?"

Melvin Hook, the owner of the diner, nodded and pointed toward the register. Early on, Melvin discovered that people preferred to eat at Melanie's more than Melvin's.

Turning to watch the mayor, I let my gaze linger on the other patrons in the diner. A few were paying attention to what the informal town council was discussing, but most were just eating. How many more of these people were going to end up as monster chow was what I kept asking myself. We needed to either kill this thing or drive it back into the sea.

After a few minutes, Mayor Watson stepped back over to the table. "According to Stella's niece Emma, Hattie Peterson owns five pieces of property in the county."

"Five?" Chief James remarked.

"She owns the entire point her house sits on including the road. Henry, this one will surprise you. Hattie was your landlord," the mayor stated.

The bait shop owner started. "No, I pay rent to old man Howard. He's the one that rented me the spot along with access to the fishing pier. Emma got it wrong."

"Nope. She owns Howard's house too. Along with that entire row of rentals and the marina. I've been trying to negotiate with Howard for years over access, and it was Hattie's all along. It's no wonder he was ignoring my offers. I wonder why she didn't like me?" The Mayor asked.

Chief James counted off on his fingers. "The Marina, Howard's place, and the other house next to him, her place, and what? We're missing two."

"Roadside To Go is hers as well." The mayor explained to the group.

Half the men at the table rolled their eyes and nodded.

The roadside market was one of the few eyesores in town. Its location near the highway was the first thing potential tourists saw when they entered the town. It sold souvenirs, fruit, and tacky tourist junk.

"Where's the last place?" James asked.

The Mayor sighed. "Tucker Island. She owns the whole thing."

"Is Tucker even accessible to cars? It was mostly underwater just a couple of years ago," George McCoy asked.

"Hurricane Carol in fifty-four exposed it again. The beaches are mostly gravel, but the lighthouse ruins are still there. My guys are supposed to patrol out that way once a week or so. Let me ask." The Police Chief stood up from the table and walked towards the doorway.

I perked up at the mention of ruins. "Lighthouse?"

Henry Sloan shook his head. "Was Hattie part of the Rider family?"

"It's up for debate, but she might have been. I went to school with a bunch of those kids. I know for a fact several went to war and never returned here." Melvin Hook replied as he stood behind the counter. Thinking for a moment he explained, "There was a lighthouse on the point, Agent Dalton. It fell into the sea in the mid-1920s. I'm not sure of the exact date on that one. The Rider's were the family that ran the place. At times they used their house as an ad hoc hotel or hostel during storms. If I remember correctly, they had twenty kids out there."

"That actually makes a bit of sense now. If Hattie were raised there, she would know how to survive. The Rider's lived off the land out there," Chief James remarked.

"Is there anything else out there? Someplace Hattie could store cheese or the thing we're hunting?" I asked.

"It was starting to be a resort town until the lighthouse was destroyed. Storms took the rest of the buildings after that. I remember these really wide and deep pilings that the structure stood on. Mary and Eber Rider used to use them as root cellars in the summer. That might be what you're searching for, Agent," Melvin explained.

Chief James stepped back to the table and sat down. "My guys said they've seen a car out there a few times but didn't see anything else. Do we need to check it out?"

Mayor Watson quickly filled the man in on our findings, and he called his officers back.

"Field trip anyone?" I asked.

THE MAYOR INSISTED on coming with us for the hunt. Police Chief James called in two more of his officers who showed up in a former military all-terrain-vehicle.

"Haven't seen one of those in a while. I grew up in Texas, and they had a few down there. Where did you get it?" I asked the Chief.

"The local guard unit. They had two inoperable ones. It cost too much to repair both, so they scrapped them. My guys had some free time and made one from two." The chief pointed out the many welds and repairs.

I was familiar with the design. Reservation police used them to hunt down runaways and rogues in Texas. It was ironic that I was the one that would do that task in the future.

Since we were taking the ATV, I grabbed the SKS and one of the ammo pouches for it. I didn't think what we were hunting was super-natural, so I left the crossbow and magic ammo alone.

"What kind of gun is that?" Chief James asked. He was gripping a Thompson in his right hand.

"Samozaryadnyj Karabin Sistemy Simonova or SKS for short. It's what the Russians designed to kill Demons," I held the gun out to him.

Handing his gun to one of the deputies, the chief gripped the SKS with both hands. "Light. What's it use for ammo?"

"7.62X32mm It's a bit lighter and more accurate than the .45 you use. I picked it for the greater range." I pointed to the Thompsons they carried. "Those are only accurate to about a hundred and fifty yards or so."

I took my SKS back from Chief James. "This can hit something at four hundred yards easily."

"To each his own I guess. Let's get moving." The chief pointed me toward the rear seat of the ATV. His officers were going to follow in a pair of beach capable trucks.

The south end of the island was nothing but tracts of houses. Large sections of scrubland were being cleared for future development as well.

"Your town isn't going to stay small anymore," I remarked.

"Progress. Can't stop it. You can only embrace it and hold on. That's part of why I'm tagging along. This whole area's the future of Beach Haven. I need to be here," Mayor Watson explained.

The construction areas gave way to a broken down road behind a tumbled-down gate.

"This whole area was a newly built resort in the 1920s. Storms took the buildings and ocean the rest. Not a surprise that the island came back. Some things are hard to destroy completely," Mayor Watson pointed out some ruins.

An older model sedan sat just behind a large sand dune. It was sunken halfway up its wheels in the sand.

"There's her car. She might still be around," Chief James pointed out.

I slipped a ten round magazine into the SKS. Patting my cargo pockets, I made sure I still had the extra ammo for my pistols. This was not the place to run out. "Where are those foundations they mentioned?"

"If I remember correctly, they're a hundred yards or so that way. The lighthouse used to be right on the water's edge and then one day it just fell right over. We've got pictures of it in the historical section of the town library. There was a photographer on hand when it happened," Mayor Watson explained.

"Check the car, we'll take the dunes. One of you keep an eye on the mayor." Chief James told his deputies.

A casual glance at the interior of the car showed it was ripped up pretty good. Whatever was once in the rear wasn't there now.

There was a long row of sand dunes near the edge of the water. I didn't know much about beaches and such, but it looked like a good sign for the continued existence of this island. A slight path was worn down across two of the smaller dunes. I could see where sea oats and grass was crushed.

Half-buried in the dunes were four round pilings. They were at least ten feet around and open on the top. A rough cut doorway was cut through the concrete on the island side of the closest one.

"Over there." I pointed.

The hole was covered with an obviously homemade door secured with a large padlock.

"Anyone bring cutters?" Chief James asked.

The officers tried kicking the door, but it was secured too well.

"We could bring the ATV up and pull it off. I think we can attach the chain right here." Chief James pointed to sections along the edge.

Reaching into my pocket, I pulled out a lockpick kit. "Let me try first."

For most people simply owning burglary tools meant a trip to the police station. But I was a federal officer, and my charter implied I was to use EVERY tool at my disposal to complete my missions. This was just one of those.

"Fancy." It was the only comment Chief James made about them as I popped the lock and opened the door.

Smelly. That's the word I would use to describe the 'root cellar' Hattie Peterson was using. Clicking on our flashlights, we started scanning the room. Makeshift shelves with unrecognizable home-canned food stacked on them covered all the interior walls. In the center of the room were wooden crates of store-bought groceries and a large glass bottle. It was the jug that the smell was coming from. More like what was inside the bottle.

"Have you ever seen anything like that before in your life?" Mayor Watson asked me again.

We'd dragged the thing out of the storeroom and set it on the bed of one of the trucks. Exposed to the sunlight, it looked like an alligator bobbing in alcohol. It wasn't until you looked much closer that you realized it was something more ancient and dangerous.

"Only in a museum," I replied. My episode in Maine was Top Secret. Washington is pretty dull if you aren't a politician so one weekend I explored the Smithsonian before my first assignment. Something like this critter was on display in one of the exhibits. But much, much larger. The small creature in the bottle was either a Plesiosaur or a Thalassomedon. Both were bad news if real. If I remember correctly, they could get up to twelve meters long. Dealing with a forty foot dinosaur armed only with semi-automatics was going to get really hairy. What is it with these creatures, anyway? This is the second time this year I've seen them.

The three of us leaned on the truck staring at the dead baby sea monster. Somewhere, somehow, Hattie found these things and tried to sell them. It was the only explanation that made any bit of sense. Momma or Daddy followed her back to her house and then to the Todd house.

"Did she kill this thing or did it die of natural causes?" Chief James peered into the jar.

"That we may never know. What we need to find out is if

momma is still around because she's eaten human flesh now," I explained.

Mayor Watson paled. "It may still be winter, but we've got a fair coming next week."

"Exactly. So, if we take the lid off the jar..." I trailed off and looked to Chief James.

"You think she's this close to us?" He asked.

"Not so much us, but the last place she either saw or smelled her baby. If this thing can smell anything. Remember those derelicts said the head was all teeth. But they remembered it had a nose," I harkened back to the Todd investigation.

Chief James reached over to the jar and started to unscrew the cap.

"Wait!" Mayor Watson exclaimed. "You're going to do this now? Right here without the military or anything?"

"Johnny, they aren't going to come here on just my say or even his. Am I right, Agent Dalton?" Chief James pointed at me.

I grimaced but also nodded. The Coast Guard or Navy might come at my request, but I would need more than a baby dinosaur to get them here. It would have to be an active threat to public safety.

"But, but what about safety? I'm not a gun guy, and you only have those rifles," Mayor Watson protested.

Chief James motioned to his officers, who jumped up into the large truck. Grabbing a wooden box out from under the seat, the two dragged it to the edge and opened it up.

"That is my extra firepower right there," James pointed.

Peering into the box, I took a full step backward almost instantly. "You had those the whole time over the bumpy roads and everything?"

"Yeah, why? They're just grenades," Chief James pointed out.

"Those are Mark Two grenades. They have to be at least thirty years old and unstable. You do know you could have blown us all up, right?" I replied.

"We use them for fishing sometimes. It's safe." James looked in the Mayor's direction to see the man was also horrified by the contents of the box. "Johnny, they're safe. My boys are in the New Jersey Guard."

I flipped my vest up exposing my own M26 explosives. "I have my own. Keep those away from me please."

"Let's get this show on the road then. Using the butt of his Thomson, Chief James shattered the glass jar. A strong alcohol smell permeated the air along with the smell of rotting flesh. The baby lizard hadn't been dead very long.

"Take that up to the top of the sand dune over there and expose it to the wind. The rest of us should get into position," James ordered.

The mayor scrambled back to the ATV and actually crawled under it in fear. It was all I could do to not laugh at his antics. Chief James and his deputy walked to the notch between the two most massive sand dunes and crouched down to wait.

I took a position near the concrete footings. Bits of rotted wood and brick were half buried everywhere all along the water's edge, but I could see where the monster came ashore before. This was a water creature, not a land dweller, but when it's young were in danger, all bets were off. Looking up I saw the deputy waving the carcass in the air. I could only shake my head. Here was something incredibly rare and now we were being forced to kill it. If I tried to save it, I ran the risk of alienating an entire town and giving the Bureau and the Director himself the ammunition to shut me down.

Propping my weapon up beside me I ran both hands through my hair in frustration. I was just starting to like these folks, and then they break a bunch of local, state, and federal laws. Police Chief or not, owning grenades was illegal, especially really old ones. The ATU was going to freak when I informed them about this. Using them to fish even broke the new game laws that I was just told about three towns north of here. Idiots.

We sat and waited for several hours in near silence. The deputy up high switched off with his partner but continued to wave the dead animal. Chief James yelled comments toward me from time to time.

"This your first sea monster, Agent Dalton?"

I stood up so I could see the man. "It is. I've seen a lot of other strange things though."

"Like what?" James asked.

"Nothing I can speak about. Has your officer seen anything?" I asked. I really didn't want to talk to these guys now.

Chief James called out to his man as I scanned the waves in front of me. The way the fading sunlight sparkled off the water and sand demonstrated to me the allure of this place. I never went to the beach as a child. Rivers and ponds yes, but not the sea.

"Peter says he saw movement out there an hour ago. Could've been a rogue wave or porpoise. Lots of fish in the sea," Chief James explained.

"Is he sure of anything?" I was getting a bit testy being out here. If Chief James responded to my question, I never found out. It was at that moment that our monster attacked.

Peter Mayberry had been with Chief James since he was appointed to the position. Waving a dead monster while looking for its momma wasn't the strangest thing he'd done in the commission of his job. Some things out here are better off left unsaid. He was looking east when the enormous head and neck reached out of the water.

Thalassomedon was a relative of the Plesiosaur, but only a pale-ontologist would know the difference. Its three-foot long head was filled with dozens of razor-sharp teeth. Teeth that ripped Peter's arm and most of his shoulder right off his body. In the creature's proper time it was an apex predator. Top of the food chain.

Peter's gurgling scream forced my attention away from the chief and toward the now dead man at the top of the dune. The creature was just finishing its second bite of the man when Chief James opened fire on it.

The chief was using his Thompson submachine gun. I'd had a chance to look at his weapon on the way down here. It was an M1 model, meaning that it was one of the ones produced for the military.

The cops had made disparaging remarks about my SKS saying it was too long or too bulky to use, but the Thompson had its own problems. Problems that Chief James was just now realizing.

BRRRRAAAAAATTTTT!

Firing from the hip gangster style, the police chief sprayed his gun in the general direction of the monster. The Thompson is really only accurate up to fifty yards, and the creature was farther away than that. It roared, a sound not heard upon land for millennia. Smelling its young on the other deputy, the head and neck thrust straight at him.

The officer ignored the rifle at his feet and pulled out his handgun. Blasting away at the dinosaur he tried to shield the chief as he reloaded.

Chief James dropped the stick magazine and scrambled in his carry case for the drum magazine. It had taken a few months to find one, but he had always wanted a hundred round fire capacity. Ammunition was expensive so this would be the first time he'd ever used it.

"Chief, I need some help here!" The deputy fired all six shots with his revolver and then rolled off the edge of the dune to avoid being bitten. He slid down through the sand, landing next to Chief James.

The chief had pulled out the used stick magazine and was jamming the drum into the hole. Unlike the magazine on my SKS or one for most rifles, there was no catch or clip to hold it in, and only the original Thompsons could use the drum. I should know since I have a specially-refurbished FBI model Thompson in my van. The M1 can't use them.

"Chief!" The second deputy screamed as a mouth full of teeth clamped down on his leg yanking him off his feet and toward the water's edge.

I stepped around the concrete piling and took aim. Not at the head but at the enormous body that was half in and half out of the water. Aiming carefully I started firing. Each of my magazines held ten rounds, and it was on the fourth shot that I got a rise from the creature. It reared up shaking its head in pain. The roar, similar to the earlier one, was a cry of pain. It broke off its attack on the chief and turned its attention toward me.

Unlike the other men, I had very large obstacles to hide behind as well as the improvised root cellar to duck into if needed.

The aquatic dinosaur was huge! More than forty feet long with the neck alone more than half that. The body of the beast was resting on the shoreline partially submerged. My shots penetrated the thick skin and hurt it internally. How much was unknown as I ducked and wove to avoid the razor-sharp teeth.

This wasn't a movie, and I wasn't an actor. In all the films I'd ever seen the monster would charge after the hero, either killing him or dying a horrible death. This creature didn't have legs, only flippers, so unless I went into the water, there would be no charging. I just needed to put distance between me and its long neck!

Crack! Crack! Crack!

Chief James drew the creature's attention away from me as he opened fire with his handgun. I ducked behind the nearest concrete piling. The dunes covering the pilings were less than twelve feet from the water's edge and within range of the creatures head and teeth. Choosing to not be a movie hero, I retreated in the opposite direction. Unlike the Chief, my rifle has a four-hundred meter range.

Crack! Crack! Crack! Crack! Crack! Crack!

I didn't have to fire all ten rounds this time. The creature let out a roar, and its head and neck slammed into the sand.

"Is it dead?" Chief James asked.

Looking past the bulk of the creature I could see the man standing atop the sand dune, blood running down his body from a shattered right arm. He wouldn't be firing a Thompson again anytime soon.

"Maybe," I shouted. Carefully I approached the monster. Blood still oozed out of the holes I put into it, but it seemed to be dead.

Using the tip of my SKS I gave it a jab. Nothing. No movement whatsoever. Reaching out I ran my hand down the unmarred side of the animal. It was both smooth and scaly. Not something I would forget for a long time. "Not your time anymore."

The police chief needed care. A tourniquet only goes so far before you lose the limb. Fortunately for us, the mayor drives fast. At the first sign of the monster, he hightailed it to the nearest phone and called in everyone.

When I say everyone, I do mean everyone. Barely an hour after the last shot was fired, we had TV crews, firefighters, ambulances, State Police, local FBI, and a Coast Guard cutter at the site.

"Are you sure you're OK?" I asked Chief James. We were both in the back of the town's ambulance.

"I'm OK for now. Those were good boys with me. Without them, we both might be dead. No idea how I'm gonna tell my sister about her sons! Got anywhere I can hide, Dalton?" Chief James asked.

I could only blink at him. Nepotism isn't dead in New Jersey for sure. Shaking my head, I replied, "Just the van I drive. It's a bit cramped back there. Besides, don't you want to speak to the press? Mayor Watson has a whole flock of them around him." I pointed towards the sand dunes.

"Press?" Chief James pushed past me at a run.

The local FBI boys gave me a wide berth once they found out who I was. Apparently, my adventure in Boston was making the rounds. Maybe the dumb ones would straighten up some.

"Agent Dalton, do you want us to take control of the scene?" The local SAIC asked.

"You can have what there is of it. I suppose you're going to have to wrestle the locals and the Guard for it. One thing you can do for me though." I stated to the man.

"What would that be?" The SAIC asked again.

I smiled and pointed toward the police vehicles. "Chief James has an entire case of Mark Two hand grenades on that truck over there. They look a bit unstable, and he may have acquired them illegally. Can you either confiscate them or notify the boys at the ATU about them? Firepower like that doesn't need to be in his hands. If I could take the Thompson too, I would."

Glancing to where I pointed the man signaled the other Agents. "Was it that bad?"

"Not really. I'm sad for the loss of life, but we needed to stop the killings. Chief James was more likely to hit me than the creature. Did Washington send me any orders?" I asked the agent.

He shook his head negatively and spoke, "Nothing. You're welcome to stay and work the scene if you like."

I laughed at the look on his face. "Thanks for the offer, but you and I both know you would rather I move on. I think I make these folks nervous around here. At least it wasn't Demons."

Shouldering my SKS, I looked for someone to hitch a ride back to town with.

"If only you could have taken it alive or even called us first! We could have captured this beauty for you."

I blinked at the voice and looked up. Several men in lab coats stood in front of me.

"Captured it how? Only the Navy has anything big enough to do the job, and they weren't here," I replied.

"You know nothing of the scientific procedure, young man. Trust me when I say we could have done a much better job than this atrocity!" The speaker took his group and headed toward the mass of people and cameras.

Eggheads and squints. I was so glad that I didn't have to deal with that part of the job. Kill the monster and move on. That was my priority now.

———

"Good work on catching the sea monster, Jack," Anastasia told me over the phone. "Expect to catch a bit of heat about killing it, but I've got your back here. I hoped you enjoyed your beach vacation because your next assignment is taking you west. It will be a new year when you get there, but keep your eyes peeled."

"Peeled for what?" I asked.

"Werewolves. Local agents in St. Louis have discovered a rogue pack, and you get to confront them. Welcome to 1960, Jack." Anastasia replied.

This ends Book Four of Jack Dalton Monster Hunter.

JACK DALTON, MONSTER HUNTER

BOOK 5

My name is Jack Dalton, and I'm a monster hunter.

Take the fight to the enemy. That was but one of the many things my step-father told me growing up. Something about the military changed a man. Both my fathers were like that. That's what mom said, anyway. I only remembered my step-father. This job was similar to being in the military at least for assignments. Go there, kill the monster, and go home. Except that home, for now, is a black and yellow van. It's not all bad.

Giving the van in question a pat on the dashboard, I smiled to myself. Whatever the squints in Washington did to this thing turned it into the best vehicle I've ever owned or driven. Tight on the turns, nice get up and go, and it got me to where I needed to be. That's all I could ask of a car or truck.

Driving from New Jersey to Missouri takes a lot out of a man. I hoped there would come a time they could just stuff my van into an airplane and fly me across the country. As if the FBI or the Army would allow that. Maybe one day when this division is more than a single person I'll be able to do that. I have been writing all my ideas down for the future, but I doubt the Director will read them. Anastasia tells me that Mr. Hoover is still pissed that I was even able to do the job. He and all his cronies expected me to fail. Nice to prove somebody wrong. I could still die though.

My new assignment took me to the heart of middle America. Right after the Great War and before what folks are now calling the Demon War, the American people were scared. Monsters disguised as humans walked among them. It didn't matter that they might have known the monsters as the local baker, policeman, or librarian. They were monsters now and not to be trusted. Many were driven from town by mobs or in some cases killed. Running them out on a rail became commonplace. It was one such case of THAT that caught national attention.

Freddie Kim was the town pharmacist in a speck of a town in Ohio. When the Great Reveal happened, he was just dumb enough to tell people what he was. They were his friends, his neighbors, and fellow members of the local Moose Lodge. None of that mattered when Fred announced he was a Werewolf. He'd been infected more than twenty years previously during a hunting trip. Unusually, he was a solo and not part of one of the local Packs. They ran him out of town on a rail after setting fire to both his shop and his house.

Typically, the victim of such a thing would straddle a beam of wood while the townspeople jeered at him. Fred's friends did him one better. He was dipped in melted tar, covered in feathers, and dragged out of town tied to a large chunk of a cut-down tree. Fortunately for the people of that small town, Fred liked them. He kept his form and didn't change. The hot burning tar stayed one step ahead of his healing factor leaving massive amounts of scar tissue all over Fred's body.

Pictures of the event fed the public's paranoia for weeks. One of the local Packs claimed Freddie before much worse could be done to him. The people cried out, so Washington responded. It didn't help that it was an election year. To assuage the public's fears and protect them from the monsters, all Were folks were ordered to report to the reservations being set up all over the Midwest and California. Like this country's native population, they were locked away to be forgotten.

That came to an end when the Demons arrived in America. Conception, California was ground zero for something that could overcome the government and drive us all back to the Stone Age, an invasion. Battling a Demonic horde wasn't something the United States Army was prepared for. What few special forces troops available were already in the fight in France. For that was where the Demons first appeared. California was just the second front in a battle that would last for years. If not for the quick thinking of then Governor Huey Long, we might have lost. The Governor marshaled the National Guard forces of Louisiana and Texas quickly sending them west. With a stroke of pure brilliance, he also recruited every Were Pack he could find on the reservations. As the only Paranormal species under government control, the Werewolves were up for anything that would get them off the reservations. Even battle was acceptable. With their aid, the Demons were pushed back and destroyed.

The Weres help didn't get them off the reservations as a species, but any individual that served in the military was given a sort of parole. They were supposed to report to a government handler once a month, but it was an improvement over the reservation system. My Pack leader and friend in Texas was a veteran. Big Ron and his chief followers were all ex-military and could leave the res anytime they wished.

Now I'm off to stop a rogue Werewolf. I grew up around Weres, and they don't go rogue often. The Alphas wanted their people off the reservations so they usually kept their problems 'in-house'. As a member of law enforcement, I don't approve of vigilante justice, but I'm aware of the issues involved with putting Weres in prison. The standard judicial practice was to give them the death penalty no matter the crime. Only Crowley prison could hold them, but it's more for crazed, Demon possessed magic users than Weres who skipped town without telling anyone.

For this mission, I'm to get a partner. That was a total surprise as the regular FBI, and I don't exactly get on well. Boston will forever hang over my head. But exposing that bit of corruption was necessary.

"New assignment Jack," Anastasia told me over the secured phone line in Atlantic City.

"More Sea Monsters to kill?" I asked. I actually found and killed a gigantic monster just a few days ago along the Jersey Shore.

"Sort of. There's a rogue Were loose in St Louis. He's already infected a couple of innocents. This threatens to become a public relations nightmare if we don't stop it. The human public's been warming to the idea of Weres living among them but if incidents like this one crop up... Well, you get the picture. Drop whatever you're doing and get moving toward Missouri," Anastasia directed.

"Does the local office have any information about what set him off or anything that would help to find him? St Louis is a huge city," I asked.

Anastasia grunted, "The local office has taken the hands-off stance on this case. The Director has stated that anything having to do with Paranormals is now the sole responsibility of the Magical Division. None of the locals want exposure to the Lycanthrope virus."

I could feel my jaw drop open all by itself at her pronouncement. Every Paranormal crime was mine to investigate? I was going to be in my truck for a long, long time! "Isn't that a lot of cases for a single man to do, Ana?"

"It's what you get for succeeding in your job, Jack. The Boss is a bit peeved that you actually found a Sea Monster last week. My contacts in both the Navy and Coast Guard tell me the reported sightings I initially told you about were bogus. You found a needle in a haystack on that one, Jack. This case puts you more into the public eye, so I need you to be careful." Anastasia paused for a moment, "I need you to take Interstate 64 through Louisville on your way west."

"Sixty-four? Is that the most direct route?" I asked.

"Not really but it's the one I wish for you to go. Outside of Louisville, Kentucky, you'll be picking up a partner for this mission, Jack," Anastasia answered.

I pulled the phone away from my head and stared at it. Did she say what I thought she said? "Am I getting another agent?"

There was a chuckle before she answered me. "Another agent? No. This man isn't agent material, but he is an expert on rogues. He was recommended to us through one of my contacts in the Paranormal underworld. His name is Robert Moore, and he's exactly what you need for this case. Trust me on this ok?"

I nodded to myself. Ana hadn't steered me wrong yet. "I always trust you, Ana. Where do I pick him up and what does he look like?"

So, now I'm looking for a hole-in-the-wall barbecue restaurant on the side road to nowhere. Personally, I'm starting to think this is a wild goose chase.

The directions send me away from the highway and onto a single lane road. I turned at the red barn and then at the brokendown mill building which popped me out onto a small town street. Stopping at what looked to be the only stop sign in this town, I craned my neck around to see where I was. There was a small, almost tiny, town park to the right of me and a big white sign atop a house that read Ookami Barbecue.

Pulling into the parking lot beside the house I could only shake my head. Even Big Ron wasn't this bold. I wondered if the town elders knew.

Climbing the broad steps, I opened one side of a double screen door leading into the house. Tables and chairs were scattered across the wide porch to enjoy the cool breeze. The front door was propped open, so I walked on in.

The place was set up like a diner with a counter at one end of the room. Several families with small children were eating off to one side along with men that had a local feel to them. A man sitting at the counter matched the description of my ride-along.

"Coffee?" The waiter asked me as I slid onto the swivel stool at the counter.

Shaking my head, I replied, "Water and sarsaparilla if you've got it please."

The man nodded and turned back to the fountain counter area to get it.

I wiggled my back and shoulders to relieve some of the road stress as I waited. The insides of the place reminded me of a favorite bar back in the city. It seemed strange to find it inside a house in the middle of nowhere in Kentucky. I think it was the sense of familiarity in the place that made me think of the only one that had ever made me feel that way before.

"Need a menu?" The counterman asked as he slid a short bottle of soda in front of me with a water glass.

For a split second, I watched a bead of water glide down the frosty glass. My entire attention was on that drop.

"Menu?" The man repeated.

Looking up I could see him staring at me, "Sorry. Not right now, thanks."

Grabbing the glass with one hand, I took what started out as a sip and turned into a gulp of the water.

"Ahh. That's the stuff." I opened my eyes to see both the counterman and my possible contact staring at me. "Sorry. Long drive."

The man behind the counter turned back around but not before I heard his muttered comment, "City people."

My possible ride along continued to stare at me. I ignored the man and started drinking my soda. Sarsaparilla used to be a home remedy for hangovers and headaches more than a century ago. Big Ron, my friend, and Pack leader introduced me to it when I was a kid. They called it Birch beer in some parts of the country. Very similar to true root beer. Not like that sugary stuff everyone served now at all.

"So, does the town know or do you just fake it?" I asked the man sitting next to me without looking at him.

"Fake it, Agent Dalton? All of these are my people." The man waved his hand at the other patrons in the room.

All movement stopped behind me. The families in the corners were deathly quiet, and every head in the room was looking straight at me. Even the counterman, still in my sight, watched me with shrewd eyes. There was just the slightest hint of yellow to them. Not one agent in five would have caught that little clue. This entire town so far was nothing but Weres.

Noting my non-reaction, the man I assumed was my contact spoke. "When did you know?"

I chuckled and glanced to my right. It really was too easy. "When I stopped outside before pulling up. Other words would have worked as well. Japanese is a bit out of place for backwoods Kentucky after all. I expect that few catch it though."

Robert Moore smiled, his teeth were shiny white and gleaming. "I told Henrietta that name was too dubious, that she should have used an Indian name or something. Japanese is a bit out there for the FBI to be fluent in isn't it?"

"I had an eclectic education. My mentors made sure I knew lots of strange words. My suggestion if you plan to go with a similar theme is to use Susi as a replacement," I replied.

Robert's eyebrow went up on his forehead as he looked at me. "Susi, like a girl's name?"

"It's Finnish for 'wolf.' A double meaning. But it's your place, who am I to mess with it. I'm assuming you are Robert Moore?" I asked.

The room came to life again with the families and others now ignoring me and my companion.

"That would be me. A good friend of mine informed me of your situation and what you can expect in Missouri. Hunting down a rogue by yourself is not a task for a human to do. Didn't you think to ask for help?" Robert asked.

"From whom? Mr. Hoover himself said I was it for this division. Besides, most regular FBI Agents only shoot to kill Paranormals. Don't we want this one alive?" I asked.

"Hmm, you are an interesting man, Agent Dalton. I was given details about you but didn't believe them," Robert replied.

I cocked my head to one side. "Who is it that gave you information about me? Was it Anastasia?"

"Ana who? I don't know anyone by that name unless you mean the Tsarina of Russia, but I only met HER in passing. The... person that sent me to you has connections but not that kind. Power isn't always political after all," he replied. Moore had a look on his face that my mother would call the 'I've got a secret' look.

I had a secret as well and now was the time to use it. I smiled and replied. "No, it isn't. This is going to be such an interesting trip, Alpha Moore."

Once again it was as if time stopped in the entire restaurant. Everyone froze. Only the ticking of the clock on the wall told me time didn't actually end.

Robert rotated his head to look directly at me. He stared into my eyes, and I felt a sort of pressure building inside my head. To me, it felt as if I suddenly had the world's most massive sinus headache. As if the only relief would be for my head to pop like a balloon at the circus. And then it was gone.

"Interesting. By all the Gods in the heavens, how did they manage that? You really do have Pack ties. I wouldn't have believed it if I hadn't just seen it. Big Ron is to be commended," Robert commented. "Will you tell me when you sensed it?"

Reaching up I rubbed my face. Right above the sinus channels on both sides of nose, my face ached like a gigantic bruise. "When I entered the room. This isn't MY Pack, but it has a similar feel. Whatever that was you just did was more powerful than anything Ron ever did to me. What was it?"

"Just a test, Agent. Just a test. You must allow me some secrets. Are you ready to go? Or do I need for Patrick here to make you a sandwich or something?" Robert asked.

———

It took a bit of manipulation, but we managed to move the file cabinet on the passenger side to the rear of the van. Washington didn't configure my official vehicle for passengers. My small cooler sat between us filled with sandwiches and more of that tasty sarsaparilla.

Robert patted the dashboard of my van. "Nice setup you've got here, Agent Dalton. Everything compact and easy to find."

"I like to think so. It's all come in handy so far. Someone in logistics really planned this out for me. And it's Jack. Agent Dalton is too big a mouthful all the time. Does that make it easier for you?" I asked.

"It does. Call me Robert. So, who are your people, Jack, and what brought you to me?" He asked.

Keeping a firm hand on the wheel of the van, I reached into the small cooler with my right hand and pulled out one of the sandwiches and a soda. Slipping the soda bottle between my legs to hold it in place, I unwrapped the wax paper sandwich covering. "The US government brought me to you, Robert."

"Patrick makes good sandwiches. That one smells like roast beef. May I?" Robert pointed down at the small cooler.

"Be my guest," I took the distraction to open the bottle using an opener I had secured to the door.

Robert pointed past me at the device, "Handy."

"I do a lot of driving. Want me to open yours for you?" I gestured.

Using his thumb, Robert popped the top right off his bottle. "No thanks."

I shook my head in disbelief. Weres.

"Do you have any clue to the whereabouts of this rogue? I know that they wouldn't just send you along for comic relief now would they?" I asked.

Robert chuckled at me and shook his own head, "Comic, no. I volunteered actually. What do your orders say about the attack?"

Keeping both hands on the wheel as I steered through traffic I thought for a moment. "I was to confer with the local office, but they described an encounter at the train station. Our subject was spotted after two servicemen were attacked and infected during a USO stopover. There weren't any details provided beyond that. He's supposed to be a local agricultural purveyor."

Robert barked out a sharp laugh. "Agricultural purveyor? That has to be the FBI's way of saying farmer. Why can't they just say 'farmer?'"

"Politics most likely. Something I try to stay as far away from as possible. So, the report's a bit thin. I assumed we would pick the station's attendees brains along with whatever the local office has and figure out a plan. How hard could that be?" I asked.

Two hours later I found myself eating those simple words. How hard could it be?

It turns out there were hundreds of station employees to choose from, and all of them apparently saw nothing.

"I don't understand how the people you had in that area of the station didn't see anything at the time of the incident. How?" I asked the station manager.

The St. Louis trains administrator was a short round individual with a severe problem with law enforcement for some reason. He smiled. "Have you looked at the station here? St. Louis is a major freight line for all things west of here. During the war, we shipped and prepped troops traveling west faster and more efficiently than any other station. This place was vital to the war effort," He waved at the window in his office looking out at numerous train cars moving about.

"There isn't a war going on anymore though. Why all this activity here?" I asked.

"Everything comes in by rail. Food, merchandise, people, and fuel are the chief items. We're a distribution point for half the businesses in the state. I have dozens of employees whose sole job is just to keep track of the trucks that pick things up. The people that come through here are anonymous. Don't get me wrong Agent Dalton. I feel for the families of the two men bitten. It's why my company provides an insurance benefit for those killed with the LV virus. Putting them down is the only option for those workers. It was luck that our protection team was on hand to take care of the task. The FBI boys around here are too squeamish to do it." The administrator grinned suddenly. "The bounty was nice too."

Quickly I gripped Robert's arm and pulled him back. I could see that the Alpha was going to be a problem here.

"What is the bounty for Weres here in Missouri?" I asked, not really wanting to know the answer.

"Fifty bucks a head. It used to be lower, what with the war and all. Some of those beasts were actually working with the troops that protected us. A few of us made a profit even then. Have to protect the nation and all that. Did either of you boys serve?" The administrator asked.

"Only with the FBI, it's my calling," I answered.

Robert nodded and spoke a single word. "Army."

"Excellent. I did a tour as a quartermaster for the Missouri Volunteers. We ran the USO efforts and kept everything running properly." The administrator nodded and smiled.

As what the man said worked its way through my brain, I watched Robert. He acted as if he was stalking the administrator by carefully stepping and looking, his eyes taking in every tiny detail about the office and man.

"Did your protection team question the men before 'putting them down' or did they just kill them?" I asked.

"I was told they were part of an illegal card game in one of the older club cars out in the storage yard. A Were had been involved in the game and bit the two men as he escaped the car. That's all I know," he replied.

Stepping sideways, I blocked Robert's access to the man for a moment. "Did you know that only half of those bitten actually become Weres and that there's a new vaccine that, if administered in time, will prevent transformation? You murdered those men without any provocation. Being bitten is not a death sentence like it used to be. Missouri just passed a bill two weeks ago eliminating the bounty system on Paranormals. You broke the law, and I intend to see you prosecuted for it."

The administrator's smile dropped away when his mouth opened to protest. I didn't give him time to do anything. Quickly I hauled him out of his chair and cuffed him. "No use struggling. Those cuffs were designed to control Paranormals. I doubt you could break them. Sit quietly until I have someone here to arrest you."

I shot a glance in Robert's direction, but he only stared back at me. Shaking my head, I pointed towards the waiting area outside the office. Robert took my hint and stepped outside.

Using my authority as Director of the Magical Division I had the man's own secretary call the local police for me. He was in shock as they hauled him away charged with murder for hire. The law was new, but I was sure the local district attorney would throw the book at him and those that helped him. Defrauding the federal government was the least of his worries. Now that the result was under arrest I continued to need the cause. Only Robert could help me track down that portion this hunt.

The man in question sat in my van staring at me. He hadn't said a word since local St. Louis police took the rail administrator into custody and tracked down the security force.

"Are you ok?" I asked him.

Robert reached up and stroked his beard for a moment as he watched me. "I'm not sure. You stopped me back in the office but made sure justice was served. Did you know?"

"Did I know what?" I asked.

"That the railroads were killing my people? I can show you figures if you like, but there have been literally hundreds killed in the last couple of years. We don't have rogues, Jack. At least not in the sense that humans think of them," Robert waved toward the train station and all the people milling around.

I let out the breath I was holding. "Sort of. Ana, my boss, filled me in on some of it as background. I didn't lie to you that I knew little about this specific rogue or where he might be. I'm aware that most Packs don't have rogues. My Pack in Texas had a few lone wolves, but they weren't considered being rogue. That term is something entirely different."

"Your boss sounds like someone I'd like to meet someday," Robert replied.

I laughed. "She's something, I'll tell you. Ana has a multitude of jobs at the main office. One is collecting little bits of information and facts that don't always make sense in the beginning but later prove worthwhile."

"It's hard for me to classify you as Pack and I do apologize for it. I'm not sure if Ron told you, but there have been only a small handful of non-Weres admitted into any Pack. Friends of the Pack, yes. But not full members. It's very rare. I've seen it happen twice in my life," Robert informed me.

"I heard you say you'd served. May I ask what branch? My dad was in France in 1946." I asked him.

"You should really ask what war. I was a brand spanking new lieutenant in Fifth Kentucky when it was formed in 1862. We were attached to General Breckinridge's command initially. We fought from Vicksburg to the retreat at Atlanta. Sherman's boys were just too tough to push back." Robert had a look of longing on his face. He turned to look me in the eye. "Having men die under your command is one of the hardest things you can ever witness. April twenty-ninth, 1865 was the last time I fired a musket in anger. It was a different time. My convictions were different. We were trying to make a different world for our people. All our efforts failed, and the cause was lost."

"You're not talking about the Confederacy, are you?" I asked.

"No, I'm not. It was a different world two centuries ago. States' rights and slavery might have been the human reason for the war, but not everyone who was in command of the Southern forces was human. History is written by the victors, Jack. Always remember that," Robert instructed.

All I could do was nod. It was easy to forget that many Paranormals were long-lived. Vampires and Weres especially. This man in front of me had seen much in his life.

"Forget I said anything kid. The past can be overwhelming sometimes. Thank you for what you did back there. The local Alpha might have a lead on our fugitive. Do you want me to contact him?" Robert asked.

I looked over at my companion. "I didn't know there was a reservation around here."

"There's not. You're going to have to pretend you weren't ever in the town or met any of these people. If you truly want to catch the guy and continue to do your new job the proper way, you have to pick a side here, kid." Robert was using the tone of voice that behaviorists at the Academy warned us about. Add a little Alpha kick, and he could control just about anyone. I'm was surprised I even caught it.

Shaking my head to clear the imaginary butterflies, I responded. "What if I say no and go it alone? I told you before that your tricks didn't work on me, Alpha. Doing my job is my side."

The subtle power stopped and made Robert smile. "I had to try. We all answer to someone, Agent Dalton. Those that lead me told me to make an effort. If you report it, we'll deal with it then. If you still want my help, head northwest. The town we're looking for is called Foley. If the Alpha there doesn't know where to look or who our culprit is, then it will be like looking for a needle in a haystack."

I pinched the bridge of my nose to try to take some pressure off my head. It really did feel like someone was squeezing it like a grape. I wasn't ready to become a mindless servant just yet though. Letting out a sigh, I shook my head. "Let's go to your contact. If I involve the FBI, law or not, they may shoot you, and then MY boss will be upset. You might be the scariest man I've met recently, but she truly scares me. Which way do I go?"

Robert gave me directions as we pulled out of Union Station. "That station is pretty neat. What was it like in its heyday?"

"You've got balls, kid. That'll serve you well in this business. It was built in the 1890s. It became a showplace of a station. It had restaurants and a hotel right there inside the station. It was an innovation for the time. Before the war even started, twenty-two railroads were using that station. It may be a bit rough around the edges now, but once upon a time it was magnificent." Robert motioned with his hands as he spoke.

"It sounds like it." We were heading north, but there was a total mess of construction equipment and detours everywhere. "What's going on over there?"

Robert spat out his open window in disgust. "Humans. Your people spend money on the damndest things sometimes. About thirty years ago, the city council along with the mayor of St. Louis had a brilliant idea to build a monument that idealized Western Expansion. The President even set aside prime riverfront property for its use. They've been raising money forever and only found an architect ten years or so ago for it. All this mess is the result of having to move several lengths of tracks and building a tunnel under the whole thing as well."

"A tunnel? Right next to the river? Is that even possible? They've got some kind of chutzpah then. That's crazy. What's it supposed to look like? I can imagine a gigantic horse-drawn wagon up there," I pointed.

"'Chutzpah,' that's a good term for this project. It's a bit crazy, but they made it work somehow. I think Fredrick Douglass said it best, 'If there is no struggle, there is no progress.' It explains why they threw themselves into this." Robert looked at me and laughed. "You wanted a description, didn't you? Sorry. Sometimes I talk just to listen to myself. It's supposed to be an arch. Sort of like a gigantic silver horseshoe in the sky."

"Interesting. At least it'll be big with this much of mess. What highway did you say I needed to look for?" I asked.

Robert looked up from the map in front of him, "I didn't, but stay on Interstate 70 until we cross the Missouri river. Once we pass through St. Charles and St. Peters, we'll take the interchange onto State Highway 79."

————

CORN, wheat, wood, and hay. Those were the fields I saw off of Route 79. Lots and lots of farms at work out here. We were on a two-lane blacktop heading north along the river.

"So, where am I going, Robert?" I asked.

"I told you already. A little farming town called Foley. It's not that much further. If I were you though, I'd slow down a bit before you pass that next rise. The local sheriff thinks he should be in the State Police and likes to find reasons to arrest people. Just a warning," Robert explained.

Nodding I started looking for speed traps. The speed limit was fifty-five and to be sure I was doing less than that, but I looked up when I heard the sound of a siren.

"I told you. You better get your credentials out because if he looks in the back, you're toast," Robert informed me.

Carefully I pulled over to the side of the road and waited. My van was clearly marked FBI on all sides. It would be interesting to see how this local officer reacted.

The patrol car pulled up behind us, and the officer got out. He wore the typical peaked cap with aviator sunglasses that many departments were now wearing. You have to hand it to Hollywood for making them so popular.

"License and registration please," the local asked.

I flipped my credentials out the window showing him the badge then the identification, "FBI. I wasn't speeding so why pull me over?"

The officer started to stutter so badly his glasses fell off his face, "Eff bee eye? I... I... I... Di... Didn't know."

Putting on my best smile I looked out the window at him, "It's ok. Was I speeding, officer?"

Scooping his glasses up, the man straightened up and peered into the cab of my van. "The chief told me to pull over any out-of-towners. Sorry." The man leaned down more and looked past me toward Robert.

"Is that you there, Mr. Moore?" The officer asked.

Robert chuckled at my expression, "That it is, Roscoe. Now I know Chief Dan didn't tell you to pull over everyone. Not after you tried to arrest those state investigators. This man really is the FBI, so you best be turning us loose now, you hear?"

It was my turn to smile when the seemingly well-educated man sitting next to me slipped into a slightly southern sounding local dialect.

The local finished his conversation with Robert and ran back to his patrol car. I could hear the engine start up and it suddenly tore past us heading north. The car was at least twenty years old and at one point had been a taxi. I could see the faded words peeking out under the police logo. "Something I should be aware of?"

Robert shook his head no. "That was Roscoe. He's actually a part-time officer for the Winfield Police Department. That's the next town up ahead."

"Part-time? I can't imagine how that works. Do I want to know?" I asked.

"Not really. This area is all farming. Money's tight and city budgets are even tighter. He won't bother us again," Robert answered.

"Hmm. How is it you're known here? I assumed you were from Kentucky since that was where I picked you up and you served. Was it all a lie then?" I asked as I slipped my left hand down towards one of my sidearms.

Robert pointedly looked at where my hand was and replied, "I'd rather you didn't shoot me, Jack. I paid a lot of money for this suit, and bullet holes will only ruin the line. You're safe. Trust me. Foley's the very next town. Now don't blink or you'll miss Winfield."

He was right about the town. There was only a stop sign between the next local highway and where the one we were on started. Just a couple of local storefront buildings and a small train station. Nothing to write home about. A few of the houses near the tracks looked prosperous, but the rest were a bit run down. We crossed a small bridge nestled up close to the railroad trestle, and then we were back to cornfield country.

"Farming is hard on the farmer and his entire family. Locals keep to themselves as well. It's the perfect place to hide a Were Pack as long as you keep it private," Robert said.

Foley was worse than Winfield. I was surprised they even bothered to build a town there. There wasn't even a stop sign.

Robert pointed to my left, "Pull up next to the post office. The man we need is in that bar over there."

Peering out the window I could see there was a very small establishment just to the right of the building proclaiming to be the post office.

"How many people live around here?" I parked the van in front of the postal building.

"Officially?" Robert asked.

I nodded as I got out and grabbed my everyday bag. I'd started carrying it after my adventure in Jersey. You never know when some things might just come in handy.

"One hundred-eighty-three at the first of the year. That's about four clans of Pack with a few stragglers thrown in. If you count hangers-on and the older folks, we've got double that here unofficially. I told you this was a refuge, not a reservation," Robert pointed out.

I could feel the others as soon as we stepped inside. The bar was simple and to the point. A real bar took up the longest wall with three small tables and some stools. No pool, no darts, no dancing. It was all about the drinking and Werewolves. A large man sat at the bar with what appeared to be two big dogs at his feet. I knew better.

"You bring me to all the nice places Robert," I commented pointing to the wolves on the floor.

"I thought we weren't doing this anymore, Addison? This man is on our side," Robert told the man at the bar.

Reaching down, the man called Addison patted the wolf on his right, "He's a stranger to us. Why bring him here? We know he's FBI."

I studied the wolves on the floor as I prepared myself. They didn't look like they were about to attack but with Weres looks could be deceiving. All I was armed with was my two modified sidearms, a couple of knives, and a silver nitrate grenade.

Carefully I slid one hand into my pocket gripping the handle of a knife. "There was a Were attack in downtown St. Louis last week. Two innocents were bitten. I've been sent by Washington to find the one that attacked and either arrest him or put him down."

"Put him down? What gives you the right to just kill one of us out of hand, Mr. G man?" The man Robert called Addison slid out of his chair and approached me. His arms were slowly doubling in size while claws formed on his hands.

"The FBI created a special branch for dealing with Paranormals. I'm sanctioned by Congress and President Long in this. It's my way or the highway. You know the standard policy on what the regular FBI considers rogue Weres. Do you really want to die? I need to bring him or her in. It might the only way to save all of you from detection," I explained.

"Now you threaten all of us with death. Who will know if I just kill you now and dump the car you came in with? We don't give up our people, Agent. We'd rather die first." Addison paused and glanced at Robert who only stood there. He made the tiniest motion toward me with his hand. "Take him."

Like I practiced, my hand came out of my pocket knife in hand. It was flying through the air toward the local Alpha as I drew my pistols. I kept them in a cross draw under my arms for easy access. I fired to the left even as the gun came loose of the holster, hitting the Pack member just now getting out of his chair. My other weapon fired at the first charging Werewolf. A miss.

The two wolves charged straight at me so fast that most humans wouldn't have even seen them. But I'm not most humans, and I was trained both by the FBI and my Alpha Big Ron.

My guns were loaded with silver, but they were only every other round. Lead bullets will just piss off a Were unless you hit them in a vital spot like the head or heart. Then you have a few minutes more before they jump up and kill you. But silver, silver burns like the fires of hell and slows the regenerative process enough for the wound to kill. Damage a Were with silver sufficiently, and they might die.

I dodged a claw swipe from my left and hit a Werewolf with my right pistol. The impact of the silver-plated weapon momentarily confused the Wolf. It's nose stinging it let out a yip and retreated just a bit to give me time to fire at the one on the left. A silver bullet this time it pierced the wolf's hide and struck near the head.

Alpha Addison attacked the very moment I fired the first

round. He transformed into his battle form almost instantly. My friends back in Texas used to tell me that the process took more than a minute and was excruciatingly painful. Addison came straight at me claws extended. I braced myself. This was going to hurt.

The world slowed as time seemed to stop. I could feel immense pressure in the air. Addison froze. I could see his eyes moving as if in panic, but his body stood immobile. The others were in similar states of stillness.

Robert spoke up, "This ends now."

Slipping my pistols back into their holsters I looked at Robert. He wasn't waving his hands or muttering curses like a Witch would. He just stood there staring at the local Alpha.

"I bring someone to you to help, and this is how you repay me? Addison, I thought we were friends. This man, this agent of the FBI has connections. You know who I work for. Didn't you wonder how I was in a position to help the FBI? This is now Council business. Attacking representatives of the government doesn't get us anywhere. Rogues make us all look bad, now change back so we can talk or complete your challenge," Robert explained.

The amount of power it would take to control four Weres at once boggled my mind. Who exactly was Robert Moore and what Council was he speaking of?

Alpha Addison started shrinking. I could hear moist sounding pops as his battle form shrank, and the human form emerged. Two of the other Weres began transformations as well.

Stepping to one side and kneeling, I checked on the man I shot first. He was writhing on the floor but was at least breathing. "Hold on, buddy."

Where the bullet hole in his chest had been now showed cleanly healed skin. The bullet remained inside. "Do you know where it went in? We could try cutting it out?"

"Leave him alone Jack. The first time he transforms the lead will pop right on out by itself. Our bodies don't like impurities. He'll be uncomfortable for a few days, but he'll survive," Robert told me. "Come back over here please."

The best word to describe the Weres in front of me was naked. All three of the ones that attacked me were just naked humans.

"Getting yourself an eyeful, are you?" The former Wolf was now a human woman and staring right at me.

Weres, as a rule, were blasé about nudity and other human morals. They usually only paid faint lip service to the laws surrounding them. So, naked was pretty typical in Were society.

"Put some clothes on, and we can talk like civilized beings," Robert ordered.

"Like we're civilized, Consul Moore," Addison replied.

A sudden pressure filled the air. It pressed down on everyone in the room including me.

Addison held up his hand as if in surrender. "Stop, please. I get it."

The pressure relented and everyone in the room sighed in relief. Grabbing a stack of clothing from behind the bar the Weres got dressed.

"The rogue?" Robert asked.

Addison shook his head. "Not one of my boys. An outsider. Lone wolf. He said he was passing through from roundabout Jackson way down in Tennessee. They run a high stakes poker game in the storage yard at Union Station almost every weekend. He claimed he could win and promised us a twenty percent cut for room, board, and protection. If we'd have known he was a biter... Well, you know. He was already here and under my protection when the word went out. I'd heard rumors about the kill squad at Union Station, but it didn't sound real. You remember how it was back in the day. We used to run that place. We had respect. Even the Dons didn't stand in our way then."

Robert grimaced, "Times change."

"Yes, they do. The rogue is up at the safe house. Macintosh Hill Road down in the lowest part. One of my boys will show you. Robert,

I swear to you, we didn't know. Please don't hurt my people for this. Please?" The Alpha begged.

"He's not in charge of this little mission. That would be me. At the moment I don't care about your internal politics or whatever Robert is in your world. I only need the rogue," I demanded.

Robert looked at me, "Kid..."

"No. I told you about my precarious position in the FBI. The regular boys hate me with a passion right now. If this case gets bumped to them, they'll hit this town with military precision. Do you really want that? I'm your best chance at living. Kill two birds with one stone. My job and your town. Paranormal rights are what this is all about," I replied.

Addison pointed to the man I tried to help. "Take him to the safe house. If you have to put down the rogue, do it."

To me, he explained. "Hollywood here will take you down there. Go in heavy. A cornered wolf..."

"... is a dangerous wolf." I finished for him. "Yes, I know. Thank you, Alpha Addison."

"It's Foley. Addison Foley. Believe it or not, I founded this town. Things just aren't like they used to be." Addison turned away for a moment. "Do we have more to say, Robert?"

Robert looked from him to me and then back again. "No. Let this be a warning to you though. Tell us next time you have a ... visitor. This might have been a takeover move by Jackson. Did you think of that?"

Addison looked shocked, "And I fell for it. We'll be more careful."

The Were called Hollywood stood at the door and motioned for us to follow him.

———

MACINTOSH HILL ROAD was one of the worst dirt roads I'd ever been on, and that's saying something since I was from Texas. There were ruts and giant holes at just about every turn.

"How does anyone even use this road?" I asked as my van lurched to one side yet again.

"It's not that bad. You should see it in winter," Hollywood replied.

Robert chose to sit this one out and stayed in Foley with the Alpha. I winced at the thought of it. He got scarier and scarier the more time I spent with him.

Having seen Missouri winters before from the Illinois side, I could only nod. I found it ironic that I didn't know about this little enclave when I was here as a kid. Some secrets really are secret it seems.

"Why Hollywood?" I asked.

The man next to me laughed, "I went west in my youth and worked as a stuntman for some early films. Buster Keaton was a genius. Those films were so much fun to do. But with the stock market crash and then the war, the industry wasn't what it used to be. The not-aging thing doesn't help either. When I came home, they started calling me that, and it stuck. The humans around here all think I'm the town drunk."

"That's a good cover. Robert didn't mention it, but I'm part of a Pack out in Texas. One of the few humans ever to do it," I explained.

"So I'm not crazy then! You move fast for a human. Good to know," Hollywood replied.

"What sort of place is this safe house we're going to?" I asked.

"It's in a low spot near the cliffs. We stuck a small travel trailer painted green up against the rock wall and planted trees and bushes to shield it from the road. It doesn't get used very often by the Pack," Hollywood replied.

I waved my hand in a circle. "Can you expand a bit on that? What's the terrain like, things like that? I don't have the advantage of fur and claws."

"You must be one badass human to do this for a living! What other Paras have you taken on?" Hollywood asked.

I steered the van around an unusually large pothole and glanced at the redneck Werewolf. I just knew that Anastasia would laugh at this report. "Most of my missions are classified, but I was in New Jersey last week and tangled with a Sea Monster."

"Now I know you're lying to me. Those things don't exist." Hollywood pointed through the windshield at a wooded area. "Just around the bend is the spot."

"You can check the national papers if you like but it was there. Seriously though, anything I need to be concerned about up there?" I asked.

Hollywood scratched his head, pursed his lips, and looked to the right out of the window. "A few Packs have been using this side of the property for construction dumping so you might run into some piles of... stuff. There's a creek just past the hedge at the opposite edge of the lot. Watch out for snakes. It's the season for them out here."

Slowing down, I parked just off the road but out of sight of the safe house. "You're just full of fun things aren't you, Hollywood? I want you to stay with the van. I need to load up."

I hopped out of the van and opened up the back. Hunting Weres was a tricky proposition. They heal so fast if you don't put them down the first time you can wind up dead. The mechanics that modified the van added a few crazy modifications. My favorite was the pull-out floorboards that gave me easy access to my weapons. I didn't like to show off what was in here, but I figured if I told Robert to keep it a secret, he'd lay down the law on these people. Just writing about him was going to take all day.

"Holy Crap! You planning on starting a war or what?" Hollywood cried from over my shoulder.

Gone was my suit. I'd already pulled out my modified flak jacket and slipped it over my fatigue shirt. Cargo pants replaced the slacks along with high topped leather boots. My jacket looked like something a hunter would wear out in the field, but mine took its inspiration from something the U.S. Eighth Army came up with during the Demon War.

Soldiers and sailors were at risk from the blowback of shrapnel being fired by artillery and flak guns at Demon Bats and other monsters. They created specially designed vests lined with nylon fibers and manganese plates. The main issue was they were heavy at twenty-two pounds and couldn't stop a direct shot or claw attack. The newer version was what I was wearing. Similar in design but lined with fiberglass reinforced panels called Doron, this vest was lighter and much studier. Unlike the standard issue for the military, mine was leather.

My sidearms stayed where they were, but I added a long silver knife at my hip and pulled out my Thompson. Unlike the gun the sheriff had in New Jersey, mine could use the drum magazines. It could also use the military 'box' magazines. I was now armed for bear... er, wolf.

As an afterthought, I grabbed the helmet I picked up in a surplus store. It was called an Adrian helmet. The French used it as a main-line helmet, but I'd had it painted in US Army colors with 'FBI' added to the back. This way if there was anyone out there besides myself they might see it.

"Stay here. If something happens to me, take the van back to Robert and your Alpha. Do not try to take the rogue by yourself. Understand?" I asked Hollywood.

The Were nodded with wide eyes and leaned back against the van as I carefully worked my way across the field and into the trees. As a teenager, I'd spent a lot of time in the woods of Illinois and Texas with my friends, so stalking prey wasn't new to me. The FBI Academy I went to actually taught the basics of what I was doing, but they really didn't have a clue. Maybe that part will improve now that they were actively recruiting Paranormals for teaching there.

True to his word the camper was tucked in under the eaves of a dirt and rock wall cliff. I'd checked and was sure to approach the place from downwind. Weres could smell the making of a sandwich a block away if the wind were just right.

Unless the place had a trap or back door, he was stuck inside.

That worried me because Big Ron always told me that a trapped beast was way more dangerous than one that was not.

Setting up toward the front of the place I yelled out, "Hello the camper! This is the FBI. Come out with your hands up, and this won't get messy!"

I could see the curtains flicker and the door opened. A voice yelled back, "Come out to my death? You G-men are all alike."

"I represent the Magical Division, I just want to talk. I'm here about the guys you changed at Union Station," I shouted back.

"That was an accident! You'll never take me alive!" The trapped Were yelled.

Cursing under my breath, I pulled back the handle of the Thompson and pulled out the grenade. From inside the camper, I could hear growls and cries of pain as he started his change. The fact it was taking so long was a good sign he wasn't an Alpha. Pulling the pin, I reared back and tossed it through the open door.

Unlike standard Mk2 grenades, this one was constructed of a silver alloy. The knobs on the little pineapple shaped explosive were there so it could be gripped easier. It shouldn't kill the rogue, but it was going to hurt. A lot.

There was a loud pop sound followed by a small explosion. Unlike the movies, these grenades were designed for maximum damage, not power. But it was followed by an even bigger detonation as the propane cylinder exploded as well.

Staying as low as possible I approached the wrecked camper. Chunks of burning aluminum and insulation were scattered in every direction. I could hear cries of pain as I stepped closer.

The rogue lay where the floor used to be. His transformation was almost complete. But he had explosive wounds over half his body, and they weren't closing. Silver fragments were everywhere.

"I didn't want to do this. We actually have facilities to hold Weres now!" I muttered as I cleared debris from the man.

The man's body never made it to full transformation. What little there was of him undamaged was changing back to normal. If a body bleeding out could be considered normal.

"... me." I barely heard the words over the fire crackling around me.

"What was that you said?" I asked as I leaned in close to the man's head.

"..." He said the words so silently I couldn't hear him.

Getting down on my knees I could see he had lacerations over half his face. Both eyes were gone and half his right arm. Placing my ear right on top of his face I listened.

Faintly he spoke again, "Kill me. Kill me. K..."

I pulled back in shock sitting on my knees. There were hospitals that I could take... My head dropped down onto my chest. There was no way this man could use them. They didn't take Weres, and if he survived, local law would put him down at the first chance they got.

From the stories that the locals and Robert said, this man was in the wrong place at the wrong time. He may have been here to stir up trouble, and I would investigate the Pack group in Tennessee to find out, but he didn't deserve the pain this was causing.

Getting to my feet, I pulled out my automatic pistol and put two shots in his head and another through the heart. Watching carefully, I looked to see if his healing factor continued to work. Patting the body down I removed his wallet and personal items. I'd need them for the report.

"Did you get him?"

I looked up and over my shoulder at Hollywood. He'd driven my van up and was standing not ten feet away. I nodded, "Will your people take care of the burial? The FBI will pay for it."

"I'll have to clear it with the Alpha, but I think we can do that. What'd you hit him with? I bet they heard that explosion all over the county!" Hollywood exclaimed.

"It was a grenade. I have some made of silver," I replied. Stepping over to the van I opened up the back and carefully unloaded the

Thompson and stored it away. I didn't put back on the standard suit. From now on I thought I'd wear the fatigues.

———

Robert was waiting for me outside the bar in Foley. None of the other townsfolk were present, but I assumed that he knew what had happened. Not much is hidden from Weres inside their own territory.

"Good work, kid. Too bad you didn't arrest him though," Robert stated.

I looked at the older Were through the open window of my van without getting out. "You knew he'd fight, didn't you?"

"The law may have changed but not how law enforcement treats us. Our people are rotting on the reservations. Getting them off is my number one priorities. The same goes for many of the other free Alphas as well. Rogues give us all a bad name. We try hard to cut down on any exposure. We could've taken care of this mess easily here, but we needed you to do it. Your new Division gives some of us hope for the future, Jack. We want you to succeed. Don't worry about giving me a ride out of here. I've got a funeral to plan and another Alpha to see. Take care of yourself, Jack. We'll have a drink sometime," Robert reached through the window and shook my hand.

I watched him re-enter the bar and just sat there for a moment. Politics and real life never mix all that well. This job just took on another dimension that I was unaware of. Who Robert was precisely and who he reported to were but two facets of a much bigger picture than I was allowed to see. I needed to have a face-to-face with Anastasia, and I needed to do it soon.

This ends Book Five of Jack Dalton Monster Hunter.

JACK DALTON, MONSTER HUNTER

BOOK 6

My NAME IS Jack Dalton and I'm a Monster Hunter!

Today I'm driving down Route 666 on my way toward Springfield, Illinois. Headquarters and Anastasia have requested that I investigate a rash of poltergeist activity in and around Lake Springfield. This will be my first otherworldly investigation since taking the job.

Ghosts are one thing that aren't counted as paranormal by the government. Shortly after the great reveal in 1914 there were a wide variety of fakes and cons that unscrupulous types used to bilk honest folk of their hard-earned money. We have a list of confirmed species that is taught at the academy and ghosts aren't on it. But I'm supposed to investigate, regardless. Spiritualists and mediums are illegal everywhere, due to their complicity in the Demon War. Communication with the other side is but one way that Demons can be contacted. The Germanic leader who brought the Demon Prince across was a member of one such spiritual group. Most countries thought they would "bite the head of the snake" early, and forbid any and all practices. Witches and Wizards are exempt from the ban but are supposed to limit themselves to approved activities. I can just imagine Marcella Blackmore turning herself in. Pulling out a notepad, I made a note to investigate what the approved activities actually were. It might prove interesting.

"This report is from the local sheriff, Jack. Springfield is the state capitol of Illinois. Time to show the flag and prove your worth to the Director," Anastasia said.

I winced. "Is he reconsidering my job?"

Anastasia paused for a moment. "You have exceeded expectations, Jack. He was of the opinion the job would be too much for you. There was actually a report saying just that, waiting for his signature. The Director hates competition and the Magical Division could potentially be just that. But President Long wants it because it's an election year, so he's given you a free hand so far. Don't color too far outside the lines, Jack. What his replacement will do is a complete unknown. Stay the course."

"So ghosts?" I asked.

"Don't exist. I've never come across one in all my years. But I'm just a lowly Vampire. There are more paranormals than you can shake a stick at in the world," Anastasia replied.

I scratched my head. "Then why send me to Illinois?"

"Politics. Governor Stratton wants this cleared up in time for the next session. Paranormals aren't very popular in the state," Ana replied.

"May I ask why?" I asked her.

"It's complicated. During Director Hoover's very public fight against corruption and organized crime over the past few years, some evidence was found that implicated them. The Italian Mafia bosses are part of a group called the Strega. As far as we can tell, they are dark Witches based out of Italy. As you know, our interaction with the Witches Council is almost nonexistent. They don't care for our laws and won't give our representatives their location. The Strega are but the tip of the iceberg. Fae warriors have been spotted in some of the downtown areas and there are reports of Gargoyles on half the older buildings," Ana replied.

"Those are all Magical things. Why wasn't I called in on them?" I asked.

"Have you ever seen the list of corruption arrests for Illinois? Let me tell you, it's huge. Add in a Magical component and it could be a disaster. The Director wants to put a patch on it in Chicago and move on. There is way too much popping up in other areas to draw his attention. He needs to appear to be making a difference. Having you shooting up most of downtown would negate that. You are better to be seen taking care of happenings locally in Springfield. In this case, Mr. Hoover's word is final," Anastasia said.

"What am I up against this time?" I asked.

I could hear a rustle of papers as Anastasia pulled out my assignment. While I waited I wound the telephone cord around my fingers. The twistiness of the cord was irritating. "There are several years' worth of strange happenings, but the most recent ones are centered around Lake Springfield and Highway 666. You should investigate those first."

"Do you know if the lake is associated with anything other than the highway?" I asked.

"The lake itself isn't a natural formation. It was created by the state in 1930 to provide drinking water to the surrounding area. That stretch of Highway 666 has actually been renamed Interstate 55. Fifty-five is part of the reorganization plan the president requested of the military. It took far longer to get troops in place after the Demon incursion than was planned. The Generals failed to take into account lack of interconnectivity of the highway system. There is a master plan to make it possible to cross the entire country by highway in less than five days," Ana replied.

"Five days? That would make my job unreal," I stated. Even now with all the conveniences of 1960 like televisions and highways, driving across the US was monotonous and could take weeks.

"The future is now. That's what they're saying about it here in Washington. Get to Illinois and stop the hauntings," Anastasia ordered.

So that's why I'm on the new highway fifty-five, crossing over Lake Springfield at this very moment. Looking out to my right, I could see a small lighthouse sitting on the edge of a vast lake. Road-side signs proclaimed motels such as Sabattini's, Bedini's, and Polands. Each boasted of having access to clean nude bathing beaches. That both intrigued and disgusted me at the same time. Whenever I sunbathed naked in either Texas or Missouri, I ended up with sand in unmentionable places. Not as fun as it sounds.

My orders from Ana were to meet a fellow FBI Agent by the name of James Randi at a place called Cozy Hot Dogs. It was, according to Ana, a local favorite and an excellent place to start my investigation.

Agent Randi stuck out like a white cat in a pile of coal. Still wearing his FBI suit in hundred-degree Illinois weather, the man looked like he was about to drop dead of heat prostration. He was surrounded by townsfolk in beachwear, shorts, or cut-offs. If eggs weren't frying in the parking lot, it was for lack of trying. I found it amusing that the place was right next to an ice cream shop. Something cold would feel good right about now.

"Agent Dalton? I'm James Randi." The Agent stuck his hand out to me as I climbed out of my van.

Looking Randi in the eyes, I took his hand and gave it a strong but brief squeeze. The hand, like the rest of him, was just dripping in sweat and felt clammy and moist. I resisted the urge to wipe my hand off, and patted him on the shoulder instead. It too was damp. "Let's go over to the shade, James. You look like you're dying in that suit of yours."

On closer inspection, the building in front of me was actually two structures, joined by an open-air-of-sorts dining room. I pointed toward an empty table in the darkest part of the room and the local Agent followed me. "Take that jacket off and let your body cool down. Even Director Hoover will understand if you need a break from the heat."

There had been a directive bandied about when I was up in Boston about active duty Agents looking professional at all times. I wasn't regular FBI, and I was the head of my own Division, so my standing orders were comfort over professionalism. I wore light grey Army fatigues with a jacket over them, every day. Easy to hide my guns and lots of extra pockets for things like grenades. I only had my side arms holstered today. It was hot, but I'd had a seamstress modify my jacket with mesh underarms and cooling slits along the sides. It resembled a duck hunter's gear, but comfort was my goal, after all.

"But..." Randi started to object.

I whipped out my credentials which listed me as a Division head. "I outrank you. You can put it back on when I leave. The Director will never know. Cool off."

I stood and went to the hot dog window. 'What's a corn dog?' I said to myself. Corn and hot dogs don't go together, or at least they don't in Texas. Fifty cents got me two cups of pop, a corn dog, and a paper tray of fries. So much has changed over the past ten years. A nickel could've gotten me half of that by itself.

"This has to be the strangest thing I've seen today," I remarked to the other Agent as I held up the corn dog. "I assume this thing is fried?"

Agent Randi cocked his head to one side and looked at the thing on a stick. "They're pretty famous around here. You have to dip it in mustard to enjoy it. Where are you from, anyway?"

The vendor had included a small cup of both ketchup and mustard, so I experimented. "Texas originally. I move around a lot. My office is the van behind me."

"My boss got a call from Washington and told me to brief you on the ghosts around here. Do you think you can stop them?" Randi took a long drink, but his eyes never left mine.

I wasn't ready to answer him just yet, so I asked my own questions. "What makes you think it's a ghost?"

Randi looked around the small dining area and lowered his voice. "Things move. Sometimes it's just a tiny bit, but we've got reports of bicycles flying through the air and lights flashing in the sky."

I smiled. "You can speak up, Agent Randi. What I do isn't a secret. These lights, have you seen them yourself?"

Randi shook his head. "Not the lights. I've seen things move, though. Over at the high school a whole rack of basketballs flew into the air and started bouncing into the hoops all by themselves."

Pursing my lips, I gave him a wry look, "Are you sure?"

"Ask my wife. It happened. It was the last game of the season and the Senators were up three points. Suddenly every ball in the place was flying through the air. Scared half the town silly," he replied.

"I assume the Senators is the name of the team?" I asked.

Agent Randi nodded yes.

"Were there lights as well as floating balls?" I asked him.

Randi leaned forward and frowned. "You don't believe me!"

Holding up my hands I tried to calm him. "I've seen lots of unexplained things over the past year. I'm just trying to get all the details now. Are the hauntings only at the high school?"

Agent Randi shook his head. "No. We thought it might be isolated to the school at first. It's built on top of a cemetery."

The investigator in me perked up. "A cemetery?"

"Many of the locals think that Abe Lincoln is the one haunting the school. They tell stories about how he's angry at the city and wants justice for his child. In 1850 one of his kids was buried in what was called the Hutchinson Cemetery," Randi answered.

"I'm confused. Why did they build on top of graves and why would Lincoln want justice?" I asked.

The agent took a sip of his drink and motioned toward my fries. I nodded to him and made a motion for him to continue.

Agent Randi finished chewing and looked up at me. "They moved the bodies to Oak Ridge in the early 1900's but there have always been rumors that they just moved the headstones. The school's been there since 1915, so unless we tear it down, we'll never know the truth. You did know that Lincoln got his start here?"

"Of course. History has always been my thing. It's part of what makes me good at my job. So where else have there been hauntings?" I asked.

Randi started counting on his fingers. "Here at Cozy's, out near the lake, one of the malt shops in town, the town library, some of the bathing beaches, and a few of the neighborhoods."

I gripped my chin as I thought. "If it was our former president doing the haunting," I said, "you would think he'd be at his old house and maybe the Capitol building. Those places you mentioned all seem too modern."

Agent Randi ate more of my fries and got up for another soda. I looked out between the buildings at a group of teens playing stick ball while I thought. If a ghost was responsible for this, it couldn't be one of the ones from the cemetery. The places he listed didn't exist prior to 1900. Even the lake was artificial. The Park Service supervised the

Lincoln home. I made a note to speak with them, if only to put that rumor to rest.

"I was thinking about what you said." Randi sat down at the table. He set a bottle of soda down along with a fully loaded hot dog.

"What was that?" I asked.

Gesturing with his hands, Randi explained. "Basic FBI craft. Look for the common denominator. What do all the places have in common? Not Lincoln."

"No. Our sixteenth president is not in search of revenge. I made a note to check with the Park Department, since they would know for sure if the graves were actually moved or not. But if it is a ghost, it isn't Abe. From what you told me, all the locations have something to do with either children or families. We should concentrate on that," I explained.

There was a sudden clatter as Agent Randi dropped his soda bottle onto the table. Looking sharply in his direction I could see he looked shocked. "What's wrong?"

Randi shook his head. "There is no we, Agent Dalton. My boss was super clear on that one. I'm to fill you in and split. They refuse to pay me for more time than that."

I spread my hands. "It's the story of my life at the Bureau. Don't worry yourself about it. Do you have the files associated with the case?"

Randi nodded. Quickly, he shoved the remainder of his hot dog into his mouth and stood up. He grabbed his coat, slipped it back on, and said, "I'll get the box."

Turning my chair, I watched him reach into the rear of a parked car and remove a large cardboard box. Agent Randi set it down next to my van. The Agent stared at me expectantly.

Sighing, I policed up the trash and slipped it into a receptacle. No need to make work for the kids behind the counter. At least I was able to get a full rundown this time. Usually, they just dump the information on me and run.

———

"THERE's no such thing as ghosts," the Park Service officer replied.

I smiled and said, "No, there isn't. But I have to follow up on every lead and this is one of them. Can you confirm they actually moved the bodies like they said they did?"

The man in the brown uniform glared at me. "You boys at the FBI don't know how to do a lick of research, do you? It's all on the plaque at the tomb. When the State of Illinois reconstructed every-thing in the 1930's, they moved the Lincoln and Todd children's bodies into it. Only the eldest is buried elsewhere, and that is at Arlington National Cemetery."

"Have you seen any ghosts, ranger?" I asked.

"Question time is over. Would you like a tour of the house?" The man asked.

———

THE FILES that Agent Randi had left me were extensive. The reports of poltergeist activity went back a bit over ten years. Like the more recent reports, the older occurrences were in some of the same spots. If it wasn't a ghost it could be something Fae or Witch kin. Both groups like to play jokes on humans. This was the state capitol. There was supposed to be a Witches Council representative on site some-where around here.

In the oldest part of the Capitol building, I found their office. The entrance to their chambers was near the restrooms. There were two sets. In some way, I think there should have been a sign or some-thing. Just as Lincoln's house is preserved, maybe these should be as well, and not just for famous poopers. Racial divide is something we try to sweep under the rug and forget in this country. The Civil Rights Act of 1925 changed everything. After the great reveal, followed by the Purge, Americans were scared. People all around them could turn into monsters. Color and race took a backseat to species. The CRA granted complete equal rights for all HUMANS and intended to put us on an equal footing with the Paranormals. Certain phrases and lines inside the Act placed restrictions upon known Paranormals like the Weres, and were instrumental in starting the camps and reservations. Humans were united, but the Paranormals were pissed.

Before I could even knock on the door a voice spoke to me. "Come in, Agent Dalton."

I opened the door and stepped inside. The office looked like any other office that I might find in this building, save for the magic. A cup was stirring itself while lunch was being prepared by invisible hands. Bread floated to a plate while a knife sliced a chunk of corned beef. Each slice floating onto the bread with ease.

"Please have a seat. Would you like a sandwich?" The man behind the desk was wearing a three-piece suit with wide lapels. He motioned with his left hand and a plate, napkin, fork, knife, and glass appeared in front of me. Another wave of the hand and a sandwich, complete with pickle, floated itself onto my plate.

"I almost forgot," he said. With another wave of his hand, a bottle of soda appeared and poured itself into the empty glass. "Now we can eat."

If I hadn't just recently been amongst Witches up in Maine, I might have needed one of those restrooms outside. This was more magic than most people ever see. I picked up the sandwich that looked way better than a corn dog, and I took a bite.

"Good?" The Witch asked.

I nodded and quickly swallowed. "It is. Good corned beef is so hard to find on the road. Thank you."

"You're welcome. I know why you're here and the answer is no," he replied.

"Why no? I haven't asked for anything yet," I explained.

The Witch behind the desk laughed. "You don't need to. I can read it on your face. You want us to help you catch the poltergeists haunting the town. I have to admit, though, you have serious chutzpah. Asking the Park Service if Lincoln haunts the town? Brilliant."

"Spying on a government Agent could be construed as espionage, you know," I stated.

The Witch laughed again. "Like your Director Hoover would even dare! He'd make you do it since it is your job to police us. How's that going for you, Agent Dalton?"

"I'm doing ok, I think. Killed a sea monster," I replied.

"Congratulations for that. But the answer is still no," the Witch stated.

I shook my head. "You keep putting words in my mouth. I'm not here for that sort of help."

"Hmm. Of that I doubt. Ghosts can be hard to catch if you don't know the trick. If your government is willing to pay, we can work something out," he replied.

The sandwich I'd just eaten turned to ash in my mouth. This man was actually trying to shake down the United States Government for personal gain! His arrogance was unbelievable. "You seem to know all about me, but I know nothing of you. May I know your name?"

Again, a smile. "You can call me Montgomery."

"Thank you. My purpose here isn't to chase ghosts. I'm completely aware that ghosts don't exist. Only a Spiritualist is able to call a soul forth from the beyond and Witches don't usually have those sorts of powers," I replied.

"Aren't you a busy little bee. Someone's been speaking out of turn." All friendliness was gone, and Montgomery was now all business. "What is it you want?"

I explained the occurrences and my thoughts and speculations on them. My exposure to magic in all forms was limited but I read a lot and when I was in Maine I asked questions. Fortunately for me, Marcella Blackmore answered them truthfully. So I had a baseline of what was believable or not for investigative purposes.

Monty rubbed his chin and nodded. "What you are describing fits for adolescents in a Magical community. But these are humans."

"I've never met them, but don't human Mages exist?" I asked.

Montgomery frowned and looked disgusted. "Half-breeds and genetic thieves is what they are. This council has no control over them."

"I'm not asking you to at all. These could be signs of someone coming into their power, right?" I asked.

"Or the Fae playing tricks. They get off on that sort of thing. Are we done here?" Montgomery waved his hand and all the plates and food vanished.

"I think so, thanks for your help..." I barely got that out when the lights went off, the door opened behind me, and I felt myself being pulled through it. My interview was over.

Staring at the closed door, I plotted my next actions. Where did human Mages come from and how do I find the one plaguing the town?

———

"ARE YOU SURE, JACK?" Anastasia asked.

"Pretty sure. The Witches Council representative didn't actually confirm it, but he was pretty quick to kick me out of his office as soon as I mentioned human Mages. There is at least one human Mage here, and they are just now coming into their full power," I explained to her. The only place in town I could call from, other than the Governor's secure line, was the police station. I was sitting in the Chief's office.

"It's an open secret that Mages were used by the military to stop the Demon invasion," Anastasia said. "What most don't know is that they were human. I'm surprised you knew about it. I'll pass your information along to the OSS and SID. They may or may not send support your way. It really isn't the FBI's purview. But you still have to track down those occurrences. Mage or not, this assignment came from the Director. Solve it. We'll deal with the Mage, or whatever it is, after. Understood?" Anastasia asked.

Knowing more than my boss was a surprise. My father fought in the Demon War in Europe but many of his companions were Weres, and they told me stories of what it was like. Mages played a huge part in ending the war. I needed one more bit of information though, and for that I needed to make one more phone call. This time to Maine. Dialing the number from memory and listening to the click of the rotary dial, I wondered how she had known I would need her, and how many times I'd be doing this. "Hello? This is Agent Jack Dalton of the FBI. I need to speak to Marcella, please."

There was a knock at the door. I looked up from the now silent phone and sighed. The chief of police must want his office back. Someday in the future I wish for those very imaginative equipment creators at the FBI to make some sort of mobile phone. It would change the way law enforcement does things forever. I doubt I'll live to see it.

"Come," I called out.

The door opened and Chief Herring stepped inside. "All finished?"

I smiled at him. "I am. Thanks for the use of your office. Sometimes Washington wants to know every tiny detail the very moment that I know it."

He snorted. "Isn't that the truth. You see where this station is? I have to report to both the mayor and the big man across the street. Have you had any progress on tracking down our spook?"

I didn't miss the man's pointed look or direct question. Normally the FBI refuses to comment on open investigations. However, I was on my own and didn't want to alienate the ones who could help me find the Mage. "It's not a ghost. Everyone I've talked to, including the Witches Council representative, has told me it isn't a spirit."

"You spoke to that jackass Montgomery?" the Chief asked.

It was my turn to laugh. "Yeah, he is a bit of an ass. He tried to shake me down, but I got the information I needed from him."

"Well, son, that's a first for this department. His predecessor was a woman named Raye. Never got a last name. She would at least make a few suggestions and actually helped take down a smuggling ring. This guy though... He hates humans with a passion. It makes me wonder what he did to end up here," the chief mused.

"I've met a few Witches since starting this job. They come in all sizes and temperament. The best advice it to steer clear of them whenever possible. When I was in Maine..." I trailed off. I thought for a moment that the fact I was attacked by dinosaurs in a gigantic garden that has a soul and can think for itself might sound just a bit insane to the man in front of me. I changed course a bit. "There was an entire town of Witches up there. Trust me when I say if you can imagine it, they may have done it."

"Dalton, you're a hoot. Seriously, though, son. If it's not Witches or Ghosts what is it? We've got some seriously upset people out there," Chief Herring said.

Sometimes the truth is the best option, so I went for it. "You have a Mage in town somewhere and he's just come into his full power."

"A Mage? Is that some sort of new Paranormal thingy or something?" Herring asked me.

I shook my head. "No, sir. What do you know about how the Demon War here in the US ended?"

The chief leaned back in his chair with a strange look. For just a moment he looked as though he might not answer, but he stuck his tongue in his cheek. I could see he was deep in thought. "Son, I was a lowly private sitting in a three-quarter ton truck just outside of what used to be Los Angeles in 1949. The Illinois National Guard was called out to watch the perimeter, shoot stragglers, and rescue whatever the Demons left behind. It wasn't much, let me tell you. The nightmares only stopped a few years ago for me. What does the end of the war have to do with this?"

"The Army used human magic users called Mages to stop the Horde and close the hole. I've been told that the trait only pops up in humans occasionally. There might be one in every million people.

During the war, our country was able to find and bring together enough to make a difference. What has been happening here has all the signs of a Mage coming into power. They start early. The power leaks through as the child grows. Before they reach puberty, they would have cast several spells by accident. Depending upon their strength and class of Magic, they might not even know it was them who did it," I explained. "Almost every report centers around places a child or family would go. The fact that there are reports of flying bicycles and trash cans tells me we're looking for a teen. He or she might have been either in the basketball game or in the building somehow."

Chief Herring nodded. "Well hell, son! Why didn't the local FBI guy, Randi, figure that part out?"

Agent Randi might be great at his job, but I knew from experience that the supernatural information we are told to read during training doesn't stick with us. Something about our brains and disbelief. My being raised partially by Werewolves helped me overcome the block. It might be why the Paranormals were able to hide for so long. "The locals aren't trained in the same things I am. I'm sure he's competent in his own job, but most regular FBI know very little of the Paranormal."

"You people should talk to each other more. We're all in this one together. So how do we find the Mage?" Chief Herring asked.

"If I was fifteen years old or so and realized I had Magic powers, where would I go? That is how I'm looking at this problem," I replied.

"So?" Chief Herring motioned.

"The local library, the school library, the Witches Council representative, and who else? Other than Monty, do you have any Paranormals in town?" I asked.

Chief Herring tapped his finger against his lips for a moment. He looked at me and winced. "Sort of? There's an old lady out on Lake Shore Drive who everyone says is a Witch. I've spoken to her a few times, but I wouldn't know a Witch if she bit me."

"That's who we talk to first, then. If public opinion says that she's a Paranormal, then that is who a kid might talk to rather than Monty across the street," I answered.

Herring nodded and said, "Come on kid, we'll take my car. That thing of yours attracts too much attention."

Within a few minutes we were turning onto highway fifty-five and Henry was telling me all about Lake Springfield and all the unsolved crimes it held.

"...water levels. They got so low we started to see remnants of the old route sixty-six bridge, sunken cars, and odd metallic items. There was actually a car, some cash, a cash register, and weapons found in one spot. That case is still open, by the way. The lady we're going to see is named Caroline Barnes. As far as I can tell she's lived here since at least 1914. Most folks around here keep their distance from her," Chief Herring explained to me.

The area he was taking me was close to where I'd seen the light-house as I was driving in. "How will she take this visit?"

"Not well. This whole area next to the highway is one of the Governor's new proposed projects. He wants to build the state's first Police Academy. I'll admit we really need one. I trained half my officers myself. The rest were either former military or went over to Missouri for school. Why he wants this exact spot is beyond me but trust me when I say the old broad isn't selling." Chief Herring shook his head and stopped the car. "I'm not at the top of her hit parade so watch your step here, son."

Getting out of the patrol car I looked around. The area in question was slightly elevated and overlooked the lake and the bridge. A small cottage sat at the top, surrounded by vegetation. The lighthouse I'd seen was out on a point of land jutting out into the lake.

"What's with the lighthouse?" I asked.

Chief Herring turned away from the house, "Eh?"

"The lighthouse?" I repeated.

The Chief chuckled. "Advertising gimmick for one of the hotels. It's not really a draw, but tourists stop and take pictures anyway. It has a light and everything. Not something you see every day."

I gave it another glance and could see the revolving top. Stepping around the car, I joined the chief as we walked up to the cottage.

"Get ready," Herring commented as he rang the bell.

Caroline Barnes looked nothing like the stereotypical Witch. Of course, Marcella didn't either. Caroline was trim, fit, blond, and very young looking. If I didn't know better, I'd have thought she was a local college student.

"Chief of police Henry Herring. Come to force me off my land at the whim of the Governor again?" The Witch commented. There was a slight burr to her voice. My trainers at the academy might say it was Scottish or possibly Welsh. It was hard to tell.

"Now, Miss Barnes, you know his plan is only hypothetical at the moment. I was only told to talk to you about the land. There are other locations being considered," Chief Herring started to defend himself.

Caroline Barnes bristled. "Those others don't have the highway, now, do they? They're just a smokescreen to put me off while you steal my land out from under me. I warned you already, Henry. Try it and you'll be eating flies for the rest of your life right out there in the lake. You need to ask yourself what happened to those engineers that made that lake. They stole from me as well!"

I glanced over my shoulder at the lake in question. It was manmade.

"Who's your friend? Another flunky sent by the Governor?" Barnes asked.

"Caroline, this is Jack Dalton of the FBI. He's here investigating the hauntings around town," Herring replied.

Caroline Barnes snorted her disbelief. "Good luck with that one. FBI huh, where'd they dig you up at?"

Ignoring her question, I asked my own. "Do you know why the Witches Council representative failed to tell me about your existence here?"

The Witch frowned and her eyes narrowed. "You're different. Montgomery only got the job here because he's the biggest kiss-ass around and that's really saying something in a town full of politicians.

He knows better than to cross me. I doubt he has the power to do a damn thing to me."

"He seemed pretty powerful to me. Made food appear and was able to move things around with a wave," I replied.

"Just tricks. Every class of Witch can do that. It's called telekinesis. I will bet you he had the food already prepared and just sent it to you. Trust me when I say he failed teleportation." She looked at me and then over at Chief Herring. "Why's he here for real?"

Chief Herring replied, "I told you. The hauntings."

"Hmm. Why is the FBI so interested in Spirits?" Caroline asked.

"We're not. I was sent here to stop the poltergeist activity and I've discovered that a Mage is responsible," I explained.

The Witch nodded. She started rubbing her hands together like she was trying to warm them. Maybe a nervous habit. I watched almost enraptured as she began circling her palms together, rubbing them back and forth.

Pulling my eyes away I spoke to her. "If that's a fireball I'm going to shoot you."

She looked up from her hands to see my forty-five-caliber pistol aimed at her head.

Chief Herring jumped as if shocked, and looked at me with wide eyes. "Son, be careful with that thing. Caroline here didn't mean whatever you think she said!"

I caught a brief flash of light as she reabsorbed the Magick in her hands. Caroline spread her hands to show they were empty. "See, no threat."

"I know there's at least one budding Mage in town. Nothing else matches the description. Their Magic's been growing for at least ten years now. You and I both know that without training, they could level the town by complete accident," I replied.

Chief Herring said, "Destroy the town?"

"What's it going to be Caroline? Chief Herring didn't mention that I represented the Magical Division of the FBI. I can and will take you in if I have to. Crowley Prison has plenty of empty rooms in it," I threatened.

"How did you know?" Caroline asked.

"That you were training the Mage? I didn't. Your reaction gave it all away," I explained.

She shook her hands in the air. "Not that. The fireball. How did you know?"

"I spent a few days in upper Maine last month. Nice little town named Briarwood. The locals gave me a crash course in what Witches could and could not do. In this job, I pay close attention to all things unknown," I explained.

Caroline shook her head. "You're lying. We don't discuss the craft with human authorities. It's against the rules."

My eyes widened at that. "It is? Marcella never told me that."

"Marcella? Do you mean Marcella Blackmore? That Marcella?" Caroline asked.

I cocked my head to one side and answered her. "Yes, I played ambassador to her coven a month or so ago. Nice lady."

"Well, that changes everything now, doesn't it? If Marcella Blackmore spoke freely to you, then I may as well. I'm not surprised that Montgomery gave you the runaround. He's been a right pain for years," Caroline said.

"Why would he do that?" I asked.

"Because he can. He and Marcella don't really see eye to eye. Ever since she resigned as head of the American Witches Council back in '18 he's had his panties in a wad. Never you mind about that wanker. I can answer your questions now. The one you are looking for is indeed a youngster. It's pretty unusual for humans to come into power. I've only know one or two in my life," Caroline explained.

"Marcella ran the Witches Council?" I asked her.

Caroline smiled at me. "Mmm, did I say that? I must have misspoken."

I nodded to her. She was telling me something I wasn't explicitly supposed to know. "Will you tell us the child's name?"

"Of course. His name is Eugene Tarbell. I noticed his aura several years ago down by the lake. You know the boy, I believe, Chief? His father is Morton Tarbell the newspaperman," Caroline remarked, with a wry smile on her face.

Herring groaned, "The press? You're killing me here, Caroline. Does his father know?"

"I don't believe so. The boy came to me in secret the first time he made something move by accident. He, like every other child in this area, reads the paper and knows what 'powers' are when he sees them. This modern world of yours is so much easier than a century ago. I could go on for hours about dealing with lunkheads wanting me to marry them or proving their honor. So much easier to just drive away." Caroline was starting to stray off topic and ramble.

"How powerful is he, Caroline?" I asked.

"I'm quite a good teacher, you know. If he wanted to, he could move that monstrosity you call a Capitol building and toss it into the lake. I doubt he'd do it, though. Wants to join the army, he does. Apparently, he knows quite a bit about the Demon Wars. A curse of having a literate father. In my day you were lucky if one person in twenty could read more than a sentence or two. So much easier. Was there anything else?" Caroline asked.

Chief Herring glanced in my direction and I ever so slightly shook my head. "That's it, Caroline. I'll pass what you said to the Governor, but I expect you'll be seeing me again pretty soon," he said.

"That's fine, I can always use more frogs for me pond," Caroline pointed toward a bubbling fountain next to the cottage. It had appeared as if by magic, and we could now hear the chirp and croak of its inhabitants.

Grabbing the chief by his shirt sleeve, I dragged him toward the car. "Interview's over. Thank you, Miss Barnes."

Once we were in the car and back on the road the Chief spoke up. "Would she have really turned me into a frog?"

"No idea. The Witches I know haven't demonstrated that power to me, but I was surprised she knew my contact in the community.

Marcella has more pull than even my bosses know about. What do you know about the Tarbell family?" I asked.

Springfield might feel like a small town, but in 1960 but it had more than eighty-thousand people living in it, and Chief Henry Herring didn't know everyone. But someone from the local paper he did know. Especially an outspoken reporter like Morton Tarbell. Tarbell had been behind the movement to censure more than one local politician over tax overruns or spending. Telling the man his son had supernatural powers was going to be a blast.

"Base to Chief Herring, come in Chief." A voice over the police radio interrupted our conversation.

The Chief grabbed the microphone, flipping the talk switch in the process, and said, "This is the chief."

"Chief, Sergeant Sennett here, are you available to come back to base?"

"What is it Mack?" Herring asked.

"Got a fella here that says he's with Army Intelligence. I tried to tell him he had to go through the Governor's office, but he insists he speak to you and that FBI guy, Dalton," Sergeant Sennett explained.

"Roger that. Tell him fifteen, twenty minutes. I'm on the other side of the lake," Herring stated.

"Understood, out," the sergeant replied.

Chief Herring looked over at me. "Something I should know about?"

I grimaced. "My boss warned me that they might show up. The same reports I got go to them. Unlike me, they know what an emerging Mage looks like. We can either work with him or against him. I suspect he has the power to go to the Governor and go over us if he invokes public safety."

"Then we better get to it." Chief Herring hit the lights and sirens and I got to have one of my childhood dreams satisfied. A screaming ride in a police car!

My van was less ostentatious and more functional. It stored all my weapons and gave me a safe place to sleep. Watching the cars pull over to the side as our car weaved in and out of traffic gave me a thrill.

Our car screamed into the parking lot and Herring switched off the siren and lights. Several officers stared our way until they saw it was the chief. "Let's get this over with."

Entering the station, we found a man dressed similarly to me but in pressed fatigues with all the military do-dads attached. He smiled at us and held out his credentials. "Captain Right at your service."

I only glanced at the credentials, but Chief Herring carefully studied them. "This doesn't say where you're stationed out of."

Taking his things back, the Captain replied, "I'm a floating Agent. My job is to investigate certain occurrences and recruit where needed."

"Anything you'd like to share with us about these occurrences you speak of, Captain?" I asked.

The Army Captain smiled. His teeth were the whitest I'd seen in a while. Instantly I didn't trust him. "Not really. Seems so far you've done a good enough job. I thought I'd ride with you out to the Tarbell house."

"The hell you say! How'd you find out about that!" Chief Herring snapped.

I shook my head and turned to face the Captain. "He obviously bugged your car somehow. I was under the impression your group wasn't supposed to actively work inside the United States."

"The Magical Act of 1959 changed that. We are allowed to actively recruit wherever and whenever we see fit. Human Mages are as rare as hen's teeth around here. I have a lot to offer. Are we working together or not? We are on the same team, gentlemen," Captain Right stated.

So back into the car we went, only this time we had a backseat passenger.

"We could have taken my car, you know. These bars back here are a bit unnerving," the Captain remarked.

Chief Herring snorted and let out a chuckle. "Son, you are not the first to say that. Watch where you slide around. Night shift used this car for drunk duty and they have a tendency to leak a bit back there."

The Captain looked down at the floorboards and started to bend and twist.

I couldn't help but chuckle. This Illinois cop was pretty funny.

The Tarbells lived on a nice quiet street with well-kept houses. In some ways it resembled the set of that TV show I'd watched as a kid. Otter something. I can remember wanting to Mr. Wilson to be my next-door neighbor. As we pulled up, I read the street name on the sign. It matched up perfectly to several of the early reports of flying trash cans and other disturbances. Maybe we should have looked here first.

The Chief got out of the car and said, "Let me do all the talking here. This guy hates the establishment, and his kid might not be any better."

We both watched the police chief walk up to the door. I glanced at Captain Right. "You going to listen?"

"No. How about you?" He replied.

I shook my head and got out of the car. Chuckling, I watched as the other guy struggled with his door. "Funny thing about police cars. The doors don't really open from the inside back there. Nobody likes catching someone twice."

"You need to let me out, Agent Dalton. Trust me when I say that I need to be out there with you," Captain Right replied.

"I don't think so. This is my case. The FBI can use this kid just as much as the army can. Director Hoover directed me to see it through, and I intend to do just that," I stated as I walked toward the house.

Captain Right muttered something to himself that sounded a bit like "stupid psychics" but I ignored him. I could see that Chief Herring wasn't having much luck just by watching what was going on at the front door. A small man was waving his hands in the air and pointing. I heard a noise that could've been glass breaking and I looked up. There, climbing out the window and onto a tree branch, was a young man in a striped shirt and jeans.

"Hey kid!" I shouted out. As the words left my mouth I realized my mistake and paid for it.

Quickly forming a fireball in one hand, the teen tossed it at me and jumped toward the ground! "You're not taking me!"

Fast on my feet, I dodged the poorly thrown ball of flame and chased after the kid. He'd hit the ground running, almost an impossibility for a non-magic person. As I ran, I could hear Herring and the older Tarbell yelling at each other about the burning yard.

Like a jackrabbit the boy jumped the fence into his backyard. To do my job I needed to be athletic, so I followed him at a slightly slower pace. Climbing instead of jumping.

Eugene waved his hands and tossed an entire set of heavy patio furniture and a grill at me. He was panicked, and his aim wasn't the best. I dodged what I was able. "I just want to talk to you, Eugene. No jail cell. I promise that you will be able to go free afterwards."

"I don't believe you!" Eugene readied another fireball, this one even bigger than the previous one.

Looking around I could see the pile of furniture in front of me, the fence behind, and a small inground swimming pool. I was trying to judge the distance to the pool when the explosion knocked me off my feet and into the fence.

There was a bright flash and all I could see was bright light. My ears were ringing like the bells on Sunday.

I wasn't dead, and the backyard wasn't on fire. Looking toward where Eugene had been standing I could see Captain Right. He was checking the boy's pulse. "I got tired of waiting in the car."

Picking my way around the wreckage strewn yard, I approached the scene. "What happened?"

"He's out. You ok?" Right asked.

"I'm fine. What was that explosion?" I asked.

"Stun grenade. Special formula. I'd brought one along just in case. Good thing I did, too. You were just about to become a crispy critter," the Captain remarked with a smile.

"A grenade? You seriously had a live grenade on you in the car with us?" I asked.

"Not my first ballgame, Agent. The kid is fine. It all worked out," Right replied.

By this time, the overexcited parent and Chief Herring had run through the house and were in the picture.

"Is Eugene all right? What happened?" Herring shouted at me.

"He's out cold. The kid was tossing fireballs and one misfired," I said with a shrug. The boy's father was hunched over his son, calling his name and checking him over for injuries. I'm not sure why I covered for Captain Right. His use of military hardware against a civilian was almost criminal, but it was like the pot calling the kettle black. I had a whole van full of weapons. Some of them were originally military as well.

We all stood by as Eugene was revived by his father Milton. As a forethought, I had a small bucket of water from the swimming pool standing by. And a good thing too. Just as soon as the kid's eyes opened, a fireball formed in hand.

Splash.

Down went the bucket and the now the kid's hand was soaked. So was Mr. Tarbell.

"What'd you do that for?" The adult Tarbell exclaimed.

"Eugene had a fireball in his hand. You have to face facts here, Mr. Tarbell. Your son's a Mage," Chief Herring replied for me.

"Dad... They're telling the truth," Eugene spoke up from the ground.

"Son, you need to lie still until we get a doctor for you. Who knows what these men have done to you?" Tarbell replied.

The kid shook his head. "No. I attacked them. I didn't want to go to prison."

Milton Tarbell looked down at his son in shock. "Why would you go to prison?"

Looking up, he glared at the three of us. "Why would you put my son in prison?"

"I'm here to offer him a job, not sure what they want," Captain Right replied, catching us off guard.

Chief Herring glared at the army officer but still answered. "Milton, we just wanted the activity he was causing to stop. Half the town was getting antsy about it all. Hell, there were rumors that Abe Lincoln was haunting the place. We just came to talk."

"I don't understand this. Why did you run then? What crime did you think you'd committed that was so bad?" Milton Tarbell asked his son.

"It was you, Dad. You told me to do it," Eugene replied.

"Me? I never said such a thing. I taught you to respect the law, not to attack it!" Milton exclaimed.

"But what about the things you've said at dinner and all those articles you've written? You told me that Paranormals should be locked up and that people with Magic powers were a menace. I just listened to you. When I realized that I was the one causing things to move, I was scared. I was afraid you would make me leave or something. Miss Barnes down by the lake gave me some advice and a bit of training. I was gonna tell you but not until I could control it a bit. The night of the game, I ran into Clarence and his gang. They tried to take all my money and I got excited. Everyone was saying it was the ghost of Abe Lincoln, so I just went along," Eugene explained.

"Clarence Rutherford? That boy is a menace," Milton stated.

"That boy, as you call him, is the star quarterback of the Senators. I'll have a chat with him. Can't have bullies running the school, now can we?" Herring asked rhetorically.

I glanced at the chief. Football was a big deal in the Midwest. I seriously doubted that they would reprimand or arrest the athlete. But day-to-day laws and practices weren't my concern. Unless it involved Paranormals.

"Eugene, I'll overlook you running and then attacking us if you at least speak to the men here with me. This is Agent Dalton of the FBI and Captain Right from the US Army," Herring said as he waved his hands in our direction.

I hadn't forgotten Caroline Barnes' comment about the military, and wasn't all that surprised by the gleam in Eugene's eyes at the mention of the army. "I really only wanted to discuss your future," I said. "The FBI and the Magical Division, which I represent, are always looking for potential Agents. Now that we understand that the happenings around town were caused by you, I can report to Washington that there aren't any ghosts."

"I should've come forward, but I was scared. Sorry," Eugene apologized.

"Don't go FBI, Eugene," Captain Right said. "Join the army. We need people just like you to fight the threats that no one ever sees. It was human Mages, not Paranormals, that really won the Demon War. We have trainers and an entire program already in place. You're what, fifteen or sixteen?" Captain Right asked.

Eugene looked at his dad who nodded. "Sixteen. My birthday is in a couple of months."

"Easy. We have your dad here sign a statement releasing you to us and we can start your training in a week. By this time next year, you'll be a private in Uncle Sam's army. Does that interest you at all?" Right asked.

"Dad, can I?" Eugene asked.

Morton Tarbell looked around at his scorched backyard and nodded. "Let's take the Captain inside and discuss it. Come on."

Captain Right all but smirked and even tipped his hat as he followed the two into the house.

"We do the work and he gets the boy. Not my day," I remarked to myself.

"I wouldn't say that, son. You did a bang-up job investigating, and you stopped the occurrences in town. Recruiting is harder than it looks. Let me tell you about finding officers sometime. Look on the bright side, you didn't have to kill anyone this time," Herring said.

The chief had a good point. I wasn't sure how I would explain losing the kid, but the recruitment thing was wishful thinking on my part. Even Anastasia had said I was on my own. Still, having a Magic user on my side would make all the difference. Maybe one day. It was time to go back to the station, borrow a phone, and call it in. Another day, another monster.

———

Captain Right watched as the two members of the Tarbell family hashed out the plan he'd given them. Planting those bugs at the local station and on the FBI had been an inspiring idea from Mr. Left. Eugene was a rare prize. Arcane was going to need talents like his in the next couple of decades.

He'd watched Agent Jack Dalton very closely during the chase. If he'd pegged to the name 'right' he was a better actor than anyone gave him credit. The Arcane program was blacker than black, set inside America's military. It was based on magical humans defending regular humans. The Paranormals could take care of themselves. But Jack would still need to be watched. There were a couple of new lookalike girls that might be able to do the job. He'd have to check when he got back to base.

JACK DALTON, MONSTER HUNTER

BOOK 7

1897 EXHIBITION

1897 Exhibition

My name is Jack Dalton and I'm a Monster Hunter.

Once again, I find myself driving down the backroads of America. I keep hearing stories about the new interstates they plan to build, but the only one I've seen so far is in Missouri. Nothing like that down here in Tennessee. After dealing with actual sea monsters and rogue Witches, I'm hoping for less of a challenge in Nashville.

Nashville, Tennessee is an interesting place. It was founded by Overmountain men in the late 1700's. They were called that because they usually lived west of or over the Appalachian mountains. I knew that Davy Crockett was an Overmountain man, but not that his father was one too. The entire area was the frontier until the early 1800's. More settlers brought industry, commerce, and government. What became Tennessee was right in the forefront of all that. Now, Nashville is a huge city and because of that people can get really lost in it. Normally that isn't my problem, except when it happens on government property.

"Jack, I've got a new mission for you," Anastasia explained over the phone.

I'd stopped at a roadside cafe and market after leaving Springfield to make my preliminary reports and check in. The local FBI offices are supposed to allow me to use their secure lines, but the word was out on me. Unless I pulled rank and forced the issue, they were starting to deny me any sort of help or assistance. The excuses they came up with were comical. Get one SAIC arrested and everyone is scared. If they're on the up and up, what do they have to worry about? The whole country can't be on the take, can they?

"Is it in Illinois?" I asked her, since I was familiar with it and already nearby.

"Just a bit south, in Tennessee. The Director himself sent this one to you actually." Anastasia paused for a moment. I could hear paper being shuffled and moved about. "Jack, it's a missing person case."

"Boss, that's way outside my purview. Why can't the local office handle it?" I asked.

"Forget it, Jack. I just told you it came from the Director himself.

Before you get upset, you need to know I did some digging on my end. The Parks Department and the State Department are the agencies who asked Mr. Hoover for help," Anastasia replied.

"WHO THE HELL IS MISSING, Smokey Bear?" I asked. A few years ago, the Parks Department found a lost bear cub after a big fire in New Mexico. They started using him in their advertising about conservation. There was a song and everything. Maybe one day I'll go see him at the zoo in Washington. If I ever find time, that is.

"A bear might be easier to find. No, this is worse. An entire tour group of visiting dignitaries vanished from inside the Parthenon in Nashville's Centennial Park two days ago," Ana explained. "This one's pretty high-profile, Jack. The local office and you have been assigned to this together. Mr. Hoover wants them either found or the disappearance explained in simple terms that he can understand. This has the potential for a major international incident."

I shook my head. Working with locals, especially in a big city like Nashville, was going to be bad news. "Who's in the delegation?"

There was silence on the other end of the phone for almost a full minute. "Ana? Who is it?"

My Vampire boss sighed into the phone. "Keep this one under your hat, Jack. The Athenian government sent out an Ambassadorial team a couple of months ago. Every country they've visited has agreed to keep it very quiet. There are still many refugees and political groups protesting their existence. According to my sources, they informed State that they'd heard of the Parthenon there and wanted to check it for accuracy."

"Accuracy? It couldn't be that accurate could it?" I asked her.

"Jack, it was originally built for the 1897 Tennessee Centennial and was made of plaster and wood. They built it as close to the original, even using plaster casts of the original so-called Elgin Marbles that once graced the one in Athens. Years after the great reveal and the loss of Greece to the paranormals, the city of Nashville tore down the crumbling wooden structure and replaced it with a concrete one. They rebuilt it exactly. It's one of the showpieces of Nashville today," Anastasia explained.

I concentrated for a moment. World history wasn't really my strong point. I knew all about the Purge and what it entailed for this country, but the rest of the world might as well be dots on a map for all I cared. Except for Greece, or Athenia, as they called it now. Nobody who went inside its borders returned and nobody ever came out. "Why now? What is so important to bring them here?"

"We don't know. If you find them, you can ask. Get to Clarksville, Tennessee as fast as you can. The local office can fill you in more. Good luck, Jack," Anastasia said, even as she hung up the phone.

"Clarksville?" I asked as the dial tone sounded. Staring at the phone in my hand, I shook my head. Something was off here.

"You still got that amulet I gave you, boy?"

Spinning around in surprise, I saw the old man I'd met months ago in another little out-of-the-way place. "What are you doing here?"

Still dressed like a vagabond, the old man smiled as he brushed his shaggy hair out of his face. Even though he kept his hat down low, I could see the scar tissue around his left eye. The last time we met, he claimed to be a war veteran. Knowing he lied to me, I wondered which war he was talking about.

He swept his hands forward and waved at the food mart. "I get around. Keeping places like this up is sort of a family thing. An oasis in a storm. So do you still have it?"

Silently, I nodded my head. It was impossible for this man to be here at this time. But here he was.

"Not speaking to me?" The old man nodded, "I can see that. Keeping your cards to yourself. Good plan when threatened. When it comes to what matters, you are in a pivotal position in this world. There are choices to be made and plans within plans. You got a taste of it with those Witch friends of yours. What you do next could change everything."

"Choices? What sort of choices? How could something I do change the world?" I asked.

The old man shifted his shoulders and cocked his head to one side. For just a moment I would almost swear there was a faint gleam coming from his scarred eye. Clearing his throat, he said, "Can't tell you that. Think of me as a sort of advisor. It's my job to point you in the proper direction."

I shook my head. "Who in the hell are you? I didn't ask for any of this! I just want to do the job."

There was a loud cawing as a pair of very large ravens flew overhead. The old man's single eye tracked them until they passed out of sight. Turning his head, he stared at me. A sudden chill ran up my spine as his eye seemed to pierce my soul. "The story of your life was written when you were born, boy. Hide in a hole if you like, but the ending will still be the same. Life is to be lived. Do your job, but be cautious of the choices you make." Pausing for a moment, he bowed his head. Then he looked up and said, "Trust the owl. He won't steer you wrong."

"The owl? How is a bird supposed to help me?" I asked.

The one-eyed man shook his head and looked skyward. Muttering almost to himself he said, "Yeah. Yeah."

He looked me in the eyes again. "I've said enough. Beware your actions and good luck."

"Who in the hell are you?" I asked again. This guy was freaking me out.

He looked past me and pointed. "Who's that?"

Following his finger, I turned my head and peered across the road, "I don't see anything. What was it?"

Nothing but silence answered me. The old man was gone. Stepping into the doorway of the store, I expected to find him there, but the place was empty. Completely empty. Ghost town empty. The cafe and the market were gone. "What the freaking hell is going on?"

All the way to the outskirts of Clarksville, I pondered what the old man had told me. I had no idea how I could be a pivot point. I just knew I was missing something.

————

THE FEDERAL BUILDING in Clarksville was impressive. Granite blocks, stone columns, and heavy leaded glass panes on the windows. It made me wonder when it was built and which state senator had it placed here instead of in Nashville proper. It seemed like something a politician would do. At least the ones I'd met so far.

I parked my van on the street and approached the front. Looking around, I could see the town's charm, but this office looked out of place.

"Good afternoon, sir. Can we help you?" The receptionist asked. Her desk was stationed just inside the door. It was a smallish lobby with marble floors and ornate wall sconces.

I cleared my throat and said, "FBI special agent in charge Jack Dalton. I'm supposed to coordinate my division with the office here."

The woman stood and held out her hand. "Agent Dalton, we've been expecting you."

Taking her hand, I replied, "Thank you, good to be here. Do we have a team assembled?"

The woman laughed and gestured to the doors behind her. "We're a bit laid back here in Clarksville with only a half dozen agents, but everyone is in the main conference room."

Stepping through the doors, I could see what she meant. The whole office was a conference room with three doors on each side. Everyone had an office here. All six Agents were clustered around the main table. Chalk and pin boards surrounded them. I could see maps and photos everywhere. Several heads turned in my direction. Jaws dropped and eyes widened. All conversation stopped dead.

I had to smile. My outfit didn't scream FBI to anyone. Even though the director himself had decreed the dress code for the regular

FBI, he turned a blind eye to my activities as long as the job got done in a timely manner. And as long as I didn't make the bureau look bad in the process.

"Gentleman, I'm Agent Dalton from the Magical Division. Do we know anything new? Washington wasn't very clear?" I asked them.

A tall man at the rear of the table raised his head and stared at me for a long second before speaking. "Not really. Some park staff members have reported that there were feathers and mud found tracked around the building the week before, but they thought it was either kids or the night watchman goofing off. At the time, no one followed up on it. We dug into the visitor logs and interviewed everyone, both present and off duty, looking for any clue or possible scenario that would explain this."

Remembering the old man's comments, I raised my hand and rubbed my chin. "Hmm. Do we know what sort of feathers they are?"

A man dressed similar to me perked up and pointed to the board. "We don't deal in birds at Centennial Park, but I sent the feathers to an expert over at Rocky Fork. According to him, they are a..." The man paused and lifted a piece of paper. "The feathers come from an owl. Our expert wasn't completely clear on the exact species, but he's sure of the genus. The real mystery is how they ended up here, in Nashville."

"Why? There are owls all over the place," I replied.

"Not this kind. According to our man, these feathers can only be found on owls native to Europe, North Africa, and Korea. A similar species was introduced to the British Isles a century ago to cut down on rodents as well." The Park Ranger held up a longish feather, almost a foot long. "But none of those owls have feathers this long."

"Could they be dyed or part of some sort of outfit?" I asked.

Trying to regain control of the discussion, the local Agent cleared his throat. "We're checking into that. My team has calls into all the local costume and hat manufacturers for that very reason. They may have cased the place earlier. The mud we cannot explain, but a sample was sent to the labs in Atlanta for testing."

I walked over to their boards. The investigative technique was textbook, right out of the FBI manual. There were geographical reports, extensive interviews, charts, and even weather reports tacked up. Ignoring the feeling of being watched, I perused the reports. "It looks like you have everything covered here. What does the Paranormal community say about it?"

"There are no Paranormals in Nashville," the Agent said.

I turned around to see everyone at the table staring. "Really? I doubt that. There are Paras everywhere. You seriously never looked?"

"The shifters are all locked up, and the Vampires are dead. What else is there?" the lead Agent said, haughtily.

Unable to help myself, I snorted. "Not to put you down or anything, but you're wrong. I will admit that the Vampires may have been reduced by what we call the 'Purge', but they are not all dead. I mean, they're dead, but not really gone. Neither are all the Weres on reservations. Every state in the union has Witches and there are Fae in some of our deepest forests. If you know what to look for, there are paramormals everywhere."

Completely serious now, I swept the room with my eyes. "This is a classic locked-room mystery that's on the verge of being an international incident."

Refusing to be made the fool, the lead Agent avoided eye contact with me, and looked at his people instead. "Did any of you know about Paranormals in Nashville?"

All the men except one looked at each other with blank faces. The Parks Department representative raised his hand just a little. "There is what I think is a Vampire working at Fair Park and I've seen unusually large wolves in some of our parks."

Giving the man a pointed look, I responded, "Exactly my point. Have you spoken to any of them?"

The representative paled. He obviously didn't like being the center of attention. "Unofficial Government policy is to ignore them.

But the ones here in Tennessee have been known to help here and there."

"Unofficial? I just don't believe that!" Lead Agent Kenneth Klarkson replied. "We shouldn't be helping any of the monsters."

I started to respond but stopped myself. Capturing the hearts and minds of the nation wasn't my job. Neither was defending the paranormal community. My job was to enforce the law. Putting on a forced smile, I looked at the lead Agent. "That may be your opinion, Agent Klarkson, but the law says otherwise."

"There are quite a few free Weres, both authorized and not. If I run across the latter I can enforce the law, but for now think of them as citizens. What sort of help have they provided?" I asked.

"We are the law around here," Klarkson retorted.

I cut my eyes toward him. "I can call Director Hoover, if you like. For clarification purposes only. But you can guess what he'll say. If we can't work together, I'm sure your assistant can take over for you..." I let that statement hang.

"How dare you come into MY office and threaten me!" Klarkson replied.

Shaking my head, I glared at the now fuming man. "How dare YOU. This entire case is supposed to be a joint effort. Not some prima donna's platform to fame. What do you suppose the State Department would say about your outburst? Aren't half the missing foreign nationals paranormals?"

Klarkson paled. "I..."

I looked to the Parks department man. "What have the Weres helped with?"

Warily watching the other Agents, the man sat up straighter in his seat. "Lost hikers have reported that strangers guided them out of the forest several times. We've also had a lost child or two show up unexpectedly, talking about glowing people helping them."

I nodded. "So you have at least one pack or a lone wolf and what sounds like Witches helping you out. They've managed to stay off the FBI's radar, at least. Anything else?"

The Parks Department man shook his head.

"What about the Parthenon? Is this event the only thing that's happened?" I asked.

"Most of the current staff think it's haunted. Ever since the concrete structure was built, we've had reports of strange smells, sounds at night, and doors left locked found open in the morning. There's something not right about the place," the man said.

Pulling a chair out, I sat down facing the men. "Recently I made the acquaintance of a Coven of Witches up in Maine. According to their leader, there are things called Gates that can be opened to other worlds and realities."

All of the other men in the room either just stared or shook their heads. I smiled. "Trust me when I say I didn't believe it, either. But there's a dinosaur head mounted inside the back of my van that says otherwise. These things are real and may be responsible for the disappearances here."

Looking around the table, I could see they still didn't believe me. "You don't have to believe me. But Director Hoover personally sent me here, so you should at least listen to me."

———

"So no one has been inside that room since the disappearance, not even to look and see?" I asked the Agent assigned to me.

"No sir. According to the people here, that door leads to a broom closet. It's the only door we didn't open. Kinda like looking in a dog house for a horse. Way too small a space," the young local Agent stuttered out.

I scratched my head. "You'd think your boss would've searched every inch of the place already, including this room?"

The Agent sighed. "KK didn't want the assignment in the first place. When Washington told him to supervise the Greek delegation, he assigned the newest, rawest agents we had to do it."

Turning my head, I just stared in response. I'd run into this sort of reaction before. "Let me guess. He has a beef with Paranormals?"

"He thinks they're all animals and not worth the FBI's time. There is way more crime and stuff we really should be chasing down out here. Just last week someone stole an entire truckload of whisky right off a loading dock. That's an interstate crime," the Agent explained.

I studied the man before speaking. Technically, I was a supervisor but not one of his. "My advice would be to treat them all like people, because before long there WILL be some of them in the bureau."

The local snorted. "Yeah right."

When I didn't laugh or change my expression, the man's eyes widened and his mouth dropped open. "Seriously? Why?"

"The Magic Security Act. I'm sure you read about it last year when they enacted it. One of the codicils was the establishment of an academy to train Paranormals for FBI and military service. My division was created by it as well," I explained to him. "Trust me when I say we need them. Desperately."

"Is Washington truly insane?" the agent asked me.

"Maybe. I had the chance to work with a Were recently. We were chasing down a rogue in St Louis. The man was a civilian, but having the advantage of a partner who can take a bullet and live, track almost anything across any surface, and can handle himself against some of the monsters is a partner you'd want to have! I look forward to the day when I can recruit someone like that," I explained. Reaching out, I opened the broom closet. Other than a broom and some cleaning supplies, it was empty. "Did the agent with the group disappear as well?"

"No. He'd stationed himself outside the building as ordered. The initial report came from him as well," the local explained.

I looked at the young agent in surprise. "Why am I talking to you instead of him then?"

"State has him. Both they and Agent Klarkson think he was in on the kidnapping. Why else bring them here?" The young agent motioned to the museum around us.

"No idea. It's my understanding the delegation's from Greece. Maybe they wanted a taste of home?" I stated.

"Washington is much more impressive than Nashville. Most people here forget this place is even here. They'd much rather spend time at the Opry chasing after their favorite singer," the young agent pointed out.

"Something brought them here and I need to know what that was." I shook my head. "This wasn't a kidnapping."

———

"I DON'T KNOW!"

Those were the first words I heard when entering the room. The speaker, Agent Asem, sat facing a trio of men in black suits. Wires that I perceived to be part of a lie detector were attached to the Agent.

"How many times do I have to say the same damn thing?" Agent Asem cried out.

All three men in black looked up at me with anger in their eyes. "This room is closed!"

I shook my head. "No, it's not. How about you let the Agent here have a break?"

"Agent Asem is under our jurisdiction. Who are you to say otherwise?" one of the men asked.

Holding up my credentials, I mimicked a favorite movie character of mine. "Dalton, Jack Dalton. I'm the Magical Division Chief. Director Hoover himself placed me in charge of this operation."

"Hoover has no jurisdiction over the State Department. We're in charge here," the taller of the three men answered.

Shaking my head, I replied, "No. The Agent there is a member of the FBI and falls under our control. If anyone is to either reprimand or remove him, it will be us. Now either release him or be arrested. We are on the same side here. Let me do my job."

"Your job?" The tall man approached me, getting so close his suit touched mine. "We have an entire delegation of foreign nationals missing and you're telling me that this is your job?"

"I am. The I in FBI stands for investigation. It's what we do." I pointed to Agent Asem. Hanging his arms off the chair, he had the look of someone whose day had been very long. "That Agent is now my responsibility. If I find something within State's realm of influence, you will be the first ones I call."

"Not acceptable. We get our orders from the State Department and only the State Department. FBI has nothing on us," the tall man replied.

Cocking my head to one side, I changed tactics. "Eventually there will be a report written explaining all of this...mess. I'm not known for exaggeration. The Director usually believes what I give him, however far-fetched it might be. So unless you can top sea monsters and rogue Weres, I think I've got you. Do count on me telling him how you and your associates here delayed the investigation for hours while you tried to push blame off onto the Bureau."

"State doesn't respond to threats, Agent Dalton," the tall man bristled.

Hooking a thumb over my shoulder, I pointed to the door. "Report me if you like, but this is now my case. We are just as concerned that a delegation disappeared from the building, but I don't see you doing anything constructive to help, other than trying to blame one of our agents for it. Now is the time for you to leave. Do I need to call in Agent Karlson and his men to remove you forcibly?"

The man glared at me with fire in his eyes, but he backed down. Motioning to his two goons, he stormed past me. "This isn't over!"

Without turning, I waited for the door to slam behind me before commenting, "I'm sure it isn't."

Agent Asem's head was bowed and for just a moment I thought

he was sleeping. Touching his shoulder, I gave him a gentle shake. "Agent?"

"Which answer do you want to hear again?" the very tired agent whispered.

I stepped around him and squatted down to his level. "You tell me."

Asem slowly raised his head to look me in the eye. Glancing to one side then the other, he gasped. "They're gone?"

"Yup. This is an FBI investigation, not State. Trust me when I say that the Director himself will hear of this." I smiled at him to try and gain his trust. "My name is Jack Dalton. Stuff like this is my bread and butter. So you might say I get all the creepy cases."

"Dalton," Asem muttered my name and scrunched up his eyes as if in concentration. "The one from the Portland office?"

With other regular agents, it always came back to the experiences I'd rather not remember. Trying to play it off, I was light about it. "I've been there. Nice town."

"What do you want from me?" Asem asked.

I shrugged. "The same thing those bozos wanted. Down deep we're both FBI. Investigation is in our blood. I'm completely confident that you can walk into a room and remember all the details down to the color of the wallpaper. It was training one-oh-one at the academy. Those fools only cared about one thing. Where the diplomats went. What they really should have asked is why come here? What's so special about this place? Why would Magical creatures cross the ocean and journey to a copy of a place they own the original of? Those are the sorts of questions that I want you to answer for me."

Agent Asem leaned forward and stood. Looking down at me, he stretched his arms out to both sides. I could hear his joints pop as he did the maneuver. He stepped over to the wall and gave it a push with both hands. At the academy, Isotonic Exercises was a course taught as an elective because many of us would spend long hours sitting or standing without really exercising.

I stood as he limbered up.

"Did you know they've been grilling me for more than a day? My wife and kids must be losing their minds in worry," the Agent commented as he pushed off from the wall.

"I'll have the local office send them a note and see if there's a phone here you can use. We take care of our own," I replied. "Do you want to move to a different room? This place is supposed to have a cafe or something downstairs. At least that's what the Park folks told me."

There was a water cooler with cups in the corner of the room and Asem stepped over to it. "Water's fine. Let me tell you what I can before those... people return. Team players they are not. Makes me wonder how anything gets done on their end."

Processing what he was saying, I only nodded. International politics and policy weren't things I was familiar with, and to be truthful, I didn't want to get involved. Director Hoover was irritated with me enough already. Changing direction, I asked a few questions of my own to get things started.

"Talk to me. Start with meeting the delegation and we'll work from there," I said as I pulled out a chair and sat down.

"Whew! Was that a crazy day, let me tell you," Asem started. Avoiding the chair he had previously sat in, he selected another. "So I get this call from the Washington field office to meet up with a party of foreign diplos and their State handlers out at Berry Field. As you might know, Clarksville is way out there, so it took me forever to get to the field. Dodging the construction traffic, I took more than one wrong turn. They have that place ripped up all to hell."

"Why is the airport all torn up? Bad storm or something?" I asked.

Asem shook his head. "You must not have come in that way. The city's expanding the place. I've heard the plan is to add a couple of extra runways and triple the size of the main terminal. Nashville's getting a jet service. Can you believe that? This place will turn into New York before you know it. So back to my story. I get there and use my credentials to park. Washington didn't tell me a single thing about the group, not even how many or what was in the party, and most importantly what country they were from. You can imagine my surprise then."

I snorted. "That must have come as a shock."

"Ya think? Who knew that Greece even still had an airline, much less one that could cross the Atlantic ocean. The airport mechanics and State Department weenies were crawling all over the thing after it landed," Asem answered.

"I think the country's called Athenia now, like the city," I commented.

Casting me a look, Asem chuckled. "That's what the State Department guy told me at the terminal. It seems these folks flew all the way to Washington to deliver some document from their queen and were supposed to see the sights, according to the one man I spoke to about it. Little did anyone know that they didn't mean just Washington."

"Why here? The Director's office told me it was to check the accuracy of the building here but that can't be right, can it?" I asked him.

"I don't know anything about that. When the State Department guy chose to speak to me, he told me that half the delegation set up an embassy while they were in DC. The rest came here and only here. Nothing was said to me about accuracy. They just wanted to visit and see the inside of the place," Asem replied.

I frowned. Something was off and I didn't know what it was. "Why you?"

Asem frowned and then looked at the floor. "Once upon a time I worked for the diplomatic corps. I was young and my parents got me the job. You have to understand, Agent Dalton..."

Raising my hand, I interrupted him. "Jack. My name is Jack."

"Ok. Jack. What you have to understand, Jack, is my family were or are part of the government in exile from Greece. My great-grandfather was a regional governor, and when the Gorgon appeared, he fled the country. According to my father, things were easier back then. Less complicated than today. Finding and boarding a ship was easy if you had money. Even buying your way into a country was possible. They just appeared, you know, the Paranormals. Trees and rocks that had stood the test of time for millennia were suddenly creatures that could speak. Things from nightmares were giving orders and seizing towns, all in the name of myths and legends. My family told tales of when the Turks ruled us, and they didn't want a repeat of it. So after much travel and turmoil, they ended up here, in the United States. I'm a first-generation citizen here. But to answer your original question, it might be that I speak Greek and Italian. Italy was the first and only place I was assigned while in the diplomatic corps," Asem explained. "I wasn't there long, though. The church controls pretty much everything except for the very top of the government there. I can't blame them. The destruction of central Europe hurt just about all the surrounding nations. Losing a good chunk of their Northern region didn't help either."

I nodded. The Demon War was pretty devastating to Europe. It was one of the major factors in turning their governments against Paranormals and those that supported them. My own father was testament to that. His army unit may have saved many lives, but once the locals found out his men were of the Were persuasion things always got ugly. My mom told me many times that he's written in letters to her that he wondered why we went overseas in the first place. Too many lives lost for no reason."

"I understand. My father served in the tank corps in France," I replied.

"Then you know. So the airport. The group was way bigger than I expected it to be. Even the State guy was shocked. My first thought was where was I going to rent a bus!" Asem shook his head. "We were all surprised when one pulled up out front. They'd somehow arranged for one already. You should have seen it, Jack. It was one of those Greyhound Scenic Cruisers. The ones with the funny upper deck? Two of the diplomats were Satyrs and getting those little guys up the stairs to the observation deck was a real challenge. It was more like a circus act than a diplomatic mission," Asem laughed.

"How so?" I asked.

"Two Satyrs. A faun. Three humans or at least I thought they were human. It was hard to tell with the costumes they were wearing. They'd brought along a three-person team of...well...the best I can say would be gladiators, for security. They wore tin pot helmets and carried swords. Sort of like that Charlton Heston movie last year, Ben Hur. Airport security had a fit when they refused to give them up," Asem chuckled again. "The State weenies did their jobs and talked everyone down. We finally loaded up and came here. They knew exactly where they wanted to go, Jack."

"Hmm." I grunted. Looking the man in the eye, I asked him, "What makes you think the humans weren't human?"

"The way they moved. You know how we're taught to read people. They were sinuous. I thought they might be women under the cloaks, but it really was hard to tell. Something was really off about them and their status as diplomats didn't allow me to look," Asem replied.

"They were wearing cloaks? That's different. Could they have been Arabic or Egyptian?" I asked him.

"I don't think so. The language they spoke was pure Greek like you'd hear if Homer himself was speaking to you. I learned more about the mother tongue sitting on that bus than I did my entire childhood speaking to my grandfather. They were the real deal," Asem explained. "We got here, stepped inside, and all hell broke loose."

———

"...AN attack! We've got an incursion on the Plain of Meggido!"

Callimachus, known as Mack in these modern years, looked up from his work in the library. A new batch of books, some old, some new, had recently appeared in the middle of the main entryway. That was how it worked with the Gods of Light. Preserving the knowledge of the ages was the task he was given, after all. Trust the Gods to make it difficult at times. This collection must have come from a library somewhere. "How bad is it?"

"Scouts are reporting two cohorts of infantry at least, with a possible squad of Ogres and Trolls in the rear. We won't be completely sure until they reach site of the wall," the messenger reported.

Mack sighed, "If it's not one thing it's another. Send your commander my regards and tell him to do his best. Owl and our Mage corps are dealing with an incursion of another kind. A random Gate opened in the middle of Athena's temple here in the library. The moment we are able to send help, we will. Understood?"

The Centurion saluted and raised his submachine gun to his chest. "Sir!"

Mack watched the soldier leave, murmuring to himself. "The Gods have it in for us today."

It started like any other day, in what some called Otherwhere, and Mack called The Library. He had books to catalog. Always more books. Mankind in the worlds above seemed to be both creating new and disposing of old. All at the same time. The Gods of Light collected things that they deemed useful in their eternal fight against the Dark. Books, weapons, people, whatever they thought would bolster the fight. It was both of the caretakers' jobs to enforce the rules and give whatever assistance they could. That being said, they did slip and fall occasionally. Mack was human at one time.

There were five permanent Portals in town. The two inside the library were closed off. Athena had informed the duo that their locations would one day be revealed. The town square held the largest and primary entrance. All food and most travelers came this way. It led directly to a place called The Garden, located in the middle of a valley controlled by Witches. Owl, the ruler of Otherwhere, claimed it was one of the most protected spaces upon the entire Earth and having been there once, Mack believed him. Otherwhere was a waystation. A hedge against the Dark on the path of the great hallway of doors that spanned the universe. If you knew how to travel them, it was possible to pass from one reality or time at will, but it was very, very, dangerous to do so. Only the brave went there and lived.

The Library came from Egypt, but the tavern was Germanic. Mid to late eighteenth century is what Mack's research had shown. Its bartender just appeared one day, many years after the building. A closet that wasn't a closet was one of the last remaining doors. It led to Russia, a permanent link to the cities controlled by Vampires. It too was rarely used anymore. On Earth, aftereffects of the Purge destroyed many of the doorways.

Where there is Light there is also Dark. Those that fought to protect the place called The Library were soldiers from many eras of Earth. Ties of brotherhood and admiration won in battle tied them to each other and formed the core of the Legion of the Damned. They held the gap and fought on the plain that lead to the final Portal in Otherwhere, Drakon the realm of the Dragons.

Athena, the leader of the Gods of Light, built Otherwhere from nothing. She took fragments of power from all the Gods, creating a storehouse of knowledge. Her only mistake was not making it self-sufficient. Portals and gates needed to be used to transport food and other necessities to the small pocket universe. They say that information is power and clues about the place's existence abounded, for there were those who constantly searched. One day no enemy Portals, the next a big one.

Tiamat's children, the Draconic Empire, once ruled Earth with a scaled fist. Only the combined power of the Gods of Light and a few scattered Mages were able to push them away. Tiamat's death at the hands of Marduk shattered the Empire, leaving it rudderless for centuries. But the Dragons hadn't forgotten about Earth. All pathways were blocked to them except Otherwhere. It was there that they could push through and return. Once upon Earth they could find Tiamat's treasure and rule for all eternity.

With all of that as a background, Mack was incredibly surprised when a small group of people and creatures appeared inside the temple, one of the safest and hardest to reach areas in the entire Library.

Rumble...

"What was that?" Mack asked as he looked skyward.

Owl swiveled his head from side to side clicking his beak. "No idea. Did you lock down the new row of book shelving? You remember what happened last time."

Mack looked back at the giant bird perched on the chair across from him, and said, "Not helping. And it wasn't my fault that time. Besides, this is just a rumble, not a crash or a boom."

The bird cocked his head to one side as if listening. "There are voices in the air. Language I haven't heard...in millenia. Get up. We need to check the temple."

"The temple? Why do we have to go there? Athena hates me," Mack whined as he stood up. Owl had already launched himself from the table and was gliding down the hall toward what was once the main room of the Serapeum. As the library grew, the original building, called by some historians the daughter library of Alexandria, had been encircled and enclosed. The statue of Serapis was long gone but Athena had taken his place.

Running after the owl, Mack stumbled and almost fell as his sandals caught on his toga. He made a mental note to excuse decorum and wear t-shirts and shorts from now on. It wasn't like this place was the hottest spot on the town tour.

Reaching what they called the temple, Mack came to a screeching halt as three men dressed as gladiators pointed what looked like very sharp swords at him. Looking past the men he could see Owl speaking to a large group of mixed beings.

"Who are you?" Owl repeated. He'd tried several dialects already, including English and had now settled on Greek.

One of the Satyrs bowed and motioned to the others. "We came here at our Queen's behest. Her Majesty the Gorgon wishes to re-establish a connection with the Goddess Athena and the Lords of

Light. Now that the great divide has been severed, we are moving, making the connections needed for the future."

Three extremely beautiful women revealed themselves, shedding their cloaks. They moved to encircle the large owl and each curtsied. The Satyr rose and continued to speak. "These are three of the Hoisioi, the attendants of the Pythia. Our oracle has foreseen what is to come and wishes to aid your kingdom."

Owl blinked his large expressive eyes as he gazed upon the people in the room. Spying Mack at the entrance, he snapped his beak a few times. "Please allow my friend entry."

The Satyr waved his hand negligently and the three gladiators removed their swords. Giving Owl a wave, Mack stepped into the temple area. "Who?"

Owl swiveled his head to one side and looked at his longtime friend. "That's my line. These are travelers from a distant land. They've come seeking the Goddess."

Without even blinking, Mack responded sarcastically, "Did you tell them she rarely speaks to us?"

"Not yet," Owl responded.

"Where did they come from?" Mack asked, eyeing the pretty girls.

"Greece, or Athenia, as they call it now. The Gorgon sent them to us if you believe that," Owl explained.

"Hmm. Sent them to us from where? It takes a special place to be able to build a Gate with enough power to get here. Did they say?" Mack asked the large bird.

Owl flapped his wings a bit and looked to the Satyr again. There were two of them and a Faun milling around the temple area. The one he'd spoken to was prostrated before the statue of the Goddess.

"Excuse our leader," the Faun said. "It's been his life's goal to visit a true temple to Athena."

"You come from what was once Greece? Are there no temples left there?" Owl asked, speaking in the Faun's mother tongue.

"No. The humans destroyed them years ago. The White God

remained supreme and encouraged the destruction. Even the temple at Sounion was destroyed. Poseidon's still stands but in name only. Our people could only watch from afar as the destruction went on and on for centuries. It was only through the actions of our Majesty, the Gorgon, that we have regained the culture we lost," the Faun explained.

Owl repeated the conversation in English for Mack so he'd understand. While he might read ancient Greek, speaking it fluently was a different matter.

"English? You speak that even here? I will tell them and adapt," the Faun spoke up in the aforementioned language. "We knew YOU were here but made other assumptions as well...Forgive us."

Stepping closer and laying a gentle hand on the Owl's wing, Mack spoke to the creature before him. "You seek the Goddess. What of her temple in Assisi? It's under her guise as Minerva but..."

"NO." The Faun made placating gestures with his hands. "Sorry. That temple is one of his, the White God. It's attributed to the Goddess, but our research says it was actually built to honor Hercules. Trust me when I say that we have done our research on this. Your temple here is the last true site. Even the center of the universe, Delphi, was looted and destroyed. They built a church to HIM upon the ruins. All is gone now. The Gorgon has restored worship, but the Pythia still received warnings. The Goddess needed to be warned and given access to the people. We chased her off and now beg for her to return. How else may we give our power to the Gods? Without us they are nothing but empty shells."

"What sort of warnings are they getting that are so serious?" Mack asked.

"Such things are the matter of state and diplomacy," the original Satyr replied as he gently pushed the Faun aside. Giving the small creature a look of reprimand, the leader of the small expedition said, "This is my task. Being here I needed...Forget what I needed. My assistant spoke the truth to you. We searched and researched for years before attempting the crossing here. There are rumors and speculation of this place. In some circles it's called a haven from persecution. Did you know that? What the humans call Europe has become almost unbearable for any of our kind. The Paranormal peoples are being driven from the land by followers of hatred and pain. Our Queen has taken many of them within her bosom and sent others to the kingdoms of the Vampires. What our oracles have seen is destruction and chaos. They are returning and nothing in this time can stop them. Not yet at least. With that being said, the Gorgon wishes to open up one of the lost Portals and send what aid she can in your fight against the enemy. It might not help in today's fight, but the future is fluid."

"When you speak of the enemy, who is it you mean?" Mack asked the Satyr. "We have many against us, including the Gods of Darkness."

"We think of them as the children of Typhon, but you call them the Draconic Empire," the Satyr explained. "Even now they fight, do they not?"

Mack looked over his shoulder to the doorway as if expecting one of the Legion or the enemy to appear suddenly. When nothing appeared, he turned back to the conversation. "You didn't answer my question. Where did you come from, other than Greece?"

"Ah. Forgive me. Yes," the speaker turned to Owl. "You have traveled to Earth numerous times in the past. The Owl of Athena is legendary to us and artifacts of your passing are treasured. Using prized forgotten feathers from your body, we built the Gate in the only place that the energies of the Goddess herself were proper. The Parthenon in the land called Tennessee."

Owl clicked his beak a few times before speaking. Muttering a curse under his breath he shook his head. "That is a museum, is it not? You did this amongst Humans in broad daylight?"

The Satyr shrugged his shoulders. "Only the guard the humans insisted accompany us was present. What matter, they've seen Magic performed before, have they not?"

Mack sighed. "Not like that, they haven't. There is an unspoken rule about showing the Humans Gates and Portals. Having them appear here more than once in force is enough for me."

"Marcella must be informed," Owl instructed.

"On it." Hiking up his robes, Mack ran for the door. He had a Portal to cross and a Witch to find.

"While it's an honor to be sought out, you may have triggered events that cannot be repaired. Mack will seek out our representative in the United States and inform her of your presence. She might be able to head off any repercussions, but I doubt it. The Humans are more capable than you give them credit," Owl replied.

———

"BY HELL, YOU MEAN WHAT EXACTLY?" I asked the Agent. We'd gone up to the main floor and he had shown me exactly what and where the diplomats had gone.

"There were nine of them altogether in here. As a group, they scurried to and fro, as if looking for something. To me it was just a big empty room, but to them it was something else. The robed ones clustered in a circle suddenly and started to chant in a language I didn't quite understand," Agent Asem explained. "Linking hands, they all vanished in a flash. It was as if a great wind came out of nowhere and sucked them right up! Damnedest thing I've ever seen."

His description rang a bell within me. I'd seen something very similar one afternoon in Maine, only the flash of light had brought forth dinosaurs trying to eat me. Marcella Blackmore had called it a Gate. Somehow these people had opened one of them here, inside the museum! Shaking the man's hand, I hurried to leave. "I've seen it before. Thank you Agent Asem. You've been a big help to me and the investigation."

The agent's mouth dropped open and he looked at me in shock. "I have? What did I say?"

"That you're innocent and unless you are secretly a Witch, that you didn't do this," I said even as I hurried from the room. The temple reproduction was huge, and sound carried like an echo through it.

Spotting one of Klarkson's men at the door, I slid to a stop. "Phone? I need a phone with long distance calling right freaking now."

The local agent looked at me in surprise and it was all he could do but point to his right. I could see the restrooms and a small kiosk of payphones.

"Great, thanks!" Sliding the booth door open I grabbed the receiver. Waiting for a dial tone, I dug into my pockets looking for a nickel. "Huh? What did I do what it?"

Cursing, I stuck my hand out the door and yelled at the Agent. "Coins! I need some change!"

The local agent must feed a lot of meters, because suddenly my hand was filled with silver. Dimes, nickels, and quarters were bouncing out of my hand. I could see a few red cents mixed in as well. Those were pretty useless in these machines. We'd had a class at Quantico on how they worked, and it had to do with conductivity. Pennies could overload the early phones, so silver was better. Plus, the way the old Crosley phones were set up was that each coin's shape or denomination only fit a certain way. A bell would ring telling the operator or switchboard how much you had put into the machine. They were actually equipped with a string cutter as well, to prevent cheats from trying to take the coin inserted back out.

Dropping in a nickel, I stuck my finger in the rotary and dialed zero.

"This is the operator," an older woman's voice said to me.

Knowing that telling her I was FBI was useless, I just stated who I wanted to speak to. The last time I did that, they had to involve a supervisor and it took what felt like hours. "I need a person to person connection to Marcella Blackmore in Briarwood, Maine. That's a 207 area code."

"One moment please." There was a pause and I could hear several clicks on my end of the call. "Please deposit thirty-five cents."

Dumping the coins in my hand onto the small shelf under the phone, I grabbed a quarter and a dime. Careful to not lose them, I dropped them into the phone. The voice of the operator came on again. "Sir, your party is on the line."

There was a click and I could almost hear breathing, "Marcella? It's Jack. Jack Dalton. I need more information and some advice from you."

"Jack. It figures you'd be behind this mess. Marcella's not here at the moment. She went..." Minerva paused. Internally I sighed when I heard the much older woman's voice. She wasn't quite what I wanted right now.

"You still there, Jack? Marcella went through the Portal to visit some folks you might be missing. They're safe, if that is what you wanted to know," Minerva explained.

I leaned back into the wooden bench. It was some relief that the people Agent Asem brought with him were safe, but it didn't explain where they were and why. "Where are they? This is the very brink of an international incident with a country we don't exactly have good or any relations with. I need to speak to them, Minerva!"

"Not unless you can get to Maine all of a sudden. I'll pass the message along for you. Goodbye, Jack," Minerva hung up the phone, leaving me with nothing but dial tone.

"Dammit!" I exclaimed. Reaching up, I started to put more money in the machine but stopped. Knowing Minerva, she'd just refuse to accept the call. This left me with nothing useful. Concentrating for a moment, I thought of something. I knew another person who at one time mentioned Gates and Portals to me. Anastasia.

My halfway boss's number I actually knew by heart. It was a special line used only for emergencies and our own personal communications. How she'd set that up without the Bureau knowing about it was a puzzle.

"Did you find them, Jack?" Anastasia was short with me on the phone.

"Sort of. I've been told they're safe, just not where they went," I explained.

There was silence on the phone for just a moment. "Explain that, please."

Clearing my throat, I launched into the story. "I spoke to the Agent assigned to the part and he told me..."

My part of the conversation took almost ten minutes to get out with Ana making almost no comments at all. As I finished, the phone was so silent, for a moment I thought she'd hung up. But her chair has a distinctive creak and the sound of paper shuffling was very distinctive.

"What am I supposed to do with you, Jack? Hmm?" Anastasia asked.

"This time it wasn't my fault—" I started, but she cut me off.

"He won't see it that way and you know it. What did I tell you the first day on the job, do you remember?" she asked me.

"Survive." I did remember. Director Hoover didn't want a separate FBI group. Especially one he didn't control completely. Congress and the President were the ones who formed the Magical Division of the FBI. The Director put a total rookie in charge with the hope of having it fail in the first week. That freshly graduated rookie was me and I've managed to last almost a year now. Many of the assignments were impossible for a simple human to overcome, but I did, and now had gained the respect and hatred of fellow agents across the nation.

"Exactly. Survive. You've done a pretty good job so far, but this isn't a simple rogue or sea serpent this time. The Gorgon has ruled for almost a half century with no outside contact. Do you understand what that means Jack? Not even the OSS has been able to penetrate her borders. Now we have half the delegation setting up an embassy here in Washington and the other half has vanished. Now you say you found them but not where?" Ana shouted at me.

Wincing I could see her point but how to explain it? "I called Marcella Blackmore."

"I know who she is," Ana replied.

"Right. Her maid answered and told me that the delegation was safe, but Marcella couldn't speak to me and unless I could get to Maine it was impossible to speak to anyone," I explained.

"Did she tell you where Marcella was?" Anastasia asked me.

"According to Minerva, she'd gone through a Portal. I wasn't sure, but does that mean the group went through a Portal as well? There was that flash that Agent Asem mentioned," I explained to her. Thinking back, I tried to remember all the details of the Gate I saw open in Maine a few months ago. That one had been full of dinosaurs.

Anastasia breathed heavily into the phone receiver. "Portals are permanent while Gates are temporary. The Nashville Parthenon hasn't been there all that long. I visited the original in the twenties. It was made from plaster and didn't hold up all that well. Something like that isn't suitable for Portal work. Someone summoned a Gate. From what you've described, they may have used energy collected there to power it."

"That sort of makes sense, but how did they know the power was here? Greece is a long way from Tennessee," I replied.

"Don't ask me how I know of this but sometimes there are… traces…or afterimages left when a Gate is used. It depends upon the creator and the destination as to how much or how little is left. You could try whispering the Gorgon's name and walk the hall as much as possible looking for those traces. If and I do mean if an echo of the Gate remains, the group you are seeking may hear you. Regardless of what happens, you better prepare those folks there for the full weight of the FBI and all the other agencies to come barreling down on top of you. I won't be able to save you this time, Jack," Ana explained.

"Then cross your fingers and toes boss, because I'm going to search for a miracle." I hung up the phone and smiled. She really did care for me.

———

"You NEED to have the other half of your delegation explain things to the humans. This could cause a major incident," Marcella explained to the lead Satyr.

When one of the Legion appeared at the Garden gate Marcella immediately followed him through to Otherwhere and the Library. It was very rare for them to come to her this way.

"Eh, humans get too excited about things. Our visit here is what is most important. My Queen has said we can wait them out and try the next generation if need be. What use is this United States to one such as her? She would prefer not to wait. There are rumblings in the beyond that she says puts this world in peril. Having friends is a must for what is coming," the Satyr replied.

"What is coming, can you tell me?" Marcella asked him.

"Chaos and wonder. As my companions would say, to know too much is to open yourself up to change. Do you truly wish that upon what you carry? Knowing the outcome will make things much harder for them," the Satyr commented. Meeting Marcella's, eyes he dropped them towards her belly for just an instant. Knowing the outcome will make things much harder for them. Raising his his eyebrows he stated, "stay ignorant for now. The Pythia will welcome you if you waver."

Marcella froze for a moment as what the creature in front of her hit home. Only Minerva knew that she was pregnant. Not even science could tell yet! But a Witch that wasn't in tune with her own body wasn't a Witch at all. Part of her wanted to just let it go, but as the head of the World Species Council it was her job to prevent issues with the Humans, and this was a major one.

"What about if I contacted them for you? Would that be acceptable?" Marcella asked.

The lead Satyr cocked his head and looked up at her. "Why risk yourself in this, knowing it might change the outcomes of things?"

Marcella grimaced. The fact the Council even existed was one of the world's biggest secrets, and by contacting Washington she would be threatening it. Just getting on their radar was bad enough. "Because I must do something..."

"Hold that thought a moment. Did you hear that?" Owl spoke, cutting her off. The giant bird cocked his head to one side as if listening.

Marcella waved her hands. "What am I listening for?"

Half the people in the temple shushed her. "Shhhh."

Owl looked at the Satyr. "How powerful a Gate did you build, and did you leave it open?"

The lead Satyr motioned to the others. "Tell him."

It was the Faun who spoke up. "We used what power resided there. It coupled well with what we had in reserve. Tying it to the local ley line was Phil's idea. There remains but a small trace of it on both sides."

Marcella came to life suddenly. "You tapped a ley line directly and combined its power? Are you insane? I've seen Witches fried alive for doing such things!"

"And how much practice did they have in doing so? I was alive and prancing across Palodes when those you call heroes walked the Earth. Two thousand years you reach, and we can have this discussion again. I do know what I am doing, youngling," Philoctetes replied with a snort.

"Reopen the Gate," Owl ordered. "Do it now. Someone is calling."

The Satyr named Phil cocked his head and listened. Snorting again, he replied. "Smart. He calls for you and he speaks Her name at the same time. Not all humans are dumb."

"Take my power if you need it," Marcella offered.

"Why else use the ley line? There is power here enough. Much more than in the human's temple," Phil closed his eyes, holding his short stubby hands skyward. Smiling he spoke a single word. "Mellon."

There was a flash of light, and the swirling Magick of a Gate between the worlds opened before them. Like a rip in reality, it brought with it dust and dirt from Earth.

"Mellon? Seriously? I thought your country didn't have access to the modern world?" Marcella asked Phil.

"Some things such as books are allowed. It's only this country and those far off that we haven't visited officially. Tolkien is a master and should be accorded greatness for his work. Were he to come to Athenia we would raise him up to the highest peak," Phil replied.

"But would he be allowed to leave afterward? Would anyone be?" Marcella asked.

Both Satyrs laughed but Phil was the one that spoke. "You have only to come and find out for yourself. Who she cross and find our caller, will it be you?"

———

I LOOKED LIKE A FOOL.

Here I was, walking in circles repeating the name of the Queen of Athenia. Halfway through the second lap, I took inspiration from the old man that keeps appearing to me, and I spoke the name Owl as well. The other Agents, including the ones from State, thought I was insane. I'm sure their reports would reflect it as well. Goodbye, Magical Division. And goodbye, Jack.

Whoosh!

There was a flash of light and a huge wind. Dust and debris flew everywhere like a small bomb had gone off. A man-sized hole just appeared in the air, smack dab in the middle of the hall. Just like Agent Asem had reported.

The acoustics inside the temple were still echoing the Gate's entry into our world when I heard a commotion behind me. The State Department weenies were yelling at each other and me as I approached the hole. I can only imagine that they had forgotten that I represented the Magical Division and this thing was what I was here for. Without another glimpse or order to the contrary, I took a step inside.

Everything that I had read and what Marcella and Anastasia had told me of Gates and Portals was wrong. Traveling through them wasn't a chore or like stepping into a room. No. It was like traveling through a wind tunnel while your hair was on fire. The colors and sights of that infinitesimal moment when I left Earth and traveled to Otherwhere was something that I would see in my dreams for the rest of my life.

"Jack! What did I tell you about Gates?" Marcella yelled at me as I appeared in what, to me, looked like a real ancient temple.

"Not to go into them without you. But you're here and I'm sort of following directions. Are these the people I'm looking for?" I asked her. Asking was dumb on my part as I could see the Satyrs and other folk. True to the old man's comments, there was a giant Owl there as well.

"Is this the human you've spoken of, Marcella?" Owl asked.

Marcella nodded. "He is. They didn't know when they sent him. He has promise."

The giant bird stared at me for a moment. "You are correct. Welcome to the Library, Jack Dalton."

"Thank you, I think." I looked around the room and could only see statues and books. Lots and lots of books. "Should I ask where this is, exactly?"

Marcella smirked. "No. Some knowledge is best left unknown."

I gave her a nod and directed my attention to the party of diplomats. "Gentlemen and uh, ladies? My government sent me to find you. Did these...people here...did they kidnap or harm you in any way?"

"Humans. Always expecting the worst," the lead Satyr snorted. "We are fine. This is where we wanted to go."

Thinking on my feet, I quickly responded. Washington would want answers they could understand. "And you couldn't get here from your own country or any of the others?"

"I mean, this mess could cause an incident my government doesn't want with your Queen," I went on. "Can you explain it to me and maybe go back through to Earth again?" Looking to the Gate, I noticed it had closed. "Or not."

The Satyr looked at me and then the bird. Shrugging, he looked back at me. "We were sent here. It's none of your business what we do here or who we speak to. Our Queen is aware of our mission. She acquired the transportation needed for this. But I do see your dilemma. Underlings are usually the first to be sacrificed for the greater good, and you seem to have some standing with those of greatness here. Tumnus will go with you."

I only stared. All the players, the people in the room, stood stock still except for Marcella, who seemed to be chuckling. I was sure there was a joke somewhere, but names were not my strong point. "Who?"

Motioning to one side, the lead Satyr pointed to the smallest member of the party, the Faun. "Tumnus. He is my appointed representative and can speak for us with all the powers of our embassy. Is that enough for you?"

Bringing back at least one person would appease the State Department, at least. Getting them off the FBI and my back would help. "Sure. That will work, I guess."

One of the humans in the room, a man dressed like an extra from a cheap Roman movie, stepped over to Marcella and whispered in her ear. My hearing wasn't enhanced like a Were's so all I caught was the word "wiped."

"Mr. Dalton. Marcella tells me that you, a human, are in charge of policing the entire United States' Magical community all by yourself. Is that true?" The giant bird asked me.

I sighed. "Pretty much. The cases I've handled so far have been interesting, to say the least."

"Keep your eye on the prize then. Stay on the side of Light as much as you can and avoid temptation. There is much that one such as you can learn if he puts his mind to it," Owl responded.

"Uh, ok," I replied. The big bird thing was creeping me out a little.

"Are you ready, Agent Dalton?" The Faun asked.

I looked down. He barely came up to just above my knee. "Sure, Tummy."

"It's Tumnus," the Faun replied.

"Tum tum. Got it. Is someone going to open the Gate back up, or do I have to use Marcella's?" I asked them.

Marcella stepped closer to me and laid a hand upon my cheek. "Jack, you are a dear friend and for this I am truly sorry. Remember."

Her hand felt cold on my skin but it sort of tingled a bit. "Remember what?"

Smiling, the Witch removed her hand and kissed me, then said, "Don't worry about it. You'll get it."

Okay. I shrugged and watched as the Gate surged open once again. Tunny went first and I followed. I could see Marcella speaking to the Owl as I looked back. The light show wasn't as cool as the first time, but it was more sparkly if that was even possible.

Tummy and I emerged to a room full of cops and guns. The State Department weenies had called in the cavalry.

"Freeze!"

Tum Tum hit the floor with a screech and I jerked my hands up. "We come in peace?"

The next couple of hours went by in a blur. Agent Klarkson, while happy I'd found the diplomats, was very unhappy I didn't bring all of them back. The State Department boys were even more upset.

"Reopen that gate thingy and go get them!" The tall man yelled at me.

"How am I supposed to do that?" I replied.

The man threw up his hands and said, "You did it last time successfully. Do it again."

I shook my head. "No. You and your people watched me walk around and around inside, calling out a name. Did that look like

Magic to you? I'm not a Mage. The Gate was opened from the other side. You have Tummy. He can explain."

"Tumnus," the man said.

"Right. Taun Taun. He came back with me. The Satyr said that Tommy would explain everything to you," I replied.

"The Faun said his name was Tumnus," the State Department man repeated.

"If you say so. I'm terrible with names. This interview is done. I've got my own reports to write and wire to the Director's office. If you need something else from me, you can get it from Mr. Hoover." I stood up.

"You can't leave!" They yelled at me.

"Watch me." I opened the door to the interrogation room and left. Agent Klarkson and his boys were still sitting in their little command center when I exited. All heads turned in my direction. "Can you direct me to your secured lines? I have to call the Director."

"Use my office. Down the hall to the left, last door on the right. The phone is the only secured line in the building." Agent Klarkson pointed.

Thanking the man, I followed his instructions. What a day it had already been, and I still had to call it in. Using Director Hoover's name in vain was going to bite me in the ass one of these days but since nobody but the big man knew that Anastasia was my boss...I figured I was safe for a little while.

Dialing the number from memory, I accessed the ultra-secure line again and began my report.

"Why only one, Jack?" Anastasia asked me as I finished the report to her. My procedure in most cases, including this one, was to write out the basics of the report for filing purposes and leave the details to Ana. She would record any top secret or eyes-only information and take care of dissemination to other offices.

My cheek and face were still tingling from where Marcella touched me but the moment Ana asked her question my whole face went numb for just a moment. It was like a heavy weight settled down upon my head and all thoughts and memories erased. My mouth dropped open and my eyes glazed over. Only Ana's voice roused me.

"Jack! Are you still there?" Ana yelled into the phone.

Reaching up, I massaged my cheek and jaw. "Yeah. Sorry, I had the strangest feeling come over me and now my head hurts. What was the question?"

"Why only one diplomat?" she asked me.

"Why only one diplomat what? I don't understand the question." I told her. Diplomats, why would I associate with those?

"Read the report in front of you. What's the last thing you remember?" Ana asked me.

Looking down, I could see a complete report on a case that I apparently conducted not three hours ago. It even had my signature on it. No idea where it came from or even remember writing it. Concentrating, I didn't recognize any of the names or anything at all. "Did I do this?"

"You said that Marcella Blackmore was there. Did she touch you in any way?" Anastasia asked.

Holding up the paper in my handwriting, I could read that Marcella was indeed involved. It made me wonder how she was doing. Thinking of her brought a memory of her kissing me forward. "I think she kissed me. Is it important?"

"Not really. File the report as usual and pack your bags. I've got a real doozie for you this time," Ana replied, and I thought I heard her mumble something about keeping me away from Witches in the future.

"Oh? where am I going?" New assignments are always fun.

"The Pacific Northwest. There's been a rash of Bigfoot sightings and we want you to find him," Ana explained.

JACK DALTON, MONSTER HUNTER

HUNTER

BOOK 8

MY NAME IS Jack and I'm a monster hunter.

Imagine walking into a strange office and confronting people you don't know. They approach you, confused that they haven't seen you before and instead of identifying yourself you ask them a question. "Do you believe in Bigfoot?"

Naturally, the reaction I got was a crazy one.

"What? Who the hell are you?" the San Francisco California FBI Agents yelled.

I stuck out my left hand. "Special Agent in Charge, Jack Dalton. Nice to meet you." In my right hand were the credentials to prove it.

The trio of Agents in front of me only stared. I will admit that I didn't look like what most in the FBI would consider a proper Agent. My clothing looked more like I was in the military than the Bureau. Khaki colored pants and shirt was my norm on most cases that I handled. Standard FBI suits and shoes just didn't work for chasing paranormals through the woods. The Director was very firm about the dress code for all offices, but I wasn't directly under him. Even though I reported to his assistant, Anastasia, Mr. Hoover had to make monthly reports to a small sub-committee of Congress and the president himself about my activities. As a result, I figured a few rules could be broken in the name of comfort and ease of motion.

"I'm here for your files on the entity known as Bigfoot? The main office in Washington was supposed to have called ahead a week or so ago for me?" I asked.

Two of the men in front of me snorted and the third laughed, "You're on the wrong floor for that. You want the Agents for Humboldt County. Get back on the elevator and go up to the fourth floor. Just follow the signs."

"Uh, thanks. You have quite the office here," I replied.

THE SNORTING MEN joined the other in laughter as they brushed past me, continuing down the hallway. Only the speaker remained.

Shaking his head, he smirked at me. "It's all a big hoax anyway. Ape men in America? This isn't Africa, after all."

"We have Werewolves and Vampires already, why not Bigfeet? There have to be paranormals that we have yet to meet," I answered.

"If you say so. Here in California we have enough trouble with emerging crime and Demons. There were far too many of those things that slipped past the boys down in Conception. Good luck with your 'Foot' hunt," the Agent stated as he walked past me.

For just a moment I could relate to what he'd said. I wasn't a part of the law enforcement world in this part of the country. Only the internal gazette that all SAIC Agents received even mentioned events here. Organized crime was the big bad in this office. Unlike the East Coast, it wasn't the Mafia. Here in California, it was Yakuza and Chinese triads. They controlled the ports and who or what traveled through them.

Finding the elevators, I went up to the proper floor. The building was huge. In my limited experience, it seemed that only the office in Washington, DC was bigger. The San Francisco office was responsible for more than seventy-three thousand square miles of territory, including more than a dozen federal parks and facilities. There were more than a thousand people reporting in to this building alone.

One such person was the elevator operator. Unlike Portland, there were still operators in the elevators and they were armed. It was a unique merger of security and maintenance that made a certain amount of sense. Why pay two people to do a single job?

"Floor?" the man asked.

"Fourth please," I responded.

Moving his handle forward, the elevator man applied pressure and the car moved upwards. "You're new."

I glanced at him for a moment. "Jack Dalton, Magical Division. I'm just passing through."

"Interesting. Too bad you're not cleaning house, then. This place could use it," he replied.

Dropping my head forward, I sighed. My reputation had

preceded me. "Portland was an accident. If they had just cooperated as instructed, that mess might never have happened."

The elevator man shook his head. "Nope. In my position, I see it all. Hoover up in his kingdom has created tiny little fiefs. None of these folks want to give up the power that he's given them. Not even a little bit. You're an outsider to them, a threat, someone outside their control. Watch yourself when you come into contact with them. Portland scared them. They won't be as easy the next time...and here's your floor. Good luck."

The large metal doors opened with a slight screech and I stepped off. Looking back over my shoulder, I gave the elevator man a small salute. I was slowly getting used to strange advice coming from unusual places. Believing in otherworldly spiritual entities wasn't a prerequisite for this job, but it was trending that way. I knew the Gods existed, because I'd met at least one already.

I followed the signs in the hallways and finally found the office I was looking for at the end of the hall. Since the door was already ajar, I didn't knock. "Anyone here?"

Peeking inside, I could see two desks facing each other from opposite sides of the room. Filing cabinets lined the room, taking up all available wall space. Even the lone window was partially covered. Each desk had an agent behind it. But only one was awake. "What do you want?"

I pushed the door open and stepped inside. Whipping out my credentials, I said, "Special Agent Jack Dalton. Washington sent me to you. I'm investigating the Bigfoot issue in Humboldt County."

The scowl dropped off the Agent's face to be replaced by mirth. It started as a giggle that turned into a bold-faced laugh. "Simon, wake up!"

Simon, who I assumed was the other man, didn't budge. A faint snore could be heard from him.

Reaching behind him, the first agent grabbed a book from a small shelf and lobbed it at the desk across from him. Landing with a boom, the book bounced off the desk and hit the sleeping man in the head. He jerked awake with a "...the hell?"

"Nice of you to join us, Simon," the first agent replied.

Simon rubbed his eyes and glared at him. "What did I say about throwing things at me, Arthur."

The menace in Simon's voice when he spoke Arthur's name was clear even to me. I doubted these two would draw down on each other at work, but I was a stranger in a strange land here. I kept a small caliber weapon in a rear holder at the small of my back, and I was seriously considering reaching for it now.

"That you'd hurt me. But I know you didn't mean it. We have *company*." Arthur pointed in my direction.

Turning his glare to me, Simon spoke. "And?"

I blinked at him. "And what?"

Making a motion with his hand, Simon looked back at Arthur. "Don't keep me in suspense here. I have a lot to do today."

Arthur snorted but answered him, "He's here about the Bigfoot problem. Remember that order we got from Washington?"

"Seriously? I thought that was a joke." Simon reached into one of his desk drawers and pulled out a wrinkled and torn sheet of paper. Squinting at it for a moment, he looked back at me. "Dalton?"

"That's me," I replied.

"Arthur and I looked into this case and couldn't find any definitive proof of anything. More than half the reported sightings and 'evidence' collected for more than sixty years, if you can believe that, is pure fiction. Fake footprints and men in monkey suits. That's what this office has concluded in more than one report. As my dad would say, pure hokum. But what Washington wants Washington gets. Those three cabinets behind the door are what you want." Simon pointed.

Looking to my left, I could see three overstuffed file cabinets with even more stuff piled on top of them. I shook my head and looked back at the agents. "How far back do they go?"

Arthur smirked. "Officially? Since 1958 when the Humboldt

Times wrote an article about footprints and unusual sabotage at logging and mining sites in the area." Pointing at Simon, Arthur continued. "Our predecessors did a ton of research into the subject. Not much else to do around here. Our assigned area is pretty boring. Some of those reports go back at least a century. Not sure if you'll believe them, though. We didn't."

"There is more in our country than just heaven and hell. The Demon invasion should've proved that to us. What sort of Paranormals are around here?" I asked them.

Both men gave me surprised looks. "We don't have any of those here."

"Not possible. Paras are just about everywhere. With this much open space there has to be at least one or two Were Packs," I informed them.

Simon shook his head. "I don't think so. The tribes around here would've said something by now. Both the state and national parks take up a huge portion of our area. If they exist, they're hiding really well."

Arthur tapped his finger against his lips, then frowned. "There used to be a small reservation of Weres on the site of Fort Bragg. It was just a couple of buildings that included a really old barrack complex. Nobody had been interned there since the fort was abandoned in 1868. The Mendocino Indian Reservation was closed then, as well. The Army reopened it in the 1920s but closed it when the Magical Act was passed. I assumed that the Weres there left, but it's possible they might still be in the town." He looked at his partner for a moment then back to me. "We never thought to check."

"So, there might be Weres. What does that matter?" Simon asked me.

"A lot, actually. Werefolk are very observant, especially when it comes to their territory and hunting grounds. If Bigfoot exists, they would've run across it by now," I replied.

Simon slapped his desk. "Then why isn't there a report somewhere about it? We have Weres in the FBI, don't we?"

I smiled. "We do. But they, like most other Paras, don't trust us all that much. We did put them in camps for more than thirty years."

Arthur shook his head. "We let them serve in the military and alongside us."

"To do that they had to swear loyalty to our government and were not allowed to go back to the reservations and their families for more than five years without permission. We treated them like third-class citizens for years," I explained.

"Still, they do take the same oaths that we do," Simon stated.

"They do, and they respect them. What takes precedent for you, family or government?" I asked him.

"Family," Arthur blurted out even as Simon said, "Government." Both men glared at each other.

"See? It's a hard choice for some. I was raised by a Pack in Texas, one of the few humans to even do so. Most Weres trust Pack, family, friends, and then government." I explained to them.

Simon cocked his head to one side and gave me a strange look. "How did that come about? Being raised by them."

I chuckled, "It's a long story, but one I'll tell if you help me move these into one of the conference rooms." I hooked a thumb at the file cabinets.

"Now, that's just not fair, but you've got me interested. Come on, Arthur, let's get our exercise for the day." Simon stood and motioned to the other agent.

———

MOVING the cabinets took the better part of an hour because we couldn't find more than one hand truck. Walking them from side to side wasn't feasible as they were so heavy. Once we got them moved across the hall, I told them all about my dad, his service in the war, and the Texas Pack I was initiated into.

"So they just accepted you, like that?" Simon snapped his fingers.

"Pretty much. My dad was considered to be family by his men. Have you spoken to any Demon war vets?" I asked him.

"Just my own father, but he was in an artillery division, not on the front lines," Simon replied.

Pursing my lips, I nodded. "Not exactly the same thing. There's a saying that there are no atheists in a foxhole. According to my dad, that's how it was, fighting Demons. It was non-stop contact with the enemy. They were able to rip a tank open like it was made out of paper mache. Only the Weres in his unit kept him alive. The average lifespan of a tank crew was just under three days. Can you imagine what that must have been like? Knowing. Knowing for sure that your death was coming and that it would only be a statistic. Fighting for the greater good of humanity. That's what my mother told me was the justification for throwing troops into the maw of Europe. Don't get me wrong. I respect our government, but some things were just wrong. The Weres are what saved us. Something about their makeup or abilities enable them to kill Demons and make sure they stay dead. Four tanks were ripped from his personal unit. Four. When it was all said and done, the men that fought with him loved and respected him as much as anyone they grew up with. And when the last battle finally came they gave their all to keep him alive with their last breath. The Battle of the Line. It was the allies' last great push against the large mass of Demonic forces threatening France. No matter what the newsies say, or the historians portray, we, as in our government, didn't know what the Russians were planning. Like throwing a switch, they destroyed the Demon Gate and just about every Lord and Prince along with it. But it came too early to save my father and most of his crew. Tank number four was cut from beneath him and his men. In the aftermath they swore to protect and care for his family." Casting my eyes downward, I drew a mystical symbol on my chest with my finger. "We didn't know that at the time. So, you can imagine my mother's surprise when she got an invite to Texas. It seems that one of his crew was a Pack Alpha. The rest, as you say, is history."

"My dad and grandad don't speak of that time." Simon shook his head. "Dad spent several months in the hospital after the war ended. I don't know why. It's some big secret in the family."

"Demon shock. It was pretty common among those who served. In a few rare cases, there were possessions. Most of those were sent to secret army hospitals run by army intelligence or the VA itself," I explained.

"Really?" Simon asked me. He looked stunned.

"Pretty much. The Pack that took us in numbered among them a great many veterans. I had a good education on the supernatural world. It's one of the reasons I was selected for this job. I'm only starting to really see that now, actually," I answered.

"It was the Pack that suggested I join government service instead of the military. Because of Dad's service, I could have gone to West Point or the Citadel. I went to the Academy at Quantico instead. The mixed one, not the strictly human one. It was the first year for it." I leaned back against the conference room table. Rubbing my hands to shake off the dust, I looked over at Simon. "I like to think I made the correct choice. At least I get to see the country," I mused.

Simon snorted. "From what I know about you, I guess that's true." Nodding toward the door he gave Arthur a nudge. "We'll be down the hall if you have a question."

"Ok, thanks," I answered with a small wave of my hand. They closed the door behind them, leaving me alone with the files.

"Where to start," I mused as I scanned the drawers. They were labeled by year with the earliest being 1958. Using that as a starting point, I dove in.

———

"Whoever these guys were, they were really meticulous," I said as I closed the bottom drawer of the first cabinet. I could see where someone, possibly the two Agents who'd signed off on the initial reports, had been collecting this information for years. As Simon had stated, there were news articles and police documents going back to at least the turn of the century. Many, many, years before the great reveal in 1914. From what I knew of Paranormal society in that time, just these reports even existing was a rarity. I'd need to ask the guys down the hall who Gannon and Friday were.

The really early reports were from the 1800's. They consisted of Native American myths and legends. Many tribes believed in a wild man of the woods. Those in this area called the creatures *Stick Indians, Bush Indians, shampe, siatco, and sasquatch.* So far, my favorite of all the legends listed in the files was the one from the Lakota. *Chiye-Tanka* was the name given to what they called the shaggy men of the woods. *"Big elder brother"* is the literal translation. All the legends agreed on one thing. The creatures in the woods were non-violent spirits of nature, guardians of the woods.

So jump ahead a century or so and the reports change. European settlers and travelers took the legends and twisted them. No longer a guardian of the woods, the Chiye-Tanka was now a "woodland ape" or monster that kidnapped young girls or attacked trappers and miners. In 1860, a German explorer came across the name *"Wendigo."* He took this to be a version of the Sasquatch legend and propagated it. In his reports, the Wendigo was a monstrous creature that consumed those he caught in the woods. More a Demon than a woodland guardian. My own research, both at the FBI in Virginia and in the files, Anastasia gave me, claimed that the Wendigo was something else entirely. Something that I was sure to run into eventually.

In 1924 a group of miners in Washington state reported that they were attacked by a "group of seven-foot-tall ape men" that tossed rocks at them. The men were exploring the area looking to start a gold mine and spotted the creatures. One of the men, Fred Beck, fired off a shot and the apes attacked. The large creatures threw themselves at the miners' makeshift cabin and tossed boulders into the camp. The men claimed it was the ape men's revenge for being shot at. They moved their operations farther south. Later, investigators searched the canyon where the men had been encamped and found nothing credible proving the story. The site of the campground is now called Ape Canyon as a result.

There wasn't a credible report until 1958, but there are many unverified stories. Loggers and miners up and down the Pacific Coast were reportedly attacked and sabotaged by tall shaggy creatures that were able to move thousands of pounds of equipment at will and left large footprints everywhere.

A Northern California newspaper called the Humboldt Times printed a story about someone who'd found enormous footprints. They jokingly reported that the Abominable Snowman now had a cousin. Yeti was the name that indigenous people in the Himalayas called their own race of shaggy mountain people. The creatures, similar to Bigfoot, were supposed to live in unreachable areas and leave large tracks. Considered sacred by many, there were no known pictures of them. Agents Friday and Gannon gave the Asian reports little credence, but the Humboldt report was just the beginning. The Northwest was suddenly seized by Bigfoot fever and footprints were showing up everywhere!

Now there were new tracks, complete with pictures of a site in Weitchpec, up on the Klamath River. They were found by an ortho-pedic doctor who swore the tracks weren't a hoax. This was the report Anastasia referred to when she assigned this case to me. The doctor and his family had some pull in Washington and made it known that he wanted the instance to be investigated. Hence the reason I was here. But first I needed to talk to the guys down the hall.

Simon and Arthur weren't surprised, and actually anticipated my questions.

"Those guys. Yeah..." Simon gave Arthur a look. "They followed Bureau policy to the letter except when it came to the Bigfoot case. Friday was obsessed with the idea of those creatures. He and his partner Gannon spent a lot of off-duty hours working on those files. It wasn't until we had an upper management change that they were forced to stop."

"How so?" I asked them.

Arthur snorted. "They got caught red-handed with reports piled up in their desks. The new guy just happened to be checking on open and current projects for all agents. You know the rules. No off-duty work in the office."

Simon took up where his partner left off. "They didn't get fired though. Just reassigned." He barked out a laugh.

Arthur giggled. "They got volunteered for a Hollywood production. They wanted real-life experience to build on. Do you know how boring and tedious Los Angeles is these days?"

I shook my head. This was actually my first time in California, not that I was telling them that.

"We talked about the war already. LA was where most of the refugees went. The army closed down and declared most of Southern California off limits, including most of the valleys surrounding the city. It's a mess. Most of the big studios lost their back lots to developers, and housing is at a premium there. Television is the next big thing as well. The positions came up and at first it looked good until you factor in the cost of living. Four hundred dollars a month? Even gas is mega high down there. We pay about thirty-five cents a gallon here, but I hear they pay almost fifty cents. Too rich for my blood. Most of my pay would be gone," Arthur explained. "It was either transfer or quit."

"And the files?" I asked him.

"Government property. Way too hard to delete them. You're the first to request them since then," Simon replied.

"Ok, thanks. I'll try to do them justice."

———

"The attacks aren't working, sire," Cenulf informed his war leader. "The humans continue to encroach upon us. This technology of theirs is too powerful for our weapons. They use cold iron in everything!"

"Then think of something else. You are far older and smarter than the short-lived fools. Look at the Bans and figure a way. We will not bow to them, Cenulf. No matter what my cousins or the Council says, I will not yield my birthright to them. We were here first!" Jharak Forestbuilder slammed his spear into the ground and glared at Cenulf before storming from the glade.

Cenulf sighed as his lord left him. For more than a century, he and his scouts had protected the forests and fields from any and all interlopers. The natives of this land were easy to fool. Any sound or strange occurrence was blamed upon the Watchers in the Woods or, as the natives called them, the Guardians. He laughed to himself. Guardians. When his people came to these lands there was nothing here, no humans, no paranormals, no other Fae. There were reports of shaggy creatures in the woods, but that was a made-up fiction of children. No true sign of any such creature had been found. At least that is what the elders claimed. They made a good decoy against the humans, though. Fae Magick could be both beautiful and deadly if wielded in the proper hands. His hands. The human park rangers and road builders they could divert and wipe their minds but only so many at once. It was the lumbermen and the miners that were the worst dangers. Like most humans, they had little regard for the land and what was here before them. Slash, burn, rip, and mine was all they knew. His recent demonstration near the river hadn't worked. Maybe his lord was right. More force might be needed after all. Tonight, he would gather his warriors.

———

"ANA, this seems so much like a wild goose chase up here. I have the reports you'd requested. They go back way longer than just a couple of years." I explained to her the personal hobby of the two Agents and the three bulging file cabinets.

"You still need to try, Jack. This one comes down straight from the Director. The latest victim, a Doctor Charles Johnson, has been screaming at everyone he knows here, and it's working. For someone from San Jose, he knows a lot of powerful people," Ana stated. "Just go up to Weitchpec and poke around. Use your judgement and your training. If it's all a hoax, then write it up and send it to me. But if it's not, I expect you to do your job. You chose this life, Jack. Live up to it."

"Is the Director warming to the idea of the Magical Division yet?" I asked her.

Ana laughed. "What do you think? He's obstinate that way."

"I really only ask because of something someone here said," I explained.

"And?"

"He said that the bosses here are creating their own fiefdoms beyond the control of Washington and the Director." There was complete silence on the other end of the line. I couldn't even hear her breathing.

Finally, Ana spoke. "Interesting. It might be time for Mr. Hoover to make a journey out there, then. Call it a fact-finding mission. Was it one of the Agents that told you this?"

"No. They still have elevator operators in the building. It was one of them," I answered.

"He would know. Fine. I'll take care of it. Complete your mission and all will be right with the world, Jack. Take care of yourself and watch your back. If what you just told me is true, you might be in danger. I have big plans for you, so don't go and get yourself killed," Ana informed me. And then she hung up.

I stared at the phone receiver for a moment before hanging it up. Plans? It was easy to forget that while Anastasia was my direct boss, she was also Director Hoover's personal assistant. Speaking to her was like talking to him. Gathering my wits about me, I said goodbye to the office here and set out for Northern California and my actual case.

———

Weitchpec.

What a name. Some of the collected research said that the whole area was part of the Yurok tribal lands, and many of the names in the region reflected either ancestral villages or their districts. Technically, most of Humboldt County was part of the reservation set aside for them after the Klamath and Salmon River war of 1851-1856. It had only been a century since they had been settled. The reservation was created by executive order, as well. Something quite unusual for the time period. Despite pressure from miners and loggers, the tribe was allowed to remain upon their own land, mostly.

The area wasn't just Yurok, though. Civilization had come to the area, and so had the Parks Department. Both national and state departments lay claim to large portions of territory. Loggers and miners still ventured into the territory, but now under state or federal mandate. It was considered progress.

I took highway 101 North up through the redwoods all the way to Eureka. It was my first real look at the Pacific Ocean and all its glory. My brief time in San Francisco was entirely too busy for me to have visited the bay there. Eureka called itself the Queen of the Ultimate West. It was a hub of fisheries, logging, mining, and tourism. Literally thousands went there to just get away. So much history and so little time. Maybe one day I'd come back.

Cutting east, I entered the Yurok reservation and the city of Weitchpec. Calling it a city was reaching. It was more of a hunting camp, crossed with a ghost town. A few old buildings mixed with hunting camps and run-down houses made up the town. Doctor Johnson owned what my briefing papers called a vacation home on the river.

Two hours of wrong turns and dusty roads brought me to my destination. I had to rub my eyes a few times. The 'vacation home' was actually a huge Victorian mansion that would've given Marcella and her family a run for their money. Looking around, I wondered how they got all the building supplies up the goat road I came in on.

I pulled up to the massive home in a cloud of road dust. Climbing out of home and office, I glanced at the outside of my truck. It looked dull in the bright sun. If I didn't know better, I wouldn't have believed it was supposed to be yellow and black. It was so encrusted with mud, crud and leaves, it looked to be camouflaged. So busy looking at all the dirt, I completely missed the man standing on the porch watching me. So much for my situational awareness.

"Are you with the FBI?" a voice asked me.

Shielding my eyes, I looked up at the porch. "Special Agent Jack Dalton, Magical Division. And you are?"

"Charles Johnson, Doctor Charles Johnson. Come on inside and I'll explain the situation." The doctor waved at me.

Thirteen was the number of steps I climbed to reach the porch. I hoped it didn't mean I was in for an unlucky day. The porch was wide and seemed to stretch out far into the distance. Looking closer, I could see it was an optical illusion as it wrapped around the house. Whoever built the place was very skilled. Holding out my hand, I smiled at Dr. Johnson. "Nice to meet you."

Cautiously, the doctor took my hand and squeezed it. I could tell right away he was going to be trouble. Trying to assert dominance over a government Agent was not the way to start the day off properly. He led me to a table and we sat down.

"My family has owned this house and much of the land around it until that thief Teddy Roosevelt took it away from us in 1905," he said. "It was bad enough that the Indians we fought off for it were being given entire sections. We took this to mean that we should take a more 'active' role in government to prevent more loss. Now this." Johnson slammed his hand down on the table. Scowling, the doctor continued. "Thirty years or so ago my father started a logging and mining interest. He wanted to profit from our land before more of it was taken from us.

"I don't see..." I started to say.

Johnson pointed his finger at me. "Stop right there. I'm getting to it. There was vandalism right from the start. Footprints. Wrecked equipment. Even a few injuries. But local law enforcement stopped it. Indians were arrested, and it stopped for a few years. Now the prints are back and my foremen are telling me that entire swaths of land that I own are damaged beyond all repair!"

"How do you damage trees and rocks?" I asked him.

"Do they teach you nothing in the FBI? Spikes! Someone drove iron spikes into ALL the old growth trees. Every. Single. One of them! And the mines? Flooded. It's going to cost hundreds of dollars to pump them out. That is, if we're even able to!" Johnson shouted at me.

I nodded. The logging industry wasn't something I knew a lot about, but sabotage I could smell a mile away. It was only a small matter of discovering what sort of tricks were being played here. For trees, iron spikes seemed to be it. If not found they could seriously damage a sawmill.

"So, what are you going to do about these beasts plaguing me?" Johnson asked.

"Other than telling me about your troubles, you have yet to show me any evidence that Bigfoot exists or that paranormals are the ones damaging your property and business. How would creatures that exist only in the forest even know how to sabotage trees like that or divert a creek to fill a mine with water?" I asked him.

"They had help, obviously. The savages around here deny it, of course. I've had the sheriff, CBI, and the parks department out here. Indian affairs didn't do squat. Bigfoot is an obsession around here," Johnson fumed.

Cocking my head to one side, I watched the doctor. "Still no hard proof. What did the Yurok elders say? I assume you or Indian Affairs asked them."

Johnson barked a laugh. "They actually support me. 'Forest dwellers' is what they said. Damn troublemakers."

That brought me up short. All the research Friday and Gannon had done called the creatures *Elder Brother or Stick Indians*. Terms like that didn't equate to forest dwellers. Did something else live there? "What did they say exactly, do you remember? It might be important."

Scrabbling through the papers in front of him, he pulled out a form. "The BIA wrote it all down. Something about liability. Read it for yourself."

I took the paper from him and gave it a look. Little tree dwellers, or Canotila (chawn-oh-tee-lah,) was the exact wording. That word made me frown. There'd been a note about that in the files I'd copied. Looking at the doctor, I raised one finger. "Let me check something in my van."

I stepped outside and popped open the passenger side. I had my own form of filing and tried to stay as current as possible. The two small cabinets where the seat used to be helped me do that. After searching three files and an envelope of pictures, I found what I remembered. Native terminology. Canotila was what the natives around here called the Fae. Rocking back on my heels, I took a deep breath. Fairies were a different sort of problem than a big shaggy thing with big feet.

The Fae had an interesting history in America. They had established an embassy in Washington practically the day after the world discovered that paranormals existed by purchasing a house and setting up shop. A few treaties were signed and deals made shortly before the start of the Demon war, and then nothing. No one went in and no one came out of the embassy. Not even the staff. But figures could be seen from the windows and somehow the shrubbery was trimmed. OSS and FBI investigations failed to discover anything and since it was still foreign soil...Needless to say, people forgot they existed. Someway, somehow, they have this effect on some humans.

Me included.

I investigated and battled a Fae creature just last year and don't remember a bit of it. There are reports though. Ana hasn't mentioned my loss of memory, but I kept a copy of the primary report and at the urging of Marcella Blackmore of all people, I started keeping a diary. Anastasia once told me that there are those in the government that know the Fae are real, though. It made me wonder if those mysterious officials know about this place?

Writing myself a copy of the information, I placed the original, still unfiled, back where I found it. With luck it might even stay there. As I walked inside, I thought about how I would present this to Johnson.

"Sorry about that. A word you said rang a bell and I needed to check my notes. The office in San Francisco had a file on the area up here and I took notes from it," I explained to the man.

"What word?" he asked me.

"Canotila. It means people of the woods, or people of the trees in Lakota," I replied.

"Woods, trees, forest, whatever the hell you like to say, these things are destroying my property and I want it stopped right now!" Johnson thundered at me. "I asked for help and they send me one, snot-nosed kid up here. I'm going to call my congressman and give him a piece of my mind!"

I held up both my hands palm out towards the man. "Call them. Be sure you explain that I was given no hard proof and no chance as of yet to look for proof. Investigations take time. Nothing is as instantaneous as shown on television. That, sir, is a fantasy. Be sure to give whichever congressman you call my best. Unlike the sheriff or the parks departments, I work at the behest of both Congress and the president. Director Hoover gives me direction but even he is technically NOT my boss."

I smiled inwardly as Johnson's mouth dropped open in surprise. If there was more than a handful of men who'd stood up to the man in his lifetime, I'd have been surprised.

"Now. Do you want me to still look for evidence or are you making that phone call?" I asked him.

————

THERE WAS TOO much rock at the mining sites to find any hard physical evidence, but I at least needed to look around. At first glance, I knew what Johnson was doing was against the law.

Modern mining techniques involved the heavy use of explosives and excavating machines. Basically, they would dynamite and dig up the mountain in search of whatever mineral they sought.

What he and his company were doing was very much old school. The mine tunneled into the earth like a mole. The rough-cut entrance was shorn up with heavy-cut timbers and steel girders. It was something out of an old movie.

"What are you digging for here?" I asked Johnson's foreman, Richard Gryb.

Pulling out a handkerchief, Richard wiped his entire face off before answering me. He motioned to the mine and said, "His nibs would say we're looking for copper, but it's a gold mine. Nothing good ever came from lying to the government. It's an old mine started by the boss's father. We ran a few tests last year confirming the presence of quartz and a minor trace of gold. Whoever it was that started this mine was on the right track."

"Have you found any?" I looked around the area. "Gold, that is?"

"Some. Lots of quartz and a few gemstones as well as garnets. Not enough to bring in the really heavy equipment just yet. We'd just hit a good vein when all the trouble began. At first it was little stuff, sugar in the gas tanks, cut brake lines, things left to spoil. We didn't think much of it except for the gas part. Then the footprints appeared. They were everywhere around the camp. A rockslide closed shaft two and partially covered the main one." Richard made a stop motion with his hands. "Before you say it, we did have protections in place. Netting was placed all around the entrances as a precaution. Someone or something removed them first. My boys didn't find neither hide nor hair of the nets."

I scratched my head. None of what was being described sounded like a mindless beast. To open a gas tank and insert sugar meant some sort of mechanical knowledge. The same with the nets. "The locals were questioned?"

"First thing. We had guards posted early on and they didn't see anything. Johnson doesn't know this, but we'd placed lights all around the mine entrances beforehand and somehow like magic the nets disappeared! That isn't the worst of it." Richard shook his hands. "How did they flood the mines? Even my engineers can't figure that one out."

"How so?" I asked him.

"There's a creek about a mile north of this site, way over on the other side." Richard waved past the large rocky hill. "It used to flow into the Klamath river, but someone or something diverted it underground. How is that possible? My guys say it's something they couldn't do overnight with all the equipment in the world at their fingertips. So how did the bigfooted things do it? This place is haunted. It's the only answer that fits."

"What about the logging part?" I asked him.

Richard snorted. "That operation is more screwed than mine is. Some of the same issues mechanically, but add in lost loads and trees falling the wrong way and you have more injuries and utter disaster."

"Lost loads?" I asked him.

"Sure. Basically, they load the cut trees onto flatbeds and haul them out to the main roads and then on to the sawmill. The boss had his own operation, but too many spiked trees shut it down for weeks. I think they're using one in Hoopa now. The loads are supposed to be strapped down, but somehow the straps fall off or are cut. They have trucks with braces like this." Richard held up his hands like forks. "The braces holding the trees in fail somehow and it all falls off the truck onto the highway. So then the state and the local police get involved. It's a big ass mess I'm glad I don't have to deal with. This is enough."

I nodded. This was so much more than the good doctor had failed to mention. "Just how flooded are the mines?"

Richard frowned. "Pretty bad. This valley we're in is about a hundred feet above sea level. Go down, like our mines, more than that, and there's water. My guys have enough to worry about without having to do their jobs in ankle or waist high water. I've got pumps being brought in, but unless we can dam up the creek, we're screwed."

"And you can't do that because..." I started to ask.

"...it's part of the reservation and Indian land." Richard finished. "They claim they didn't do it but as I've said before, they won't help fix it. BIA won't help either."

Thanking Richard, I stepped away and walked back to my van. Almost none of what I'd learned read as Bigfoot to me. It was either an outside influence, members of the Yurok tribe, or the Fae. I did consider that there could be combinations of the three as well. Fake footprints were nothing new. Ever since the 1958 news article, there'd been prints found all up and down the state.

Heading back to the Johnson estate, I heard the sirens and smelled the smoke before I saw the actual fire.

———

"IT'S A COMPLETE LOSS! A hundred years of history, gone in an instant! Who would do such a thing?" Johnson rubbed his temples with both hands, his eyes clenched shut as if in pain.

There wasn't all that much left of the house. A couple of anti-quated fire engines were pulling away, heading back to the towns they'd come from. Park Department tankers were hosing down the surrounding acres to prevent wildfire flare-ups but from the looks of things, it was really bad.

"It's a god damn conspiracy is what this is! Everyone is involved, too. You, the Yuroks, BIA, Bigfoot, and the damn parks department. Everyone!" Johnson pointed at me as he raged.

Leaving Johnson to his madness and his children, I walked past him, surveying the fire. The house and everything within a ten-foot radius was burned. Interestingly enough, it didn't look as though it had spread farther than that. You would think sparks coming off the structure would have ignited the woods and fields.

"You'd think that, wouldn't you," a man behind me replied.

"Oops. I didn't realize I said that aloud," I told him. Holding out my hand, I said, "Jack Dalton, FBI."

"Bradshaw, Ted Bradshaw. I'm the county's fire marshal and I know who you are. News around here travels fast. Johnson over there should just quit now. He's pissed off the forest people enough."

Interested, I turned and looked him in the eyes. "How so?"

"I grew up here. My people are here. Folks like Johnson don't understand. They come with their money and their influence and they lord it over us all. You don't ignore local customs and people. This plan of his," Bradshaw paused and looked at the smoldering ruins, "It was doomed to fail. They won't stand for it. He should have asked first, made an offering. Tried to accommodate them first."

"So not Bigfoot then?" I asked.

Bradshaw burst out laughing. Slapping me on the back, he chuckled. "Only city folk believe that hokum. If you want tourist money, you have to do...things. Big shaggy monsters that live in the forest that no one ever sees? Hollywood, the town drunk, swears he saw one once, but he also says he saw a dragon once. Trust me, they're a myth. This was caused by something else."

"If someone wished to make an offering to the forest people and possibly meet with them, how would you go about it?" I asked the man.

Bradshaw shut up, immediately realizing he had said way too much. "I..."

I held up my hand and shook my head. "You aren't in trouble. I don't work for Johnson, regardless of what the rumors might be. It's my job to police the supernatural in this country. If the forest people are causing trouble, then they are who I need to contact."

"This won't get back to him, then?" Bradshaw nodded toward where Johnson stood.

Looking over my shoulder I could see the man screaming at his hired help and berating whom I assumed to be his wife and son. I looked back at the local. "Nope. Not my circus or my monkeys. Help me out here, please."

———

Oak, Ash, and Thorn. That was what I was told would protect me. I had a couple of twigs bound together with a sprig of blackberry vine and an old nail in my pocket. Cold forged iron was a sure thing. The rest, not so much. I just needed to remember to not shove my hand in my pocket.

The meeting place was several miles inside Klamath Park, along the river. Not on any of the maps I'd been given, the spot could only have been found with local assistance. Johnson couldn't have been a help for this.

It was something like you'd see in a European forest, if you could find one untouched, or from Salisbury plain. A small circle of dolmens surrounded a stone altar. I wasn't part of any of the earth-based religions that had sprung up in the years since the big reveal, but as an FBI agent I was aware of them. According to Bradshaw, I was to lay an offering and say a prayer to whichever deity I wished and one of the people would appear. He claimed he himself had never done this, but his familiarity belied his own words.

Patting my pocket, I approached the stones. Looking closer at them, I was reminded of pictures I'd seen of Stonehenge. That very fact was impossible! Dolerite was a type of rock formed around volcanos, but not something commonly found in this part of the world. Unfortunately, that was the complete extent of my geology knowledge. How they got here, set up like this, was a mystery to me.

I laid an apple on the altar. Unable to decide who to pray to, I sent good thoughts towards the old man I kept running into. He was either a figment of my imagination or some sort of entity. Rocking back on my heels I looked around. "How long is this supposed to take?"

"What is time to those who don't age? You are but an acorn compared to an Oak," a voice answered.

Reverting back to my training, I used the corners of my eyes to search for glamours and hidden shields. The FBI might not have any magic users in it, but we did hire good consultants. Sensing rather than seeing someone to my right, I spun around to see a faint shimmer. "Even acorns can hurt if fired from the right gun. I know where you are now. Come out so we might talk."

"We don't talk to humans. Your people are the destroyers," the voice said from the opposite side of the clearing.

"You're speaking to me now," I replied. "This won't end now. You've taken it too far. Johnson will retaliate the only way he knows how. If you were trying to save the land, you've lost. Burning the house was the wrong move."

"Getting our point across is important," the voice replied.

"Only if the question is understood. His father started the project. Did you ask him to stop? The son was never told, if you did. You forget the shortness of our lives," I explained. "If you are who I think you are, you won't be able to fight him when he retaliates. Machines of iron will lay waste to the land and explosives will destroy it."

"This is our land and we are allowed to protect it!" A different, more forceful voice spoke close to me.

Spinning around, I came face to face with who I assumed to be a Fae lord. Motioning to the forest and river, I spoke. "This is part of the United States now. You've had your chance for almost fifty years now to tell us about your people and ask for recognition. Why didn't you?"

"Who are you to dictate to me?" The elf pointed his finger at me. I expected to die right then and there. The mythical 'elf shot' was a doomsday type spell that had a 100% kill rate. My pants pocket warmed up suddenly and the amulet bag around my neck actually burned me.

The elf gaped when I didn't die.

I'd forgotten about the old man's charm, or it was the prayer I sent. The protection I seemed to be getting wasn't going to make me start worshiping the one-eyed God any time soon either. I did appreciate it though and if given the chance would thank him. "Now you've attacked a government official. I'm actually trying to help you here. Answer me this. Are your people behind the Bigfoot vandalism? That's my mission. To find the truth."

Jharak Forestbuilder waved his hand, canceling the now failed curse. "Argh! Human magick. I sense a God around you as well. The truth? You wouldn't know the truth if it bit you. You humans will believe anything. Create belief in the unknown and you fall for it so easily."

I smiled at that. "Not if you step away from the myth itself. Opening gas caps and using sugar betrays the myth you've created. The Indians here won't take the blame for the house. Not after the fire marshal writes his report."

Jharak snorted, "He won't blame us. The people here wouldn't dare."

"No, he won't. But he knows the truth and it will come out eventually. Secrets are like that. Nothing stays hidden forever. I convinced him to call it faulty wiring or something similar. It won't stop Johnson, though. He really does want a hunting lodge and resort built here, and he doesn't care about the reservation or state park boundaries to do so. Unless you harm him directly..." I looked the Fae in the eyes. "Don't plan on it. It's my job to police you. If I have to level the forest for miles around, I will."

I gave the elf a speculative look, then asked, "What are you protecting so much?"

"We came here before there was anything. Our job is to protect. This is a sanctuary for our people," he replied.

"Underhill or other?" I asked.

Jharak's eyes narrowed. "You know much for a human. Look past the altar and unfocus your eyes."

Doing as I was told, a city came into view. Above or below the ground, it was spectacular. Architecture beyond what man can even imagine. They did indeed have something to protect. If you ever dreamed of visiting Oz this might have been what you'd see. Glass towers that seemed to reach the sky joined with plants and trees not seen by humans, ever. Paradise on Earth.

"So you see, then," he said.

"Contact your embassy and have them make a deal. Forget about your act of silence and whatever rules you feel you need to enforce. Johnson has far too much leverage in Washington for you to stand up directly against him. He doesn't control me, but he could. Go to the president directly if you have to. He has the power to circumvent Congress through executive order. The Magical Act of 1957 gives you plenty of power. You just need to act upon it. If, and I do mean if, I tell Johnson of your people's existence, he will do his damnedest to destroy you. He is a vengeful man," I explained. "Dying for principal is stupid."

"Why help us?" the Elf asked.

"It's my job. Yes, I hunt monsters for a living. But I'm also supposed to coordinate with the paranormal communities. I might be one man but I've the entire government behind me," I answered.

The Fae lord shook his head. "You need to learn to lie better. Come see us in a century, if you still live. We will teach you."

In an instant the Elf faded from my view. Searching the area, I couldn't find a single shimmer or trace that they'd even been there. Not even a footprint, big or otherwise.

"Did we make a deal or what?" I asked into the forest. Utter silence was my answer. "Damn elves, I swear they're worse than Vampires."

Hiking back to my van, I ran through the entire conversation. The notes I had on the Fae said they were tricksters, but I think they were being incredibly frank with me. It made me wonder just what was in that city of theirs that was so important. Whipping out my journal, I wrote down everything I could remember. It would help with my official report as well. Writing my reports and trying to explain the craziness of them took longer, much longer.

For the entire drive back to the Johnson place, I considered my options. If they did go through channels, then I should try and slow down the doctor on my end here. Even though he held the high ground politically, I could report his mining and logging infractions with the Department of the Interior. Any report I made would add to the file as documented infractions. It would help in the future. Without the Faes' aid, though, I would be fighting an uphill battle all by myself.

Things had changed since I had been gone. There was now a shiny new airstream trailer parked on the site, along with a bulldozer and work crew. Johnson himself stepped out just as I pulled in.

"Hey! Did you talk to the tribe elders?" Johnson asked.

I frowned. "Elders?" When I'd left, the man was red with anger and swearing up a storm.

"Sure. You were going to spread the word about the hooligans that burned down the house. Had they seen them at all? Sheriff Mays and the fire marshal told me it was definitely arson. Who knew that escaped prisoners from Sacramento were hiding up here?"

I felt myself blink a couple of times. What was happening here? "So no more Bigfoot?"

"That old legend? Only out-of-towners believe that," Johnson replied.

I first rubbed my eyes, then my forehead. Somehow in the time it took me to drive from the meeting place to here they'd altered the good doctor's memory completely. Did they now wish a treaty?

"Do you still plan to build the lodge your father dreamed of?" I asked him.

Johnson frowned at me. "That old plan? No way the Parks department would let me do it. How'd you find out about that?"

I muttered a nonsensical reply about a rumor I'd heard that placated him. "Do you think the convicts were the source of the other vandalism as well?"

"That's what the sheriff thinks. I guess we didn't need you after all, Agent Dalton. Sorry you made the trip up here." Johnson shook my hand, dismissing me.

What just happened? I asked myself that as I sat watching a bulldozer clear the house site. If the Fae could twist someone's memory so much, why hadn't they done so before? What was the purpose of dragging it out so long and letting it go so far? All I could think about was something one of my Academy professors had once said. Paranormal cultures might as well be alien, as much as we understand them. He meant humans, but I got the big picture. Even though I was raised by Wolves, partially, I didn't completely understand them. Maybe you just had to be born that way.

———

"SHOULD I ASK WHY?" Cenulf asked his lord.

"No. Our Seers held the answer I searched for. This man is important and his 'solving' our problem is, as well. Erasing the matter should've been done in the beginning." Jharak held up his hand to stop Cenulf's protest. "'Twas done in my father's time. It's done. The humans will remember what they need to as will this Jack person. Are our people in place?"

Cenulf bowed before his lord. "Of course. He won't leave the valley with his memory intact."

"Warn your team. He is in possession of a very powerful amulet. They won't be able to touch him physically," Jharak commented.

"They will accomplish the task or not return," Cenulf stated.

"It will have to do, then." Jharak looked out at the river near the place of the meeting. "I have betrayed my father's memory and contacted our brethren to the east. Promises will be made and treaties respected because of this."

Cenulf stayed silent. It wasn't his place to correct or comment on what his lord was saying.

———

NONE of what the Fae cared about bothered me. As far as I could tell, there was no Bigfoot and the Fae issue was solved. It was a huge question as to why bother in the first place if they had the power to just alter everyone's memories like that. Why wait so long?

Looking ahead of me, I could see brake lights. The tiny bit of traffic around me was slowing as I came upon a massive tree across the road and road maintenance chopping it up. Rolling down my window, I questioned the officer who approached.

"Will this take long?" I asked.

"Not that long. You'll hardly remember a thing," the blue clad officer replied. The sun was so bright it sparkled off the shiny buttons and badge of his uniform.

"You'd be surprised…" I started to say.

———

"…SURPRISED." I said. Blinking a few times, I looked out the front windshield. "Why am I on the side of the road?"

Glancing up at the rearview mirror, I couldn't see any traffic behind me. "What was I thinking about?"

I looked at the map beside me and could see the route traced out in red, but it didn't register why I was on it. Flipping up the center console lid, I looked at the safe contained inside. It appeared to be locked. My report and diary should be inside there. I always wrote in triplicate, filed the copies and put the original under lock and key.

Spinning the dials, I opened it up and gave my journal a read.

I might not remember it all, but the highlights were in my report. No one but Anastasia would see it, though. Stuff like this was why my job existed, after all. I checked my mirrors, put the van in gear, and pulled out onto the highway. There was a large FBI contingent in Seattle. I would head up there to file this. Something this hot couldn't be trusted to the main office in California. Way too political and way too cutthroat, if my notes were to be believed.

————

MORE THAN A THOUSAND feet above me, up on a hill, a shaggy form stepped out of the dense woods. The creature's soft brown eyes watched me as I researched my missing memory. Wiser than most living creatures walking the Earth, it missed very little. The Fae's game was tedious at best and maybe it was time for the Elder Brothers to up their own game and break some rules. The so-called Paranormals needed to be brought to heel, regardless. Using Magick not seen for millennia, the creature transported himself to the hidden realm known as the World Species Council.

The time of seclusion was over.

JACK DALTON, MONSTER HUNTER

BOOK 9

My name is Jack Dalton and I'm a Monster Hunter!

"Jack, I need you in Washington as soon as humanly possible," Anastasia informed me over the secure line.

I was in San Francisco at the main FBI headquarters, wrapping up my reports. Every large office in America had a secure line to the Director's office. They had to. As the country grew, so did the criminal element. J. Edgar Hoover liked to be on top of things at all times.

"What's going on there?" I asked her.

"Trouble. Our investigative units responded to a series of deaths in and around the DC beltway area. We've got a serial killer on our hands here, and everything points to a Vampire doing it," Anastasia explained.

"How many Vamps are in your area, anyway?" She was the only one I'd ever met, outside of the guy at the Academy. He was supposedly the go-to guy for Paranormal interactions.

There was a long moment of silence on the other end of the phone. "Two that I'm aware of, counting myself. Jack, you have to understand something here. Other than the Director, no one knows I'm a Vampire."

Now that explained a whole lot. In this country, Vampires were a rarity. Eastern Europe and Russia were their primary haunts, especially after the great Purge. If she wasn't known..."Boss, that makes you one of the primary suspects."

"You think I don't know that? The Director is on my side, but this is Washington. Backstabbing is almost an Olympic sport here. The Magical Division must be here to run the investigation if it is a Vampire. Get here as soon as you can," Anastasia directed even as she hung up the phone.

I stared at the receiver in my hand. It could turn into a Witch hunt if Ana was suspected of the crimes. And it would signal the death knell for any other Paranormals in government service. I needed to get moving.

Finishing up my reports, I pulled out all the maps. From here, the fastest way east was Highway 50. Up through Sacramento and across Nevada, the highway followed the old horse and wagon trails. Not a lot of towns between here and Denver, Colorado. But if I was going to get there fast, it would have to do. For a moment, I considered catching a flight, but I'd have to leave the van here in California. I seriously doubted the guys at the semi-secret garage would build me another one so soon. Drive it was.

Hunting Bigfoot had been a bust. Other than footprints and rumors I'd found nothing. It was too bad that Johnson's house burned down, but faulty wiring will do that. Sitting in the file room, I tapped my finger to my lips. Something about the report in front of me wasn't quite right though. Notes that I didn't write were in my journal saying I *did* find something up there. But I had nothing to prove it. No pictures, notebooks, interviews, or anything other than the same reports saying there was no proof of Bigfoot or other creatures.

"Screw it. I need to go." I scrawled my name at the bottom and dropped the file in the outgoing mail. Copies would be distributed to the office here and in Washington, per procedure.

————

HIGHWAY 50 WAS a nice scenic sort of road. Once I got through Sacramento and into the Eldorado National Forest, the traffic thinned out considerably. Looking at all the trees, it was really hard to believe that just a couple hundred miles to the South lay what the locals called the Demon Wasteland. Grinding the Demon advance to a halt... the army had held that from Salinas, to Fresno, to just outside of Las Vegas. Our world and the Demon Wasteland were the antitheses of each other. Anything the Demons touched was despoiled. Trees, cities, people, everything, were turned into mutated or twisted forms of themselves. Much of the area, even now, almost fifteen years later, was still under martial law. Fortunately, no one had seen a living Demon in about that long.

Kachunk! Kachunk! Rumble, rumble, rumble. Kachunk!

"...the hell?" Glancing down at my gauges told me absolutely nothing. The noises continued but weren't as loud as before. Reaching out, I patted the dashboard of my trusty delivery van. "That's a good girl. Please hold on so I can get you fixed."

I checked my mirrors and slowed down to a crawl while I checked the map. Stopping wasn't an option; it might not start up again! I'd passed a place called Eureka, and it was too far back to return to. The towns of Ruth and Ely looked too far away to push the engine. I was screwed. Folding the map a couple of times, I scanned it for anything that might help me. A ranger station, military post, Indian reservation, something. Moving my thumb, I spotted something. Belmont Mill. A tiny speck on the map, it looked to be just a bit south of my position. Speeding up, I looked for a turn off or sign for one.

"White Pine County Road #5." There was a sign and an arrow pointing toward possible salvation, Belmont Mill.

Rumble, kachunk, kachunk, rumble, bump!

The dry and dusty county road seemed to be making it worse! Having second thoughts about this side trip, I almost turned around, but then I saw the beginnings of civilization, a town in the desert.

In a cloud of dust, I rolled into town, parking in front of what appeared to be a boarding house and diner. Belmont Mill was an actual mill. I could see a four-story building up the hill with assorted mining equipment in use. Steam from a pair of smokestacks shot into the sky not too far away. A few small houses and shops were scattered about with no sense of city planning.

Saying a small prayer to a new-found God, I shut off the engine and climbed out.

"You get lost?" a big burly man asked as he and three others stepped out of the diner.

"Engine trouble. I saw the sign for town and took a chance. Is there anyone available to look at it and is there a phone I can use?" I replied to them.

The first man glanced at the others before speaking. "We've got a small garage for the mine. I can have our guy take a look if you like. It's quite the ways to the next biggest town."

"That would be dandy," I replied. "Is there a phone too?"

Maggie's boarding house had a phone, as well as a spare room I could use. A very talkative sort, Maggie seemed like she didn't see very many new folks here in town. She wouldn't shut up about the town and how they came to be here.

From what I'd been able to decipher, the town was built in 1925 when both silver and lead had been discovered here. Most of the residents dated from that time period with the exception of a few dozen of the miners. They'd come as refugees from the Demon incursion. Something similar had occurred all over the Southwest. People just looking for a place to go that was safe. But now the moneymaking part of the mine was petering out. More lead than silver.

"Can't they try digging in other spots?" I asked her, remembering my last assignment and the mines there.

"They tried that. Bunch of times. Disaster it was," Maggie replied as she put new sheets on my bed.

"Cave-ins?" I asked her.

Maggie gave me a sharp look and shook her head. "Not my business. Ask about it if you want. Them's not my problem."

As the small woman scurried out of the room, I looked around. Bed, water basin, and dresser took up the whole room. A window looked out over the town, but it was nailed shut. Curious. It must get as hot as a furnace in here in the summer.

"Your phone?" I asked Maggie. The woman frowned but pointed down the hall from where I stood.

To say that Anastasia was mad at me would be the understatement of the year. But she understood my reasoning for driving instead of flying. In the year or so we'd been working together, she'd barely told me any of her story. I'd thought that Vampires all had resources all over the world they could use, but somehow she was exempt from all that. Not to worry though. just as soon as my van was fixed, I'd be back on the road.

———

"Two DAYS?" I looked at the grease-covered man in surprise.

Arlen, the town's only mechanic, nodded. "Drive shaft section. I've got nothing here that fits right. I could jerry-rig it, but you might find yourself in a worse situation than this. Lots of desert out there."

"Fine. Whatever. I'll wait it out. Thanks, Arlen." One thing I'd learned out on the road by myself was to not unnecessarily piss off the locals. At least not this early in the game. Maybe I could get caught up on my paperwork.

Maggie only nodded when I told her I'd need the room longer. Money from out-of-towners was apparently rare here.

"Anything to do in this town, Maggie?" I asked her.

Barely looking up, the mousey little woman busied herself with cleaning the front room. "We gets the random prospector here and there. Them don't like it though, don't stay long."

Listening to the words she was speaking I caught something. "Maggie, you mentioned them before. Who is them?"

Maggie's hands shook as she stopped wiping the table in front of her. "Them don't like to be bothered."

"Them who?" I asked her again.

Looking up at the ceiling, Maggie muttered something I didn't quite catch. Something about night. Giving me a frightened look, she ran from the room.

"Good work, Jack. Scare the landlady on your first night," I muttered to myself. Something sure scared her though.

I sat in the corner of the small diner and began digging into my paperwork. I filled out all the stuff the FBI required of Agents. I swear that Washington must float on a sea of paper, as much as everyone has to fill out. It was almost a blessing it was just me in the Division.

The sound of a steam whistle going off forced me to check the time, four o'clock. Quitting time at the mine, I assumed. Several dusty, dirty, and mud-covered men stumbled into the small diner. Bellying up to what served as a bar around here, the men began sucking down beer and liquor shots. Out of habit I half-listened to them as they talked. So much information is available during people's unguarded speech.

"...no sign in the new tunnel..."

"Rafe... too bad about him but more money..."

"I'm out as soon as I get my stake..."

"... them. I can barely sleep through it without..."

The conversations around me went on for several minutes until they noticed me sitting there. "Stranger..."

Looking up from my paperwork, I gave the men a nod with a smile. It was returned with frowns and outright anger. I shrugged and went back to work. The forms wouldn't fill themselves out.

There was a blast of the whistle again, and the men at the bar couldn't get out of there fast enough. Almost as one they threw money down and left. Maggie stepped out from behind the counter and started locking large metal shutters over the windows. I'd missed them as I sat down, but now that I was looking, they were obvious. Half sliding out of my booth, I asked if she needed help.

Holding up a hand she replied, "I can manage."

The shutters covered the windows and door completely. They resembled blast curtains I'd seen in books about the 1914 war in Europe. Why someplace like this would need them added to my questions about this town.

"Anything I can get you, Mr. Dalton," Maggie asked me.

"It's Agent, actually," I replied to her.

"Agent..." Maggie looked at me questionably.

"Of the FBI. I'm a government Agent, Maggie." I explained. The concept of the FBI seemed to go right over her head.

The short woman cocked her head and just stared for a moment. Shaking herself slightly, she started talking again. "Okay. Never met someone like that before. Place is closed up for the night. Time for them. Stay inside tonight, ya'hear?"

Them again. I only nodded. Maggie glanced back at me numerous times as she scurried away. I could hear the sound of a door slamming shut as she turned the corner. She lived in the basement.

I knew very little of what went bump in the night in the Southwest part of the United States. Them. It could mean a lot of things. There'd been a movie when I was younger about gigantic Demon ants out in the desert. It was called *Them*.

There was only one verified instance of Demons surviving the great hunt in and around Conception after the Gate closed, and that was in Death Valley. A small group of Indians had adopted a group of Imps and were worshiping them. The Imps had eaten half the tribe by the time the military arrived. That was just a couple of years ago. It was believed they were the last remnant of the Horde. This town was beyond the range of any of those instances.

The creaking of the stairs and my own footsteps were all I could hear as I went up to my room. Peering out my lone window, I could see the town was totally blacked out. Whatever or whomever Them was, I couldn't see.

———

MORNING BROUGHT MORE questions than answers. As before, a sharp whistle blew at sunup. I'd heard many strange noises in the night, but with all the doors and windows shut, they weren't enough for me to climb out of bed and peek. They could be kids playing. I didn't see all that much to do around here.

Eddie Gord, the mine's foreman, confronted me as I was eating breakfast.

"You really an FBI Agent?" he asked. "I read the side of your van."

I nodded, but continued to eat. "Sure am."

"You know anything about strange critters?" he asked me.

Pushing my plate away, I focused on the short rotund man. He resembled Curly from the Three Stooges films. "What sort of animals are we talking about?"

"Lizards, about this long." Gord held out his hands a few feet apart.

I relaxed with a deep sigh of relief. So not Demons.

"And they fly," Gord added.

"Flying lizards. Really?" I gave the man an incredulous look. "Like dragons?"

"No. I see you don't believe me, just like the others." Gord turned to leave.

Standing abruptly, I cried out, "Wait! Are these the creatures people call Them?"

Gord looked back at me nodding. "They are a pestilence upon the Earth here. But no one wants to believe us."

I sat down and gestured to the chair in front of me. "Sit and tell me about it. Please."

The heavyset foreman sat down. Looking bashfully at the floor, the man cleared his throat. "I've tried to tell people. Corporate doesn't care as long as we keep sending them silver, but the mine's petering out. The governor blew me off, as did the Nevada National Guard. We're too far out of the way for people to care about."

I gestured for him to continue.

"It started a year or so ago. The mine started to dry up, so we did some exploratory digs. Two out of five showed promise, and the bosses in Vegas gave orders to shift operations to them. At first, everything was great. Silver output was a bit higher than the original Belmont mine. We normally get a high concentration of lead, zinc, and silver from the mines around here. Some even yield a tiny bit of gold, but not these here. The amount of work to extract it is too costly, anyway. So we dug deeper and started blasting," Gord explained as he picked his nose. It made me squirm a bit watching his dusty hands repeatedly reach for his nose. "As expected, we started getting high concentrations of lead, but then we hit a silver vein and followed it. Over and over we blasted the rock, until most of the hilltop was in ruin. The mining engineer Belmont hired suggested we strip mine instead of blast, but the boys in Vegas said no. We kept at it as ordered."

"And," I asked him.

Gord sighed and slumped his shoulders. "And we broke into a cave complex at a hundred feet down. Caves are pretty common in Nevada, so we didn't think anything of it at first. We sent a guy down to check for obvious minerals, but he claimed he didn't see anything. So we continued with the blasting. Opened the hole up really big. We'd left a security guard onsite overnight. Nothing to steal out here, but we didn't want anyone poking around too much. Come morning, there was no sign of the man. At first we thought he'd run off or got drunk. It happens out here. A couple of local kids found him a day later out in the desert, stripped to the bone. Dead."

"Coyotes," I asked.

"No. They don't kill like this. The sheriff thought he wandered off and vultures took care of him. It was a mystery, until it happened again. Another watchman, this time one of the guys in charge of the generators. All we found was a bloody shirt and a foot," Gord explained, his eyes crusty from last night's sleep. "It was a boot with a foot inside. Once again, they wrote it off as an accident. Mine equipment is dangerous, after all."

I frowned at him. No sign of a body was bad. "What about the lack of a body?"

"We lost a guy a few years ago? Got stuck in the grinder. All we found was a finger and some blood, and not all that much of it. This is a dangerous business. But both of these new deaths were when everything was off!" Gord looked down at the table for a moment. "Weird stuff began to happen. There were some unexplained break-ins. Stuff like baskets and sheets being stolen from houses with open windows or doors. We're such a small town, we know everyone here. Then pets started disappearing. If you walk out into the fields around here, you won't find a single mouse or rabbit. Even birds are rare."

"Lizards?" I asked him. Mentally I'd started a checklist. If it was Demons, they'd have ravaged the town by now.

"Right. Mothers were keeping their kids in after dusk, but adults still had to work. One of our shift crews got stuck at the mine late and paid for it in blood." Gord caught my eyes and held them. "As they left the new mine, a swarm of...things came pouring out of it. We'd blown up the entrance to the caves and instead of mining down, we'd gone both left and right. The flying lizards hit my guys like a freight train, biting and clawing them. Unable to fight, my guys ran for it."

Grimacing, Gord continued, "Nobody died, but too many were hurt. About half walked off the job the next morning. Miners are a dime a dozen out here, as are the dangers. What is up there, though, is something else. Corporate doesn't care. I've kept the mine hours from dawn to dusk, but as the days grow shorter and we dig deeper, the men...they're scared. Scared for their families and their lives. You might have noticed, we board up the town at night."

"I saw that, even helped Maggie close up last night," I explained, mentioning the nailed-shut windows as well.

"Yeah. The lizards come out at night. They've gotten bolder the past few weeks," Gord explained.

I licked my lips. This was starting to sound like my sort of thing. A monster hunt of some kind. Right up my alley. "How so?"

"At first? They would only hit the windows and doors out of what seemed an accident. But a week or so ago, they chased Hannah over at the general store into her shop. She'd stepped out for just a moment to enjoy the night air and they were on her like bees to honey. Only her slamming the door saved her life. Now they're pounding on the doors and windows at all hours of the night trying to break in. People are scared to send their children to school. When we realized it was getting this bad, I called the state police, the National Guard, and the governor's office. Nothing. No one in this state wants to hear the words 'Demon' or 'Paranormal monster'. There are enough accusations made as it is," Gord explained.

Nodding, I agreed with him. "If those Indians hadn't captured those Imps... Have you killed or captured any of these lizards?"

The foreman shook his head. "We had one dead one, but it dissolved right before our eyes a day later. Damnedest thing I've ever seen. Since then, most are afraid to go outside to look."

"So no pictures then?" I asked. Hunting ghostlike creatures was going to be hard to do. Justifying it to Anastasia would be harder. Nervously, I ran my fingers through my military style crew cut. "I guess I'll have to try and catch one, then."

"Catch one? You and what army?"

———

An army of one, apparently. Not many volunteers were to be had in town. Once again, I was proving that monster hunters are both crazy and solo.

I spent a few hours in the mechanic's shop preparing my gear before the hunt. The foreman had reported that the last time anyone had direct contact with the beasties, they'd been bitten and torn up. Since I like my health, I thought I'd make some armor.

"You want to do what?" Arlen exclaimed. He didn't have any issues with using his gear. As the mining company's primary repairman, Arlen had some unusual stuff.

"I want to make some armor. Maggie was kind enough to give me a couple of weeks' worth of old cans. I'd like to use your welding rig and make something to cover my arms and legs. Once that's done, I've got a couple of tin pot army helmets in the van. If we can weld a grate or basket over one, my face would be covered too," I explained. It did sound a bit crazy. Like a three stooges skit.

"Don't use the welding rig, I've got one of those new-fangled acetylene torches over in the corner. It burns hotter and will do the job way faster. What about your body? That uniform of yours won't do the job," Arlen pointed out.

I smiled. Talking gear was something guys like to do. "Chainmail. I've got a gambeson for under and some fitted leather armor for over. It's a long story, but I took on a couple of critters on the east coast that almost killed me. I smiled remembering my time at the Academy...a colleague of mine hooked me up with a group that makes period pieces for museums. This will be the first time I've used them. For defense I've got my sidearms and my Chicago Piano."

Arlen looked up from the box of cans and things. "Piano?"

Laughing, I reached behind the file cabinet on the passenger's side and pulled out a violin case. Popping it open, I displayed the Thompson submachine gun inside. "The FBI had this in storage. I'm told it was seized from Dillianger's gang."

The mechanic stepped over and started poking at the gun. It was a really nice weapon. One side of the case held the actual gun, the other side a stock, drum, and stick magazine. I only had two drums for the gun but if one hundred rounds of .45 ACP didn't kill these things, then I was in big time trouble.

Arlen blew out a breath and laughed. "Mister, you're crazy. But I'll help you if you like."

The finished product was ugly. Really ugly. Up close I looked like a shopping ad for every grocery store in America. Tomato and bean cans lined my arms with flexible ducting at the joints. Large #10 cans made up my new leg armor. In a perfect world we would've painted the cans, but I didn't have that kind of time. Add in my chain-mail and girdle and I felt like the tin man on his way to Oz.

"Where'd you find this thing, anyway?" Arlen asked as he welded the wire onto my army helmet.

"Maggie. She had an old bird cage in the attic, said it was there when she moved in," I explained. Maggie had told me in no uncertain terms that I was insane for going after what she called Them. Gord hadn't known, but the lizards had chased her as well.

"This helmet we're making reminds me of gear for that jai alai game. You know the one with the scoop thing?" Arlen stated, his voice muffled by the welding helmet.

I wrinkled my nose. "What game?"

Arlen stood up, pushing the face mask up. "Jai alai. They played it at the world's fair in 1904."

"How old do you think I am? I wasn't even a gleam in my parents' eyes that long ago," I told him.

Arlen laughed at that. He was apparently from Florida. He'd come west looking for work in 1926 and just never went back. "Jack, it was a combination of many things that brought me way out here. You're too young, but we'd had two hurricanes in a row in South Florida and then this tiny little fly caused a shutdown in the groves by killing off all the fruit. No job, no prospects, no place to stay, I just packed up and kept going. California looked like the promised land, but I never made it that far."

"You've been in Belmont that long?" I asked him.

"Pretty much. I spent some time in Ruth and Ely getting established, but that was before most of this town was here. Don't let Maggie fool you, she built much of that place herself," Arlen remarked. "Hell, I ran half the electrics. Those were the days. The mine was booming, new folks were coming here with that sparkle of greed in their eyes..."

"Sounds nice," I said.

Arlen snorted then laughed. "No. This was a boom town. When the silver dried up so did the sparkle. We're all just hanging on here 'cause we've nowhere else to go. The new mine was supposed to save us."

From what I'd seen of the town, I could agree with that. No one seemed to care about upkeep or looks. The town was fading away.

"Let's see how this fits you." Arlen lifted up the helmet he'd been working on.

Slipping the thing on, I turned to him. "Well?"

Arlen laughed again. "Looks like a birdcage gone wrong but it should work. Don't let them hit you too much in the face, though. That wire is cheap. What about your neck?"

Reaching up, I could feel what he was asking about. There was a space about six inches or so all the way around my neck and shoulders.

"Hmm, a gorget would be ideal, but I don't have one. I've got some heavy-duty canvas that used to be part of a life raft that I picked up somewhere. Maybe I can have Maggie make me a focale or something," I stated.

Arlen raised his eyebrows and looked at me. "Fo-what? I can barely understand you, son."

"Sorry, it's my love of history shining through. The ancient Roman soldiers wore a sort of a scarf thing called a focale around their upper shoulders and neck. It wouldn't stop a sword strike, but it was to protect from ashes and insects. They were jaunty, as well." I demonstrated with a shop rag.

"You best get moving then, if you're gonna catch her before dinner. Just to let ya know, the part we need for your vehicle is coming in with the supply run truck tomorrow from Ruth. At first they said it would take longer, but I told them you were a G-man and they put a rush on it. Had to send to Crystal Springs, but it's coming." Arlen pointed to the open hood of my van. "So if you survive tonight, I should have you back on your way this time tomorrow."

Nodding my thanks, I explained my job to him. "If these things are a threat, I'll stay and take care of it. I'm not in the habit of passing the buck. I appreciate the help, Arlen."

———

THE SUN WAS GOING DOWN and third shift at the mine was rushing to get home. No one, not even Gord the foreman, wanted to see what was coming out of the mine at night. Surprisingly, no one laughed at my costume.

"For a government man, you're crazy. Try to stay alive." Gord patted me on the shoulder as he practically ran down toward the town.

From all the accounts I'd received, the main entrance was where the flying lizards would come from. Using the submachine gun seemed like overkill to me now. While I had a couple of shotguns, I didn't think they'd be as effective as the Thompson. Still, shooting at what might look like a flock of birds with a Tommy gun sounded odd.

Leaning against an old mine cart, I watched the entrance. The sun had dropped behind one of the distant mountains, plunging the entire area in darkness. In a few moments, even the sunset would fade. Gord had said these things liked full dark. I was starting to wonder how I would pee in this outfit when I heard it.

The flapping of wings.

At first, it was just one or two. Then hundreds of small winged snake-like lizards poured out into the night air. Not giving them a chance to get away, I sparked a road flare and whipped up my gun, pulling the trigger.

It takes a strong arm to fire a Thompson, which is why most Agents use sidearms. Bracing the weapon to my shoulder, I started firing.

Bam, bam, bam, bam, bam, bam...

Using all my strength, I held the Thompson down as it fired. Brass was spitting out everywhere to my right as the drum magazine went through all fifty rounds. The flying lizards reacted to my attack like a flock of sparrows running from a hawk. They moved as a single cloud, up and away from the bullets.

At nine hundred rounds a minute, the machine gun fires super fast. Dropping the first drum, I scrambled to attach the second one. This was one of the original 1921 Colt guns, so I had to feather a lever even as I attached the drum. I was using fifty-round drums. There were some twice that amount out there, but they made the gun too heavy.

Looking skyward, I could see the swarm of creatures turning and twisting in the sharp light of the flare. They were moving closer and closer to me.

I pulled out another flare and waited until the last possible moment to start firing.

Bam, bam, bam, bam, bam...

Blowing through the second drum, I barely had time to move as the swarm plowed into me. Frantic creatures with long undulating bodies, sharp teeth, and bulging eyes hit me head on. The wire framework that Arlen had put together didn't buckle as they rammed into me repeatedly.

The bulky mechanic's heat resistant gloves I had cut the fingertips from made it too hard to draw my pistols, so I did the only thing I could think of. I dropped face first onto the ground. I could feel every instance of the lizards hitting my body, trying to dig in. I'd tucked my fingers underneath my chest for protection.

I only chanced a look once and was immediately attacked again. It wasn't just nature that drove these things. They had some bit of intelligence to them, as well.

As the night progressed, the attacks lessened except when I moved. So I stopped doing that. No need to spend time figuring out how to pee in the suit, either.

"You alive, G-man?" Arlen's voice woke me from a dead sleep. Raising my head, I could see just the faintest glimmer of sunlight.

"Yeah...sort of." Pulling myself up to my knees, I looked around the mine entrance. Dozens of dead lizards surrounded me.

Arlen picked up one of the dead creatures. "Wooee, son! You did a number on them for sure. The whole town was pulling for you when the shooting stopped. I thought for sure you got eaten up here."

I stood and dusted myself off. Picking up my fallen Thompson, I pulled the drum off and checked it for debris. Seeing it was empty, I replaced it with one of the stick magazines.

"Good thing you had that," Arlen commented as he made a pile of the dead lizards.

"I'll have to thank the special armaments guys. I can see why the gangsters liked it so much. How many do you figure?" I asked him.

"At least a couple dozen here. There might be more wounded in town," Arlen replied. "What are these things?"

Giving one of the bodies a careful inspection, I shook my head. "Not a clue. Dangerous things, though."

Nothing but teeth and scales, they looked like a cross between a snake, a dragon, and a piranha fish. Bad news all the way around.

"What's next?" Arlen asked me.

"Call it in. Short of blowing up the mine, they're too much for little old me to handle on my own," I started to explain to him.

"The hell you say! Closing the mine would kill the town!" Gord yelled as he came up the hill.

Turning, I gave the mine foreman a look. "You asked me for my help, remember. If blowing it up is the only solution, it's what I'll do. But I intend to ask higher for help in this."

———

"DAMN IT, Jack! I told you why I need you here in Washington asap!" Anastasia admonished me over the phone.

"I can't just dump these folks' problems on the local police. Boss, these little monsters have killed people. I need the guard at the very minimum. I'm not sure I have the power to just blow up the livelihood of the entire town," I explained.

"Fine. Tell me what you need but let me be clear. You will document everything, including sending as many of the creatures as you deem necessary to the labs here in Washington. Understand?" Anastasia ordered.

Paperwork wasn't my strong point, and she knew it. This was punishment as much as it was help. "Got it. Thanks boss."

"Uh huh. Get here when you can, Jack. I'll just have to hide more than usual." Anastasia hung up the phone.

I was using the mine office for security's sake instead of the boarding house phone. Looking out at the roofs of the town, I cringed a bit, considering what was coming. The army might just shut it all down. No one wanted another Conception Point in their state.

"Is help coming?" Gord asked as he walked into the office without knocking.

Scowling at the lack of courtesy, I shook my head. It was his office, though. "Maybe. My boss in Washington promised to contact the local officials as well as the military. I'll be staying until someone takes over, though."

The foreman plopped down in one of the office chairs. "It burns me up that you can get them to respond and I can't."

"It's not really me that's asking though, is it. My division of the FBI is under the Director's purview. The request to the Nevada guard will come from Mr. Hoover's office," I explained without really explaining. Bureau business wasn't open for discussion.

It took two days for "help" to arrive. Two days of constant attacks by the lizards, or Quetzalcoatl, as the locals were calling them now.

As I wrote my reports, the corpses were examined by the towns-folk. A few of the newer miners from across the border cursed when they saw the lizards, calling them Quetzalcoatl and making the sign of the cross as they did. The name stuck.

"Feathered serpent" was a rough approximation of the name. My only problem was that the name was associated with an Aztec God. Odin was bad enough to have to deal with. I didn't need more strange Gods in my life. According to the men, there were paintings of flying lizards on some of the old temples down in Mexico that resembled these creatures. Bigger ones, though. Much, much bigger ones.

All the town had seen were the smaller variety. It really worried me that maybe these were babies and a big one was lurking somewhere.

———

THE ARMY WAS EARLY.

Everyone in town heard the rumbling before any of the vehicles came into view. Two large half-ton trucks, followed by a flatbed truck, led the way. Jeeps and several half-tracks brought up the rear. None of the equipment was front line, which told me this was a National Guard unit.

A jeep pulled up to the boarding house and stopped. The other equipment spread out as if to surround the town. Two officers and a couple of armed soldiers came inside. The soldiers took up guard positions by the door.

"We're looking for an Agent Dalton," the colonel said.

I stood and approached the men. "That would be me. Thanks for coming so quickly."

Taking my hand, the older man snorted, "When the governor of Nevada and the president call you in the middle of the night you spring into action pretty quickly."

Standing stock still for half a second, all I could do was blink. Rousing myself, I felt my jaw drop open. "The president? Really? All I did was call it in to my boss, Director Hoover."

"You kicked over an anthill is what you did. Nobody wants Demons in their state. Can you tell me what we're dealing with here? The bigwigs weren't all that clear." the colonel asked me.

Ushering the officers into the dining room, then ushering most of the locals except Gord and Maggie out, I started pulling out my reports and the dried Quetzalcoatl creatures. "...how many there are or how big. Mr. Gord here can explain the hole they made and just how big it is. The cave system down there could go for miles. I was afraid to just blow it on this end. These things could pop up anywhere."

Colonel Horton frowned as he examined one of the small corpses. "You did this with an unmodified Thompson? You're either the craziest FBI Agent I've ever met or the stupidest. Those old 1921 models jam at the drop of a hat. You might've gotten yourself killed. Luck was on your side, for sure. Mr. Gord?"

Gord sat up straighter in his chair for a moment. "Yes, Colonel?"

"The governor himself is supposed to be contacting the owners of the Belmont Mine about this situation. If we are unable to contain these things, I need you to get the word out to the town and all your employees. Evacuation is very possible."

Gord grimaced. "We've got a lot of time and money tied up in this place to just have to leave it."

"Just let them know, please. We'd like to do this peacefully." Colonel Horton gave me a sharp look before continuing. "Captain Falconer here has some engineering questions for you about the mine. He'll go with you, if you'd like."

Gord shrugged and led the Captain outside. I caught the tail end of one of the questions as they walked. "...connect to the old mine? If it does, we need to trace it."

Horton glanced at Maggie, then back at me, a question in his eyes. I shook my head. "She's fine. This is her place."

The Colonel nodded and tapped my stack of files. "Containment is what I was told to do. Anything more you're not telling me?"

"Not really. These things are fast and intelligent. They reacted to my gun and my movements. I would suggest your men cover up as much as possible." Reaching behind me, I pulled out sections of my homemade armor. Showing the teeth marks I explained, "Their teeth are razor sharp. If I didn't have this on, they might have stripped me to the bone like the others."

Horton rubbed his jawline in thought for a moment. "We don't have anything like that on hand. I brought one tank and most of my rolling stock with me. You fired off a hundred rounds and killed a few dozen?"

"Yes, and it was like trying to kill a flock of moving sparrows at night with a pellet rifle," I explained.

"I was part of the San Bernardino breakout in 1948, and I remember what fighting Demons is like." Horton remarked. He took a deep breath. "I don't want to do it again. Our brigade has a couple of flamethrower units. We'll see how they do against these things. Like you, I'd hate to blow the mine shut, not knowing the exits. Captain Falconer's a good man. He'll find out what he can. This is a hell of a mess you've brought me, Agent Dalton."

"Do you want me to stay and help?" I asked. Ana would kill me more, but this was my job.

"Initially, yes. Let's get through the night and we can plan. So what do the people here do when it gets dark..." Horton asked as we both dug into the files I'd prepared.

LIKE BEFORE, the Quetzalcoatl poured out of the mine entrance in a flowing mass of feathers and scales. This time, they met gouts of flame rather than lead.

"Let them have it!" Horton's subordinate gave the order.

Just before dusk, the guard had set up batteries of guns and flame on opposite sides of the entrance, hoping to catch the creatures in a crossfire. The very moment the men spotted the lizards, large electric lights switched on, bathing the rock face with light.

Like the fires of hell, gouts of liquid flame shot out at the Quetzalcoatl, catching them alight. As before, the swarm suddenly changed direction, and like a living entity, jinked to one side, coming in from behind to attack the battery on the right full on.

"Look out!" The man holding the flame gun fired a controlled burst over the heads of his companions at the diving lizards. He only had seven full seconds of fire to use and barely fluttered the trigger. Like puffs of smoke the flame broke up the attack. Other men in the battery directed their guns skyward and began firing.

Horton and I were a hundred yards back inside his command vehicle watching the Quetzalcoatl attack the troops.

"You need to pull them back. They don't have the correct sort of armor against these things," I told the colonel. Seeing American troops torn apart and not being able to stop it wasn't on my agenda.

"The plan here is to thin them out. Let the boys do their jobs," Horton remarked dispassionately. "This is what they get paid to do."

The second battery started puffing out more gouts of flame, aimed at the entrance to the mine. I watched as the men began throwing grenades at it as well. Looking to the officers I asked, "Why grenades?"

Horton didn't bother to turn around. He kept his binoculars on the entrance. "White phosphorus. If you should happen upon any of that white smoke, run the other way. It will burn out your lungs in but a moment. They wanted containment, I'll give them containment."

New additions to the swarm were stopped at the entrance, but the ones already out were moving on to easier prey, the rest of the Guard forces camped around the mine. Gunshots and screams echoed across the small valley for hours.

By dawn, the once stern colonel was a shadow of himself. Showing his age, the military leader sagged in his command chair. "I should have listened to you, Agent Dalton. That's one of the problems of leading large groups of men. You forget the little people, and they're the ones that got you there. I've already ordered an evacuation of the valley and the surrounding area. We'll take it from here on out. You're free to return to Washington now."

I didn't like being referred to as little, but I knew how to take a hint. Anastasia would be happy but at this moment, I wasn't. I didn't like to lose, and this case I'd stumbled upon counted as a loss to me. The monsters weren't supposed to win.

———

"LIKE YOU PREDICTED, ISN'T IT?" Arlen asked me as he handed over my keys.

"Pretty much. Maybe you could go back to Florida, watch some of that strange game you told me about," I replied.

The grease-covered man shook his head. "That's a pipe dream, my friend. I think I'll go see the other ocean. California is calling me home."

Taking the keys and starting up my van, I listened for the sound in the engine that had brought me here in the first place. Nothing. "You did a good job. Thanks, Arlen."

"I did mine, and you did yours. The way of the world son, the way of the world." Arlen shook my hand and looked me in the eyes. "You watch your back out there in the crazy world. And stay safe."

I chucked my duffle bag into the back and pulled out of town. More and more Army and National Guard troops were pouring in now. The word was out on this place, and somehow they would contain the threat. Belmont Mill would fade from existence and the world would be none the wiser.

"You can't save the world from itself." My step-father used to say that all the time while I was growing up. It took this instance to really drive it home to me. My job was to hunt the monsters that disturbed society's rules, not to right the wrongs. Seeing that those goals were different meant I was growing up.

It was fifty hours or so to Washington. What would I find when I got there?

JACK DALTON, MONSTER HUNTER

BOOK 10

My name is Jack Dalton and I am a Monster Hunter.

Vampires. I don't know all that much about them beyond what Anastasia's told me, which makes me almost blind to this next assignment. The files I was equipped with describe them as one of the few truly immortal species. Barring the removal of the head, heart, and a massive exposure to sunlight, of course.

According to British intelligence, the apparent origin of the information, Vampires were ranked in a sort of caste system. Elders known as Ancients were the ultimate top of the Vampire rank system. It was their magical destruction that both ended the Great War and caused the event known as the Purge.

In 1914, war broke out in Europe. The governments of the world rushed to battle each other. Paranormals for the most part stayed far away from it, except in Germany and Austria. They wanted war, and they wanted power. What they wanted was control of a country and of an army. They coerced the Vampires to help them by using forbidden spells on them. The Vampires then attacked the allied troops at night, devastating them. How do you kill something that is already dead? The Witches used magic to control the skies by enchanting German planes and bringing forth minor Dragons from the nether realms.

Since the cat was out of the bag, so to speak, English paranormals then revealed themselves to governmental authorities and volunteered to help. The allied governments, once they got over their shock, begged the paranormals to do something about the Vampires. All they wanted was a solution to the Vampire problem; they didn't really care about the Witches. The British Paranormal Council decided to create a great spell. Other councils around the world warned them of the consequences and problems that could arise, but they pushed forward, anyway; they wanted to help their government. The leader of the London Vampire Coven volunteered to be a part of the spell. The goal of the Magickal folk of Britain was to separate the two races and shield the innocent Vampires from the Fleisch und Blut Witches. No deaths were intended at all. That was not the point. So the spell was triggered and something unexpected happened: the Vampires died. The paranormal races call the Great War "The Purge." The Vampires that were being used to attack allied soldiers died along with every Vampire in a 5,000-mile radius surrounding Paris, France. The Generals and the Allied leaders were ecstatic and patted each other on the back. The British Council was devastated. Not a few hundred, not a few thousand, but tens of thousands, hundreds of thousands, of Vampires were killed. The only Vampires to survive were those that lived on the far Western coasts of North America and those in Japan and parts of China. The Germanic Witches of Flesh and Blood were also wiped out completely. The British suspected it was by surviving Vampires, but even they deny doing it. The British Witches' Council were put on trial on charges of genocide by a council made up of elders from all the races. Those directly responsible for creating the spell were punished.

Of all the information in my files about Vampires, the Purge was the most interesting. I found it fascinating that the FBI, with a Vampire resource in the main office, didn't have reports of our own. Anastasia could've updated them from her perspective. She had to have been alive then, but there was nothing about her in them. To the FBI, she didn't seem to exist as a Vampire.

———

WASHINGTON HAD CHANGED a bit since I was last here. Construction projects put on hold by the recent elections and political foibles were underway again. Scaffolding and large tents hid much of the Capitol building from sight. It was undergoing the first real restoration in more than a hundred years. Add it to all the highway work and tract housing going up and the whole town was a mess.

"Sorry I'm so late, there's construction delays everywhere," I explained as I walked into Anastasia's small office. The FBI building was the still the same, but all the faces were different. I knew from my studies that many of the higher ups or department heads could change when a new president was sworn in, but this was the first time I witnessed it.

Anastasia glared at me before speaking. "Explain to me again why it was so important to you to disregard my orders and help those miners?"

On my way here, I'd had engine trouble mid-way across the country. Instead of catching a bus or asking for one of the local offices to pick me up, I'd stayed around the area, fighting monsters. It was my defined job to do so, but I'd ignored both Anastasia's and the Director's orders to do so and as a result lost. The military was forced to step in.

"My job?" I started. "I understand that this is important, but you told me in the very beginning to make this job my own. To stand up to the Director if need be and prove him wrong. How can I do that if you are micromanaging me the entire time? Some cases I need to find on my own. Building up a network of informers and those I've helped is just part of it all," I answered back. It was hard to hold her eyes without flinching. I'd knew that some Vampires were powerful but not that Ana was one of them!

Suddenly Ana was within inches of me. I could feel her breath on my face, her eyes peering into me. "Your job is what we say it is. Do you understand me?"

Raising my hands, I made to a motion to ward her off but froze. It was like my entire body was slowing down. Only my brain seemed active. Frozen in place, I could only watch as she examined me. Sniffing she moved in close to my neck.

———

A sharp prick and nothing.

That was what the entry in my secret journal read. I'd made the entry the very moment I climbed into the van. Like watching a movie, I'd witnessed my boss and confidant suck the life out of me, literally.

The very act of feeling my blood leave my body and her blood red eyes forcing me to forget everything I thought I knew was a betrayal I could never, ever, forget.

"Why do I remember everything then?" I muttered to myself. Ana's instructions were to travel to the first murder site and take over the investigation. I was to forget everything about our meeting except that the Ripper case was paramount. Track down the rogue Vampire and arrest him. If I was able to track him to his lair, then I was to inform Ana immediately.

Closing my eyes, I tried to remember if this was the first time she'd done this to me, but I couldn't remember. "What's different this time?" I murmured to myself. Shaking my head, I made a promise to figure it out later. Right or wrong, I still had a murderer and monster to catch.

Five murders in as many weeks. In each case, the victim was a part of the Washington political machine: senatorial aides, interns, or staffers. An equal opportunity killer, none of the deaths were along party lines so far. Washington police were stumped as to motive, according to the files Ana had given me.

———

"Who are you again?" Chief Sylvester asked me. I went straight to the top before doing any investigating in Washington. A turf war between the locals, the bureau, Bureau, and any of the alphabet agencies that seemed to be everywhere in Washington these days wasn't something I wanted. Too many elements of this case were hotter than hell already without adding more trouble to it.

"FBI Magical Division. We're the ones you call for any and all Paranormal activity or crimes," I answered, handing him my badge and credentials.

Squinting, the chief glanced from my badge to me a couple of times before handing them back. "Supervisory Special Agent. That's a pretty big title for such a young man like yourself."

"The Director himself recruited me for the job. He wanted someone with intimate contact with the Paras as well as the training for the job. So far, I've been a part of both the sea monster and rogue Werewolf investigations. I was dealing with some nasty demonic creatures when Director Hoover called me. These Ripper cases are priority now for us," I replied, ignoring his comment about my age. Nothing I said to him was a lie, from a certain point of view. One thing I'd learned in this job was that if you were going to lie, you had to make some part of it the truth. Just that little bit would throw off truth verification or mind readers. The things you learn in this business.

"Did he now? You going to get in my officer's way here son?" Sylvester asked.

"I can't control the main office and the Director, but I myself will try to stay out of your way. All I want is closed cases and justice for the victims. I leave the politics to others," I explained the best I could.

The chief snorted and shook his head as he tried not to laugh at me. "Everything is about politics around here. Just catch this monster and leave your boss to me. J. Edgar and I already have a unique relationship together."

"He's a hard man to warm up to." I stated. Most local police didn't care for the FBI, as we took credit that they thought was theirs for cases we assumed.

Chief Sylvester chuckled and pulled out a bakery box. "You have to use the right sort of leverage with him. Donut?"

Reaching in and pulling out a pastry, I thanked him. "I don't know if donuts work on the Director."

"If he ever walked a beat they might. It's why we all love them so much," Sylvester replied, motioning at the box with his donut with a hint of powdered sugar on his face.

"Come again?" I asked.

"It's not a cliché, kid. The reason donuts and cops go hand-in-hand is that pastry shops and diners are the only places open late at night or early in the morning. After a long shift of walking the streets, sometimes you just want to sit down for a moment, understand? Why not have a donut if it's just sitting there in front of you? Besides, after all that walking, it's not like we're going to gain any weight." Sylvester laughed at the look on my face. Staring at the donut in my hand, I could see what he was saying was true.

THERE'D ACTUALLY BEEN seven murders, but only bodies for five of them. Deaths six and seven were technically still considered missing persons. Looking over the official files, I could agree with the assumption that they were dead. Nobody loses that much blood and still survives.

"We found it over there in the nave, never seen anything like it," the park ranger explained to me. We were standing in front of Lincoln's statue inside the Lincoln Memorial building. "To me it looked like someone killed a big ol' hog and butchered it. We couldn't believe it was a man or two men."

"Were there any remains other than blood?" I asked him.

The ranger shook his head. "Not a bit. Fortunately, it was us and not a tourist that found it. Opening up the bathrooms is first on our list in the morning."

The police file I'd gotten showed it all in graphic black and white. Color photography was available, but I was almost glad they didn't use it here. The entire area to Lincoln's right was a charnel house, blood everywhere, coating the walls like it was painted on.

"Did anyone see anything unusual leading up to this? Strange activity, funny looking people, maybe folks who don't want to leave?" I asked him.

"None of that. I told all the other officers the same thing, just the regular tourist groups. We've got a few artist types that hang out around here but that's it," he explained.

"Artists?" I asked.

The ranger motioned to one side. "I'll show you."

Walking to the entrance, he pointed to the young people below, sitting on the steps. More than one of them held sketch pads. "We're a popular spot."

I nodded. "And none of them are missing?"

The ranger cocked his head to one side. "None of the regulars...I'll ask around, though."

"Good, you do that. If you think of anything else, contact the bureau. I'm in charge of the investigation now," I replied, shaking his hand.

For this to happen here in one of America's holiest of holy monuments was either the work of a monster or someone trying to send a message. At this point I wasn't sure which it was. But I was going to find out. I needed to look at the other five murders and find the intersection point.

———

"WE THOUGHT OF THAT AS WELL," the chief replied. "Detective work 101, find the connection. Of the seven deaths there's two unknowns, a senatorial aide, two secretaries, a night watchman, and one of ours, an off-duty cop. I knew him, too. Which is why this case is so crazy and personal for us around here. Look at the map we put together..."

Now that we were all sharing, I could see two rolling boards in the conference room. A map of the city with push pins was most prominent. It was surrounded with news articles, photos, and evidence reports.

"No real pattern to it all. We know the memorial murders were first, but the timeline becomes muddled after that," he explained by pointing out the different locations. "These three were killed over the recent holiday. The coroner can't be completely sure of time of death for any of them, other than more than twenty-four hours."

"How modern is your forensics team?" I asked.

Sylvester frowned, giving me a sharp look. "Why? Washington is a big city. We've got fingerprints and some analysis available."

Motioning with my hand, I pointed toward where FBI headquarters was. "I'm not a regular agent, but even I know the field is becoming more scientific. A good entomologist or one of the sensitives would be able to answer time of death easily. Or you could hire a Witch to cast a spell."

"You would seriously use freaks for this investigation? There's no way to ensure they wouldn't cover for each other and let this killer go!" Chief Sylvester yelled at me.

I looked down at the floor to hide my anger. During the course of the past year, I'd met a lot of good, decent, hardworking paranormals whose ethics were beyond what this man in front of me might believe. Without his support, though, my own investigation of the case would be doomed, so I stayed silent.

After a moment, the chief settled down. He was still audibly grumbling so I could hear him. "I understand your position, but it will be a cold day in hell before this department allows that. Understand?"

I nodded. Clearing my throat, I mentioned the FBI forensics laboratory.

Shaking his head, Sylvester said no. "We went over this already. No way I'm letting your boss take credit for this investigation. If I allow him his foot in the door he'll take it. Bugs we can do, though. We've got a squint at the university already on the payroll. Good thinking. Once we establish a timeline, we can track this monster down."

Taking my silence for agreement, the chief proceeded to show me what they had and explain most of the boards of evidence. A Witch on staff would've helped, though. *Fight the battles you can win.* That was something my stepdad used to say.

————

"And?" Anastasia asked me. "What do the locals have?"

"Not a lot. The timeline is way off and most of the evidence available to enhance it is gone or ruined. I broached the idea of bringing in a Witch or specialist..." I started to say before she cut me off.

"I bet that went over like a lead balloon. Chief Sylvester is very inclusive of his department. He and the Director clash constantly," Ana explained.

"He wasn't happy. I did convince him to talk to an entomologist at the university, but with none of the bodies still on site that might be a lost cause. We..." I motioned to her, "know it was a Vampire. Of that we're certain. Correct?"

Anastasia crossed her arms and leaned back in her chair. "Yes. I'm able to sense these things."

"I think...I think the murders at the Memorial were the first ones. They are sloppy. Something angered him or her and the victims were torn to pieces. The other five read like random kills, but I think even that is wrong. There is some small detail, a link or common theme that we're all missing. I just have to figure it all out." I shuffled through the files for a moment. Looking up suddenly, I asked, "Did profiling take a look at these?"

"Sort of. Because you were taking so long to get here, I had them do a basic work-up of the first four deaths. They didn't have the memorial killings or the most recent one," she explained with a scowl. "At the time, we didn't have the complete evidence report either, so the psychologists could only examine the kills themselves. According to them, we're looking for a man filled with some sort of rage."

"Rage? That's all they could come up with?" I asked.

"These are medical professionals, not detectives. We use them to get into the mind of a killer, not track them down. That's what you and the others are for," she replied.

I shook my head. "Why pay them then? If we're going to use them, they should do it all, be trained to do it all. Can you imagine what a whole team of trained professionals could do? Suggest that to the Director sometime."

"Let me tell you a little secret about J. Edgar. Ideas like that have to come from him before they are enacted. Look at your position. How's your assigned staff working out?" Ana said with a smile.

"Gotcha. I get it. What can you tell me about Vampires? How would you track one down if you could?" I asked her.

Anastasia leaned forward in her chair, placing both hands on the desk and staring at me. For just a split second I could've sworn her eyes flashed at me. "We are an ancient people. Older than most recorded history. For us, the powerful rule the weak. Like Witches, we have a few mental powers as well as extended lifespans. Planning plays an important role in everything that we do as both individuals and a species."

"What kind of powers?" I asked.

"Persuasion, telepathy, and necromancy are just a few. It depends upon who brought you across and when. The older a Vampire is, the stronger they are. To stay hidden like this, I suspect we're dealing with an old one," Anastasia explained.

"Why do you say that? The murders that have happened could've been caused by either a human or a Were. There's nothing so remarkable about them that they scream Vampire deaths to me. Half the Were I know could do the same," I explained to her.

"There's an aura about them." She paused for a moment. Rubbing her hands together, she looked me in the eye. "I can feel him. It's so hard to explain. It's like...I know, you spent a lot of time out West. Did you ever go hunting? Hunting for something other than a prey animal?"

"On the reservation, I helped track down a cougar once. It had killed some of the local tribe's sheep and our Alpha volunteered us to hunt it down. The local tribes out there have a knife-edge relationship with the Were Packs. They don't like sharing what little government resources they receive, and they constantly accuse one another of wrongdoing." I shook my head as I remembered that hunt. "We set out early, the six of us. The Alpha chose only the strongest of the boys to hunt. His instructions were to chase it down and either bring it back alive or mostly intact to prove it wasn't one of his people. I went along as both a witness and a test of loyalty. They may have gone into battle with my father, but I wasn't him."

"Feeling another Vampire's aura is very much like that feeling you get hunting a predator," Ana said. "It's that small itch right between your shoulder blades that's screaming at you. Someone or something has you in their sights. It's when the hunter becomes the hunted. I know he's out there because I can feel it." She thumped her chest. "I can feel it right here inside me."

I let out the breath I'd been holding in. Licking my lips, I asked my real questions. "That feeling I know. Can you tell where he is? Who his companions are? Maybe how old or what part of the world he comes from? Just how accurate are your feelings?"

Ana chuckled. "That's one of the things I like about you, Jack. You're straight to the point. He's old, older than me. The powers of the Elders are beyond most Vampires. As I've said, depending on lineage, our powers increase with age. If he's one of our ruling classes, then he can do almost anything. All the powers are open to him. But he doesn't... taste... that way to me. His psychic imprint is familiar, but not. I'm sorry I'm not much help here, Jack. I just know he's here. And he's dangerous."

"How old are you?" I asked her.

"Don't you know you should never ask a woman her age? It's just not done, Jack," Ana cocked her head and smiled seductively.

"Seriously, your file doesn't say," I explained.

Her eyes widened just a bit and she nodded her head. "Impressive, Jack. I didn't know you had it in you to track that down. Personnel files for those working directly for Mr. Hoover are kept under lock and key. I'm not going to ask how you did it. Everyone is allowed a few secrets, especially in our business. I'm just a bit over a two hundred. If you have my actual file, you'll see I've worked for the bureau since 1945."

I nodded back. Much of what I'd been able to find was redacted, but she'd been a huge help to the FBI since she joined. "Why'd you stay? Even at a couple of centuries you must have hidden wealth beyond what was destroyed in California by the Demons. Why stay with the bureau?"

Ana stirred in her seat. She seemed to shift her weight back and forth as if considering both sides. "I made a promise to someone." She held up her hand in a stopping motion. "Don't ask me who, I won't answer you. The FBI was a means to an end that led to a very nice career. I've met good people here in America. People who've gained my trust and respect. My interaction with humans was much more limited before I came here. We Vampires are the ultimate loners. It's the right fit for me."

"So if I find this creature, what happens? Do I call in support or what?" I asked her.

"No. As I said before, this is Magical Division only. If and when you find his lair, you are to contact me and me alone. Trust me on this, Jack. You are not capable of taking him down by yourself," Ana explained. Once more I caught a slight flash from her eyes. "Are we clear?"

"Understood. You never said how you'd track him, though."

"Oh, that's simple. Look for the places he's not. They'll feel silent, almost abandoned to a human. You'll have the strongest feeling that you need to be somewhere else, that you've forgotten something important. It's very similar to a repulsion spell. For Vampire Elders, it's just another tool. A way to protect their lair. Find that feeling and you've found him, or at least you've found the general area. Fifty yards is about the farthest we can project. Once again it depends on age and strength," Ana explained.

———

So THAT's how I found myself tracing back and forth, on foot, the areas between all the deaths, looking for those "dead" spots.

"If the Lincoln Memorial is there..." I traced my hand across a map the Park Service gave me. Contrary to what Chief Sylvester's people had, all the deaths were in sort of concentric circles around the park. They were using math and logic, while I was using Magic and guile to figure things out. Much of what I did as a Magical investigator relied on gut and instinct. It's how I've been able to stay alive this long doing this solo.

Well, that and certain gifts from the Gods, I said to myself as I stroked the necklace I'd been given.

Magical amulets of any sort were extremely rare. They existed, everyone knew that. Finding the ones that actually worked the way they were advertised was the big trick. Lots of shysters and con men out in the world. Which made me question the one I'd been given by the old man. The old man I suspected to be Odin.

"Keep your distance from those beings of power, Jack. The Gods are fickle and cruel. They play games only they understand." That one bit of wisdom from Marcella Blackmore stuck in my head. Witches were the minor leagues when it came to divine beings, and they knew it. The thing I didn't get was why they were helping me in the first place.

And not only the Gods. Why were the Witches helping me as well?

I was deep in thought and muttering to myself when I felt a strong hand grab me by the shoulder and spin me around.

Suddenly I was face to face with two uniformed police officers. Dropping his hand, the officer who had grabbed me asked, "You Dalton?"

Reaching up, I brushed off where he'd touched me with my hand. "FBI Special Agent in Charge Jack Dalton. Who wants to know?"

I suppose it might've been my lack of the standard black or grey suit or even my demeanor, but both cops could only stare at me for a moment.

"You boys forget how to speak?" I asked. Carefully, I reached into my shirt pocket and pulled out my credentials. I flipped them open and displayed my badge and identification.

Exchanging meaningful looks, the two men took a step back from me before responding. "Chief Sylvester would like a word, sir."

"Ok. Do you know what it's about?" I asked.

The first officer looked both left then right before saying anything. "Some people were killed last night, and we think they're related to... Well, you know."

I pointed toward my van just down the street. "There wasn't anything on the radio or reported to our offices."

"We're keeping this one quiet. Or trying to." He motioned for me to follow them.

"Fine, have someone keep an eye on my rig over there. I'd rather not lose it. How far away is this?" I asked, even as I climbed into the front of the old patrol car.

"A couple of blocks over in Foggy Bottom near the river."

We headed down Constitution and turned onto 26th street. Police and emergency vehicles filled the streets. Figures were moving in and out of a group of run-down buildings. "All this out here is either unclaimed or government property. The Saudi Embassy is a bit farther down on the right. Just across the river is Mason's Island."

Tapping on the bars separating the seats, the officer in the back tried to get our attention. "We're supposed to call it Roosevelt Island now, remember?"

The driver, whose name was actually Smith, let go of the wheel for a moment. "Fine, what he said. Some do-gooders bought the place up some years ago and want to build a monument to him."

"And this helps me how?" I asked the both of them.

"Just passing the time. The chief told us to find you after what we found..." pulling out onto the road, Smith drove up to the first barricade. "You get out here. We'll wait for you."

Surprised, I asked, "You're not coming with me?"

Smith snorted. "And see that mess again? No freaking way, buddy. I can still smell it on me. You're on your own here."

"Fine, thanks for the ride." I climbed out and scanned the crowd.

Government officials and cops were everywhere, but no FBI were in sight. I flashed my creds and was passed into the interior of the scene.

———

"GOOD, THEY FOUND YOU," Chief Sylvester remarked the moment he saw me.

"Chief, what's happened?" I asked him.

"We think we found more victims. Or what's left of them. They don't resemble the other kills, though. These are...I need to show you, hope you have a strong stomach." Sylvester led me through the crowd of cops to an open doorway into a half-ruined brick building.

Peering into the dark doorway, I could feel eyes on me. Pretty sure I wasn't a sacrificial victim being fed to a bunch of lions, I walked up the steps and into the building.

The air was thick with the smell of decay and rot. A miasma of vomit and other unsavory smells hit me like a rogue wave. Initially it was all I could do to keep my insides in. Sucking it up mentally, I relied upon my training. Now wasn't the time to put on a show for the locals. The dark hallway led to a great room that might have once been offices or something. The entire area along the river was filled with ruined warehouses and old industrial buildings, some left over from the War Between the States.

Lying in heaps, bodies or parts of bodies were everywhere. Small groups of gowned doctors were poking and prodding the deceased. "Who were they, do we know?"

Looking up from a mangled corpse, one of the white coats caught my eyes. "And you are?"

"Dalton, FBI," I answered.

"Well Mr. Dalton, these used to be members of one of our city's finest Rotary clubs," he explained. "We've found at least ten so far."

"You've already identified them?" I wondered how. Some of the piles were of just arms or heads.

"I'll show you." Introducing himself but not shaking my hand

Doctor Fenn, a coroner working for the city's morgue system, directed me to a small ruined desk along the wall. A camp light hung above it with medical tools and things on top of it.

Pulling the cloth off one of the lumps on the table, the Doctor revealed a man's forearm. "Do you see the rings?"

Looking closer, I could see the hand wore two rings. Both gold.

"The one on the left is from West Point, class of 1920. The other is only given to state senators or representatives. Add in the age of the arm and this can only be former State Senator Todd Manderle from Texas," the coroner explained. "We checked his house and spoke to his wife already. The group were supposed to be surveying the land all weekend."

Tuning the man out, I ran both my hands through my hair. This was bad. Really bad. Doctor Fenn was still talking, though.

"...hotels in the area. When they didn't return, alarms were raised. At first, we thought animals had gotten to some of your creature's kills but there's no way one man could do all of this, Vampire or not! And we don't have major predators in this area, haven't for at least a century. Did you see the forearm? It might be wild dogs." Doctor Fenn held up the ragged end of the arm so I could see.

Ignoring the really strong smell of ammonia, I looked closer at the bite wound and cursed as all the details clicked in my brain. "Damn."

"What is it? Do you know what did it?" Fenn asked me.

"First thing, has the Secret Service been called, as well as the local FBI? We're going to need resources only they can provide," I said.

Fenn covered the arm back up. "Chief Sylvester is in charge of all that. Why?"

"The ammonia smell is what gave it away. A Vampire may have killed them, but it was something much, much worse that did all of this," I said as I subconciously reached for my pistol. "We need to get your people out of here right now."

"We have evidence to gather, and all of these poor souls need to be recovered," Fenn protested.

"None of that matters a damn bit right now. Ammonia plus carnage and death only means one thing. Ghouls," I said. "Somewhere around here is a pack of Ghouls. And they're hungry."

———————

"Ghouls? Are you completely sure, Agent?" Chief Sylvester asked.

"Pretty sure. To be completely sure, we'd have to dig down into the basement here, but I wouldn't recommend doing that at all. They're extremely dangerous," I explained.

The chief's men had been busy the whole time I was inside. Local FBI and Secret Service were now on the scene, as well as a small group of Army National Guard. And all of them were yelling at each other over jurisdiction.

"We need to get a handle on this first, though." I waved at the mass of law enforcement personnel. "See if you can get all the leaders or highest ranks all in one place for me." I pulled out my keys and handed them over. "Can you have one or two of your officers go get my van for me? Smith had me leave it."

Sylvester delegated, and within the hour had all or most of the bodies and coroners removed from the scene, as well as the locals gathered. Cracking my file cabinet, I pulled out the congressional finding and the president's orders relating to my job. Better to be over-armed than not at all. Another one of my *stepdad's* sayings.

Wheet!

Pulling my fingers out of my mouth, I smiled at the group's reaction. Shock and surprise seemed to be the best way to describe it. That was before I started yelling. "My name is Special Agent in Charge Jack Dalton and I'm taking over."

Chief Sylvester, standing right next to me, rounded on me first. "Oh hell no! This is *my* investigation and *my* town. You came to *me*, remember?"

Holding up the papers I'd gotten from my van, I explained. "Both

Congress and the president approved my appointment to head of the Magical Division of the FBI. You may outrank me, you may have more experience, you may even be able to get me fired, but right here and now, I'm in charge of this circus." I pointed to the building behind me and continued, "That building, and possibly others, have an infestation of Ghouls inside them. The government of this county put my division in charge of all things paranormal and Magical. So unless any of you know more about the critters in there than I do, step out my damn way!"

"Now see here! If any FBI is going to be in charge, it will be us! Your group only has *you* in it!" A man dressed like I was supposed to be dressed pushed through the crowd.

Looking down at his shiny shoes and immaculately pressed suit, I shook my head. "Nope. Do you even know what a Ghoul is? Do you know the best way to kill one?"

Puffing up his chest and looking down his nose at me, the Agent responded, "My men are some of the finest trained in the FBI. Director Hoover will hear of this insult, sir. You aren't even in uniform!"

Even as I dealt with the self-important Agent in front of me, I'd been watching the sky. Complete darkness was almost upon us. Lifting my head up a bit, I sniffed the air.

"Wearing a suit in the woods doesn't make you a better agent. In fact, it makes you a bit of a liability. But as you're about to discover, all the crime-stopping training in the world isn't going to do you a damn bit of good when the perp is trying to eat you," I responded.

The suit threw up his hands. "Eat me? Are you on drugs or something?"

Pointing behind the crowd I replied, "Not me. Them."

Several shaggy creatures were in the process of rolling out the doorway as everyone turned to look. Ghouls are like cockroaches. If you see one, there are always more about. Dozens more of the creatures emerged. I could see their green gleaming eyes from where I stood.

Officers near the building yelled "Halt!" as shots rang out. The group surrounding me scattered like a covey of startled quail. Local cops dove for cover among the scattered Federals. Even the National Guard boys hit the ground running as the gunfire increased.

Ghouls, like most paranormal creatures, are immune to standard bullets. Shooting them only pisses them off.

Whipping open my coat, I pulled my pistols and started firing.

It was dark outside. Really dark. Only flashes of light from the firing guns illuminated the field.

Firing like I was at the range, I stood upright, out in the open, blasting away. Unlike the other shooters, I was making progress. The special rounds created for the Magical Division were working well against the Ghouls, but as a group we were losing ground. More and more of the creatures were joining the fight.

"Where the hell are they all coming from?" Chief Sylvester yelled from the cover of his car.

Edging closer to him I shifted my fire. "Ghouls live in abandoned buildings and cemeteries. With all this ruin and decay around us, this might just be the tip of the iceberg."

"My boys are getting massacred out here! What does it take to kill these things?" Sylvester asked even as he fired.

"Fire and iron work the best, but you might try heavier rounds or shotgun shells," I explained. Ducking down beside the chief, I dropped both magazines and quickly reloaded. My weapons were custom, just like the ammo, or I would've offered them to him. "I've got something in the van that might do the trick."

The Ghoul attack was in full swing now. If we didn't get a handle on them, they might spread out across the city. While these things were super-dangerous, they didn't usually attack people in large groups. Something or someone was stirring them up.

Leaving Sylvester in the lurch, I ran for the van. There were only so many Magical bullets in the world, and I didn't have them all. What I did have was a flamethrower!

According to my files, Ghouls were hunted in the olden days by archers with flaming arrows. It was the best and most classic way to kill them. Trust in the military to take an idea like that and improve upon it. Guns at the ready, I ran down the street, dodging Ghouls and human police as well. Stopping only once, I managed to reach the rear of the van intact.

After my Fae creature encounter more than a year ago when I first started this job, I wanted just a bit more firepower than human guns and arrows. Firing a crossbow or arbalest is fun, but reloading is a bitch. No human alive is strong enough to go without using the windlass. I wanted bigger and badder, the more dangerous the better. The United States Army called it the M2A1-7, the man portable flamethrower.

Reholstering my pistols, I slung the tanks onto my back and almost hit the ground. Seventy pounds of metal with leather straps isn't some light backpack. Grabbing the van doors to support myself, I locked in the firing wand. Just as I was about to close the doors, I spotted my flare pistol. Flares were what this battle really needed.

Pop! Boom!

Taking aim, I fired the first flare upwards, illuminating the entire battleground. Ghouls were everywhere! Near the first building, they had several uniformed men down and were eating them. The cops and Agents were either in the vehicles or behind them, shooting at the monsters or throwing road flares. Almost everyone blinked back from the bright light.

The firing wand was set up like that of a Tommy gun, with front grips and rear grips. I only had about seven full seconds of usage on this thing, as it fired a bit less than half a gallon a second. Popping another flare, I swung the wand up and triggered the flame.

Whoosh!

There is nothing better in life than shooting fireballs at your enemy with a wand. I felt a bit like Merlin the Magician. Keeping my bursts at barely a trigger pull, I was catching as many Ghouls on fire as I could. Seeing the creatures in the light of my fires almost made me wish it was darker. Ghouls look a bit like what would happen if a zombie made love to a hyena. But with more teeth and fur. Nasty creatures that can strip a body to the bone in seconds.

"The head! Aim for the head," I yelled as I staggered toward the first group, firing my puffs of flame.

With a roar, two Ghouls charged me. Mixed with the almost overwhelming smell of ammonia was the smell of burnt fur and death. Giving them another puff from my wand, I let go of it, letting it swing free. The creatures' claws were tearing at my jacket as I put them down with shots from my pistols.

Forgetting the now dangling wand, I lined up the others and continued to fire.

"Jack!" Chief Sylvester yelled.

I heard my name but ignored it. Just like Hogan's Alley, I was in the groove! Bang! Bang! Bang! I shot two and wounded another. Dodging to the left, I shot two more.

"Jack!"

Glancing to my rear, I saw the chief and a large group of uniforms behind the cars. I dropped my magazines and pulled reloads, then kept firing.

It was a cool night here down by the river, but for me things were heating up fast. Sweat was dripping down my face and where the flamethrower tank was, it was hot to the touch.

"Jack, you idiot!"

Spinning around, I raised my hands, guns still clutched in them, and yelled, "What?"

Sylvester was pointing at my feet and yelling my name. Looking down, I could see a stream of liquid fire pooling at my feet. The grass and debris all around me burned as well.

"Holy shit!" I jumped like my pants were on fire, which they were, and struggled to slip the seventy pounds of fuel and liquid nitrogen off my back! If it hadn't been so serious, it would've been a great vaudeville act. The pack slipped off finally with a thump, and I ran for my life. Dying in a gas explosion wasn't my idea of fun.

Several really loud explosions made me hit the ground with my hands over my head. Looking up and to my right I could see National Guard reinforcements fighting back against the monsters, using grenades and heavy machine guns. It reminded me that I actually had a box of thermite grenades in the van. But if the military needed my help they could ask for it.

"That was quick thinking, Dalton," Sylvester remarked. "If you ever want to quit the FBI, I could use a sharp man like you on the force."

"For now, I'm happy with the Magical Division." Looking around, I didn't see any of the other FBI or Secret Service Agents. "Where'd the others go?"

Several of the police officers around Chief Sylvester laughed. The man closest to me explained, "They hightailed it as fast as they could run. I saw one or two firing at the Ghouls coming out the door, but the moment they saw that bullets didn't work, they were gone. Our experience with them is they don't like to get their hands dirty."

Not wanting to disparage the Bureau, I kept my comments light. "Different strokes for different folks. Since I don't usually have any backup, I like to get my hands dirty."

"We noticed, son. I have to ask, what the hell have you been shooting them with?" Sylvester asked, pointing at my guns.

Scanning the battlefield for Ghouls, I could see that between the Guard and the State Police they were on the run. Heavy weapons were doing the trick. I looked back at the cops and explained the tricks we came up with to even the playing field. "You know how Magic exists? So we came up with these bullets..."

———

TALKING the Chief and his men through some of the FBI's procedures and how I'd modified them took several hours. Several long tiring hours.

Slumping down next to the car, I actually fell asleep until the battle was mostly over. We'd fought the Ghouls for more than four hours before forcing them to retreat back into their hole or across the river. More than a dozen cops were either dead or maimed.

When the recriminations and those playing the blame game started up, I climbed into my van and left. While I might have proclaimed myself in charge the previous night, I knew they would be looking for scapegoats today. Heading north, I looped back toward the Director's office and Anastasia.

"What by all the Gods on Earth were you thinking last night?" Anastasia thundered at me. "Did you know who you offended?"

Pulling out a chair from the nearby conference table, I flipped it around and sat down. Another of the many things my stepfather taught me was to protect your weak spots. The slats of a chair wouldn't stop a bullet, but they might stop a knife. Glaring just a bit, I explained. "I didn't catch his name, but he ran like a little girl when the monsters came out to play. He may even have fed a few fellow agents to them as a deterrent."

"Mistakes were made. That is true," Ana started.

"It was a god damn cluster is what it was. Too many cooks in the kitchen. If it hadn't been for Chief Sylvester's men keeping the Ghouls off me, things might have been way worse than they were," I replied.

Ana scowled. "I heard about your flamethrower. As a matter of fact," she pointed her finger upwards, "Director Hoover called me about it bright and early this morning!"

"It's official. I got it from the FBI armory when I picked up my guns and other supplies. If I hadn't had it, we would've been screwed out there. You yourself should know what I do isn't a simple walk in the park. It's a war, and I don't want to lose it!" I exclaimed.

"What about the case I brought you here for? Have you got a lead on it?" Ana asked me.

"Last night was sort of it. You told me that Vampires had certain powers. Can the older ones call creatures to them, like maybe a pack of Ghouls? I ask because everything I know about Ghouls says that what happened last night was strange. They don't do that. Ever. In all the files and reports we have on them there isn't any mention of pack activity like that. Normally, they are loners and big-time cowards. Something was directing them. It's the only explanation I have. This Vampire we're hunting tried to make us the hunted last night. Which means he's either desperate or I'm closing in," I stated.

"Probably both. Show me where you've searched so far," Ana directed.

Unfolding the map I'd been using, I spread it out on the table. Wrinkled from being in my pocket so long, I smoothed it with my hand. "Between the police and me, we've checked everything for four blocks to the north, south, and east of the Lincoln Monument. The Ghouls were here," I pointed on the map to just east of Roosevelt Island. "The buildings all around the monument itself and the reflecting pool are either government or embassy in nature. We only have their occupants' word that they're clear, but I detected no clues they were being persuaded. Could this creature have crossed the river into Maryland?"

Anastasia stared at the map for a moment before closing her eyes. As she cocked her head, I could see the faintest of smiles cross her face.

"No, he's still close, I can feel it. What about the monument itself? Did you check it completely?" she asked me, opening her eyes only to stare.

I shook my head. "No, I didn't, and I stupidly allowed the police and Park Service to distract me."

"There's your answer, then," she said. "Good job on the Ghouls, but you need to find this creature and stop him. Don't worry too much about the Director. He won't like it, but I'll explain what's going on."

"He won't just fire me for embarrassing him?" I asked.

"I won't ever admit to telling you this, but he can't. At least right now he can't. Your position was created and approved by both Congress and the President. That fact alone was why he picked you and expected you to fail right away. If you quit that first week, he could asked for more funds and resources, allowing him to create his own FBI team filled with handpicked Agents. The Division would become his tool to control and become just one more political show-piece. Administrations change though, so watch yourself," Anastasia commented. "Fight the good fight for now. "I'll call the Park Service, but you need to get out there now."

———

WHAT ANA HAD SAID GAVE me a lot to think about. It sure did explain why I was out here alone and on the edge so much. But I seemed to have a few allies, as well. This could be a lifetime job if I could stay alive and keep the politics at bay.

Standing at the edge of the reflecting pool, I looked at the memor-ial. The massive structure sat ninety-nine feet above the ground. It was made of marble and concrete. Looking at it made you think of ancient Rome or Greece with the Yule marble and Doric columns. Thirty-six names and dates were printed across the top edge, all states that were in the Union at Lincoln's death. It was hard to believe the entire structure was less than forty years old, having been just completed in 1922.

"Magnificent isn't it?"

Looking to my right, I smiled at the Park Service representative. "It is. While I know there are restrooms and a gift shop in the interior of the building up top, what's underneath it? I mean, it can't be solid all the way through. There has to be a way to access the electrical and plumbing."

"You mean the undercroft? There's an access door to the right of the stairs that leads down, but it's my understanding the stairs are wooden and rickety. Nobody's really been in there since just after construction," the man winked at me. "For once, they didn't use the lowest bidder on utilities."

"Can I get down there? It might be where our perpetrator is hiding," I said.

The man shrugged. "Sure. Let me grab the MOD and call maintenance. We should be able to find the keys."

"MOD?" I asked him.

Shrugging, the man smiled. "Occupational lingo. I'm sure you have fun acronyms in the FBI as well."

"Yup," I replied thinking about some of the more complicated ones like the office wienies seemed to come up with.

Finding the manager on duty took longer than maintenance. When everyone was gathered outside the door, I explained what I wanted to do.

"What undercroft?" The MOD asked.

"The basement. Where do you think the pipes all go?" the maintenance man asked.

"We don't have one of those," the MOD shook his head.

"Sure you do. You just handed me the keys for it, remember?" I held up the key ring so he could see.

"No, no, no, no, no, we don't have anything like that and if we did it's not safe to go down there. Hold up..." The man started trembling and shaking as if palsied.

Touching the man's shoulder, I asked, "Are you ok?"

"No, no, no, no, you can't go down there. Unsafe. It's locked for a reason." The MOD's eyes moved wildly back and forth.

"What the hell's wrong with him?" one of the men asked me.

"He's under the Vampire's spell," Anastasia answered from behind me.

I looked at her in surprise and pointed upward. It was daylight! "Uh, boss?"

Ana smirked at me. "I'll explain it all to you later, I promise."

Leaving the MOD with the other Parks people, Ana and I entered the undercroft.

———

"You've been holding out on me," I muttered as we climbed down the half rotten stairs.

"Everyone has secrets Jack, especially in this town. You should know that by now," she answered.

"You could've clued me in at least, though. It would've made my job here easier," I explained. Having a day-walking Vampire would be so helpful in many of my investigations! My God! I could see the potential of it all.

"My life is not my own, Jack. No Vampire's truly is. I don't need the complication of the FBI or whomever is in charge at the moment. You do these sorts of jobs for many years and you'll understand me better. Trust me on this, Jack," Anastasia explained to me. "We're close."

The memorial undercroft was dark and damp. Our voices, while kept low, echoed. Concrete support columns ran the length of the structure and small white stalactites hung down from the roof.

"You're supposed to be dead! How have you hidden yourself from us so long?" a voice growled from the shadows.

"Grigori, it has been a long time. Why are you in my city?" Anastasia asked.

"Your city? You claim this magnificent place as your own? Really, Aeliana, keep dreaming. When the master learns of your betrayal and claims... Well...You were in charge of punishments once, so you know already." A short, hairy man dressed like a hobo dropped from the ceiling. "Did you like my present? Finding that many Ghouls in one place was a surprise to me."

"The humans don't believe in them," Ana explained.

"Who are you?" I asked the strange man.

"Your pet still speaks?" the man asked. "You're slipping in your old age, Aeliana. Want me to fix him for you?"

"Jack, his current name is Grigori Rasputin and he's part of the Strigoi faction," Ana explained. She looked back at Grigori. "Your change has begun, hasn't it?"

"The Curse of the Strigoi has struck. You cannot stop me now,

Aeliana, this city is mine now. My minions will rise from the depths and the light will fall upon the unworthy," Grigori chanted. "Join me now or suffer my clan's wrath."

Ana spoke, her voice sounding like that of an angel. "I think not. Jack, now is the time for all good men to come to the aid of the party."

The logical side of my brain thought "code word" while the illogical side thought "action." My hands, moving on their own, swung the crossbow on my back around and put two bolts instantly into the Strigoi Vampire in front of me. Even as they hit home, one in the heart and one in the chest, Anastasia was ripping the man's head off his body.

"Feels like old times," Ana said as she held up the bloody trophy. "Thank you for your service, Jack."

With that, I passed out onto the floor of the undercroft, my weapon at my side.

———

"WHAT HAPPENED?" I blinked my eyes several times to clear the dust and sleepy from them. The last thing I remembered was talking to the Park guys.

Darkness had fallen on the city and there were rotating emergency lights everywhere.

"You hit your head coming out of the undercroft when the stairs collapsed," Anastasia explained from beside me. Impeccably dressed as always, my Vampire boss smiled at me. "You should be congratulated, Jack. Killing an ancient vampire is the big time."

"I got him?" My head hurt, really hurt. It felt as though a herd of elephants were stampeding through it right now.

"The emergency crew found his skull in your hands under the collapsed stairs," she explained.

Cocking my head to one side I tried to remember, but got only sharp pain for my trouble. "Ow. That smarts."

"Then don't do that, dummy. How you can be so smart as to kill a centuries-old Vampire, then be so stupid? Aggravating your injury boggles my mind. Men! When you can stand up straight and not fall down, I expect your report. Don't forget to include what happened with the Ghouls, and any other things you may have forgotten to mention about this case. Understood?" she asked me.

"I do. Thanks for coming down here to check up on me. We might be a small Division but at least we care about each other," I told her.

Ana smiled at me. "That we do, Jack. Your health and well-being is my concern as well. Don't forget to write the report.

Watching her leave, I boosted myself up off the stairs I was sitting on. The elephants came back in a hurry, making themselves well known inside my head yet again. I groaned and almost sat back down. Instead, I staggered over to my van and sat down behind the driver's seat.

Rubbing my head didn't help at all. Temporary amnesia was possible in cases like this, but unless that Vampire zapped me, I should remember something, at least. Reaching under my seat, I pulled out my journal, flipped to the back, and re-read what I'd written. Nothing unusual popped out at me, so I went back even further. Ten or so pages back, I found an entire section missing, the pages ripped completely away. "Why did I do that?" I asked myself. What happened when I first got here that made me do that?

Setting the journal aside for later, I pulled out my pad and started writing. I'd type it up when I felt a bit better, but for now I just needed my impressions and feelings, plus whatever I could remember. No matter my injuries, the job must go on.

The End.

Jack Dalton returns in Magical Probi, Book Two of the Federal Witch series of books.

UP NEXT: BORN A WITCH . . .
DRAFTED BY THE FBI

Agatha Blackmore came into her powers early as a child. Her first spell was a thing of beauty and wonder. It brought terror into the hearts of her family. Who wanted to accidentally become a pink chicken? Now that she's older her magic is out of control. She needs a teacher and none of the Witch Schools will take her. How about a career in law enforcement? The FBI needs serious help in catching law breaking Paranormals. It's a match made in heaven or is it in Hell? God only knows what happens next.

ALSO BY T S PAUL

Federal Witch

Conjuring Quantico - Now Available in Audio!

Magical Probi - Now Available in Audio!

Special Agent in Charge - Now Available in Audio!

Witness Enchantment

Path to Otherwhere

Night of the Unicorn

Invisible Elder

Blood on the Moon

Child of Darkness

Child of Darkness - The Extra Chapter

A Draft of Dragons

Cat's Night Out, Tails from the Federal Witch - Audio Available

Serpent Con

Darkness Revealed

Monster Hunter

Jack Dalton Book 1

Jack Dalton Book 2

Jack Dalton Book 3

Jack Dalton Book 4

Jack Dalton Book 5

Jack Dalton Book 6

Jack Dalton Book 7

Jack Dalton Book 8

Jack Dalton Book 9

Athena Lee Chronicles

The Forgotten Engineer

Engineering Murder

Ghost Ships of Terra

Revolutionary

Insurrection

Imperial Subversion

The Martian Inheritance - Audio Now Available

Infiltration

Prelude to War

War to the Knife

Ghosts of Noodlemass Past

Athena Lee Universe

Space Cadets - Coming Soon

Smuggle Life

Double Cross

Politics Equals Death

Cut and Run

A Grand Affair

Short Story Collections

Wilson's War

A Colony of CATT

Borscht is Boring

Box Sets

The Federal Witch: The Collected Works, Book 1

Chronicles of Athena Lee Book 1-3

Chronicles of Athena Lee Book 4-6

Chronicles of Athena Lee Book 7-9 plus the prequel

Athena Lee Chronicles (10 Book Series)

Camilla: The Collected Works

New Beginnings

Standalones or Tie-Ins

The Lost Pilot

Uncommon Life

Kutherian Gambit

Alpha Class. The Etheric Academy book 1

Alpha Class - Engineering. The Etheric Academy Book 2

The Etheric Academy (2 Book Series)

Nonfiction

Get That Sh@t Off Your Cover!: The So-Called Miracle Man Speaks Out

Study Guide and Timeline: The Athena Lee Chronicles

www.ingramcontent.com/pod-product-compliance
Lightning Source LLC
Chambersburg PA
CBHW070724280626
47159CB00023B/2659